## "Not so tentative. Try it again."

Left jab, right cross. Helena tore into him. The next shot went between Randy's gloves and landed square on that taut, sweaty six-pack he was so damn proud of.

"Hey, whoa!"

She couldn't stop. He caught her next punch on his forearms. Why didn't he fight back? Hit her? She could take it. She *had* to take it or she'd never win.

She felt herself falling as he cut her legs out from under her with his heel.

They hit the canvas locked together. She struggled against him, felt every inch of him above her, his weight bearing her down. "Hit me! For God's sake, hit me," she sobbed. "You *have* to hit me."

"I can't," he whispered.

She felt his breath against her lips, his body hot and hard.

Suddenly she wrapped her legs around him, arching her back, no longer struggling, as his mouth came down on hers....

Dear Reader,

When my last book, *His Only Defense* (December 2008), came out, readers wanted to know more about "Randy" Randy Railsback, the womanizing detective from the Cold Case Squad. He's a good detective, but a responsible guy—not so much. Randy never dates women with ex-husbands, kids, abusive boyfriends or family...or psychological problems. No baggage. And the minute the word *marriage* comes up, he's outta there.

The last woman he needs in his life is English professor Helena Norcross. She has enough baggage to fill a moving van. She's divorced from a compulsive gambler, has two frighteningly intelligent children, suffers from debilitating anxiety attacks and dangerous rages. She's fighting to get her life back on track by enrolling in Randy's self-defense class for women. Two years earlier she was assaulted by a serial rapist who comes back to kill previous victims.

Randy's breaking his own rules about avoiding responsibility. He's falling not only for Helena, but for her kids, too. She's falling for him as well, but believes the only way to be free to love again is to kill the man who raped her, setting herself up as a target.

I love to hear from readers. Write to me at Harlequin Books, 225 Duncan Mill Road, Don Mills, Ont., M3B 3K9, Canada, or check out my Web site, www.carolynmcsparren.com.

*Carolyn McSparren*

# Bachelor Cop
## *Carolyn McSparren*

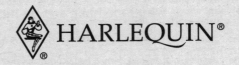

TORONTO • NEW YORK • LONDON
AMSTERDAM • PARIS • SYDNEY • HAMBURG
STOCKHOLM • ATHENS • TOKYO • MILAN • MADRID
PRAGUE • WARSAW • BUDAPEST • AUCKLAND

Recycling programs
for this product may
not exist in your area.

ISBN-13: 978-0-373-71618-0

BACHELOR COP

Copyright © 2010 by Carolyn McSparren.

This edition published by arrangement with Harlequin Books S.A.

® and TM are trademarks of the publisher. Trademarks indicated with ® are registered in the United States Patent and Trademark Office, the Canadian Trade Marks Office and in other countries.

www.eHarlequin.com

**Printed in U.S.A.**

## ABOUT THE AUTHOR

RITA® Award nominee and Maggie winner, Carolyn McSparren has lived in Germany, France, Italy and "too many cities in the U.S. to count." She's sailed boats, raised horses, rides dressage and drives her Shire cross mare to a carriage. She teaches writing seminars to romance and mystery writers, and writes mystery and women's fiction as well as Harlequin Superromance books. Carolyn lives in the country outside of Memphis, TN, in an old house with four indoor and six outdoor cats, three horses, seven raccoons, at least two foxes and one husband, not necessarily in order of importance.

## Books by Carolyn McSparren

### HARLEQUIN SUPERROMANCE

Don't miss any of our special offers. Write to us at the following address for information on our newest releases.

Harlequin Reader Service
U.S.: 3010 Walden Ave., P.O. Box 1325, Buffalo, NY 14269
Canadian: P.O. Box 609, Fort Erie, Ont. L2A 5X3

# CHAPTER ONE

"OKAY, STREAK, show me what you got." Randy Railsback stood relaxed, with an easy grin on his face.

The woman he'd nicknamed Streak came at him across the workout room like a charging rhino. At the last second, he casually moved his hands sideways. Completely off balance, she stumbled past him. He caught her ankle with his instep.

She sprawled on the big mat that covered two-thirds of the floor, and rolled over onto her back awkwardly. The other women gasped. "See, ladies," he said over his shoulder, "you use their force against them." He reached down to offer her a hand, and found himself facedown across her body, staring into a pair of brown eyes so enraged they seemed to be entirely black pupil. "Whoa!" he said as he rolled off. "Way to go, Streak. More than just a pretty face."

He came to his feet in one fluid movement. She scrambled away on the seat of her sweatpants.

"Hope I didn't hurt you," he said, and rubbed his wrist. "*You* definitely hurt *me*."

The other women tittered. She hadn't hurt him, but she might have. Out-of-control newbies were always more dangerous than pros who understood how to engage and when to stop. "Friends?" he said, and stuck out his hand. She ignored it and struggled to her feet.

Had to be a reason for all the anger she was carrying. Jessica might have an idea. As manager of a working gym, Strength for Health, Jessica often knew more about her clients than they realized.

He hadn't planned to take Streak down, but she'd come at him with such force, he'd had no choice. She toted some muscle on that skinny frame, she moved fast and she was only three or four inches shorter than his six feet two. If she learned to channel that anger, she might turn into a formidable opponent. If she didn't, she was going to get herself or someone else hurt.

"Okay, ladies, gather 'round," he said. "I'm Randy Railsback. I'm a Shelby County cop and I teach this class several times a year, and I'm afraid you're stuck with my standard introduction. After that we'll get to work. During the break, you can all introduce yourselves and tell us why you joined a self-defense class." He opened his hands. "Okay with you?"

Most of the heads bobbed. Streak's didn't.

"A competent big man will almost always beat a competent small man," he began.

"But we're not men, Randy," said the luscious blonde, with a small waggle of her estimable rear.

"I've noticed," he said, and included the whole class in his killer smile. Streak didn't react. "That's my point. Women are usually smaller than their assailants. Most men have greater upper-body strength than women, and most women have a glass jaw. A solid right will take you out every time."

"Then why are we here?" Streak asked. Voice like

velvet. Deep, almost baritone, but full of authority. He'd bet she was a doctor or lawyer or top-level manager despite the droopy old sweats. Whatever she was, she sure hadn't made it on her looks or cheerful nature.

"Excellent question. I'm not about to teach you how to start fights. I'm going to teach you how to finish them."

"And disable our attackers?" Streak asked.

"If that's what it takes. We have three objectives." He counted on his fingers. "First, get free. Second, get away, and third, get safe." He grinned at her. "And avoid a right cross while you're about it."

"Why not just shoot his ass?" asked a plump and cheerful lady who looked like Mrs. Santa Claus. "My husband says shoot until the gun goes click, click, then if you have time, reload and do it again."

There were nods all around.

"What if you don't have a gun handy?" Randy said. "How many of you have gun permits and carry a weapon in your car, or have one in your house?"

Every hand went up.

"How many of you feel comfortable shooting it?"

Everyone except Streak raised her hand. A cross section of female West Tennessee America, and every one of them owned a gun. If he were a perp, he'd be terrified. But then, if faced with shooting someone for real, so would they. He didn't usually do this until later in the course, but after Streak's little episode, he decided to move up his demonstration. "'Scuse me a second," he said.

He came back from his gym locker with the .38 Smith & Wesson short-barreled five shot he carried in his ankle holster as backup to his Sig Sauer .45. He unloaded it, checked it twice, dropped the bullets into his pocket and offered Mrs. Claus the weapon, butt first. "I carry a weapon at all times, even off duty." He winked at them. "So I can take down your friendly neighborhood ATM bandit at Kroger's. I've never shot anyone and I pray I never have to, and I definitely hope you never have to, either. Now, Mrs...."

"Ellen," she simpered. She held the gun low with her trigger finger safely along the side, even though she had just seen it unloaded. Someone had taught her well.

"Most shootings occur from six feet or less." He moved back ten feet and stuck out his hand. "Woman, how 'bout you give me that diamond ring you're wearing?"

Ellen narrowed her eyes. The pistol swung up toward his chest. Before she could dry fire, he crossed the distance, blocked her finger on the trigger, wrenched the gun up out of her grasp and pointed it back at her.

"Oh," Ellen said.

"It's not as easy as it looks."

"So we can't shoot, we can't fight. Should we just lie down and...die?" Streak again. He was certain she was going to say something besides "die," but changed her mind. He was glad he hadn't offered her the gun. She'd probably club him over the head with it. She'd relished the idea of disabling her opponent a tad too much.

"You're here to learn to avoid dying," he said. "Get loose from whoever is after you and don't stick around. We clear on that?"

"We can beat his brains out with a rock," Streak said.

"Only if you have one," he said. "Accept that you may get hurt. Don't get dead."

For the next half hour he put them through simple drills—how to move forward, backward and sideways, how to keep their weight balanced so they couldn't be knocked over easily. They were sweating when he called for a break. Everyone collapsed on the exercise mats, pulled bottles of water out of their bags and drained them.

He lobbed his empty bottle into the waste bin in the corner and asked, "Who wants to start?" He smiled at the little blonde. "How about you? First names only. Less to remember." Plus it gave them some privacy among a group of relative strangers. Before the classes finished, the ones who stayed would know one another well, but at the moment, first names were plenty.

"Everybody calls me Bunny," she said. "I have no intention of telling you the name Mama saddled me with. I have a husband and two teenage boys, and there are times I wish I could beat up every one of them. And no, I do not have a job."

"One husband and two teenage boys *is* a job," said Mrs. Claus.

She went next. "You already know—I'm Ellen. My husband and I raise Black Angus in Fayette County, and he's gone early and late with the stock. If I called the sheriff's department, they wouldn't get to me for at least twenty minutes. I'm on my own. I have to be able to take care of myself."

"Thanks, Ellen. How about you, Streak?" he asked.

She arched an eyebrow at him. "My *name* is Helena. I want to learn to protect myself."

"I like Streak," said Bunny. "It suits you and it's cute."

The look Helena gave her would have peeled paint, but Bunny grinned and shrugged.

Everyone waited for Helena to continue. When she didn't, he nodded to the fiftyish woman sitting beside her.

"I'm Francine. I live alone, I run a day-care center, and in case y'all hadn't noticed, I'm sixty pounds overweight and black. I didn't give birth to any of my kids, but I still consider 'em mine. As to why I'm here… In the last year three deadbeat dads under Orders of Protection have tried to pick up their kids when they weren't supposed to, and one drunk mama was strappin' her two-year-old daughter into her car seat ready to drive home when I stopped her. I need to know how to handle myself."

"Did you keep the dads from taking their children?" Ellen asked.

Francine grinned at her. "Being a heifer like me has to be good for something. You bet I stopped 'em."

"Good for you," said the tall, dark woman who sat beside her. She was maybe forty-five, and looked like Streak might have if Streak only fixed herself up. Expensive haircut, expensive workout clothes, expensive trainers. Sleek as a pampered Siamese cat. "I'm Amanda. I'm a divorce lawyer. Divorces bring out the absolute worst in people and sometimes they take out their nasty tempers on me." She nodded toward the girl sitting next to her, who was maybe twenty-five, with wide hazel eyes.

"Hi, I'm Lauren." She waggled her fingernails. They were neatly manicured, but so short she must bite them.

*Oh, Lord,* Randy thought, *she's* perky.

"Walter and I haven't been married all that long," she continued. "My mama and daddy live all the way over in Birmingham and Walter's got a new job where he travels a lot and works nights. He has to do it to get ahead, but we live in a town house in Germantown, and I don't know anybody to call if I get scared."

Randy was surprised to see tears threatening to spill down her cheeks. Okay, he'd forgive her for being perky, since Walter, her husband, was obviously an insensitive jerk. Lauren was lonely and frightened. He let his gaze run over his group. He'd be willing to bet, by the time the course finished, these women would have taken her under their collective wings.

The final member of the class worried him as much as Streak did, but for a different reason. She had a head of fluffy white curls without a hint of blue or purple, was nearly as tall as Amanda and Streak, and according to Jessica, was past seventy. He'd have to be careful not to hurt her when they practiced. She stood erect, with no hint of a dowager's hump. She might run marathons for all he knew, but that didn't mean her hips would hold up.

"Hello, I'm Sarah Beth." She nodded at Ellen. "I live in the country, too, but we've sold all but five acres. I have four cats, two dogs and a goat. The dogs would probably lick a burglar to death, the cats couldn't care less and, unfortunately, the goat is the variety that faints at loud noises, so I need to be able to protect myself when my husband's gone."

Everybody laughed. The tension was broken.

"You all ready to get started again?" Randy asked.

By the time he dismissed the class an hour later, the women were riding a tide of adrenaline, laughing and high-fiving one another. Except for Streak. She drove away without speaking to anyone.

Too bad Bunny, the little blonde, was married. He watched the others drive off, then found the gym manager in her office.

"You ever go home, Jessica?" he asked.

The manager answered, "I'm like a vampire. I sleep during the day and babysit this place at night. How'd your class go?"

"Pretty well. Interesting group. I'm willing to bet there's a lot they're not telling. Women don't take self-defense for no good reason. What's Helena's story?"

"She's been a member of the gym for three or four months, but she usually walks on the treadmill and doesn't speak to anyone."

"Lawyer? Doctor?"

"College professor. Why?"

"She came unglued. Lot of rage. I'd like to understand why."

"She doesn't seem like a nutcase. Should I refund her money?"

"Nah. I can handle her."

Jessica rolled her eyes. "Right."

"And I'd like to find out why she wanted to kill me tonight."

"I'M NOT GOING BACK to that class Thursday night," Helena Norcross said. "The instructor is a chauvinistic redneck."

"Tell me what you *really* think," said Marcie Halpern. "Don't leave your dirty glass in the sink after you finish your drink. Put it in the dishwasher."

"Yes, Mother," Helena said. She poured herself an inch of Irish Cream and sat at the small kitchen table to sip it.

"Thank heaven one of us is a neat freak," Marcie said. "Otherwise this house would be so knee-deep in books you wouldn't be able to find your children unless they wore bells."

"You are the best tenant in the universe, as you never tire of telling me. Where *are* said children?"

"Bathed, tucked in, read to, tomorrow's clothes laid out, lunch boxes filled in the refrigerator…"

Helena patted her shoulder. "I'll run up and kiss them good-night. God help me if you ever find a husband. I'll never have another tenant like you. All this and rent, too."

"Precious little rent. Thanks so much for agreeing to swap nannying for the cash. If that no-goodnik ex of yours would pay his child support…"

"If Mickey doesn't pay, he can't come around and mess up our lives again."

"So, tell me about the redneck chauvinist," Marcie said.

"He made me look like a fool. Told us we didn't have enough upper-body strength to fight off a man, that we had glass jaws and would never get in a shot before the bad guys turned the tables on us."

"I thought he was supposed to help you repel the bad guys." Marcie leaned back so that her chair teetered and only her toes touched the floor. "How'd he make a fool of you?"

Helena told her.

Marcie laughed so hard she had to grab the table to keep from tipping over. "It's the fool part you hated, isn't it? You spend too much time with students who don't dare talk back. God knows what they say behind your back."

"'Nasty old Dr. Norcross thinks Shakespeare's plays are worth reading. *Not.*' In another generation the entire human race will only text-message. Pronounce 'roflol,' why don't you?" She finished her Irish Cream and set the sticky glass on the table.

Marcie pointed to it.

Helena got up to rinse the glass in the sink and set it in the dishwasher.

"You should have seen him leering at the blonde trophy wife. He'll be jumping her bones inside of two weeks. Would you believe, he actually called me Streak."

Marcie spat her mouthful of diet soda straight across the table and laughed until she choked. Helena grabbed a paper towel and mopped up the spill.

"Oh, dear. Sorry."

"Marcie…"

"How many thirty-five-year-old women have a white streak down the side of their head? You're lucky he didn't call you Skunk."

"That's it. I'm going to bed."

"Wait. Helena. Please, sit down. Aside from your assessment of his character, does he know his stuff?"

"I suppose so. He took me down easily." She sank into the chair across from Marcie. "He obviously works out. He's neat. He smells very clean and was freshly shaved. His jeans had a knife-edge crease in them and he has plenty of muscles…."

"Noticed his muscles, did you?"

"I couldn't help but notice his muscles when he was on top of me."

"Say what?"

"Never mind."

"I think you should go back. Helena, you need this. It's the only way you'll ever get over your fears."

Without warning, Helena hunched her shoulders. She clamped her hand over her mouth and began to shake.

Marcie came around the table, sank to the floor and grasped her hands. "It's all right. I'm here. Alarm's on.

Nobody can get in. You're safe. I'm safe. The kids are safe. You drove to class alone and drove home alone after dark. Six months ago you couldn't have done that. You're more in control every day."

"I'll never have total control while he's alive!" She beat her fists on the kitchen table.

"It's been four months since your last panic attack, and you haven't had one in public for over a year. That's real progress."

Helena closed her eyes and flung her head back. "I want him dead."

"I know."

The two women sat silently until Helena's breathing slowed. Finally, she pushed away from the table. "I'll go look in on the children before I go to bed." She squared her shoulders. "Maybe I will go back on Thursday."

## *CHAPTER TWO*

"IF MY MOTHER ASKS ME one more time when I am getting married and giving her grandchildren, I will join a monastery," Randy said. He tossed his jacket onto the wooden coat rack rescued from the old precinct, loosened his tie, sat down and turned on his computer.

Around him in the part of the large bull pen Cold Cases shared with Homicide, other detectives clicked computer keys and talked on their telephones. A few sat with their feet propped on their desks, reading the paper. Early mornings were usually reserved for catching up on paperwork and meetings, while possible witnesses still slept or were commuting to work.

"Never happen," Liz Slaughter said from the next desk. "Monks are celibate."

"New Girl dump you?" Jack Samuels, the third detective in the Cold Cases squad, asked. He stared at his computer screen and began to fill in an arrest form with two fingers. Samuels had long since stopped bothering to learn the names of Randy's girlfriends. To him they were all New Girl, until they vanished to be replaced by the next New Girl.

"Paige and I agreed to see other people," Randy answered.

"She dumped you," Samuels said.

"She wanted to get married, have babies, a giant mortgage, the whole schmeer," Randy admitted. "Paige said it was time to move our relationship to the next level." He shuddered. "Her exact words."

"Uh-oh."

"Right up there with 'honey, we need to talk.' She said I was a dead end and she needed to move on to somebody who wasn't afraid of responsibility." He grimaced. "Baggage."

"I like baggage," Liz said, and patted her belly. She was four months pregnant with her first baby and beginning to show.

"By the time I leave Cold Cases every night, I'm up to here with baggage." Randy passed the palm of his hand over the top of his head. "Give me beautiful women who don't want a thing from me but great sex. Deliver me from *needy.*"

"You, Randolph Quentin Railsback, are shallow and selfish," Liz said. "One of these days you'll get yours."

He raised an eyebrow and leered. "I want mine and everybody else's, too."

"Damn!" Samuels held the delete key down on his computer. "Who'd name a kid Linoleius?" His beat-up desk chair screeched in protest as he swung around. "What really happened with New Girl?"

"Paige kept bugging me to talk about my job. She said if I really loved her, I'd share." He grimaced. "How do you share what we do?" He pointed to the sign beside the door to Lieutenant Gavigan's office, which said Cold Cases Squad. "Hey, honey, I'm home. I spent the afternoon digging through the North Memphis landfill for the leg that fits the foot a bum found in a Dumpster two days ago."

"At least with Cold Cases it's generally a skeletal leg and not a greasy one." Jack glanced over at Liz. "Sorry."

Liz waved her hand. "I don't barf the way I did my first three months." She leaned across her desk toward Randy's. "So she won't be going to Aruba with you?"

"Lots of beautiful unattached ladies in Aruba. No need to take my own. Anyway, Paige has left for Hawaii and won't be back for a while."

Liz propped her chin on her hand and stared out the grimy windows at the dank February morning. "If I weren't married and pregnant, I'd beg to go with you. When do you leave?"

"I'd like to get out of here today, but teaching the self-defense class is paying for the trip, so I'm stuck for a couple more months."

"Any candidates for New Girl in the class?" Jack asked.

Randy shook his head. "One gorgeous trophy wife."

"Off-limits, I hope," Liz said.

"No way would I be crazy enough to get involved with a married woman. The others range from farmers to a perky newlywed."

"All married?" Samuels asked.

"One divorcée and one widow, both in their forties. Then there's the whack job. She doesn't wear a wedding ring. Wouldn't be surprised if she's never been married." He leaned back, propped his loafers on his desk and shook his head. "I'm not getting near that one."

"Not pretty enough?"

"I get the feeling she's trying to make herself ugly. She's succeeded."

"Why would a woman do that?" Jack asked.

"Fear. Low self-esteem. Depression," Liz said. "How ugly?"

"Last night I would have said unattractive. Looking back, I'd have to say *not,* if she made an effort. Big brown eyes, eyebrows like Sela Ward, wide mouth even without lipstick. She's got this straggly, dark brown hair she keeps in a tight ponytail." He ran his hand along his skull just over his right ear.

"How's her figure?" Jack asked.

"Hard to tell under sweats, but she provided a lovely cushion when I fell on her."

"Excuse me?" Liz asked.

He told them what had happened.

"She took you down?" Liz laughed. "I'd like to have seen that."

"She caught me off guard. I'll have 'em all taking me down before we finish the course, but she won't come back. She hated me."

"Oh, sweetie, what woman could hate *you?*" Liz asked.

He spread his hands and flashed her a smile of wide-eyed innocence. "What's not to love, right?"

"Maybe she hated your aftershave. What are you wearing these days, Essence of Shark?"

"I tossed that stuff. I've switched to Love God. Want a sniff?" He leaned toward her.

She rolled her chair out of his reach. "Back, Fang. Go detect something."

WHEN RANDY WALKED INTO the exercise room at the gym for the Thursday evening class, he spotted them at once. Of course, he should have guessed. Streak didn't swing his way. He was surprised that he felt let down.

The pocket Venus who trailed her into the room stood maybe five-two, with light brown curls, eyes such a bright blue that he could tell the color from across the room, boobs he'd bet came straight from Mother Nature, narrow waist, lush hips. On top of everything else, she was laughing. She had a happy, infectious laugh. Polar opposite to Streak.

What a waste.

Venus spotted him and crossed the room with her small hand extended. No wedding ring. Long nails with pink polish. She wore jeans and some kind of silky shirt that slid over her body like cream. "Hi, I'm Marcie Halpern, Helena's housemate. I wanted to meet you."

"You joining the class?"

She shook her head. "'Fraid not. Somebody has to look after the kids."

*Kids, plural? As in more than one? Adopted? Artificial insemination? In vitro? Old heterosexual relationship gone sour?*

"Aunt Marcie, come watch me lift weights."

Streak's kids, then. More baggage. Randy looked down at them as the boy ran into the back of Marcie's legs.

"Ow, watch it, Milo. That hurt."

"I'm sorry, Marcie."

Whoever Daddy was, Streak—uh, Helena—was certainly their mother. The boy was probably nine or ten, the girl six or seven, depending on whether they had inherited their mother's tall genes. Same dark hair, long bones, high cheekbones and wide mouths. Same intelligent dark eyes.

"Should you be lifting weights?" Marcie asked the boy.

"Not heavy ones. I might tear a muscle or something. Vi's too little, anyway. She just rolls them around on the floor."

"I'm strong as you."

"Are not. Bet you can't do this." He ran over to the rack of free weights in the corner of the workout room, rolled one off the bottom and managed to heft it to his knees before Randy took it and set it back on the rack.

"We all start light," he stated mildly. The boy glared at him, then took a deep breath and nodded, though the frown stayed on his face.

Marcie said, "Milo, Viola, go say goodbye to your mother and tell her we'll see her when she gets home."

"Can't we watch her kick butt?" The boy glowered at Randy. "She gonna kick his?"

"I don't think she's up to butt kicking yet," Marcie said, with a shrug of apology to Randy. "Go."

The kid hesitated, then took the girl's hand and trotted across to Streak. Randy watched her open her arms to the children. She lit up. He must be losing not only his touch but his eyesight, as well. This was the woman he thought wasn't beautiful?

Marcie grinned. "Sorry about that. Sibling rivalry rears its ugly head. Milo and Vi are scary smart, but they're still children."

"I'm sure they make you both very happy."

Marcie cocked her head. "I rent the other side of Helena's duplex from her, Detective. I'm her tenant and part-time nanny. I'm also assistant librarian at Weyland, where she teaches, so we're colleagues as well as friends. We're not lovers."

"I didn't—"

"Sure you did. That's okay. The last time I checked we were both heterosexual. Milo and Viola's hideous father is a journalism professor."

So he was still around. "Hideous?"

"Makes Darth Vader look like Saint Peter. Should have been strangled at birth for the benefit of the human race."

"But then you wouldn't have…Milo, was it? And Viola?"

Marcie's smile was luminous. "Mickey is completely out of the picture, and they're worth it."

He felt his heart give a small kick. Streak wasn't off-limits, then. Why should he care?

Marcie waved at Helena, picked up the children and walked into the main gym, where the latest workout machines shared space with a professional-style boxing ring.

Through the picture window, Randy watched Marcie help Milo hoist a small dumbbell, then carry it one-handed over to stare at the two young men sparring in the ring.

Marcie was younger than Streak, and being some-body's tenant and babysitter didn't precisely count as baggage. Now that he knew she was hetero, he should have been on her case like a praying mantis on a june bug.

So why wasn't he reacting?

"Detective?"

He turned at the sound of that smoky baritone. For some nutso reason, he reacted to Streak. Maybe it was the slim body he could imagine under those sweats. Maybe it was the voice. She reminded him of Lauren Bacall after five years in a salt mine.

She stood at the corner of the exercise mat with his

other students, her legs splayed and her hands on her hips. She wore the same old gray sweats tonight, and her hair was pulled back tight with a rubber band, showing off those cheekbones. The look she gave him was not so much provocative as provocation.

"We're five minutes late getting started," she said.

Ellen—Mrs. Claus—sighed. "Oh, for pity's sake, chill."

"Let's get started," Randy said quickly, before Streak could react to that. "Now, we're going to begin with some stretching exercises to warm up our muscles."

"So we can do yoga while the mugger's cleaning his nails?" Streak sniped.

"Honey," said Sarah Beth, "relax. You put up with hecklers in your classes?" she asked, glancing at Randy.

"How did you—"

"Everybody knows about everybody in this gym," said Bunny. She flashed a killer smile that included the group, extended her arms and put her palms flat on the floor in front of her.

"Wow," breathed Francine. "I can't reach my *knees.*"

"Bless your heart," Ellen said, and patted her hand. "There are other talents. I sure wouldn't try to mug *you.*"

Francine shrugged. "Got to be something fine about being a heifer."

"So maybe Francine can get to take me down tonight. Game?" Randy asked.

"That mean I get to go upside your head with my purse? Probably break your skinny neck." She snickered. "I carry my life in my purse."

"I was thinking more about unarmed combat. What do you do when somebody tries to clothesline you?"

The rest of the class went smoothly. Even Streak began to relax, although she still looked ready to chew nails. Or some more sensitive part of his anatomy—interesting idea if she didn't geld him in the process. Randy worked hard to show her that force wasn't necessary. Her forward momentum landed her on the mat every time. Did she hate all men, or just him?

By the time the class was over, everyone was sweaty, but exhilarated. Even Streak glowed. Real pity. She could be a knockout. He couldn't believe she'd always been dowdy and enraged. What had screwed her up?

As they were leaving, he put a hand on her arm. She glared at it. He dropped his hand and said, "Got a minute?"

The others kept walking, but he knew they'd be gossiping.

"I wondered how long before you tossed me out of your class," she said. "Fine. I won't come back."

"I'm not tossing you out." Of all the women, she needed the instruction most. "Come with me."

This late in the evening, the weight-lifting, body-building part of the gym was empty except for a couple of hard-core musclemen who didn't bother to look up. "You must be hell on wheels as a professor," Randy said.

"I am an excellent teacher."

"But this isn't *your* classroom."

She didn't crack a smile.

"Look, Streak, if you don't lighten up and get rid of some of that anger, you're going to get hurt."

"Me? Hah. You, maybe."

"I mean it. You're the one who wound up on the floor tonight, right? Don't let emotions override your control." He grabbed a pair of boxing gloves off the rack and held them out. "Put these on."

"Why?" She stared at him with suspicion. "Planning on showing me that right cross to my glass jaw?"

"Not this time." He held the gloves until she slipped her hands inside, then he fastened the Velcro.

"This is like having sofa cushions on the ends of my arms."

"You'll get used to them." He walked her over to the light bag. "I'm sure you've seen enough boxing movies to know how this works. Try it."

She studied him, then the two-foot-long, pear-shaped bag suspended head high. Before he could give her any further instruction, she let fly as hard as she could. The bag bounced back and caught her square on her cheek. "Ow!" she squawked. "That hurt." She raised her hand to her face, but obviously couldn't feel it through the heavy gloves. "Is my cheek bleeding?"

He caught the bag before it could swing back for a second attack. "No, although it may be a tad bruised tomorrow. Sorry. I should have caught it before it hit you."

"Then why didn't you?" She rounded on him, but he grasped her wrist and held her.

"You didn't give me time. Here, try this one." He half dragged her over to where the man-size heavy bag hung, then walked around behind it and held on. "Okay, hit this one."

She tapped it gently.

"Not like that. Hit the thing."

"And get my jaw broken? I don't think so."

"This one doesn't hit back. Drive your fist hard from waist level, right smack in the gut."

She whacked the bag as hard as she could. With Randy behind it, the bag barely budged. "I felt that all the way to my shoulder," she said.

"Like the feeling?"

"Certainly not." But she whacked the leather again, then again with her other hand, for good measure. Her focused expression told him she *did* like the feeling it gave her. She hit it over and over until she was too tired to raise her arms. She was panting and drenched with sweat.

Maybe he should paste a male face on the front, so she could really enjoy herself.

"Not bad," Randy said. "Next time, get your shoulder into it. Sit down over there and watch."

He pulled her gloves off and put them on himself. He tapped the light bag with his left glove so that it swung away and back. He stopped the motion with his right glove. In ten seconds he had established a steady *poppa-poppa* rhythm.

After a couple of minutes he caught the bag. "See, you hit hard, it fights back. You tap easy and get the rhythm right, you can keep going forever. You do that to somebody's face, he'll remember."

Randy walked to the heavy bag, lowered his shoulder and slammed into it with his left glove, followed by a hard right. The bag barely swung. "Now, this one you can beat the stew out of."

"Interesting, but not germane to our classwork, surely. I have to go."

"Let's say you're earning extra credit. Can you come early on Thursday?"

"Why?"

"So you can put on these gloves and take out some of that aggression before class."

"Don't be ridiculous."

"Unless you learn to use your opponent's strength against him, you won't beat him. You'll beat yourself. That's what you're doing now."

"You afraid I'll hurt one of the others? Like Sarah Beth?"

"Sarah Beth is in better shape than you are, and she's more focused. You wouldn't go for her the way you go for me, either. The second you're off balance, she'll send you flying."

"I'm leaving now." Helena dug a towel out of her gym bag, wiped her face and shrugged into her windbreaker. She looked around at the nearly empty room, then said, "Please walk me to my car."

That cost her. Randy saw her hands clamped in fists at her sides. He'd already explained to the class that walking with purpose went halfway toward not being a victim. She was doing that, all right, but she gave off an odor of fear you could smell half a mile away. She was like a whipped dog that snarls and attacks anything that moves.

He watched her burn rubber out of the parking lot. The woman was not only angry, she was frightened. He needed to know why.

# *CHAPTER THREE*

HELENA'S SHOULDERS ACHED, her arms sagged as though they had weights on them and her cheek felt as though it had swollen all the way across her nose. She'd only hit those dumb bags a couple of times. Randy had pummeled that light bag so fast she could barely keep up with it. He'd moved with powerful grace. As much as she hated to, she had to admit he was beautiful. He probably had to beat women off with a stick.

She shivered. A male body, no matter how beautiful, was not something she ever wanted to touch again.

He'd opened her car door and checked the backseat before he'd let her get in, then he'd waited until she locked her seat belt, started the engine and backed out before he'd turned away. He seemed like a nice person, but he was a cop. She intended to commit a crime without getting caught. That made him her enemy.

Maybe Randy was right that she was sabotaging her ability to protect herself. He called it rage. She called it righteous anger.

She refused to give him the satisfaction of letting him know that she might agree with him, but she'd get to the gym early and smack those bags until she could do it without getting creamed. Then she'd relax his socks off in class.

AS THEY WERE GETTING READY to leave after the next class, Ellen asked, "Can we go to that indoor gun range over on Stage Road for a session?"

Randy saw several heads nod.

"We could meet over there, and maybe go out for a sandwich afterward. We'd bring our own weapons, of course," she added.

"As long as nobody wants to use an AK-47 or a Thompson submachine gun, and we all agree on the time and date," Randy said. "How do the rest of you feel about that?"

"Outstanding!" Amanda said, with the first real enthusiasm she'd shown. "I love my Glock, but every time I try to load the magazine, it takes me forever. You can show me how to do it right."

"Uh-huh." Randy sounded dubious.

"I have one of those S&W titanium five shots in the car," said Sarah Beth. "It's so light that after I shoot it three or four times, I wind up with a blister between my thumb and forefinger. What am I doing wrong?"

"Probably nothing. The lack of weight will cause the gun to wiggle around in your grip."

"But I've heard that a really big gun, like a .357 Magnum, which is what Walter and I have, can break a woman's wrist when she fires it," Lauren commented.

"Nonsense," said Ellen. "Try a heavy shotgun and forget to hold it hard against your shoulder if you want pain. That Magnum myth is a good ole boys' tale to keep us in our places."

"Which they sure figure is not the firing range," said Francine. "Some of those guys act like it's testosterone central."

"How about you, Streak?" Randy asked.

"I can always use the practice."

Always Miss Superior. Hell, maybe she *was* an expert. "Okay. How's this Thursday? I'll reserve some lanes and have Jessica call you if they're available. Afterward, we can discuss finding cover. Doesn't matter if you're armed, if you're standing out in the open like a doe. Now, remember what we worked on Tuesday? Line up, ladies, and let's see if you can toss me out of your way."

He noticed that the back of Helena's sweatshirt was wet. When she turned to look at him, he realized the front was equally wet. He'd been right about her curves. He could see the outline of broad athletic bra straps under her wet shirt, but it couldn't hide her nipples completely. Not exactly a wet T-shirt, but it got the point— or he should say points—across.

The hair around her face was damp, as well, and tendrils had escaped from the tight rubber band. Her moist face was no longer pale and lifeless. Beneath the sheen of perspiration her cheeks glowed, her eyes sparkled.

"I guess you came early," he said.

Her chin lifted. Instantly, her eyes went flat and cold. "I enjoyed myself." She sucked in a breath. "Thank you for recommending the exercise."

That had probably cost her more than asking him to walk her to her car.

"In your head, who were you beating up on?" He grinned. "Me?"

She stiffened. "You're merely the means to an end." She turned on her heel and strode to the back of the room to join the others.

*Oooo-kay.*

Whenever the Cold Cases squad interviewed a female, either as a witness or possible perpetrator, Randy generally led the session. Ninety-nine times out of a hundred if he didn't get a full confession, he gained enough information to find the real criminal, or enough evidence to prosecute. Women liked and trusted him. Most of the time he liked women.

Watching Streak make a point of ignoring him, he wished he could leave for Aruba tomorrow, before his curiosity about her got the better of him. He wanted to find out what made her so angry. He *could* run her name through the police database to see whether she came up as a victim of a crime. He'd be willing to bet she would, and that it had been a bad one.

What good would it do him to know? He was already close to burnout from listening to the gut-wrenching stories of desperate and angry people. He prayed he could hold out until he made it to Aruba for two weeks in the sun, with no responsibility except to choose the right wine with dinner.

And the beautiful woman to share it with. Someone new now that Paige was out of the picture.

Why should he care that Dr. Helena Norcross loathed him? Plenty of other women adored him. He vowed that before the sessions finished, she'd at least tolerate him. Call it an exercise to hone his skills. She was too loaded down with ex-husbands and kids to date, Sela Ward eyebrows or not. Streak and those kids needed somebody reliable. Responsible. *That ain't me.*

She wore different sweats this time. Still too big, but sky-blue rather than gray. He spent the next hour and a half showing his class moves, practicing with them, being grabbed, slung and generally mauled. So far nobody had "accidentally" landed one in his groin, but that was bound to happen. He just hoped he was quick enough to take the blow on his thigh.

He taught them a new maneuver, then paired them up to practice on one another. He took Streak. He still didn't trust her not to blow up and actually attack. He could handle her, but he might accidentally hurt her by reflex.

She piqued his interest, and, dammit, his libido.

Every time she tried to manhandle him, she couldn't budge him, and snarled in frustration. Finally, he asked her to watch Sarah Beth, who had what he called "the touch." Maybe if he could show Helena how this little old lady could manage him, she might begin to get it.

He reached for Sarah Beth's throat with both hands. She smiled sweetly, stepped in, moved her arms up and sideways the way he had showed her, and sent him spinning away.

"Are you all right, dear?" Sarah Beth said.

"Absolutely. Now, Streak, how about you try it again?"

She closed her eyes and took several deep breaths. "I can't. I don't get it."

"Of course you can," Sarah Beth said. "Put your palms flat on his chest." The older woman laid her fragile hands against Randy's torso. They rested there with all the weight of pigeon feathers. "You can feel when his breath comes up." Suddenly she pushed off her back foot and shoved. He stumbled backward again. "See?"

Streak stared at her with something akin to awe. "How did you do that? He helped you, didn't he?"

"Try it."

Randy could tell she didn't want to touch him at all, much less gently, the way Sarah Beth had. He watched Streak clench her fists. She was wishing he'd turn into that heavy bag, so she could let fly at him with all her strength, without being hit back. She had a real need to lash out. Maybe she'd had a bad experience with a cop. No, her anger went deeper than that. She resented his very maleness.

Maybe the ex-husband had mistreated her and still threatened her. A man, possibly more than one, had hurt her badly. Throughout his career, Randy had seen that victims of violence tended to gravitate from one such relationship to the next, so maybe hubby had come after an abusive family and abusive boyfriends.

He couldn't fix damaged goods in one self-defense class. It would be nice if he could, but people seldom changed without time and hard work. He'd tried hard enough to change himself, without a lot of success.

If she'd finally decided to fight back against her demons, he had to teach her that the only chance she had lay in skill, not strength.

She unclenched her fists, but didn't meet his gaze as she reached out and laid her palms carefully against his chest.

*Uh-oh.* He caught his breath. She opened her eyes very wide, whispered, "Oh!" and shoved.

For a second he thought he'd wind up on his ass.

Francine caught him and righted him. "You go, girl." She tried to give Helena a high five, but her classmate didn't see it.

She still had her hands in front of her, her mouth open. She held his gaze too long, then spun away with her arms crossed over her chest. She'd felt it, too.

Until this minute he'd never believed in that old saw about electricity jumping between a man and a woman. He knew she was blushing and her pupils were dilated. His own ears felt hot and probably blazed like stoplights. He blessed his jockstrap. It felt damned uncomfortable, but kept his erection from becoming obvious. Sweatpants without a fly were pretty revealing.

For the duration of the class he paired her with Sarah Beth, who was not only a natural at self-defense, but a natural teacher, as well. They were all still going strong when Jessica stuck her head in the door. "Closing time, people."

Amanda checked her fancy watch. He'd be willing to bet the diamonds were real. "I can't believe it. We've been here over two hours."

"See, Streak?" he said. "Told you I'd make up the time."

She barely glanced at him as she hurried out. He called after her, "Jessica will phone you about meeting at the shooting range on Thursday."

When he left the building, Streak's car was already gone. If she'd waited for him to walk her out, he might have tried to kiss her. Plenty stupid that he actually *wanted* to kiss her, without getting his head handed to him for trying.

# CHAPTER FOUR

"THIS IS INSANE," Helena said, and struck her steering wheel. She slammed on her brakes as the light in front of her turned red. She hadn't noticed the yellow. She had to slow down. The whole of Germantown was one big speed trap. She couldn't afford a traffic ticket, and the cops were always stopping cars like her old BMW. She looked as though she was flying even when she was driving twenty.

Mickey had resented the car, although she'd bought it used, with money she'd saved waitressing in the Grand Tetons as a grad student. "That car screams rich bitch," he'd said. "Now, if you'd been driving my old Ford…"

She could fill in the rest. She'd been raped because she drove a used BMW.

She loved her car and nobody could force her to sell it. She wouldn't sell the duplex, either. She'd kept the title in her name alone, just as she'd established her own credit from the first days of her marriage. Her parents had drummed into her head that a woman had to control her own money, because men died or divorced you. She hadn't often said no to Mickey when they'd been married, but she'd held out on handling their finances. Good thing. Otherwise she and the children might be living under a bridge.

She noticed a squad car parked in the bushes beside the road. Thank heaven she hadn't run the stoplight.

Her stomach tightened as she remembered the feel of Randy's chest. Damn her hormones, anyway. The first sweaty male she touched, and *boom,* fireworks. She wriggled in her seat. It was a miracle she hadn't tossed his skinny rear end all the way through the picture window between the workout room and the gym from sheer surprise.

Without warning, she saw *that* face in its black mask. She screamed and the car swerved. She righted it, put on her brakes, coasted into the Presbyterian Church's deserted parking lot and cut off her lights.

And shook. The memories always hit her without warning, never left her time to prepare, to control her feelings. As long as he lived, he'd hold power over her.

She got her .38 out of the center console and set it on the seat beside her, then took a dozen deep breaths to keep from throwing up inside the car. She'd never get the stink out of the upholstery.

In her rearview mirror, she saw the lights of the squad car cruising closer. She prayed it wouldn't stop. If the cops shone a flashlight inside and saw her gun, they might not give her time to reach for her carry permit before they dragged her out of the car. She willed them to drive by.

When they had turned the corner and disappeared, she started the engine and drove out of the parking lot, although she was still shaking. Her mouth felt dry, but her throat burned.

Later, as she pulled into her garage and lowered the door with the electric control, she giggled. She refused to allow herself a full-blown attack of hysterics. She'd made a new discovery. All she needed to quiet her raging hormones was a rip-snorting anxiety attack from the memory of the last time she'd been touched by a man.

EVEN WHEN HE WENT TO BED alone, Randy nearly always slept like a log. Not tonight, however. Staring up at the lights from the Memphis-Arkansas bridge reflected on the ceiling of his converted warehouse loft, he considered getting up and turning on his laptop to check the file that served as his little black book. He checked the lit dial of his bedside alarm clock. Past three o'clock.

He couldn't call anybody at three in the morning. Besides, he was lonely and restless, not horny—or no more than usual, anyway.

Streak was screwing up his life. Randy usually knew within a couple of hours of meeting someone if he wanted to sleep with her. It had taken him longer to make up his mind about his student.

He definitely wanted her, but he doubted she was into sex with no strings attached. He couldn't handle anything else.

A damaged woman with two kids, no less. An ex-husband who'd probably beat her. Somebody sure had. He wanted to hold her in his arms and assure her that so long as he was around, nobody would ever hurt her again. He wanted to heal her.

Yeah, but how long would he be around? And then what? Would she go back to being a victim?

He gave up on sleep. Climbing out of bed, he showered and dressed. Then he stopped by an all-night café for sausage biscuits and the largest cappuccino they made.

He walked into work at four in the morning, ground fresh beans and brewed the day's first pot of coffee. Unlike most squad rooms, the Cold Cases facility had excellent coffee that all the other teams tried to steal. With only himself, Liz Slaughter, who'd be on maternity leave in another few months, Jack Samuels, close to retirement age, and Lieutenant Gavigan, they could afford designer beans and a top-of-the-line coffeemaker.

Added to his king-size cappuccino, the squad's caffeine should keep Randy awake until his shift ended at four in the afternoon. He'd pulled plenty of twenty-four-hour shifts. Twelve was nothing.

Although he wasn't actually supposed to use the department's computers to check up on non-suspects, he knew the lieutenant wouldn't say a word if he checked out Helena Norcross.

The police report was extensive. Two years earlier she'd been abducted from the faculty parking lot of Weyland, the small liberal arts college where she worked, was beaten, sexually assaulted, then dumped half-naked and semiconscious beside the road through the Old Forest in Overton Park. The report said her assailant was never identified. So he was still out there. Explained a lot.

Detective Dick O'Hara from the east precinct was the investigating officer. Randy would reach out to him to find out if there had been any further developments.

He scrolled down to the medical report from the rape crisis and trauma center. As he read about her injuries, he fought to keep his rage from choking him. He saw and heard much worse, but this was Streak, and that made it immediate and personal.

The assailant had struck her at the base of the skull. She'd had a bad concussion, but no skull fracture. Her right eye socket was cracked, but not displaced. Her jaw was badly bruised.

No wonder Streak was upset by his offhand remark about women and right crosses.

Three ribs on her left side and four on her right had been broken. One had punctured a lung. Her left collarbone was cracked. She'd been struck repeatedly, probably by fists. At some point both her wrists and ankles had been tied, and were raw, although they'd been free when she was found.

He scrolled down to O'Hara's notes on his interviews with her. She swore she remembered nothing about the rape or beating. The blow to the head and jaw had apparently knocked her out for some time. She did say the man wore some kind of mask.

The forensic report was bleak.

No fibers from mask, ropes or carpet were found. Probably bound her with something like rubber-covered electrical wire. No extraneous hair. No DNA. That meant he'd worn gloves and used condoms. Possibly laid a new tarp on the floor of the vehicle he'd used to transport her.

Randy wished criminals didn't pay so much attention to the *CSI* shows on television. Those guys had fancy laboratory facilities that produced immediate results. Maybe on Mars. In Tennessee most trace had to be shipped to the Nashville crime-scene lab, which was so backed up sometimes they couldn't process evidence for months.

The Memphis crime-scene team suspected the rapist

had shaved his body to avoid leaving so much as a pubic hair, and wore some kind of rubber or vinyl suit—maybe rain gear or a wet suit. He was too damned careful for this to be his first rape. So did O'Hara know of other rapes that might fit the same pattern? Were they actually dealing with a serial?

Unless Detective O'Hara had some new developments, Helena Norcross's rape was a bona fide cold case. Lieutenant Gavigan hated rapists as much as he hated killers, so Randy should be able to look into it officially.

He poured himself a fresh cup of coffee in his oversize mug while he waited for the aging printer to crank out the report. Then he slipped it into a fresh manila folder and shoved it into the top drawer of his desk to give Gavigan at their morning meeting.

If Streak's rapist was still out there, Randy wanted to hand her his head on a pike. Although that probably wasn't nearly as romantic as red roses.

# CHAPTER FIVE

RANDY LEANED BACK and propped his loafers on his desk.

Outside, traffic noises picked up. In another hour the February sun would rise, but he still had the squad room to himself. Since budget cuts, central precinct homicide detectives only worked days.

He was no stranger to interrogating rapists and convincing them he understood and sympathized. Although he didn't. *They* thought it was about sex, the great god, orgasm. Actually, it was about dominance—assault with a deadly weapon. The rapist wanted to humiliate and destroy the victim's humanity. He exerted total control. Even if his victim healed physically, she might never regain her sense of being in control of her life.

The fact that Streak had joined his class proved she was still fighting for her prerape sense of self. He would give her all the help he could.

He doubted his other class members had similar experiences, but you never knew. He glanced at the clock. Jack and Liz wouldn't be in for a while yet. He had time to check out the other class members online.

Sarah Beth Armstrong, the first he checked, seemed like a nice old lady, but anybody could have a record.

When the screen lit up, he slammed his cup down so

hard that coffee splashed on his desk. He grabbed a handful of tissues from Liz's box and mopped it up before it could reach his keyboard. The desk had survived worse.

Sarah Beth had only a couple of speeding tickets, but when he followed the link, he found a homicide report. Eight years earlier her thirty-year-old daughter had been carjacked and killed by three nineteen-year-old gangbangers. Sarah Beth, her husband, Oliver, and two children under eighteen were listed as next of kin. No husband listed for the daughter.

All three men were now serving life sentences without parole.

Sarah Beth seemed, what? Together? In his professional experience, the death of a child, particularly by violence, was the hardest kind of grief to survive. She'd had eight years, but that kind of pain and loss didn't go away.

Next he checked Francine Bagby. Squeaky-clean, except for the 911 calls about noncustodial parents and drunks she'd already mentioned. He pitied anyone who went up against her with anything less than an antitank gun.

Nothing about Amanda Donovan, the lawyer, either. He recognized the name of her firm, however, as the biggest and toughest divorce firm in west Tennessee. No lack of material for nasty confrontations there.

Nothing on Ellen Latimer, aka Mrs. Claus.

Next he checked Lauren Torrance, the newlywed. Another surprise. In the previous year there had been three reports of loud arguments called in by neighbors. No signs of physical abuse, so no arrests.

Little Bunny was actually Gaylene O'Donnell Yates from Ittabena, Mississippi. Even though she was only five foot three, she'd won second runner-up for Miss Mississippi, and had married a plastic surgeon. The surgeon, Wilton Yates, had just won a malpractice suit over a boob job that had supposedly gone wrong. A disgruntled ex-patient was threat enough to send his wife to self-defense classes.

Her beautiful rack was probably silicone. Pity.

Finally, he pulled up Marcie Halpern. When she didn't pop up, he entered variants of Marcie and found nothing, not even a speeding ticket.

His coffee was now tepid, so he added a dollop of hot from the carafe he had made, and drank it in a single pull. Even the women who didn't show up in police reports probably had secrets they didn't want revealed.

Randy had secrets, too. Without them, he wouldn't have become a cop, and he'd be married with two-point-five children, a mortgage and a bass boat. He'd fall asleep on the couch after Thanksgiving dinner with the entire Railsback clan, instead of eating a tuna sandwich alone at his desk. He always volunteered for duty on holidays.

It was an excuse to avoid his family. He talked to his mother on the phone once a week or so, but never spoke to his father.

Maybe not all families were toxic, but his was right up there with Three Mile Island.

HELENA DROPPED Milo and Viola at the front door of their school on her way to her morning class. "Marcie will pick you up after day care. Tonight is my self-defense class. I'll tuck you in when I get home."

"Can we come with you?" Milo asked.

"Not tonight. Sorry."

"Mo-o-om," he whined. "I promise I'll just lift the little weights."

"I don't want to go back," Viola said. "Not never."

"Then *you* go home with Marcie," Milo snapped.

"Both of you go with Marcie." She kissed them goodbye and watched Milo stalk up the stairs, while Vi bounced behind him. Helena had given up attempting to bribe him into waiting for his sister. He raced ahead to join his friends. Helena watched until both children disappeared inside the school.

She pulled out into the stream of cars that had disgorged their children. Traffic was sluggish, but she'd allowed extra time before her class. She turned on NPR, listened to five minutes of one disaster after another, then turned the radio off. They never seemed to report good news.

How could she keep her children safe, yet allow them enough freedom to grow? How could she teach them to avoid monsters without destroying their trust in decent people? How could she protect them from her own fears? Her panic attacks came less frequently and were shorter and less severe, but she still had them.

She forced herself to turn into Overton Park. This early she could drive the winding roads through the golf course and the Old Forest without meeting another car. Her sweaty palms slipped on the steering wheel, and she could feel the pulse thrumming in her throat. "You can do this," she whispered.

In the two weeks since she'd begun to drive to work through the park, she hadn't dared to turn from the main road into the Old Forest. She'd promised herself that today was the day. She would stop by the side of the road where she'd been found, maybe even get out and look at the spot. Demystify it. It was only a bunch of shrubbery.

February was its usual cold, dreary self, but she started the air-conditioning to dry the sweat between her shoulder blades. A moment later she switched it off. Her teeth were chattering.

She swung right onto the narrow forest road where the aged oaks and maples met overhead. Their leafless branches drooped over her car like threatening brown stalactites. Even in winter the lane was shadowy.

She inched along the road and studied the underbrush. It all looked so different. Was it here? Farther along? Behind her? On this curve? How could she not recognize the place she'd been dumped?

When a pickup drove into view around the curve behind her, she floored the BMW, barely braked at the stop sign onto the parkway and drove ten miles over the speed limit until she pulled into her allotted parking space at the college. Undoubtedly a commuter taking a shortcut, but she'd freaked. She hit the steering wheel hard enough to bruise the sides of her hands.

She turned off the ignition and took deep breaths to calm her heart rate. Her face in the rearview mirror looked as gray as though a vampire had sucked her dry.

The bastard had sucked her *life* dry. She *would* take it back. Milo felt he was in charge of keeping her safe. He'd seen her curled up on the floor of her closet. Vi was always wary, watching for signs of an imminent attack. Children should believe their mother was in control, invulnerable, *there*.

Sooner or later, the bastard would come to kill her. She felt it in her bones. Which was why she had to kill him first.

She lifted her chin and felt her pulse. No longer stroke territory. And, finally calm, she climbed from the car, picked up her briefcase and started up the stairs toward the liberal arts building.

She'd only downed a can of tomato juice as she left the house to take the children to school. Now her stomach rumbled in protest, so she detoured to the student union for a bagel and tea in the twenty minutes before class. Since juniors and seniors avoided early classes, she had the cafeteria to herself except for a couple of bleary-eyed freshmen.

She opened the bound notebook she used for her rape notes. At the top of a new page she wrote the same two points she'd written at the head of every page for the last six months. *Find him.* The police hadn't managed in two years, with all their resources. What chance did she have?

She underlined the second item so hard the pen tore the paper.

*Make him find you.*

In the meantime, however, she had to try to teach thirty freshmen how to construct a five-paragraph essay, a task they should have perfected in junior high. Most of them acted as though she was teaching them ancient Greek.

She stopped in the faculty common room for another cup of tea to take with her to class. At this hour she was usually alone. This morning, though, Albert Barkley, full professor of American literature, sat in one of the worn blue club chairs by the window, reading the *New York Times Sunday Book Review.* He blinked at her over his glasses, then put the paper down and raised an eyebrow. "Something different about our Helen of Troy this morning. You must have launched another thousand ships."

"Not even a kayak, Al," she said as she poured her tea. He hated being called Al, which was why the faculty did it.

"There *is* something different about you. You seem, I don't know, girded about the loins. Planning to go into battle?"

"Think of me as a female Daniel headed into the lions' den," she said as she emptied a packet of artificial sweetener into her Earl Gray. "One of these days maybe I won't have to face English 101."

"Only after I die and leave a full professorship open. Until then be grateful for your tenure and your paltry literature courses, and think of Idiot English 101 as sparing you hell after you die. You've already served your time."

She walked upstairs to her classroom and thought that if Albert the Oblivious could recognize something different about her, she must actually be sending out different vibes. The self-defense course had been a first step in her plan to protect herself and kill the man she always thought of as "the bastard." The second was to change her appearance. The third was to set herself up as a target.

"I will learn to use my softness against his hardness," she whispered, and caught the startled expression on the face of a junior coming down the stairs toward her. That remark would be all over campus before lunchtime.

"IT'S A LEGITIMATE cold case," Randy said. He'd made certain Lieutenant Gavigan and the others had read Detective O'Hara's notes on Streak's case before their morning meeting.

"No forensic evidence and no suspect," Gavigan said. "Dead end. Gonna stay a dead end."

Jack Samuels and Liz Slaughter sat in front of Gavigan's desk. Randy rested a hip on the edge of the credenza.

"These guys don't normally stop on their own, Lieut," Randy said, and spread his hands. "I doubt this rape is an isolated incident. He's either moved away, he's dead or disabled, he's in jail, or he's raped others and will rape more."

"Gotta be," Jack said.

Liz had already assumed the pregnant woman's position, with hands folded on her belly. "Can't hurt to check it out. More cases equals more chances he slipped up, so we can catch him."

"I get the feeling I'm being sandbagged here," Gavigan said. "I'll go this far. Randy, talk to O'Hara. After all this time new cases will have forced him to move your girlfriend's assault to the back burner."

"Not my girlfriend. I told you, she's just a member of my class. If there's anything she didn't say during the original investigation, either because she chose not to or didn't remember, I'm in the best place to tease it out of her memory. We agree on that?"

The other three nodded.

"I like Streak. I'd like to get this guy for her sake."

"Streak?" Gavigan asked.

Randy explained.

"Prematurely gray hair?" Liz asked. "How come she doesn't dye it?"

"I kind of like the streak in her hair, although I wish she'd fix herself up so she doesn't look like a vagrant. And it's white, not gray."

"Bet you five bucks she didn't look so frumpy before the assault," Jack said. "It's camouflage. She's hiding, and blames herself. Why not? Everybody else probably blames her." He shook his head.

"Assuming we reopen the crime as a cold case, what do you plan to do that the original detectives didn't?" Gavigan asked.

"Same as always," Randy said with a shrug. "Go over everything again from the beginning." That meant revealing to Streak that he knew about her assault. She wouldn't thank him for checking up on her. Might not thank him for reopening her case—and half-healed wounds—either.

"Long shot," Gavigan said.

"All our cases are long shots," Randy said. "Look how many we close."

Liz and Samuels nodded.

"All right, talk to Detective O'Hara. He may already have info on similar assaults. And try not to step too hard on his toes, will you?"

"Thanks, Lieut," Randy said.

"Now, how's the Murchison killing coming?" Gavigan asked Liz.

An hour later, he closed the meeting.

As she passed Randy on her way to the ladies' room, Liz said, "If you need somebody female to talk to this Streak, I'll be happy to interview her." She patted her belly. "Didn't you say she has two kids? I can ask her advice about motherhood."

"You meet her kids, you might be scared off motherhood."

"Too late for that. Seriously, she might say things to me she'd be embarrassed to tell you." Liz laid her hand on his arm. "We need to get this guy before he rapes somebody else. Anything I can do, let me know."

"Ditto," Samuels said from across the room. "I hate these guys."

## CHAPTER SIX

RANDY BROUGHT LATTES and a dozen chocolate doughnuts to his meeting with Dick O'Hara at the West Precinct.

O'Hara was a big man, solid but not fat. He had the basset-hound eyes of a man who had seen too much in his forty-plus years. He wore his sandy hair in a buzz cut, and even at ten in the morning his khaki slacks looked rumpled.

"I'll accept help from the devil himself if it gets this guy off the street," he said. "This is one creep I hope shoots it out with the TACT squad, although life without parole would make me happy."

"We find him, you get the collar. No problem."

O'Hara waved a hand. "Your team makes cases we don't have time to work. The hell with jurisdiction."

The two men settled down at O'Hara's beat-up government-issue gray desk. Around them other detectives leaned on desks, chatting amiably, while another group surrounded the coffeepot. The room seemed almost tranquil this early.

O'Hara shoved a stack of folders and two loose-leaf binders to Randy. "You're welcome to look through the evidence boxes, but these might bring you up to speed quicker."

Randy set his cup down. "A hell of a bunch of notes for one rape case. What's in these that didn't make it into the electronic file?"

"The others." O'Hara narrowed his eyes. "You're saying you don't know the guy has probably raped at least five more and killed three?"

Randy choked on his doughnut. "I only started working Dr. Norcross's case officially a couple of hours ago. He's a killer?"

"After he raped three victims a second time, he killed them."

"He came *back?*" *God, Streak!* Did she know that she was still in danger from the same rapist? Randy ran his hand over his face. "Man, I feel like an idiot."

"No reason to. You're playing catch-up, and you were smart enough to start at the right place—me. Officially, we still have no forensic evidence to say the assaults are connected."

"But *you're* sure they're connected?"

"Damn straight. Like he signed his name. You got time?"

"As much as it takes."

O'Hara settled back in his chair and wolfed down another doughnut. The chair creaked under his weight. "I'd bet my pension he's sexually assaulted more than the victims we know about. Report rate's higher than twenty years ago, but women still take showers and hide what happened."

"They still feel guilty."

"Yeah, and the lawyers make 'em feel worse on the stand." O'Hara swigged his coffee and chewed half of another doughnut. After he swallowed, he said, "You know as well as I do that most rapists don't stop with one. You'd have connected the dots once you programmed the computer to kick out similar cases."

"If I knew the proper parameters to enter."

"Call me a short cut. The first one we know about was a lawyer. Six months later came a Realtor, then another four months after that the professor."

"Dr. Norcross was raped two years ago. You're saying he's been out there over three years?"

"And not one suspect in all that time. You notice a pattern here?"

Randy nodded. "Professional women."

"Take a look." O'Hara pulled a set of photographs from the top file, turned them around and slid them across the desk.

Since they were taken after the assaults, the women looked like hell. Black eyes, split lips and cheeks, blood in their hair. Randy looked away from the shot of Helena. He wanted to roast the guy over an open pit and flay him alive.

"Well?" O'Hara asked.

"These women could be sisters."

"Right. They're all over medium height, slim, well-dressed, with dark hair, although the lawyer's hair was short. She was six-one and no pushover. He didn't hit her hard enough, so I guess he was still perfecting his technique. She fought hard until he knocked her out, but she didn't draw blood, or if she did we didn't find it. A DNA match to somebody in the system, and he'd already be in prison."

"Could she give a description?"

O'Hara shrugged. "Shorter than she was, but that

could mean six feet. Total body covering including face and head mask. Something slick. Possibly a wet suit. Stands to reason he'd wear latex gloves, as well. No eye color, no skin color. He could be purple for all we know."

"What about the rest?"

"Here's number four. A pediatrician." O'Hara shoved two photos across the table. In the first, the woman looked as beat-up as the others. The second was a photo of her body.

Her head was a mess of blood and bone. Jack Samuels had once told him that if he ever reached a point where the sight of violent death didn't move him, he should retire. Randy hadn't reached that point yet.

"She's the second one he came back to kill," O'Hara said.

Randy gritted his teeth and kept his voice even as he asked, "Who was first?"

"His first victim, the lawyer. She was an assistant district attorney. Nobody connected the killing with this rapist until the second murder. It's a miracle we put the pieces together. Different jurisdictions, different detectives."

"I remember that case, but I didn't know it was a serial."

"Neither did we," the detective said. "An ADA baby lawyer gets assaulted a second time and killed, everybody starts looking at the people she's convicted, maybe out on parole or just released. Nobody fit. Then after the pediatrician was killed, we connected the original cases."

"With no forensics? What made you believe they were connected?"

"Aside from the fact that the same women were raped a second time—statistically unlikely to be two different rapists—the blunt-force trauma looked as though it had been inflicted by the same instrument."

"Could you identify the weapon?"

"Possibly the butt of a heavy pistol. Not certain, but the medical examiner thinks he's right. Then number three showed up."

"Why wasn't this all over the news?"

O'Hara shrugged. "She was actually the sixth victim, the most recent. To the best of our knowledge, she hadn't been previously raped. If she was, she never reported it."

"Why connect her with the others?"

O'Hara slid a photo across the desk. It was a professional head shot.

Randy caught his breath. She looked enough like Streak to be her sister. "So he's escalating? Raping and killing the first time?"

O'Hara shook his head. "We think it was an accident. We're not sure she's one of his, but she fits the profile. She was a stockbroker with heart arrhythmia, and her doctor put her on Coumadin."

"Blood thinner."

"Right. We think he stuns them or knocks them out so he can get them into his vehicle and leave the area. The initial blow caused a massive cerebral hemorrhage. She bled out before he could get her away."

"Did he finish the assault?" Randy asked.

Again O'Hara shook his head. "No bruising in the vaginal vault commensurate with rape."

"And since he wears a condom, no semen."

"Probably pissed him off she wouldn't feel what he had intended to do to her."

"Poor guy. Bummer."

"Yeah," O'Hara said. "Breaks my heart." He turned over another photo. "At first we thought victim number five, the one before the stockbroker, fell outside the pattern. She was older, for one thing. Over fifty, and a Germantown housewife. Then we found out that she was chairing the annual antique sale for one of the big charities."

"Not necessarily a professional woman, but powerful."

"Right. She'd also had some work done. She looked closer to thirty than fifty. So we believe he saw her somewhere without knowing anything about her."

"Checked her out, and went for her anyway?" Randy asked.

"He seems to return to the ones that reported the rape to the police. No way to know for sure, since it's impossible to prove a negative, but I've checked for any other killings in the last five years that fit the profile."

"And?"

"Nothing. As far as we can tell, he started three years ago and comes back sooner or later to kill the ones that talked, but not necessarily in order. As if they've broken faith with him."

"Does Str—Dr. Norcross know?" Randy asked.

O'Hara nodded. "They all know. Dr. Norcross and I talk every couple of weeks. She asked to be kept in the loop, and I'm glad to oblige. She's careful. Doesn't take unnecessary risks."

Randy would have to protect her without getting caught at it. "Could be he only moved to the area a few years ago. Maybe he has a record somewhere else. Part of the problem with Ted Bundy was that the different locales didn't piece all his crimes together. His crimes started in California and ended in Florida, with other states in between."

The detective nodded again. "Like our guy, Bundy also attacked women who looked alike, so we searched for matches on the FBI database. Nothing stood out."

"Are you protecting the others who talked?" Randy could only protect Streak, and she would probably freak out if she caught him following her.

"We don't have the manpower, but we've alerted them to be extra careful, and we're checking on them when we can."

After the next class Randy would not only walk Streak to her car, he'd follow her until she was safely locked in her house.

"When do you alert the media that we have a murdering rapist?"

O'Hara sighed and shook his head. "Not until we have forensic evidence to connect them. The brass says anecdotal evidence and my personal gut feeling are not enough. *They* say he takes too much time between assaults. *They* say he's probably left the area. *They* say they don't want to start a panic. Every tall, dark, powerful woman in the Tri-State area would demand bodyguards."

"*They* are wrong."

"Tell me about it," O'Hara said. "I know that, you know that, but what can we do? I can't leak it. I value my pension. So should you."

"Any woman who went public could be painting a target on her back." Even Streak wouldn't be that crazy. Not with two dependent children. "He can't be driving around this area until he spots a likely prospect."

"Could be. Planning appears to be part of the thrill

for this guy. Appears to get off on stalking and fantasizing. Afterward, he goes back to his boring little life, sometimes for months, sometimes for years."

"You send in for a profile from the FBI?"

O'Hara snorted. "Ever fill out one of those questionnaires? Hell, if we knew that much about the guy, we'd already have him in custody."

"So you didn't do it."

"Sure we did. We got the usual report." O'Hara's voice turned singsong. "Twenty-five to forty. Possibly shorter than the women, although not necessarily. Works some kind of Joe job. May or may not be married and seem perfectly normal on the surface. Probably watches cop shows on TV and reads a lot of books about serial killers. He doesn't fantasize that he's actually on a date with these women. He knows they'd never give him a glance in real life, and it burns him up. He wants to punish them. He may interact with them in some way…."

"Like what? The counter man at the local fast-food joint?"

"Yeah. Like that, but we couldn't narrow down any place the women intersected. We've reinterviewed the women several times to find out if they went to the same grocery or used the same hairdresser." O'Hara pointed to the folders and notebooks on his desk. "Somewhere in there is a grid we worked out of places where they might have encountered the guy. Nothing stood out, but we barely scratched the surface of possibles. Could be a busboy at a restaurant they went to once. We'd never pick up on something like that."

"What about his disguise?" Randy asked.

"We checked recent buyers of wet suits and bad-weather gear at the local shops, with no success. Probably bought off the Internet. No way to trace him there. Vans were a dead end. You got any idea how many SUVs and vans are registered in this part of Tennessee? We don't even know the color or whether it's the same van every time."

"You said the lawyer fought back. Anything under her nails?"

O'Hara shook his head. "You think of anything we missed, be my guest. I hate this case. I know he's out there planning the next assault and maybe going back to kill a woman he's already attacked. I want to stop him in the worst way. I mean that literally."

"The worst way would be?"

"Blow his head off."

SINCE IT WAS Wednesday night, Randy didn't expect to see any of the members of his class when he stopped by the gym on his way home, to work out. He was surprised to find Streak on the rowing machine. She had her back to him, so he watched her. If she'd been in a real boat with real oars, she'd be halfway to England by now.

Typical newbie. Too much weight worked too fast. She wasn't taking the full stroke, so her arms and shoulders weren't stretching out between pulls and her legs weren't extending fully. She could damage muscles if she kept that up.

He touched her shoulder. "Hey," he said.

She jumped a foot, yelped, twisted in an attempt to look up at him and launched herself as fast as she could out of the machine.

He dropped his hand. "It's only me. You're okay." What a jerk! He knew better.

The pulse in her throat jumped. Her face blazed. Her blood pressure was probably off the scale. "Sorry, didn't mean to…" He was going to say he didn't mean to scare her, but she wouldn't like that. "To run into you tonight," he finished lamely.

She got to her feet. "I thought I'd try some of the other equipment." She wiped her face with the towel around her shoulders. "I should take a shower and head home."

"Wait a second," he said. "Come over here where we can talk." Now did not seem the time to tell her he knew about her case. "Your body needs a break between sessions. You worked out with the bags yesterday, so take tonight off or walk on the treadmill."

"But…"

"Trust me, exercise like this makes small tears in your muscle tissue that have to heal. Otherwise you can hurt yourself."

"*You're* here. It's all right for you to work out every day, but not me?"

"I work different muscle groups on different days, and I concentrate on reps, not on weight. I'm not interested in looking like Schwarzenegger in his prime. I just want to keep my chest from winding up below my belt. Why don't you take a couple of sessions with Jessica to learn how to use the machines?"

"How can I row wrong?" Helena's head came up, her jaw set.

"Look, Streak, any bodybuilder with the IQ of a possum could tell you that if you row fast and tight that way, you're going to wind up with cramps on your cramps and knots in your calves."

She opened her mouth to tell him off, then took a deep breath and said, "You're right. I'll schedule a session with Jessica after I take my shower."

She headed for the women's locker rooms. As she walked through the door, she turned to him and said, "Thank you. I apologize." Then she was gone.

Damn, the woman moved well. She might be trying to hide her femininity, but at least from the back it wasn't working. She couldn't conceal that loose-limbed sway by wearing a feed sack. He found himself imagining how she'd look in black lace and four-inch heels, with that streaky hair falling down around her shoulders. Not an appropriate reaction of teacher to student, but definitely man to woman.

Liz always told him he'd get his comeuppance. Streak might be the one to hand it to him on a platter. Heck of a shame that that very womanly woman was so tied in knots. He would like to untie them, but couldn't work out the right method. He *always* knew the way to get to women, but not this one.

Despite what he'd told her, he wanted to impress her with his tough-guy routine when she came out of the ladies' locker room, even though he realized how stupidly macho that was. He picked up a set of free weights, sat on the nearest bench and began doing curls. He'd barely completed his first set of reps when she walked out. She didn't wear any makeup, not even lipstick, and her damp hair was pulled severely back in a rubber band. No lingering over hair and makeup for our Helena.

And not a glance at Randy on her way to Jessica's office, either.

By the time she came out, he'd cut his routine short. He rubbed his towel over his sweaty hair and body and walked over to her. She stood at the front door with her hand on the panic bar, staring out at the parking lot. Probably afraid to go to her car until someone else left, too.

"I'm leaving, too. Walk you to your car?" he asked.

He was sure she was going to snap at him, but after a moment her shoulders drooped and she said, "Thank you."

"Buy you a cup of coffee?" he asked as they walked. Good a chance as any to tell her he was working her case.

She glanced at her watch. "I really need to get home. Marcie is an angel, but it's not fair to take advantage of her."

"We're meeting at the gun range tomorrow night," he said. "You know where it's located? Want me to pick you up?"

"I know the route, thank you." She clicked her key to unlock the door of her car, opened it and let him check it before she climbed in.

"Your friendly neighborhood Smokey reminds you to buckle up."

"What do you do with the police?" she asked through the open door.

"I'm a detective with the Cold Cases squad."

"That means?"

"Old cases never go away until they're wrapped up and the criminal convicted, but eventually they get shelved as 'unsolved.' They come to us when they're moribund."

"I see. Thank you. I'll see you tomorrow evening." She shut the door and backed out.

He watched her until her taillights disappeared. Then he jumped in his car and followed her at a distance until she shut her garage behind her. After picking up a pizza, he drove home.

He loved his Front Street Memphis loft with its view of the Mississippi River. The perfect bachelor pad. Tonight, however, it felt cavernous and as cold as the cases he worked. No booty call tonight, either. What the hell? Streak was screwing up his libido. He'd never met a woman who could do that.

# CHAPTER SEVEN

"MORIBUND," Helena said, and laughed as she stowed her purse in the front closet.

Randy might be useful, because he certainly had more resources than she did. O'Hara swore he was continuing to work the case, but offered no new leads.

She would only heal completely after the bastard died. She'd even be willing to let somebody else kill him, although she'd prefer to pull the trigger herself.

Three of the women who had reported the rape to the police were still alive. Sooner or later he'd go for one of them. She had to control his choice and take him out when he made it. But she wasn't ready yet. She'd finally managed to take step one when she joined the self-defense class, although she was a long way from being good at it. Time to set step two in motion—make herself attractive enough to entice him back. Step three: pick the time and circumstances of the confrontation. Step four: blow his brains out. Step five: be certain the authorities called it justifiable homicide.

Above all: survive.

She didn't have a clue how she was going to get beyond step two. The whole plan was a big, fat fantasy she'd cooked up in the hospital while she was recovering from her injuries. She wiped away tears of frustration and quickly looked toward the kitchen to make sure Milo and Vi hadn't seen her crying.

She'd come this far. She'd figure out how to go the rest of the way. If she didn't, she'd never be safe to raise her kids.

The kitchen smelled of hot spices and ginger. Her stomach rumbled. For tonight, at least, they were all safe and together.

"Hi, guys," she said. Milo ran to accept her hug but backed off at once. "Marcie made Chinese," he said. "Chicken Pow Pow." He punched the air twice and narrowly missed his sister's head.

Vi shrieked and ducked. "Mommy, Milo almost hit me." She ducked behind her mother. Helena laughed and held her out of the line of fire.

"Did not," Milo said. "I'm hitting the chicken. Pow, pow!" He spun and slugged the air in the other direction, then clutched his throat, sank to his knees and made what Helena assumed were dying-chicken noises. She applauded and pulled him to his feet.

Marcie stood at the stove stirring something in the wok that smelled marvelous.

"*Kung* Pao, actually," Marcie said. "I made it mild."

"Can we use chopsticks?" Vi asked Helena.

Milo sneered. "You're too little to use chopsticks."

"Chinese children use chopsticks when they're bitsy *babies*," Vi said, with her hands on her hips. "I am not too little. You're just jealous because you're so clumsy you drop stuff on the floor."

Milo rounded on his sister, who dove behind her mother again. "Take that back," he said.

"Knock it off," Helena said amiably. "Yes, you can use chopsticks—both of you. But whatever you drop on the floor you clean up, including the sticky stuff, and you don't argue about which one of you did it. Deal?"

Vi stuck out her tongue at Milo, then ducked behind their mother. He took a step toward her, thought better of it and stomped out of the room. "Call me when dinner's ready."

"He sounds like Mickey," Marcie said. "Macho man."

"Hey, tiger, finished your homework yet?" Helena called.

From the living room came Milo's exasperated voice. "I did it in study hall. Easy-peasy."

Helena closed her eyes. *Easy-peasy* was Mickey's favorite expression. She hoped Milo would grow out of it.

Vi seldom mentioned her father. Her memories of him probably dimmed with each day that he didn't call or write. Milo, on the other hand, had been old enough when his father walked out to pine for him. Helena did everything she could to reassure him that he and his sister were not the cause of their dad's sudden departure.

She felt certain Milo believed her "accident" had caused Mickey's desertion, and that he blamed her without being able to admit it even to himself. He definitely realized their lives had changed—she'd changed—after her stay in the hospital.

She shouldn't have put him in this position—more guilt for her to carry around.

"I ran into Milo's teacher in the hall this afternoon when I was picking them up from day care." Marcie's tone was neutral.

Helena's stomach lurched. "What's he done now?"

"Why do mothers always expect problems?" Marcie gave the chicken a stir, then turned off the flame under the wok. "She says he has a brilliant mind when he settles down enough to use it. He's fun to teach, even if he does get ahead of her."

"That's not so bad."

Marcie burst out laughing. "It's outstanding, dummy."

"She didn't mention discipline problems? I worry he'll turn into a recluse or a bully, that I've screwed him up. I try to stay calm and relaxed. Doesn't always happen."

"He's a perfectly normal boy, which means he's a handful. He has plenty of friends, he loves animals and he even likes his sister from time to time. Lighten up."

Later, after Milo and Vi helped clean up the mess from dinner, blaming each other all the while, Helena oversaw their baths, put them to bed in their separate rooms and let Milo read in bed while she read part of a Nancy Drew mystery to Vi.

She tucked her daughter in and then Milo. As she reached for the light switch beside his door, he said, "Mom, is Daddy dead?"

She caught her breath. "No, he's just not here."

"I wish he *was* dead."

That brought her back to his bedside. He refused to look at her.

Helena heard her mother's voice in her head, saying, "You don't mean that." Whenever she said something her mom didn't approve of or agree with, that was her refrain. Helena vowed she'd never do that to her children. "Why?"

His eyes filled with angry tears. "Because then he'd have an excuse not to call us or come see us. He doesn't now because he doesn't love us."

If Mickey had showed up in that moment, she'd have strangled him. Actually, her husband had probably never been capable of loving any of them, even before the gambling. She wondered how she could have fallen for his glib intellectual cant and charm, and overlook all his weaknesses. Didn't say much for her judgment.

Milo was much too smart to accept an easy lie, so she fell back on the truth, but not the whole truth. She didn't actually *know* the whole truth. "I think your daddy is working out some personal problems that he doesn't want to dump on us."

"When he's finished, will he come back?"

She shook her head. "My darling, I truly have no idea. None of his problems are your fault. He'd never in a million years want you to think they are. Your only job is to keep being the good kid you are. Let the grown-ups worry about the other stuff."

"Sometimes I don't want to be a good kid. Sometimes I want to yell and scream and hit stuff."

"Me, too. The trick is to do your screaming where nobody can hear you and get scared, and to hit things that can take it, like Vi's punching clown. Mostly, not to hurt animals or people."

He sat up. "I really wouldn't hit Vi, Mom. I've never even hit Pete at school, and he deserves it."

"You want to join me for a scream session? We'll go out in the woods and yell our heads off where we won't disturb a soul."

He giggled. "Maybe squirrels. But we can't bring Vi. She'd get scared."

"Deal. Now go to sleep." Helena tucked him in again, bent and kissed him on the forehead.

She went downstairs, poured herself and Marcie an Amaretto, kicked off her shoes and sank onto the sofa. Marcie was reading a mystery. She had the TV on and was watching *The Most Dangerous Catch* with the sound off.

"What was that about?" she asked.

Helena told her. "I have no idea whether I handled it right or not. How do you ever know?"

"You don't. Not until they're forty or so."

"I can't tell Milo his father loves us desperately and will come home. Milo would think I was either lying or stupid. If he could see that his father was a thoughtless jerk, how come I couldn't?"

"He needs a man in his life."

"Puh-leeze."

"I'm not saying you need a man in yours, although I think you do."

"So do you."

"Don't I know it. Milo lives in a house of females. Look into Boy Scouts or Big Brothers. I've seen you throw a baseball, Helena. It is not a pretty sight."

Helena turned up the television's volume to listen to a bunch of tough men talking about fishing in the Arctic. Marcie went back to reading.

During one of the endless commercial breaks, Helena said casually, "Oblivious Al says I've girded my loins."

Her friend looked over the top of her book. "Have you? Why?"

"Semigird. It's counterproductive to look like Mother Hubbard. On the other hand, I'm terrified to look any other way."

Marcie stuck a bookmark in her volume and set it on the coffee table. "What did the counselor say?

Your clothes do not make you a target. A rapist doesn't care whether you're wearing a bikini or a gorilla suit."

"*I* was what he was after…before."

"Yes, you were."

"If I become that person again, he may come back."

"He may not. How many times have we had this conversation? I've stopped counting."

"This time I've made up my mind. I'm going to 'fix myself up,' as my mother used to say."

"I'll believe it when I see it. I do think you'd feel better about yourself, stronger, if you didn't look like crap all the time." When Helena didn't respond, she picked up her book again.

"He has to die."

"I agree," Marcie said over the top of her page. "I want him dead, too, and he didn't rape me."

"I'm making an appointment with your hairdresser."

"Have at it. Just don't get rid of the streak. We like it."

"Who's we?"

Marcie just grinned.

HELENA STOPPED RANDY in the foyer of the gun shop with the pistol range. "May I speak to you?"

"Sure. What's up?"

"Is it too early for Milo to learn to box?"

She expected him to laugh. Instead, he said seriously, "He's tall for his age, but I think he needs a couple more years before he starts sparring with another boy. Why?"

"He wants to hit stuff."

"Like mother, like son. Okay, can you bring him to our next session, thirty minutes early?"

"I was planning to come early anyway. I want to hit stuff, too."

He smiled. "Glad to hear it. You can punch out some of that aggression before class."

"I don't want him to get hurt."

"He won't. I'll put gloves on him and let him hit my hand paddles. It's a way to develop hand-eye coordination without overtaxing his muscles. Not long—say five or ten minutes. We can build to half an hour."

"I'll pay you extra, of course."

"Let's see how it goes before we start talking money." He held the inner door for her.

"Hey, Randy, Helena," said Francine from across the large sales room. "I'm thinking about buying a new toy."

They walked over to the glass-topped counter. "Planning on shooting a rhinoceros?" Randy asked.

Francine held up an enormous Sig Sauer .45 automatic. "I like the look of it. Scare the poop out of a gangbanger."

"And shoot a hole in the gangbanger, the four people lined up behind him and the brick wall. Even for you, Francine, that hog leg is overkill."

"You're no fun at all, Randy Railsback." She handed the gun back to the salesclerk, who took one look at Francine's expression and wiped the smile off his face.

"Okay, dahlin', let's see that one." She pointed to a small automatic. "Is that little enough for you, Mr. Instructor?"

"Petite, just like you."

She sniffed. "I haven't been petite since I was six months old." She turned to the clerk. "See you after our session. Come on, everybody else's already on the range." She raised her eyebrows at Helena. "This time *you're* the one five minutes late."

The range master had already passed out safety glasses and ear protection to the other students and assigned them shooting stations. Helena and Francine got theirs and took their positions. After the man gave them their instructions, they began.

Randy offered his hand to the master. "Any help you can give will be appreciated. I'm Randy Railsback."

"Harley Bitler." The man shook hands. "Any beginners in this group?"

"Some have had more experience than others, but they're all familiar with firearms." He didn't add that they'd all be more than willing to use them. "I'd be grateful for your assistance. I can't get around to all seven of them effectively."

"Sure, happy to oblige. Excuse the pun, but what are you aiming for?" Bitler slid his safety glasses down over his prescription eyewear and screwed in a set of earplugs. "Can't coach with earmuffs." He offered Randy a set of plastic plugs.

"I think they've all worked with single shots at silhouette targets. We need to train them to get off three quick-shot patterns."

"Cop style. Gotcha. Why don't I start with the little old lady at the far end and meet in the middle?"

"Sounds like a plan. Word of advice, don't call her a little old lady."

Bitler didn't look like the prototypical retired military man or ex-cop who might be expected to coach shooting. More like a high school history teacher. He wasn't quite as tall as Randy, and ran to fat around the middle. He wore his eye protection over rimless glasses, and was going bald. The short fringe that was left had started to gray.

Randy watched him with Sarah Beth and decided that he was competent and careful. He'd guessed that Sarah Beth and Ellen would be the most proficient members of the class, and he'd been correct.

Lauren closed her eyes and flinched with each shot, which meant that most of them missed the target. Randy spent a lot of time with her, and by the end of the session, she held a fairly decent pattern on the target, although she still couldn't get off three shots in a burst.

Francine fired doggedly. Though not completely accurate, most of her shots would have taken down her target.

Amanda was either a natural or had had plenty of practice, easily landing single bull's-eye shots. He merely had to coach her to get off three. She was cool, didn't flinch or close her eyes, and didn't miss often. Probably the same way she conducted her law practice.

He kept a close eye on Streak. He didn't expect her to do anything unsafe or stupid, but figured she'd fire too fast and without aiming properly. He moved in to show her how to squeeze the trigger rather than pull, how not to flinch or close her eyes and how to relax. He had minimal success. She tried too hard. Same way she went after him in class.

She'd improved by the end of the session, but had a long way to go.

"Okay, ladies, that's all for tonight," Randy said at the end of an hour. "You're going to have sore hands and shoulders tomorrow morning."

"What are we doing Tuesday night?" Francine asked.

"Boring drills. Developing muscle memory. If you have to think about what to do, you won't react in time."

They dropped off their ear and eye protection, as well as their used shell casings in the bucket provided, thanked Harley and went out, pumped as usual. Randy had already collected their tips before the class, so he could hand Harley a single envelope.

"Thanks, man, much appreciated," Bitler said. "What are they, some kind of class?"

"Something like that."

"Haven't seen you before."

"I use the police range."

"Y'all be coming back?"

"Possibly."

Harley grinned. "Come anytime. You'd be surprised how many people don't tip."

Randy found them in the foyer shrugging into coats and gloves.

"We're all going next door for coffee," Francine said. "You coming?"

*All? As in Streak, too?* She wasn't walking away, so he assumed she was joining the rest. That surprised and pleased him. He put on his windbreaker and followed them.

He sat at the end of the table between Amanda and Streak. After the waiter had taken their orders for coffee or hot chocolate, he heard Francine call from her end of the table, "Hey, Streak, how'd you do?"

She answered to the nickname. "Not well enough. I need more practice. Amanda, I watched you. You're really expert."

"I'm much more used to rifles and shotguns than

pistols," Ellen said. "I used to deer hunt in my younger days, but no amount of venison can compensate for freezing in a tree stand and then having to shoot Bambi. I don't want to think about how it gets to my kitchen."

"If cannibalism wasn't against the law and downright gross, I can think of a bunch of people who would benefit mankind by hopping right into the stew pot," Lauren said.

"We could always feed 'em to the hogs," Sarah Beth suggested.

"Poor hogs." Streak shook her head.

Randy had never doubted that the female of the species was more deadly than the male. "How many of you bait your own fishhooks?"

He was surprised that every hand went up except Streak's. When they looked at her, she said, "I've never been fishing."

Ellen patted her arm. "Come out to our place. We've got bream in our pond big as catfish."

Francine snorted. "Uh-huh. Tell you what, this spring we'll all come out and catch your bream."

"You're on. We'll have a picnic." Ellen looked sheepishly at Randy. "I keep my husband, Tom, around to kill wasps and remove dead mice, though."

"Sugar, men were put on this earth to take out the garbage," Francine said. "And a few other chores." She laughed, and a second later they joined her.

Even Streak laughed, wrapping him in her warm, caramel alto. She caught his eye and held his gaze too long. He wasn't imagining things. She felt it, too.

He wondered if the others noticed, but he didn't dare look around until his pulse slowed. He visualized the two of them drifting along the Ghost River in a johnboat with a bottle of wine. He'd be praying that the bream and crappie were on vacation in another river.

As though she read his mind, Streak pushed her seat back. "I have to get home to read to Milo and Vi." She opened her wallet, but Randy stopped her.

"My treat for everybody tonight."

When Streak protested, Francine said, "Hey, sugar, let him. We're a real cheap date."

She nodded and turned to leave, but he stopped her again. "Escort to your car comes with the service." And to the others, he added, "I'll be right back."

He followed her out and again waited while she unlocked the car, then checked no one was hiding inside. "Got your pistol?"

"I keep it on the seat beside me when I'm on the road."

"How about you give Marcie my cell-phone number. If you don't check in or show up when she expects you, and she can't get you, tell her to call me."

"I am perfectly capable—"

"I'm telling each of you the same thing. Both Sarah Beth and Ellen have a ways to drive on country roads, and you're all driving alone after dark. Just do it, okay?"

"All right." She stopped with her hand on the car door. "You know, don't you?"

"What?"

"You checked me out. I can't believe you did that."

"I checked you all out."

"And found the others had a couple of parking tickets, no doubt. If you open your mouth about what happened…"

He put his hand on hers. She snatched it away and

held it in front of her chest in a fist. "If you want to say anything to them, it's up to you," he said slowly.

"I have no intention of telling anyone anything," she snapped.

"Be careful. O'Hara says you know the guy comes back."

She slid into the car. "I certainly hope so." She started the engine.

Randy stared after her, refusing to believe he'd heard her correctly. Because that could only mean one thing. She planned to sucker him in and take him down. "Of all the dumb-ass ideas…" No way could she go up against this guy, even if she somehow managed not to be taken out before she could react.

Streak already cost Randy bed partners and gave him sleepless nights. At this rate he'd soon start hallucinating from sleep deprivation. What he needed was an uncomplicated, athletic night of sex to calm him down and convince him he was still in the game.

Problem was, he wanted a night of sex with Streak.

# CHAPTER EIGHT

"Milo," Randy said, and shook his proffered hand.

"Very nice to meet you again, Mr. Railsback," the boy replied. He sounded like an accountant, but he was bouncing on his heels, breathing fast, and his eyes were darting toward the bodybuilders.

Streak had handed the child over to him and gone to put on her gloves and work on the light bag, but she kept an eye on them.

Randy tied gloves on Milo and slid the red leather paddles onto his own hands. He explained the process, but before he'd finished, Milo whaled out at him so hard that when he missed, he spun around and would have lost his balance if Randy hadn't caught him.

"Whoa, there, tiger. I see where your mother gets it."

The child's eyes blazed and his little face set hard. "Don't you talk about my mother."

"I meant she's tough, too. But you have to learn to be smart, not just tough."

"My whole family's smart," Milo said. "I'm smarter than Vi, but she's littler." He wasn't boasting, simply stating a fact. "I am tall for my age, but I'm skinny and bad at sports."

"You haven't found the right sport, then. How are you at basketball?" Randy had bought the small boxing gloves at a sporting goods store on his way to the gym. Streak hadn't considered that gloves meant for adults would be too large for Milo. Randy didn't intend to tell her. She'd want to pay for them. They were his treat and his secret.

"I suck at basketball." Again a simple statement. "My dad tried to teach me how to shoot hoops, and sometimes he'd play catch with me, but mostly, I just play soccer at school and I hate it. I trip a lot."

"Have to work on that. But first, let's see if you can hit my hands." He hunkered down and coached Milo through his first awkward punches. The boy concentrated and took coaching much better than most kids his age. Not that Randy knew that many. His nephews were wild and drove their parents nuts.

After fifteen minutes, Randy stopped the session, despite Milo's protests. "Take it slow, kid. Don't want to damage your muscles."

"I have to get big quick," he said. "I have to watch out for Mom."

Randy stopped unlacing the kid's gloves. He saw himself at Milo's age—another skinny, uncoordinated boy carrying too much responsibility.

Because he hadn't been able to fulfill that responsibility, a child had died. Not his fault, his family said. On the Cold Cases squad, he had a second chance to catch the criminals who thought they had gotten away with it. As his uncle had.

Legally, anyway. For a while.

He reached to tousle Milo's damp hair and push it out

of his face, but the boy slipped away from him, uncomfortable with the familiarity.

"Thank you, Mr. Railsback. May I come again?"

"Absolutely. Call me Randy, by the way. You did fine, Milo."

"No, I didn't. But I will." He trotted over to his mother, and Milo the Serious turned into Milo the Supercharged. He bounced around her, punching the air, showing her what he had learned, whooping until they both broke into laughter. Streak hugged the boy to her. Her eyes caught Randy's over Milo's head. She smiled and silently mouthed, *"Thanks."*

He wanted to go join them in a group hug—anything to establish physical contact with her. Instead he nodded and mouthed, *"My pleasure."*

Milo sat on the floor in a corner of the exercise room and did homework during class, although Randy caught him checking out the moves and felt sure he'd go home and practice them on his own. So long as he didn't practice them on his family or friends, it was fine by Randy.

He walked Streak and the others to their cars. Francine and Amanda were going someplace for dinner.

Randy was worn-out. All this celibacy and extra exercise was sapping his energy instead of giving him more. He ought to feel pumped, ready to hit the clubs down on Beale Street, have a margarita or two, check out the ladies.

Instead he went home. As he watched a basketball game on ESPN, he said, "Before long I'll adopt a cat."

WHEN HIS PHONE RANG, he came instantly awake and answered.

"Streak?" he asked, and tried to keep the fear out of

his voice. He checked the dial on his beside clock. It was 1:00 a.m. Only bad news came at 1:00 a.m.

"It's Francine, Randy. Oh, Lord! I didn't know who else to call."

He sat on the edge of his bed. "What's happened? Are you all right?"

"I'm fine. It's Amanda. Somebody tried to kill her."

"How bad? Is she alive?"

"Uh-huh, but she's beat-up. We're in rape crisis at the trauma center."

"I'll be there in twenty minutes."

As he threw on his clothes, he prayed Amanda wasn't badly hurt, and hated that he was so glad it wasn't Streak. He parked illegally at the big medical facility, stuck the police ID on his dashboard and raced into the trauma center to find Francine.

When she saw him, she launched herself into his arms and almost knocked him down.

"Where is she?"

"In there." Francine pointed to one of the curtained enclosures. "The cops are talking to her."

Thank God she could talk. "What happened?"

"I shouldn't have left her. It's all my fault."

"It's not your fault. It's the fault of whoever did this to her. Settle down, Francine. Tell me from the beginning. Then I'll go talk to Amanda. Take deep breaths."

Her ample bosom rose and fell as she took in gulps of air.

"Slow down, you're going to hyperventilate."

She let out a breath.

"That's better. Now tell me."

"Amanda and I went over to that steak house off

Summer for dinner, and we had fun. When she showed up that first night, I thought she was cold and stuck-up, but she's just shy." Francine's laugh held more than a touch of hysteria. "Hard to believe that woman's shy, but she is. Anyway, we said goodbye in the parking lot and drove away. Or at least I did." She grabbed Randy's hands hard. "I should have waited. I know you tell us…but she was getting into her car and I thought…" She began to cry ugly tears.

"Go on. Don't think about that now."

"There was a bunch of traffic. I was waiting for an opening out onto the road when I looked in my rearview mirror. I could still see Amanda's car—see inside it, I mean, 'cause the door was open and the dome light was on—but she wasn't in the driver's seat and something was happening on the ground. She should have been right behind me."

"What did you do?"

She managed another laugh, "Honey, I have never been able to back a car in my life, but I backed that sucker straight into the parking lot, laying on my horn and reaching for my gun at the same time. I ran right smack into the front of Amanda's Jag." Her eyes widened. "She's gonna kill me when she sees what I did to that precious baby of hers."

"She's going to say the hell with the Jag." Randy kept a lid on his impatience. It was important for a witness to tell the story her way, but he wanted Francine to dump it all on him so he could go talk to Amanda.

"I could see she was down on the ground beside the car and there was somebody crouched over her. Looked like they were fighting."

"Could you describe him?"

"When I hit that Jag, he stood up and took off running into the bushes. He was in black, head and all."

"Did you shoot at him?"

Francine put her hands up to her face as if she wanted to close out the sight. "I was afraid if I fired, I'd miss and hit one of those little houses on the other side of the bushes. Maybe kill somebody sleeping."

"It's against the law to fire at fleeing felons. If you'd shot at him, you'd be the one in trouble."

She snorted. "You think they'd convict me if I'd killed the SOB? But I couldn't take the chance. I practically fell out of the car, didn't even turn off the engine, and got my fat self down on the ground. Amanda was so groggy she tried to hit *me*. I don't know what he clocked her with, but the side of her head was bleeding, and her face looked pretty messed up. The sleeve of her jacket was torn out." Francine shook her head. "Then she passed out. By that time, some of the kitchen people came running out of the restaurant to see about the crash, and I said to call 911. They thought I'd done it, since I'd hit her car. Took me yellin' my head off at 'em before they got it. Big black woman hunkered down over a fancy-dressed white woman? Well, what would you have thought, if you didn't know us?"

"I hope you put your gun away before the police got there."

She nodded. "In my purse. Gave 'em my carry permit first and let 'em check to see I hadn't fired. Thank the sweet Lord, Amanda was back to semiconscious by then and holding on to me for dear life, so they knew I didn't do it."

Francine gripped Randy's hands. "Cops are trying to say it was some random purse snatching, but I don't believe it. He was waiting for *her,* Randy, not just anybody. He didn't have to hit her that way, trying to drag her off."

Randy jerked up at that. "Dragging her?"

"Uh-huh. He had hold of her and was yanking her toward the bushes. I guess that's how he tore her sleeve. There were plenty of easier targets in that restaurant he could have gone for. Little old people. Why wait for somebody Amanda's size? She sure as shootin' doesn't look like anybody's victim of choice."

"No, she doesn't. Neither do you."

"*Godzilla'd* be a damn fool to go after *me.* I rode in the ambulance with her because she wouldn't let go of my hand. She doesn't remember much of what happened. Just that one minute she was unlocking her car door, the next she was in an ambulance." Francine put her plump hands over her face and began to sob.

Randy wrapped his arms around her and pulled her against him. He felt as though he was hugging a bolster that kept inflating and deflating. He patted her back. "It's all right, Francine. It's all right."

Finally, she cried herself out and sat up. He handed her his handkerchief so she could wipe her eyes and blow her nose. "What if there hadn't been any traffic on Summer and I just drove off? I probably shouldn't 'a called you, but I didn't know who else…"

"Of course you should have called me. I'd have been mad if you hadn't. I had you pegged as a superhero the first night. I was right."

She grinned. "If I'd gotten close to him, gun or no gun, I'd 'a shot the fool."

"I do not doubt that for a second."

"Detective Railsback?" He looked up to see a uniformed patrolman he didn't recognize coming out of the curtained enclosure where Amanda lay. "You don't know me, but I've seen you around." He smiled at Francine. "Lady inside says you're her guardian angel."

"Huh. Take all the wings God's got on back order and then some to get *me* off the ground." But she sounded pleased.

"Could we talk to you, ma'am? The detectives will want to interview you tomorrow, but I'd like to get your story while it's fresh. Get a BOLO out on the guy."

"What's that?" Francine asked.

"Be on the lookout." He shrugged. "Not that it's likely to do much. He's home in bed by now. We've got the lady's permission to tow her Jag down to the impound lot so the CSIs can go over it. They're keeping her overnight to get a CT scan tomorrow morning. Is your car drivable, ma'am? Do we need to take you home?"

"I drive the heaviest van this side of a Hummer," Francine said. "My rear bumper's probably messed up, but that's all. Somebody needs to drive me back to the restaurant to pick it up, though."

"I'll drive you after I talk to Amanda." Randy motioned to the cop, and when they were out of earshot of Francine, said, "The assailant doesn't know how much she and Francine saw. He could try for either or both of them. Tell your watch commander Detective Railsback suggested he dispatch a policewoman to watch Ms. Donovan tonight, then notify Detective Richard O'Hara."

"In the middle of the night?"

"Trust me. He may decide to come down here now. If she'll let me, I'll stick with Francine."

The cop nodded and reached for the transmitter button on his collar, then stopped. "You don't think this was a mugging, do you?"

"I'd rather not call it one way or the other." *Smart boy,* Randy thought. He'd mention his name to O'Hara.

He had one hand on the curtain of Amanda's cubicle when the patrolman said, "Detective, she bit him. Tore a chunk out of the latex glove he was wearing."

Randy whirled to stare at him. "You've got trace?"

"Yessir. The EMTs found a piece of latex stuck to her shirt and preserved it in an evidence bag."

"Stuck to her with blood?"

"Don't know, sir. They're holding it for the lab techs to pick up in the morning."

*Yes!* Finally concrete evidence. Elated, Randy ducked around the curtain.

Amanda looked even thinner beneath the light hospital blanket. Monitors beeped and registered heart rate and blood pressure. She was hooked to an IV drip and wore a bandage on her head.

"You're getting one hell of a shiner," Randy said. The rest of her face and her left arm looked pretty bruised, as well.

"Thanks to Francine, that's all I'm going to have." She closed her eyes. "I'm doped up and about to be out of it, so talk fast. I have one god-awful headache."

"It'll be worse tomorrow."

"You are a ray of sunshine."

He pulled a chair up to the bed, sat and took her free hand. "I feel responsible."

"You're as responsible as Francine is for saving my ass. You've made us hypervigilant."

"Not vigilant enough, apparently. I should have gone to dinner with you."

"You weren't invited." She clutched his hand. "I'm scared. I'm very, very scared."

"Your self-defense class doesn't seem to have been much help."

"I didn't believe I was in danger from anyone except an angry divorce opponent in the courthouse. There's always a bailiff around. You warned us. I didn't take you seriously." She tried to smile, but obviously moving her face hurt. "I fought the way you said. At least I think I did. You said not to let him take us to another location. Maybe I scratched him. I know I bit him when he covered my mouth with his hand. Tasted rubber."

"We have the piece of latex you tore. Can you remember anything about him? Size? Race?"

She shook her head. "One minute I was opening my car door, the next I was on the ground, scratching and clawing." She touched her bruised cheekbone and winced. "That's when he must have hit me. The next thing I remember Francine was holding me." She clutched Randy's hand hard. "What if he thinks I can identify him?"

"I've asked the department to send someone to stay with you while you're here." He stood. "I should let you sleep."

"No, wait! I want to talk while it's still fresh."

He settled back in his chair. "Okay. Close your eyes. When you clawed him, what did you feel?"

"I reached behind me the way you taught us. Didn't feel like hair or skin. Maybe some kind of a hood? They checked under my nails in case I drew blood, but I don't think I did." She looked down at her hand. "Played hell with my manicure."

She was getting groggy. "Keep going. What did you smell?"

"Oil."

"Cooking oil?"

"Can't remember…" Her head lolled, and a moment later she was asleep.

The young patrolman was leaning against the wall opposite the trauma cubicles when Randy came out. "They're sending somebody to watch Ms. Donovan," he said. "Detective O'Hara wasn't mad I called him, either. Says he'll come down first thing tomorrow morning. Said to tell you thanks and he'd phone you."

Randy drove a largely silent Francine to her car. The Jag had already been towed, but Francine's van only had a small scratch and a broken taillight. He followed her home to a neat 1930s bungalow in East Memphis, and waited in the living room while she checked the house.

"I got the world's best alarm system," she said when she came back into the room. "I'll be fine. It's nearly dawn, and we both need some sleep."

"I'll bunk on the couch."

"You will not. Go home. I got my alarm and my gun. I am worn-out, and I don't want any man babysitting me."

He gave in. "The detectives will call you tomorrow morning to set up an appointment to interview you. Can you take off from the day care?"

"If I have to. Besides, I only run the place. They can do without me. It's the teachers and the grandmothers they need."

"Grandmothers?" He stopped with his hand on the doorknob.

"Uh-huh." She kissed his cheek. "Thank you."

"What for?"

"Being there."

He gave her a bear hug and waited on her front porch until she had armed her alarm system. He was bone tired. Hardly worth driving home, but he needed a shower, shave and fresh clothes. The way he was going, he'd fall asleep over his computer in the squad room. Sooner or later all the caffeine in the world wouldn't keep him awake.

He didn't know how early Streak got up to get her kids ready for school, but he planned to call her to tell her about Amanda and remind her to watch her back.

On second thought, he'd go over to her house. With luck, the attack wouldn't make the early news, so he had a chance of telling her before she heard it from another source.

This wasn't random. Amanda looked too much like the other women, even if she was a few years older.

He detoured by the restaurant where she had been attacked, and cruised all the streets in the vicinity. He took down the license-plate numbers of the two vans he saw parked in driveways, just in case they might be connected to the crime, but found no vans on the streets. If the guy had come in one and parked it close enough to snatch Amanda, he'd long since driven away.

THE FEBRUARY DAWN broke gray and wan, and as exhausted as he felt, Randy wanted to stay in bed. An hour in a hot shower and a venti cappuccino woke him sufficiently to drive to Streak's without getting lost or hitting a tree. He was getting too old for late nights, early mornings and twenty-four-hour shifts. Wasn't that a kick in the ass? If he kept thinking that way, next thing he knew, he'd start looking for a wife.

As if.

He was looking forward to seeing Helena outside of class. His stomach knotted at the prospect of telling her about Amanda's assault. He always felt lousy when he delivered bad news. He wondered whether he'd catch her with her hair down, literally, and how it would feel running through his fingers. So he liked long dark hair. No biggie. He also liked blondes and redheads.

He sat in his car in front of her house while he tried to work out how he'd tell her about Amanda, then gave up and went to ring her doorbell.

"Mom! Somebody's at the door!" He heard footsteps thundering down the stairs even through the security door, then he saw the dead bolt begin to turn.

"Milo! Stop! Get away from the door."

"But—"

"Now!"

More footsteps, barely audible. There was a fish-eye in the door, but not large enough that he could see who was looking at him from the other side.

"Oh!" Streak's voice. More fumbling with locks. He heard the beep of an alarm system being disarmed. Eventually the front door opened, but the glass security door stayed closed.

Her hair was down, all right, and still damp. Her streak appeared luminescent silver against the dark brunette. He'd been hoping to catch her in something silky like a dressing gown. No luck. She wore a baggy gray sweater with gray slacks, and stood with her arms wrapped around herself. But she was wearing lipstick. That was new. She ought to give up and put on something that fit, because what she was wearing couldn't conceal those sexy curves.

"What's happened?" she asked.

Not even a hello. But then how often did a cop show up at the front door at seven-thirty in the morning bringing *good* news?

"Mind if I come in before the neighbors call the cops?" He gave her his biggest smile. No effect.

She opened the security door and stood aside for him to come into the front hall.

"I came to tell you—"

"Randy!"

He managed to turn fast enough to catch Milo's assault on his hip and not in his gut. It hurt, but he couldn't show the kid that. "Hey, Milo. How's the next featherweight champion of the world?"

"Heavyweight!" He aimed a fist at Randy's belt buckle, but Randy captured it before it landed. The kid could punch hard enough to bring back twenty ounces of cappuccino if he aimed just right.

"Milo, stop it," Helena said. "Say good morning properly, go finish your breakfast and get ready for school or we'll be late."

"But—"

"Go."

Randy shrugged to show Milo that he understood mothers could get their priorities screwed up. Viola watched him gravely from the kitchen door, and disappeared after her brother.

"Come back to my office," Helena said. He glimpsed

the living room as he passed. The walls were covered by well-filled bookshelves. There were more bookshelves along the hall leading to the back of the house, and more again in Helena's small office. Stacks of paper littered her desk, wedged around a computer monitor and two printers.

She didn't go around the desk to her battered leather chair, and she didn't ask him to sit in the only other chair, also battered. "What's happened?"

"Amanda was assaulted last night."

He caught her as her knees gave way, but she shook him off and sat on the front edge of her desk. "Is she all right? Of course she's not all right. Where? How bad?"

"The parking lot at the restaurant after she and Francine had dinner. Francine saw what was happening and crashed her car into the Jag. The guy panicked and ran. Amanda's got a black eye and a couple of bruises, but otherwise, she's fine."

"He got away?"

Randy nodded. "Disappeared into the hedges. They searched, but he was gone."

"Was it…him?"

"Possibly. I wanted to tell you before you heard it on the news."

"Is she in the hospital? Is she safe?"

"Under guard."

"Francine saved her? By crashing into the Jag?" Streak laughed out loud.

He wasn't surprised at that, either. The release of tension frequently brought on laughter. "I'm not sure they've told Amanda yet. It's not totaled, but the grill and radiator are toast. It's in the impound lot. We're going over it with the finest-toothed comb possible."

"But you don't think you'll find any evidence."

He shook his head. He'd already decided not to mention the latex shred. It might be weeks before the lab in Nashville processed it for DNA. "He wore gloves, mask, the usual."

"Mom?" Milo called. "We're gonna be late."

She glanced at her watch. "Milo's right. I have to go." She led Randy down the hall. At the front door she stopped and said, "Thank you for coming to tell me." She sounded cool and in control, but he could see the vein in her throat throbbing, and the hand turning the doorknob shook.

"No problem."

As he stepped past her, she grabbed his arm. "Why don't you catch him?" Her eyes blazed. "Damn you." She began to shake all over.

He wrapped his arms around her and held her hard. He could feel every muscle strain against him for a moment, then she curled into his chest and let him hold her.

"We'll get him. I swear," he whispered against her ear. "I won't let him hurt you."

She pulled back, her cheeks wet with tears. "You mustn't let him hurt *anybody*. Promise me."

"You know I can't."

"Then what good are you?" She practically shoved him out the door. He stood on the small porch until he heard the dead bolts click home.

"Not much, Streak, not much."

## CHAPTER NINE

HELENA LET MILO AND VI out at school, drove to Weyland through the Old Forest—her pulse remained nearly normal—parked in her assigned spot and sat in her car.

The bastard had gone after Amanda, who was now on the list of women he might come back to kill. Ready or not, Helena had to move to step two of her plan right this minute.

Rudyard Kipling wrote that in a tiger hunt, the hunters tethered a goat in a clearing, then waited for the tiger to attack. If they shot straight and fast, the goat survived. If not…

If Randy found out what she planned, he'd have kittens. No matter how warm his arms felt around her, no matter that when he looked at her she felt her heart turn over, he was a cop. Her libido must not get in her way.

She was surprised that she actually *had* a libido, and that Randy had caused stirrings she didn't want or need.

She took her briefcase, climbed out of the car and ducked her face into the collar of her coat against the wind. Why on earth anyone had ever chosen February 14 to honor the patron saint of lovers was beyond her.

Maybe February was warmer in Rome or wherever they worked out those things. In west Tennessee it sucked.

"Morning, Professor Norcross," called a lanky boy wearing a black knit watch cap pulled down to his eyebrows. With the collar of his coat turned up, only his eyes and nose were visible.

For a second he looked as though he was wearing a mask. She recoiled, caught the heel of her boot and nearly toppled backward.

"Hey, Professor, you okay?" He grabbed her arm and steadied her.

She managed a smile. "The wind took my breath away. Thank you, Mr. Langston. Have you finished your Ben Jonson paper yet?"

"I'm on the final draft." He let her go and struck off toward the student union.

"Believe that and I'll sell you some swamp land in Arizona." Oblivious Al fell into step beside her.

"If this cold keeps up, you've got a deal."

He held the door of the liberal arts building open against the wind until she slipped inside, and followed her up the stairs to the faculty lounge.

"What's different about you?" he asked as he took her coat. "Ah, it's lipstick. Next you'll be wearing skimpy purple charmeuse dresses with dangly earrings, and sporting a tattoo."

MARCIE PICKED UP Vi's ice cream bowl and fitted it into the dishwasher. "You're serious? You want to dress like the old Helena?"

"Much better. Hot."

"For Randy?"

Helena felt her face flush. "Don't be ridiculous. Call it rediscovering my vanity. I haven't entirely forgotten the old me, but I'm out-of-date."

"Also out of size. You can't drop forty pounds that you didn't need to lose, and keep on wearing your unattractive fat clothes without looking like a fugitive from a low-end thrift shop."

"More like fifty pounds, but I've gained fifteen back."

"I hate you," Marcie said.

"I still can't face rare steak without gagging."

"I really, really hate you."

"Help me anyway." Marcie poured detergent into the dishwasher, closed it and turned the switch, then leaned against the kitchen counter and crossed her ankles.

"What *do* I wear?" Helena asked.

"We'll go over what's left in your closet."

"I tossed everything even moderately sexy after..." Helena took a deep breath and squared her shoulders. "I need to do this fast. Will you go shopping with me?"

"I have little people to look after, remember? *Your* little people."

"We can take them with us," Helena said. "Vi likes to shop."

"Milo would prefer to have his toenails painted puce and pulled out," Marcie said. "Go shopping after work before you go to self-defense. Bring home a bunch of clothes. Return what we hate."

"I hate returning things."

"Run what you pick up by the other women in your class," Marcie said. "A couple of them are real fashion plates. They can tell you what works and what doesn't."

"But they have money—at least Bunny and Amanda

do. I'm going to have to make myself over on a budget."

"If Mickey would pay you what he owes you, you could invest in Chanel."

"Not likely to happen. In a just world, English professors would make more than a sixteenth of the salary the business admin types make."

"And do at least half the private consulting for megabucks."

"Mommy!" Vi flew into the room. "Milo grabbed Petey and won't give him back. He says he's going to drown him in the toilet."

"Milo!" Helena shouted. "Get in here and give Petey back to Vi this minute."

Milo slid around the corner with his hands behind his back. "Here." He tossed the threadbare stuffed rabbit at his sister. Hard. "Cruddy ole thing. It was a joke."

"No, it wasn't," Vi said, clasping the rabbit close to her. "It was mean. You're mean and hateful and—and heinous!" She flew past him and up the stairs. A moment later her bedroom door slammed.

The two women shared a look, before Helena said, "Knock that behavior off right now."

"She's a tattletale," Milo said. "I *never* tattle on her, and I could lots of times."

"Like I believe that," Helena said. "You tattle every chance you get. If you had stuffed Petey down the toilet and stopped it up, you'd be in lockdown until you turned eighteen or paid the plumber's bill, whichever came first. If you want to continue boxing with Mr. Railsback, stop teasing your sister."

He stared at her in horror. "But I love boxing. Afterward I feel great."

"Your choice."

"Okay, I guess." He turned toward the door, then back to his mother. "It's gonna be hard. I may forget sometimes. She's such a little dweeb." He followed his sister up the stairs, but his footsteps dragged.

When his door finally shut, Marcie said, "Heinous?"

"I have no idea where she picked that up."

"She's reading at a fourth-grade level," Marcie said. "I'm glad your ex didn't dilute your gene pool."

"Mickey's not stupid. I'd never have married a stupid man. He's just…"

"The term *deranged* comes to mind."

"*Damaged* is more like it. His mother taught him he could have anything without working for it. That's one of the reasons he gambles—to prove he can beat the system."

"Beat you, you mean."

"We weren't in competition."

"You said he only started gambling heavily when you got tenure and he didn't."

"He was depressed," Helena said. "He hated that I made more money."

"I don't think that would bother a real man," Marcie replied. "You think Randy Railsback would give a flip if you were a multibillionaire and CEO of a Fortune 500 company?"

"Why should my financial status matter to Randy?"

"Come on, I saw him over here at the crack of dawn this morning."

"He came to tell me about Amanda."

"The way he looks at you is hot enough to strip wallpaper."

"And what a romantic visual that is. Mr. Railsback, would you please focus those hot eyes of yours on my bathroom walls? I'd like to redecorate."

"His eyes aren't the only things about him that are hot."

"So go for it," Helena said.

"He's already made his choice. You're it, whether you like it or not. And I suspect deep down you *do*."

HELENA SHUCKED the three millionth sweater and hung it on the rack with the rest of the rejects. She felt sorry for the poor salesclerk, who had started out being helpful and enthusiastic. "Everything I put on feels too tight."

"May I make a suggestion, ma'am," said a new voice from outside the fitting cubicle.

She opened the door. From her chic black suit to her six-inch heels, this woman looked like the head of the department, possibly even the buyer. "Please. I can't seem to make up my mind."

"I think I know what the problem is," the woman said with a smile. She sounded genuinely helpful and not at all put out. Helena gave her high marks.

"I'll give a heads-up to Wilma in the lingerie department. You need bras that fit. That one barely touches you. No wonder everything looks strange."

Helena felt her face heat. She couldn't even pick out suitable underwear. She was still wearing her fifty-pounds-plus cotton bras that were two years old, with worn-out elastic, and her white cotton granny panties. Not exactly chic, but she'd never expected anyone who mattered to see them.

"Then come back upstairs. Would you like some help on what works for you?"

"Oh, would I!"

"You have dark hair, but your skin is fair and has no yellow in it." The lady, whose name tag read Karen, picked up a yellow sweater. "This is wrong for you. So is this gray one. You can wear taupe, but not yellow or gray."

Helena sheepishly went downstairs to Lingerie, and found herself an hour later with a half-dozen exorbitantly priced bras, a dozen pairs of bikini underpants and a pair of thigh-high black stockings with lace tops she couldn't imagine where she'd ever wear. The tethered goat better not have to strip down to underwear before she killed the tiger.

So why had she bought them? She glanced in the mirror, sucked in her gut and rolled her shoulders back. Dammit, because they made her feel attractive, and for the first time in what seemed like forever, she actually wanted to feel that way. For whom? The attacker?

Or Randy? Surely not.

An hour later, still wearing her sweats for class, she asked the security guard at the mall exit to escort her to her car in the gathering darkness.

She tossed her bags onto the backseat, checked that nobody was hiding on the floor and climbed in fast. Shutting and locking the doors, she turned on the ignition and put the car in Reverse. Only then did she set down her purse and fasten her seat belt.

That was one of the tricks Randy had taught them. If someone suspicious walked up to her car, she could back out and lay on the horn before he reached her. If she hit another car behind her, rising insurance rates were the better alternative, and chances were the guy would run away.

Francine had remembered the lessons and acted on them. Amanda had not. Maybe the guy had been too fast for her, but Helena would be willing to bet Amanda had organized herself before she locked her door. Women did. They set their purses and packages down, sat in the front seat with the door unlocked while they dredged through their handbags for keys, made cell-phone calls, put on seat belts before they locked the car doors—on and on. And every second made them vulnerable to carjacking or worse.

Some women still picked up hitchhikers.

The small things Randy taught might save a life. In a world where one had to live in a state of alert, how could you ever let your guard down when you wanted to?

The front of the gym was in shadows. Helena didn't see a soul as she carried her purchases inside and left them on a chair where the other women could help her sort through them after class. She tightened the rubber band around her hair and went to work out on the heavy bag before anyone else arrived.

As she walked by the small boxing ring set up in the back of the men's side of the gym, someone called, "Hey, Streak, you're way early."

His voice shouldn't make her heart pound. He had been sitting in the far corner, out of the light. Now he came over, leaned on the ropes and smiled at her. His smile warmed his eyes. He wore only shorts, and his hair and chest glistened with sweat. She longed to say something snarky like, "I love the smell of testosterone in the evening," but somehow the words wouldn't come.

She tore her eyes away from his belly button and below, where she could see the outline of his cup.

"I didn't notice you back there. Where's your sparring partner?" she asked.

"No partner. I'm working on my Krav Maga."

"What's that?"

"Israeli martial art. Deadly."

"Could I learn?" she asked. Deadly would be good. Better offense than defense.

He laughed. "In five years, maybe. Tell you what, come on up and we'll spar a little. Time you mixed it up. You didn't bring Milo?"

"Not tonight, and I'm not ready to mix it up. I'd make a fool of myself."

"There's nobody here yet to see if you do. I promise I won't hurt you."

"I may hurt *you*."

"I'll take my chances." He pulled her up and held her elbow as she climbed between the ropes. She caught a toe on the edge of the mat and fell to her knees.

"Easy there, tiger," he said, swinging her against his chest. She inhaled the scent of clean male sweat. She felt his heart rate speed up and knew hers was doing the same thing.

She took a step back. Her mouth went dry, and she couldn't catch her breath.

Not another panic attack, not here, not now! She'd die of embarrassment. She grabbed the rope behind her so hard her fingers went numb.

Randy watched with concern as she took slow, deep inhalations.

The heat of his body should not have wakened an answering heat in hers. That was a complication she hadn't expected and couldn't afford. Staring into his eyes and feeling her insides turn to jelly was bad enough.

"You're not wearing boxing gloves," she said, and hoped he didn't pick up on the tremor in her voice. *Stupid!* Obviously he wasn't wearing gloves. She could feel where every one of his fingers had splayed against her back when he'd steadied her.

"We won't need them. I want to teach you to move out of the way after you punch. Your opponent won't stand still. Neither should you." His businesslike tone said he was taking his cue from her, but his eyes still held hers, until she looked away in confusion.

"Aren't we supposed to wear mouthpieces?" she asked.

"You don't have one and mine's in my locker. Only body shots. Agreed?" He slid a pair of padded leather gloves without fingertips over her hands. They weren't as heavy as boxing gloves and didn't feel nearly so cumbersome.

"These are supposed to protect my knuckles when I hit you?"

He chuckled. "*If* you hit me."

"Oh, I'll hit you, all right." The floor of the ring felt springy, so she bounced around a bit while Randy watched her with a grin on his face. "So how do we do this?" she asked.

"You're working out consistently on the bags, and you've watched me spar with Milo. Remember what I taught you. Keep your distance, keep your cool, pick your shots and step away. Move left. Give me a combination—left jab, right cross." He held up his hands. "Come on."

Left jab to the body, right cross. *Smack, smack.* He caught both on the palms of his gloved hands. She felt the concussion in her fists. Not painful—exhilarating.

He nodded. "Too tentative. Try again."

She did. Punch, punch, step left. Punch, punch, step left. After a dozen steps, she caught the rhythm.

If she hadn't been working out regularly, her arms and shoulders would have screamed in pain by now just from the stress of holding them up in front of her. Although sweat ran down her body, her muscles didn't hurt. She moved faster, hit harder. He sidestepped or caught her blows on his forearms.

He was driving her crazy. No matter how fast she was, he was faster. She fought to control herself, as he casually warded off her hardest punch. Dammit, she'd wipe that smug smile off his face. She'd knock him on his tight ass if it killed her!

Tentative, was she? Careful? She'd show him superior upper-body strength.

No man was going to best her—never again! Never hide, never quail, never curl into a ball while the blows fell and fell until she couldn't scream for the blood choking her, couldn't keep his hands from tearing at her, forcing her open—

"Hey, whoa! Time out!"

Rationally, she knew she should stop, that she was out of control, that Randy wasn't the enemy. But something inside her had broken free and she couldn't seem to force it back.

He caught a right cross on his glove, tossed it away. She flailed at him with punch after punch, forcing him back against the ropes. "Fight, damn you!" She could take it. She *had* to take it. How else could she find out she wouldn't run?

She felt herself falling before his arms came around her, pinioning her own to her sides as his heel cut her legs out from under her.

They hit the canvas locked together. She struggled against him, twisting and kicking as his weight bore her down. "Hit me! For God's sake hit me," she sobbed. "You *have* to hit me."

"I can't," he whispered. "I've got you. You're safe."

The madness drained away as quickly as it had come. "I'm sorry," she murmured. "I am *so* sorry."

"I know."

She felt his breath against her lips. Part of her had been afraid of him from the start. Not because he was a cop—that was only his job. She was afraid of what he *was,* what he did to her when he looked at her, touched her. In his arms she felt longing, desire, the need to hold and be held, to come together in pleasure, not pain.

To do what she planned meant denying even the possibility of love. Afterward, she might find someone. Not now. Not yet. How could her body betray her this way?

He released her arms and brought his lips gently down on hers. Her own lips parted and answered him, exploring, tasting salt and lemons on his tongue—a margarita. Her hips lifted against the erection she felt even through his jockstrap.

She ran her fingers down the muscles along his naked spine. She longed to taste him, caress him, guide him inside her, move with him up and up until she soared to a place where her body ceased to be her enemy.

He lifted himself on his forearms to look down at her

with unfocused eyes, but she wrapped her arms around his neck and pulled him back, to kiss him deeply again. His hand slid between them, and she gasped as his palm circled her nipple to send shock waves of pleasure to her core.

"Aw right!"

She barely heard the words, but did hear the slow applause.

Randy broke the kiss. He rolled off her and onto his feet in one smooth move, reached down, grabbed her hands and pulled her up, then let her go and turned away.

For a moment she couldn't remember where they were. *Bad.* Then she did. *Worse, much worse.* She grabbed the top rope of the ring and fought to get her breathing under control.

"Man, that is some *kinda* full-contact sport. Way to go." The boy grinning up at them was one of the serious bodybuilders who won posing contests. Randy was three inches shorter, forty pounds lighter and fifteen years older, but one glance at his face warned Helena she had two seconds to keep him from vaulting the ropes, decking the boy and getting one of them hurt.

She raised an eyebrow, and said in the voice she'd perfected to quell unruly students, "Whatever you think you saw, you didn't."

The kid started to say something, but glanced from her to Randy, said, "Yes'm," and removed himself quickly to the locker room.

She watched him go. "It worked, didn't it?"

"Nobody else saw us." Randy reached for her hand, but she backed away from him.

"I've never done anything like that in my life. You mustn't tell anyone."

He dropped his eyes and said in a perfect imitation of the kid's voice, "Yes'm." Then he smiled. "I won't, but he will. We'll be the hit of the gym once this gets around."

"Nobody better hear it from you."

"Promise. Provided we can practice our new martial art until we're experts."

"Don't press your luck."

## CHAPTER TEN

HELENA HATED COMMUNAL showers, but this time she stood under one as cold as she could bear in the women's locker room, and scrubbed until she could no longer smell Randy on her skin.

How could she lose herself that way? And in public? How could she look at Randy or practice the moves he taught without remembering his palm on her breast, the heat of his kiss, the weight of his body pressing against her?

He was nothing like the few men she'd allowed into her life. Certainly not like mercurial, irresponsible Mickey, who cheated and gambled and abandoned his children, who resented her when she was successful and gloated when she'd nearly been destroyed.

She'd never wanted any man as she wanted Randy.

Nobody *allowed* Randy. From that first moment when he'd dropped her to the mat so easily, he'd been in charge.

She planned to kill the only other man who had controlled her.

"YOU GO, STREAK," Francine said. "'Bout time you decided to look decent."

"Am I so bad?"

Even Ellen laughed. "As compared to what? Come on, let's see what you've come up with."

Randy picked that moment to join them. Helena quickly thrust an emerald-green sweater back into the bag.

"Later," whispered Bunny. "After we get rid of Randy. We can look at those things back in the dressing room."

"I can't ask you to stay late."

"Get real! We are talking shopping here," Bunny said.

Out of everyone else's hearing, Helena asked Francine, "How is Amanda?" She glanced at the others. "I wasn't sure they knew."

"She swears she'll be here tonight. I told her she was crazy, but she says she can't afford to miss a session, 'specially now." Francine looked around the room. "I guess it didn't make the news because nothing really bad happened."

"Thanks to you."

"What are y'all whispering about?" Sarah Beth asked.

From the doorway, Randy said to the group, "They're discussing Amanda. You want to tell them, Francine, or you want me to?"

"I can't talk about it."

After he'd finished describing the incident, the women crowded around Francine.

"Thank the Lord you saw what was happening," Ellen exclaimed. "We ought to send her flowers."

"I'd rather have a steak for my black eye," Amanda said from the door.

"What are you doing here?" Sarah Beth cried. "You ought to be home in bed with a policeman." She giggled. "You know what I mean. Oh, dear, you do have a shiner, don't you?"

"But my jaw's not broken," Amanda said. "Several of my colleagues regret that my jaw's not wired shut for the next six weeks."

"You're taking this awfully well," Lauren commented.

"It's an act. I don't remember much about it, which makes it easier." She held out her hands to Randy and Francine. "From here on in, I'm paying better attention, in class and out."

"And not driving alone?" Ellen asked. "Who brought you here?"

"Me. I can't let this stop me from living. I waited in the parking lot until I could come in with other people."

"What are the police doing to catch him?" Francine asked.

"I had a long interview with a Detective O'Hara this morning. He says I may have been a victim of opportunity. Wrong place, wrong time."

"Nonsense," Helena stated. "You were a target, same as I was."

The temperature in the room dropped twenty degrees, as they all turned to stare at her.

"Only, I didn't have a guardian angel named Francine watching out for me. I didn't get away." She turned to the black woman. "You asked why I'm so frumpy. I wasn't before. Afterward, I hid behind sloppy clothes and no makeup. Detective O'Hara thinks he goes for women who dress like Amanda and me, but the way I did before."

"He? The same man who raped Helena tried to rape Amanda? Randy, is this true?" Ellen asked. "How come it's not all over the news?"

"The powers that be believe that until they have real evidence this is actually the same serial rapist—"

"And killer," Helena interjected.

"He kills them?" Amanda's hand went to her throat.

"Not the first time."

"But they never come *back,*" Lauren whispered. "Do they?"

"In about twenty percent of cases they do," Randy said. "You're here to learn to keep safe, so you'll never be a victim. That's what I want, too. Afterward, if you've got time, let's get coffee and talk about it."

"Within department policy?" Amanda asked.

"The heck with department policy. I'm not on duty tonight."

"Cops are always on duty, sugar," Francine declared.

"Sorry, we've got something else to do after class," Sarah Beth said.

Amanda gave up after ten minutes and sat in the corner of the room. "My depth perception's off," she said as she touched her eye. "And I seem to hurt more places than I thought I had places."

"So watch and learn." Randy patted her shoulder.

"I really, really, want to hit somebody," she said with a sad smile. "I'm not a violent person normally, although there are some deadbeat dads I'd like to throttle and some that have threatened me."

"That's the way I feel," Helena confessed. "Maybe everyone would benefit from some boxing lessons. I've been coming early and working out on the bags."

"Sounds like fun," Ellen said. "Get rid of all that hostility."

"The bodybuilder boys won't like it," Helena mused. "They seem to think they have first dibs when they're here, and that includes the ring and the boxing equipment. They consider I'm an intrusive amateur, and a woman to boot."

"And we care because?" Sarah Beth's eyes glittered. "We have the run of the place, don't we? Jessica says we do."

"They'll just have to stand in line with us lightweight contenders," Francine declared.

RANDY SUGGESTED he and O'Hara meet for barbecue at B. B. King's on Beale Street. The place was noisy, but they managed to snag a booth in the back where they could talk without being overheard.

"How's Amanda Donovan?" O'Hara asked as he slid his bulk in with difficulty. Randy pulled the table closer to give the big man more room.

"Not too bad physically, but she's more frightened than she thinks she is." He ordered a regular barbecue with onion rings and sweet iced tea.

"Make mine a jumbo with fries," O'Hara said. "But unsweet tea for me." He waited until the waitress moved off. "Assuming Donovan was one of his—"

"Come on, Dick," Randy interrupted. "She fits the pattern."

"Not perfectly. Donovan's a little older, has plenty of enemies and a reputation as a junkyard dog. Word is her husband stiffed her, then loped off into the sunset with a lucrative new partnership and a fancy new girlfriend. 'Bitch' is the nicest term I've heard from her opponents. Her clients, however, bless her and send her fruitcakes at Christmas."

"So you already knew her?"

"Met her a few times in court. I agree that she's probably our guy's latest victim."

Their waitress set down tall glasses of iced tea. O'Hara dumped three envelopes of artificial sweetener in his and drank half the glass in one swig.

"She's the first victim we know of since the stock-broker died before he could rape her, correct?" Randy asked.

O'Hara nodded.

"And because of Francine's interference, he blew it with Amanda. He must be antsy."

"Agreed."

"What the hell do you think triggers him?"

"He's one patient SOB. We haven't figured out his timetable."

"And what precipitated the first rape? Doesn't the FBI say there's always an event that kicked them off in the first place? How does he find his vics?"

O'Hara chewed his barbecue in silence. Randy waited. He didn't have much appetite these days, what with worrying about Streak.

The detective put down his napkin and leaned his elbows on the table. "Don't you think we've asked those questions? The victims don't go to the same churches, grocery stores or hairdressers, fill up at the same service stations, patronize the same shops. They don't use the same landscape or pool services. If he drives the streets until he spots a likely candidate, we may never catch him."

"Pizza delivery?"

"They don't eat the same brand of pizza. It's hopeless to think of every possible point of contact, but if you come up with something we missed, check it out. Took years to catch BTK, and they never did get Zodiac."

"He's going to do it again."

"I know."

## CHAPTER ELEVEN

LIZ SLAUGHTER STOPPED HIM in the hall outside Cold Cases as he was leaving. He was dog-tired from working his other cases, when all he could think of was Streak.

"Jud and I are having a pre–Valentine's Day barbecue Saturday night," she said. "Dig out your little black book and bring somebody. Sixish."

He didn't feel like going to a party, but felt less like cruising Beale Street bars. He couldn't think of any current or former woman that he wanted to ask to go with him. If he went stag, however, his reputation as a player would never recover.

Liz gave him a quizzical look and said, "Small group. Informal. Mostly just us." She reached across and laid the back of her hand against his forehead. "You coming down with something?"

He shook his head. "I'm fine."

"Then we'll expect you with the lady of your choice."

The minute he reached his loft he drank a Sam Adams in one gulp, kicked off his shoes and fell back on the maroon leather sectional that divided the living room from the dining room and kitchen.

He could only truly protect Streak by catching her rapist, but that might not happen soon. In the meantime, he'd stick close to her. Maybe Liz's barbecue was the place to insinuate himself.

He looked up the phone number to Marcie Halpern's side of the duplex. He expected she'd be next door at Streak's and that he'd have to leave a message, but she answered on the fourth ring. She sounded rushed and breathless.

And puzzled to hear from him.

"I need a favor," he said.

"Send Helena and the children to Barbados? Even if she had the money, she has a job she can't afford to lose."

"If I had my way, I'd send her to Outer Mongolia until we catch the guy, but that's not feasible, either. Keep as close to her as you dare."

"She'll catch on."

"Tough."

"I also have a job, plus the children to watch."

"Yeah, that's why I'm going to try to be around when I can."

"Strictly to protect her?" Marcie said. "How big a doofus do you think I am?"

"Not a doofus at all, otherwise I wouldn't be talking to you."

He heard the chair scrape as though she'd pushed away from wherever she'd been sitting, and stood up. "You may not realize it, but Helena's still very fragile. I've seen the way you look at her. If you use her or hurt her in any way, physical or emotional, I will see that your playing days are over and your particular studly genes will be cut out of the gene pool. Clear?"

"Crystal."

"Now, Helena's fixing spaghetti and I have to go next door and toss the salad. Bye."

He sat and stared at the telephone, then dialed Streak's number.

"Norcross residence."

He recognized Milo's voice even though he was lowering it to sound more grown-up.

"Hey, Milo, is your mother home?" It was a trick question. Every caller should think there was an adult present.

"May I tell her who's calling?"

"It's Detective Railsback."

"Randy? I thought it was you, but Mom says I should always ask first."

"She's right."

"Hey, Mom," he shouted in Randy's ear. "It's Randy."

"Detective Railsback," he heard Helena say.

"He says I can call him Randy."

"What can I do for you?" she asked when she picked up.

"I need a favor."

"What sort?"

"One of the other detectives, Liz Slaughter, and her husband are having a barbecue Saturday evening. Real informal. Can you come?"

Silence. "Are you asking me out?"

"Yeah." He braced himself.

"Small gathering?"

"Right."

"Well, if Marcie isn't busy and can look after the kids."

"You think I could come early? Milo asked me to toss him a few balls."

"He did?" She paused. "If it's not an imposition."

"I'd enjoy it. It's warm enough if we wear jackets." He would enjoy it. He liked the kid. He wasn't too sure about Viola, who obviously wasn't too sure about him, either.

"Just a minute while I ask Marcie." He heard mutters in the background, then Streak came back on the line. "She says it's fine."

"Tell her we'll bring her back some barbecue."

After he hung up, he slumped on the couch and closed his eyes. His pulse was racing. He hadn't realized how much he'd wanted her to come with him. He felt like a fourteen-year-old with his first crush.

Play catch with Milo? What was that all about?

Okay, so the closer he stuck to her and her family, the safer she'd be. Nothing else. Uh-huh.

"HE DOESN'T KNOW ABOUT your new clothes and your new hair," Marcie said. "I'd have killed you if you'd taken out the streak."

"Linda wouldn't hear of it," Helena replied. She wasn't used to being able to swing her hair. Now at chin length, it felt ten pounds lighter. "I had forgotten what tyrants hairdressers can be."

"So this is the big coming-out."

"Randy's expecting my usual grunge self. How's he going to react?"

"If he's like most men, he'll notice a difference, but he won't have a clue what it is."

"He'll realize, all right. He's a professional woman-izer." Helena stared at her reflection in the bathroom mirror and at Marcie behind her. "I can't do this. Look at me—I'm shaking. Remember what happened the last time I tried to go out on a date?"

"That was a long time ago. You're stronger now. Besides, he was a *blind* date."

Helena rolled her eyes. "I still can't believe I hid in the closet."

"You wrote him a very nice apology and sent him a gloxinia."

Helena laughed. "Thank heaven he never called back."

"Randy's just a friend."

Helena avoided Marcie's gaze. She would never tell her about the boxing ring, and went hot with embarrassment when she thought of it herself. Randy never brought it up, although several bodybuilders—most of whom were barely out of their teens—had asked her out. Them she could handle. Her own feelings were the problem.

"Mom!" Milo burst into Helena's bedroom. "Randy's here. We're gonna do some batting practice."

"Go to it. Stay in the backyard and don't break anybody's windows."

"Oh, Mom. We're using one of those balls that doesn't break stuff."

The doorbell rang. "I'll get it." Milo catapulted down the stairs.

"Tell him I'll be ready in a half hour."

There was no answer, but the front doors were thrown open, and a moment later she heard footsteps moving down the hall and out the back door.

Randy had a rumbly baritone that easily overrode Milo's shouts. If she went to the window, she could look down on him. Instead, Marcie did, while Helena put on lipstick and eye shadow with a shaky hand. "Too much?" she asked at last.

"You look fine," her friend answered.

"Mommy," Vi said from the doorway. "That man is in the backyard with Milo."

"Mr. Railsback is helping Milo with his batting."

"I don't like him."

Helena swung around and held out her arms. Vi walked into them. "Why don't you like him, honey?"

"I don't like hitting."

"He doesn't hit me in the gym, even when I hit him."

"He makes you mad."

Helena glanced over at Marcie, who raised her eyebrows. This child was too perceptive. She'd only watched the class a couple of times, yet she had picked up on her mother's barely controlled anger.

Thank God Vi hadn't been there the first night, when she'd gone for Randy and wound up on her butt. She pulled Vi onto the knee of her new pants and wrapped her arms around her slim waist. Vi leaned her head on her shoulder. "Randy is trying to help me, to help all of us, so that nobody *can* hurt us."

"Why would anybody hurt you?"

"Marcie, you can weigh in here any time you like," Helena said.

She raised her hands in a "no way" gesture.

"Not everybody in this world is nice." Helena wondered if she should mention her own anxiety attacks, but they frightened Vi badly. Like any child, she wanted her mother to be strong. "So Randy shows us all how to look after ourselves and you in case somebody does try to hurt us. Not that anyone will ever actually try, but if somebody should, we'll be prepared and not be scared."

"You're not really mad?"

"Not at all. I'm grateful to him. And he doesn't hit me. He shows me how not to get hit. You understand?"

"I guess." Vi didn't sound convinced, but it was a start. She slid off her lap. As she left, she said over her shoulder, "Don't hit."

Helena dropped her forehead into her hand. "I handled that badly."

"As well as you could. Talk about the elephant's child! Vi remembers every single thing that happens."

"And frequently puts the wrong spin on what she's seen and heard. I have to remember that and head her off."

"What you have to do is finish getting ready." Marcie gazed at her critically. "Earrings."

"Do I have to? The holes in my ears have probably closed up."

"That's an old wives' tale." Marcie brought a pair of small gold hoops from Helena's jewelry box. "Here."

The back door slammed and Milo yelled up the stairs, "Mom, Randy says you need to go."

"Be right there." She grabbed Marcie's hand. "I can't do it. You go. Make some excuse."

"Get your tail down those stairs. Here's your purse."

"What if you need me?"

"You have a cell phone. Go." As she shoved Helena out her bedroom door, she whispered, "If you don't come home until breakfast, I won't worry."

"What?"

"You heard me."

RANDY HAD NO IDEA how many parties Helena had attended in the past two years, so he planned to keep his distance and let Liz handle integrating her into the group. If nothing else, they could talk babies. Women always enjoyed talking babies, didn't they? At the first mention, he usually sprinted in the other direction without a backward glance.

He turned when he heard footsteps on the stairs. For a moment he thought Helena had a houseguest. He'd been gearing up to deal with raised eyebrows when he introduced her. Cops being cops, he'd even geared up for possible snickers.

No chance of that. Wow.

"Are pants all right?" she asked diffidently. "I can put on a dress...."

"They're perfect. I like your hair."

She touched it and actually blushed. "Bunny's hairstylist cut it. She said my split ends had split ends."

He'd seen her aggressive and passionate and frightened. He'd never seen her shy before. Kind of endearing.

Endearing, hell. How was he going to keep his hands off her?

"YOUR IDEA OF FRUMPY is different from mine," Liz Slaughter whispered to Randy. "I love the streak. I'd kill to have hair that thick."

Randy glanced at Streak, sitting beside Jack Samuels in front of the Slaughters' massive stone fireplace, where a crackling fire kept the February chill at bay. She looked completely relaxed and was actually laughing at one of Jack's old and generally bad jokes.

Her fair skin glowed faintly peach in the firelight. He

knew more about women's clothes than most men did, and he'd be willing to bet the maroon sweater that caressed her breasts was cashmere. He longed to do the caressing without the sweater between them, and the thought of her whole body under his touch...

He took a deep breath. He would stick to his plan. Maybe a kiss at the door, maybe not. But no invitations to his loft for coffee. Not tonight.

She must trust him. Tall order considering he was a pretty untrustworthy guy, and she was a woman who had reason to fear men. Still, she'd come a long way in a short time.

From what he could see tonight with the new clothes, the makeup, the haircut, the relaxed way she curled up on Liz's couch with her arm stretched along the back, she'd inched out of the shadows, if not precisely into full light.

She was wearing nail polish. He'd missed that. He'd caught the eye shadow and the earrings, but now he saw that the short nails of her elegant hand were a soft pink. He longed to feel those sensitive fingers on his back again, holding him, accepting him, guiding him to her.

"Your eyes are crossed," Liz whispered. "You've got it bad."

"My eyes never cross."

"I think the Bible says something about that which we have feared has come upon us. She's going to break your heart, Randy Randy. You might as well have fallen for a cloistered nun."

"Is it that obvious?"

"I'd stay away from Jack, too. He knows you even

better than I do. I don't think Lieutenant Gavigan will notice, but when I was in the kitchen with Jud, putting the dishes in the dishwasher, he said he'd never thought you'd fall in love."

"He said *that?* I'm not in love. I'm in lust."

"Of *course* you are. Pure lust and nothing else. By the way, my dear husband added 'poor bastard.'"

On the drive home, Helena sat quietly. "They're nice people," she said after a few minutes. "Thank you for inviting me."

He felt tongue-tied in a way he hadn't since he'd turned thirteen and discovered girls. "I was afraid…"

"What?"

"Well, for cops, shop talk is cop talk. I was afraid you'd either be bored or uncomfortable."

"Because I'm a crime statistic? A borderline nutcase?"

He put his hand on her thigh for a second to shut her up. She didn't flinch, but he withdrew it anyway. "Don't put words in my mouth. The guys I work with are smart, honest and dogged, but not necessarily book smart. Me, neither. I scrounged my degree in criminal justice in night school, and we didn't concentrate all that much on *War and Peace.*"

"How about *Crime and Punishment?*"

"Dostoyevsky or legal statutes?"

"Now who's being arrogant? You've profiled me as a literary snob, while you're profiling yourself as a redneck slob, which you are not."

"Who says I'm not?"

She laughed. "Have you actually read *War and Peace?*"

"Yeah, yeah, okay, so I've read it. But on my own time."

"Most of my students think they're overworked if they have to read the Cliffs Notes on *Hamlet*."

He pulled into her driveway. He didn't expect her to wait for him to race around the car to open her door for her, but he also didn't want her to sprint for her front door before he had a chance to say good-night properly. In the end it was a dead heat. She climbed out as he opened the door, so that she nearly stood on his toes. They were too close not to move closer. He wrapped his arm around her waist and held her against him. He felt her resist for a moment, then her body molded to his as he bent his head to kiss her.

He meant to give her a kiss good-night. Before Streak, he'd always managed to keep his mind a half-step back, orchestrating the seduction, building the passion. He prided himself on being a caring lover, never selfish, always in the driver's seat, assuring his lover enjoyed herself as much as he did.

The moment her lips touched his, his concentration disintegrated just as it had in the boxing ring. He wanted to crush her until her bones melted into his, to absorb her so that they would never be separate again. When her lips parted, her tongue answered his with the same passion he felt, and her hips moved against his erection.

Without warning, she tensed and pulled away. "I can't do this."

He caught up with her as she fumbled with the key, then opened her front door. "I'm sorry, so sorry," she murmured. "It's not your fault." She fled inside and shut the door in his face.

After her door closed behind her, he sat in his car

with his head on the steering wheel until his erection subsided and he could breathe normally again. He needed a woman in the worst way.

Only, sex wasn't just sex anymore.

## CHAPTER TWELVE

STREAK STAYED OUT OF Randy's way when he coached Milo, and during classes, for the next several weeks. Strictly teacher-pupil. She did join everyone for coffee afterward on the nights Milo stayed home, but sat at the end of the table farthest from Randy. He let her have her space. That kiss in the boxing ring must have rattled her badly.

He wasn't too surprised when she'd attacked him, although she'd been controlling herself much better in class since she started working out on the bags. But the sudden explosion when they'd kissed had stunned him. Maybe once she'd let all that emotion loose trying to beat his brains out, it had to come out somewhere else. Not great for his ego. At least he knew now there was a great passion inside her. He wanted to be the man to awaken it again.

One night she stopped him after class on his way to the locker room. "I have to attend a faculty reception Friday evening. If you're free, would you go with me?"

He wiped the sweat off his face. "Trotting out the tame bear?"

"Never mind." She strode off toward the women's lockers.

"Hey," he called after her. "Sorry. That was uncalled-for. What do I have to do? Put on a suit and make nice?"

"That's about it. It's a small cocktail party for a couple of big alumni contributors in town for a basketball game. I have to go, and I'd rather not go alone."

"I can talk basketball."

"I assumed you could."

THE PRESIDENT OF WEYLAND and his family lived in a Tudor mansion just off campus. Since Weyland College owned it and used it for entertaining, the living room seemed more like a gentleman's club than a home. Stiff portraits that Randy assumed were of previous presidents hung on the polished walnut paneling, and the Oriental rugs covering the hardwood floors looked antique.

A fire burned in a stone fireplace that was large enough to roast an ox, but there were no comfortable chairs in front of it, and no TV. Plenty of leather sofas, antique tables and fancy lamps, but they seemed to be more for show, since no one was actually sitting on them.

From somewhere "off stage" New Age music drifted in. Yeah, it did seem like a stage designer's idea of what a college president's living room should look like. He hoped the president and his family had a wing in another part of the house, because they sure couldn't relax here.

"I hate this room," Helena whispered as they stood at the door and surveyed the crowd. "Reminds me of the reception area in a fancy funeral home."

People were too engrossed in their own conversations to notice Helena and Randy. "I have to speak to the president," she said, "and get credit for being here. Come on, I'll introduce you." As they crossed into the threshold, a slim, gray-haired man tapped Helena on the shoulder. Randy decided from the cut of his suit that it was expensive—Armani or even Zegna.

"Helena, my dear, introduce us." He looked like an aging Puck with a glint in his eye.

"Detective Randy Railsback, Albert Barkley from the English Department."

Randy shook the man's soft hand, which held his a trifle too long.

"I'm in American studies," Dr. Barkley said. "You would add immeasurably to my studies."

"I'm sure you already cover a broad enough field," Randy said with a smile.

Barkley slipped his hand under Randy's elbow and leaned close. His breath smelled of rum and breath mints. "When I saw the way she dressed tonight, I wondered if there was a new man in her life."

"She did this on her own. I had nothing to do with it."

Barkley raised an eyebrow. "Whatever the reason, she's suddenly trying to return to the old Helena." He dropped his voice and said seriously, "I'm fond of her. I've been afraid we'd never get her back."

"Helena, who is this gorgeous creature?"

Randy turned to face a woman six inches taller and two feet broader than Helena. She wore a voluminous paisley silk caftan that looked as though it had started life as drapery in a sultan's harem. Even in flat-heeled sandals, she stood taller than Randy. Francine would seem thin beside her.

Helena introduced them. "Randy Railsback, this is Dr. Joan Witherington, chairman of the chemistry department. He's my self-defense instructor."

"Dr. Barkley said you're a police detective. What do you detect?"

"Anomalies and inconsistencies, mostly."

She tilted her head to look at him closely. "Find the inconsistency, discover why it occurs, then either fix it or build on it. I try to do much the same, but with chemicals. You can count on chemicals to react the same way every time. I don't imagine that holds true for human beings."

"Almost never."

"He's on the Cold Cases squad," Helena said.

"Really? I didn't know we had one locally. I've seen the television show. You catch criminals who think they've gotten away with it. Must be satisfying when you're successful."

"Very."

"But heartbreaking when you're not."

He nodded. "Interesting choice of adjective."

"Following a trail that leads nowhere *can* break your heart. I'm still waiting for my Nobel prize."

After a moment, Helena excused them so she could introduce Randy to the president. In short order he was surrounded by people, and he noticed that Helena had slipped away. Everyone seemed to be aware he was a detective, and was fascinated by what he did. He was used to the general public's reaction and prepared for it. He told a few funny stories. He never talked about the cases that still gave him nightmares. He was bombarded with questions about forensics, profiling, the differences between television shows and real police work, the nature of crime on the street—on and on.

Since he was driving, he was drinking tonic water without gin, and all the talking was making his mouth dry. He started looking for Helena and found her talking to a tall, balding man, one of the few wearing a well-tailored suit. One of the rich alums down for the basketball game, no doubt.

As Randy began to inch his way toward her, Barkley handed him a glass. "Tonic water. Helena sent me with this," he said. "She obviously thinks you function well on your own." He expertly cut Randy away from the others.

"Most of these people watch *Cops?*" Randy whispered.

Barkley raised an eyebrow. "Why not? The police impose order on chaos, and I, for one, appreciate the effort." He looked past Randy, smiled and waved. "Here comes Helena. She's a dear friend as well as a colleague and she's had a bitch of a time. If you hurt her I'll hang you in effigy, and I won't necessarily use an actual effigy."

By the time they filled up on hors d'oeuvres and left the party, the drizzle was mixed with sleet.

Helena took his arm, which pleased him immensely. "You were a hit. Even Joan Witherington liked you."

"Even if I can't recite the periodic table?" he said.

"She thought you were charming. She also said if she were twenty years younger, she'd fight me for you…but her nice engineer husband might be annoyed. Jake was home with their three children."

"So if you lost me to her, you'd just hand me over?" Randy asked.

"That's what the Amazons did with male captives. Passed them around, wore them out making babies, then sacrificed them to their goddess."

"What a way to die." They drove in silence for a few minutes, then Randy said, "On second thought, the sacrificing part doesn't sound that great. Wouldn't you keep me around to clean house and take out the trash?"

She laughed. "I'm not the world's greatest housekeeper, but I'll bet I beat you."

"No way. My loft is so clean you could eat off the floor." He shrugged. "Maybe not, but close." He glanced down at his watch. "It's only twenty minutes after nine. How about I show you?"

She stiffened.

He was afraid he'd pushed too hard, but after a moment, she said, "Why not?" Her voice sounded tight, and she'd clenched her hands in her lap. He considered rescinding his offer and telling her he was joking, but she had made her choice. He had to be certain she didn't regret it.

*I WILL DO THIS,* Helena thought, as she buckled herself into Randy's SUV. Neither of them seemed to want to talk.

As they drove toward the river through rain-slicked streets, she stared out the window. *Calm down,* she told herself. *I planned to end the evening this way, after all. I shaved my legs and put on my fancy underwear. Two years without the feel of a man's arms around me is long enough.*

*Besides, we're not in love or anything. We're friends. Randy is bound to be expert in bed, he knows all about me, he seems to want me, and he's the only man I've met since it happened who turns me on. He's no more interested in commitment than I am. I refuse to put my life on hold until the bastard's dead.*

*And even after I kill the bastard, I won't be completely rid of him if I can't make love. And maybe, just maybe, fall in love someday.* She leaned her head back against the seat.

Her heart raced as though she'd been jogging on the treadmill at the gym for hours.

Randy took his eyes off the road and dropped his palm to her knee.

If he took his hand off her thigh, she'd be able to outline where each finger had been from the heat of his touch.

He was a really nice man. Was it fair to use him as a test case?

She might disappoint him. Men like Randy expected women to be hot in bed. What did that even mean?

She'd never had the nerve to initiate sex, even with Mickey. She did what was expected of her and usually enjoyed it.

Suddenly her stomach lurched and a wave of nausea swept over her. Unmitigated disaster loomed ahead. How could she possibly get naked in front of a strange man? Or go back to class and face Randy after seeing *him* naked?

He pulled the car into a two-level parking garage, into a spot with his name on it, shut off the engine and turned that million-watt smile on her. Adrenaline flooded her.

She took a deep breath and smiled back at him. *I am wearing thigh-high black stockings with lace tops, black lace bikini underwear and a black lace push-up bra. I asked for it, and I am going through with it. Whatever happens, afterward is afterward. I dealt with rape, I can handle humiliation.*

On the ride up in the freight elevator to his loft, he kept his distance. So did she.

What if he jumped her the minute she walked into his apartment? The streets north of the Pyramid, where the warehouse was situated, were largely deserted after nine o'clock. She didn't know how to work the elevator, or even how to unlock the door. Once inside, she'd be trapped. Her palms were sweating.

He held the industrial steel door for her, and flipped a light switch. The loft looked half the size of a football field.

"Oh, my," Helena said. The west wall consisted of floor-to-ceiling windows overlooking the Mississippi River, the Memphis-Arkansas Bridge known as the Big M and the Pyramid, the white elephant that had originally been built as a basketball arena.

A moment later it hit her. Not only could they see the lights outside, outsiders could see in. It was like being onstage. She hugged herself and stepped back.

"They can't see us," Randy said, reading her mind or her body language or both. "It's one-way glass. Jud Slaughter has it in his house and put it in for me."

"You trust that?" When he nodded, she walked across and put her face close to the window. "It's starting to sleet. Maybe I should get home."

"Maybe you should take off your coat and relax." He went to a large fireplace in a brick tower that bisected the space and separated living room from dining room, kitchen and somewhere beyond, what must be at least one bedroom and a bath. "Gas logs." He squatted and lit the fireplace. "Can't risk a log fire, but these look pretty real."

She let him hang her coat beside the front door, and saw he'd left the key in the lock for her. If she lost it completely, she could unlock the door and sprint for the elevator. Which she didn't know how to operate. Or the stairs, only she didn't know where they were. Beside the elevator?

"Sit and warm up. I make a mean hot toddy."

Maybe what she needed was a hot toddy with a big dose of tranquilizer.

*Coward!*

What did she *want* to do tonight? She sank onto the black leather sectional sofa that screamed bachelor pad and looked around. Neat, but not too neat. He'd probably hired a decorator. No bookshelves. Maybe there were books in the bedroom.

"Here you go. No GHP. No roofies." He sat beside her, but not too close.

She took a sip of the toddy. It was probably stronger than it seemed. A couple more of these and she'd be drunk enough to lose her inhibitions.

Actually, if she ran true to form, one more toddy and she'd wind up sprawled on the bathroom floor.

"I'm trying to make it easy. Don't seem to be doing a decent job."

She set the drink on a coaster on the black glass coffee table. "You've read up on me, but who are you? More than a cop, certainly."

He took her hand and brought it to his lips. "Tonight I'm a man, not a cop."

*Oh, Lord. Stall, girl, stall.*

He leaned across the space between them and kissed her. His lips felt so tender. So warm… She stiffened and leaned away from him. "I'm so nervous I'm ready to jump out of my skin."

"Clothes I'm up for. Skin, not so much." He sat back against the square throw pillows on the sofa. It was a gesture to tell her she was off the hook…for the moment at least.

"Why would someone like you become a cop?" She

sounded as perky as a freshman at a sorority tea. She wanted to crawl under the sofa and die.

"Someone like me?" He chuckled.

"Oh, God, what a dumb question."

"No dumber than why did someone like you decide to teach college. Relax. I followed along in the family business," he said. He pointed at the toddy she'd barely touched. She shook her head. Drunk would be cheating. She would do this sober or not at all.

"One of my cop ancestors died in the yellow fever epidemic in 1878 because he wouldn't leave Memphis when most everybody else in the police force did."

"Proving no good deed goes unpunished." She turned away.

Randy sat forward, leaned his elbows on his knees and stared into the fire. "I try to make certain people are punished for their *bad* deeds, no matter how long it takes."

When he opened his arms, she slipped into them. Natural, no thinking involved. She did want him, ached for him, not as a convenience or a stopgap, but as a man, *the* man.

SHE FELT SO SOFT. He ran his tongue across her lips and tasted rum, then her tongue met his and teased him. Tonight he would strip them both naked in his bed and coax her with gentle caresses until he uncovered the passion in her he'd only glimpsed.

He'd never felt such pressure to go slow. Her haircut and chic clothes didn't fool him. She was the same Streak who'd tried to knock his block off.

He was no altruist when it came to sex, but tonight had to be about her. He took her hand and pulled her to him. She came willingly, even eagerly, and leaned against him as he led her past the kitchen and into the space he used as a bedroom.

On the chance that tonight she'd come home with him, he'd remade his bed with new Egyptian cotton sheets with the highest thread count he could find. He'd even added a little lavender to the dryer. That was a trick one of his old girlfriends had taught him.

He wanted the atmosphere to be fresh, clean and relaxed. No pressure. Streak must feel in control, that this experience didn't happen in the same universe with rape.

Not that *he* could relax. It was taking every bit of restraint he possessed not to tear her clothes off and explore every inch of her with his lips and hands and tongue until she begged him to take her.

She responded to his caresses. She didn't break their kiss when he unzipped the back of her dress. He relished the feel of the silk material and the equally silken skin of her back as the zipper opened to her waist. He froze when she stepped back a pace. Had he lost her already?

He held her gaze as she let him ease the dress off her shoulders, to fall in a puddle around her feet. Her dark eyes half begged him for approval, half begged him not to look at her.

So he closed his eyes, drew her against him again and kissed her gently, deeply. He felt her arms around his shoulders, her hips moving against him. He unfastened her bra and dropped it, then moved his palms to cup her breasts. She gasped and arched her back as he bent her away from him so that he could kiss the hollow at the base of her throat, and then lower until his tongue circled first one, then the other nipple.

When he felt her hand move down his back to his waist and below, he swung her into his arms and laid her on the bed.

She wore black lace panties and thigh-high black stockings with lace tops.

How could he stay sane, much less in control? He yanked his shirt out of his pants, tore it over his head, heard a couple of buttons pop. He unbuckled his belt, kicked off his shoes, pulled his black silk socks off and flung them into the darkness, reached for his zipper...

And stopped. Helena lay beneath him half-naked, her eyes boring into his. Instinct warned him that she had to accept the feel of him, find her ecstasy as he made love to her, before she saw him. He knelt above her and slid his fingers down her body and beneath her panties. He parted her, touched her, felt her wet and swollen.

She closed her eyes, moaned softly and opened to his touch. He leaned over her and pulled her hips under him....

In an instant she became a writhing, clawing hellcat. She kicked at him as she twisted away, battering his shoulders with her fists. Bucking beneath him, she arched her spine and screamed.

He rolled off the bed with his hands out in front of him. "It's all right," he said. "You're all right. Helena! Streak!"

She covered her mouth with her hands, shuddered, and flew off the bed to the windows. "Oh, God. Oh, God."

He stood still in the shadows.

"I'm sorry," Helena sobbed. "So sorry." She leaned her forehead against the cold glass. "That was unforgivable."

"You didn't do anything."

"Yes, I did." She started to turn to look at him, but couldn't meet his eyes and went back to staring out at the sleet. "I swore I'd go through with this. I want so much to move on, to be a normal woman again. I had to try with someone."

His stomach roiled. He didn't want to hear this. He'd always played up his reputation, so he shouldn't be surprised she'd picked him. Served him right. That didn't cool his indignation. "I was your test case? Randy Randy, the original sex-for-fun guy. No baggage, no strings, no fault, no foul. Safe."

"You were a *friend*. I trust you. I thought I could trust myself with you."

At least she considered him a friend. That shouldn't feel like a bullet to the gut, but if anything, it hurt worse.

"I thought you'd probably be an expert lover, and I'd know."

"If you could endure sex again?" he snarled.

"I had to know if I was ready. Obviously I'm not. I may never be. Oh, God, I am so sorry." She covered her face with her hands. He watched her naked shoulders hunch, pulled the coverlet from the foot of the bed and crossed to her.

She flinched as though she was afraid he intended to strike her, and her arms came down to cover her breasts. Wordlessly, he draped the quilt gently around her, then returned to prop himself against the pillows at the head of the bed. He felt tired and wounded, but his anger had drained away. "That's why the makeover," he said.

She nodded. "Partly. You would never give me a second glance the way I looked, but when I was attractive Mickey thought I was worth marrying, and *the man*—" she shuddered "—liked me enough to—"

"That's the least ringing endorsement I've ever gotten from a woman."

"That was before I knew you."

"You may not believe this, but I wanted you almost from the moment I saw you." He chuckled. "Maybe from the moment you tried to kill me."

"Even looking and acting the way I did?"

"Hey, I'm a first-class womanizer, remember? I can spot the dancing girl beneath the sweats."

"What else can I say except that I'm sorry, and you're not really like that."

"I'm exactly like that." His voice sounded harsh in his ears. Damn straight he'd always been like that, and wished he could be again. Liz Slaughter was right. He was finally getting his and it tasted rotten on his tongue.

"Tonight you were so marvelous at the party and so sweet and…I went crazy on you," she murmured.

"Not crazy."

"From the moment you kissed me I wanted you," she said. "I did."

"Then you thought of *him.*"

"I stopped thinking. I was truly feeling!" She reached out behind her without looking at him. He leaned over to take her hand, and her fingers clenched his. "It was wonderful. *You* were wonderful. I wanted you to hold me, make love to me, but when I felt your weight on me…"

"Suddenly it stopped being me and started being him."

She pulled her hand away and became all business. "Let me get dressed. I can take a cab home. I won't come back to your class."

"A cab in a storm? In Memphis? Fat chance." He patted the bed. "Come sit. I won't touch you, I promise. And of course you'll come back to class."

She lifted her head but didn't move away from the window.

"I pushed too fast," he said.

"No!" She spun to look at him, bracing her hands on the window behind her. The quilt slid off her shoulders, but she didn't try to cover her breasts. "I'm messed up, not you. I thought I was past it, I really did."

"So we have to find out how to *move* you past it."

She picked up her bra and dress from the floor beside the bed. "How? I've talked to counselors and other victims, told them my story and listened to theirs."

"How many of those counselors were male?"

She gave him a puzzled glance. "None of them."

"Then tell *me*. It would be simple to say I understand, that I've heard it all, but I haven't heard it from you. You ever talk to *any man* about the experience rather than the facts?"

She turned her back and fastened her bra. The finality of the gesture saddened him, but he already knew that tonight he'd failed her.

"Mickey didn't want me to mention any of it." She slid the dress over her head.

Randy forced himself not to volunteer to zip it.

She wriggled and managed without his help. He'd never been able to understand how women did that. Watching her dress was almost as exciting as undressing her. She had the most beautiful back....

"I suppose he felt guilty that he hadn't protected me, which was dumb, and even more guilty that a part of him thought I deserved it." She stooped and picked up her pumps.

"Did you talk to your family?"

"I don't have any close family left. I didn't know Marcie then, and they wouldn't let Milo and Vi come to the hospital, so it was just my husband and my best friend, who, it turned out, had been having an affair with Mickey for months. We had a happy marriage the first few years, but by then it was falling apart." She turned to Randy with tears in her eyes. "Most of us learn to handle failure when we're children, but Mickey never experienced a real ego-crusher until he didn't get tenure. That's when he started gambling so much and had an affair.

"I tried to help, but suddenly he saw me as a competitor, not a partner. In a sense, being supportive after the assault made him feel superior."

"Not an unusual reaction," Randy said, although he thought Mickey was a jerk. "Men feel guilty they weren't there to protect their wives, then when they can't handle that reaction, they start to blame the woman." He wondered whether O'Hara had ever considered Mickey a viable suspect. He resented his wife. Maybe he *wanted* her taken down a peg and hired someone to do just that. Maybe he wanted her dead, but his hired killer lost his nerve and stopped with rape. Not likely, but he'd have to check it out before he could cross the ex off his list.

"You think you walked into it tonight. You should have seen my first anxiety attack. I went for Mickey like a tiger the first time he tried to touch me."

"The hell with Mickey. Sit and tell me." If the two of

them were ever to have a chance—a chance Randy wanted—then he had to know everything about what made her what she was. Maybe eventually he'd be able to open up about what made him what *he* was.

She stood silent so long he couldn't be certain she'd heard him. Then she took a deep breath and dropped her pumps, which bounced on the concrete floor.

He patted the bed beside him. Instead, she sat at the far end against the footboard, and pulled her feet under her. The dress rode up above her knees, to the edge of the lace at the top of her stockings.

She had no idea how much she turned him on. He leaned over the side of the bed and pulled the quilt across his lap.

"It's funny that the television shows talk about the psychological damage of rape, but gloss over the actual physical pain." Outside, ice crystals ticked against the window and slid down like cold sweat. She shuddered, but her voice grew stronger. "You sure you want to hear this?"

"Yes."

"Rape is like being jabbed over and over with a jumbo hot curling iron."

He couldn't begin to imagine what this was costing her, but he knew enough to keep his mouth shut and let her take it where she wanted to go.

"Just since I started your class, I've begun to remember what it was like when he beat me. I must have blocked it out. Remembering the beating was what set me off while we were boxing."

"So you were conscious during the assault, after all?"

She shrugged. "Who knows? In and out, I guess. I'm not *trying* to remember. The counselor says some women can go somewhere else mentally. That must be what I did, because I still can't remember a thing about the man. A black face mask, period."

"O'Hara says he leaves no trace."

She blew out a deep breath. "He *takes.* My sense of security, privacy, and most of all, my sense of control. I was his…creature, not even human. He made the call whether I lived or died." She wrapped her arms around herself and leaned against the footboard. "He still does," she whispered.

"Were you conscious when you were found? There's precious little traffic on the Old Forest Road after dark."

"I came to in the bushes, but I must have been groggy, because all I could think of was finding my underwear and pants before someone saw me. Isn't that weird?" She met his eyes and shook her head. "Weird. I could endure what the rapist put me through, but after all that, God forbid the cops or EMS should glimpse my pubic hair."

He didn't dare move, although he wanted to take her in his arms and simply hold her.

"I found my pants, not my underwear. O'Hara thinks he took them as a souvenir." She giggled. "Mothers always tell their children to wear clean underwear in case they wind up in the hospital. I did end up hospitalized, and I didn't have any underpants at all."

Randy wondered if she could ever break through that last hard place.

"He took my cash, but he left my purse and didn't find my cell phone in the pocket of my pants. They traced my 911 call, and took me off to the rape crisis center in an ambulance to do a rape kit, and wasn't *that* a real picnic! The morphine was a blessing. I didn't go home for a couple of days or back to work for a month. Mickey started his digs at me almost at once, mostly when we were with other people. He pretended he was kidding, but he wasn't. I supposed he was keeping me in my place."

Randy hated the SOB already.

"If I didn't wear so much makeup, if I wore my hair short, if I didn't swing my hips, if I didn't drive a BMW, if I didn't treat my students as equals…

"Intellectually, I knew that was crap, but on some level I bought into it. Most women blame themselves, at least a little. If I'm partly to blame, then I still have power over my life."

Randy leaned forward and propped his elbows on his knees. "Why'd you join the class?"

She bounced up, grabbed her pumps and shoved her feet into them. "Sooner or later he'll come back for me. When he does, I intend to be armed and waiting for him."

It took Randy a second, then he got it. "My God, you're planning to kill him."

"Don't be ridiculous." She walked away. "If you're going to drive me home, better put on your clothes. I'll wait in the living room."

He lunged for her and twisted her to face him. "You'll go to jail."

"For shooting a rapist who's trying to kill me? Justifiable homicide, Your Honor."

"Dammit, Streak, you don't have a chance against this psychopath. You want to leave Mickey to raise Milo and Vi? You can't stay on alert 24/7 in hopes that he'll show up with a target on his chest. He's patient and he's crazy. How do you expect to find him, when the police don't have a clue who he is?"

Tears began to streak her makeup. "Then *you* kill him, so I won't have to."

## CHAPTER THIRTEEN

"WHY ARE YOU HOME SO early?" Marcie put her book on Helena's sofa to come to meet her in the front hall. "Uh-oh."

"Thank you for staying," Helena said. "Go home."

"The kids have been asleep for hours. Want to talk about it?"

"Not now. I'm going to bed."

"It went badly."

Helena started up the stairway, pulling herself up by the banister. "I am so tired. *I* went badly."

"How?" Marcie said from the bottom of the stairs. "Let me make you a cup of cocoa."

"Cocoa won't cut it. Arsenic might, but I don't have any in the medicine cabinet. Good night."

THE MOMENT HIS HEAD HIT the pillow, Randy fell into an almost drugged sleep. He awoke to Sunday-morning sunshine, and when he looked out the window, the glint from icicles that had formed around the telephone wires nearly blinded him. The ice was already melting, but the schools would probably be closed on Monday. The city wasn't set up to handle ice or snow, and made its decisions based on the remote possibility that a school bus might crash.

Surely Helena would keep Milo and Vi in today. He had no idea whether she regularly attended church, and if so, which one. But when he checked the Weather Channel, he read on the crawl line that most services had been canceled.

He called her and was relieved when Milo picked up.

"Hey, buddy, could I interest you in some hot doughnuts?" he asked.

"Yeah! Mom, it's Randy. He's bringing doughnuts."

A moment later he heard her voice. She sounded cool, then he heard the catch in her voice. "That's kind of you, but you shouldn't drive in this mess."

"I'm a cop. We drive in everything."

"Last night…"

"Was last night. See you in an hour."

He was glad to find she hadn't reverted to the baggy sweats. Even so, her eyes looked bloodshot. Crying? Lying awake thinking about him? He handed the doughnuts to Milo, who whooped and ran off to the kitchen.

"Mom made coffee," he called. "Come on."

"We'll be there in a minute, sport. Morning, Vi," he said as the little girl came down the stairs.

"Good morning, Mr. Railsback," she said. "Thank you for the doughnuts." She followed her brother into the kitchen without taking her eyes off him.

"Why doesn't she like me?" he whispered.

"She thinks you play too rough."

"With Milo?"

She grinned. "With *me*. I explained about the classes, but she's still suspicious."

He looked after Vi. "Any suggestions how I can convince her I'm harmless?"

"Who says you're harmless? Let it go. I'll bring her Tuesday to see what we're actually doing. Let me have your coat."

He handed it to her and she hung it on a brass coat rack by the front door.

"Doughnuts are a cop's traditional peace offering."

"I don't need a peace offering." She turned toward the kitchen.

"Yeah, you do. Consider this a professional visit."

She stopped in midstride. "Has something else happened?"

He held up a hand. "No. I want your promise you won't try to find this guy on your own."

She widened her eyes in pure innocence. He wanted to shake her. "How can *I* find him when the police can't?" she asked.

He pointed her to the living room and followed her. Through the open kitchen door he could hear Milo and Vi squabbling. That meant they could hear him, so he whispered through clenched teeth, "You think it's easy to kill another human being?"

"If he's trying to kill me and take me away from my children, yes."

"Trust me, it isn't. If you help *me* find him, the police can take him down." *And you will be safe.*

She looked at him suspiciously. "How do you plan to do that?"

He pointed to the red wing chair beside the fireplace.

A log fire burned in the grate and Sunday newspapers were strewn on the couch. Clean mess in a living room that was actually used for living. So unlike the college president's living room, which had seemed mothballed and opened only on state visits. Randy could feel at home here.

She sat unwillingly, poised to leave if he said anything she didn't want to hear.

He sat opposite her, leaned forward and dangled his hands between his knees. "Somewhere, all the victims have met or seen this man, possibly talked to him, maybe even hired him or worked with him. I'm doing what we always do in Cold Cases. I'm going to reinterview all the victims, people who might know something to point us in the right direction."

"We've been over and over—"

"Then we'll go over and over it again. Please."

"Oh, why not."

From the kitchen, Vi said, "No! It's a *yellow* claw, see? It goes here."

"You're supposed to be working on the monkey," Milo said. "Leave my dragon alone."

Randy pulled a yellow steno pad from the hip pocket of his jeans and clicked his pen. "You're going to tell me everyone you can remember talking to the week you were raped."

"Randy, it's two years ago. Besides, O'Hara already has the same list."

He ignored her. "Where did you buy your groceries?"

After thirty minutes he went into the kitchen to refill their coffee mugs, while Streak leaned back in her chair with her eyes closed. People never realized how wearing police interviews could be. But they solved cases. She was surprised not only at his questions but how much information he teased out of her.

Milo and Vi were on their knees in kitchen chairs on

opposite sides of the table. Between them lay a half-finished jigsaw puzzle. The picture on the box looked like a complicated rendering of Chinese zodiac signs. He filled the mugs while they squabbled about which piece went where, then he went back to the living room and gave Streak her cup.

"Can we please take a break?" she said. "My head is killing me."

"Sorry. Five minutes, then we start again."

When she was seated once more, he asked, "Why college? Why not high school? Better job market, isn't it?"

She opened one eye. "I couldn't fill out a lesson plan if my life depended on it, and you have to take boring education courses to teach high school. My parents were both teachers, so believe me, I know what it's like to spend every night and every weekend grading papers. Yuck. They did pass along the family curse." She waved a hand at the bookshelves. "We have a genetic predisposition to hold on to every book we've ever bought, and to keep buying new ones. A lot of these are theirs."

"So they're both dead?"

"My first year of graduate school. A tornado crushed the gym at the high school where everybody was hiding. Twenty students and teachers were killed. Like to have killed *me* when it happened. I swore I'd get my Ph.D. for them if I had to scrub floors to pay for it. I waited a lot of tables, but I managed."

He wrote "stubborn, self-sufficient, goal-oriented." She wouldn't back down easily. She'd lie to him in a heartbeat. He glanced at his watch. "Time's up. Back to work. Now, where did you have your car serviced two years ago?"

He kept up the same line of questioning, and then

dropped in the query he'd actually come to ask. "If you'd been killed during the attack, I assume your husband would have inherited your estate?"

She opened her eyes and sat forward. "Excuse me?"

He repeated the question.

"It's not much of an estate."

"Five cents is an estate. You had a will? Life insurance?"

"We both did. We were each other's beneficiaries and executors. Standard husband and wife stuff." She shook her head. "Mickey had nothing to do with what happened to me. The man was a stranger."

"You're positive?"

"Yes."

"Your husband could have hired someone."

"How could he benefit from that?"

"Maybe it wasn't supposed to end the way it did."

"You think Mickey hired someone to kill me? Someone who lost his nerve at the last minute? Someone who coincidentally turned out to be a sexual predator? That's ridiculous."

"How about now? Who inherits?"

She wrapped her arms tight around her body as though shielding herself from the idea. "My estate is in trust for the children. Marcie's the executrix and legal guardian."

"Not Mickey?"

"Definitely not."

"Do you know where he is right now?"

"Not really. He doesn't send me child support, and if he's not in Tennessee the state can't do anything to collect. He could be in Gulfport or Vegas or Reno or Monte Carlo for all I know."

"Or Tunica or Memphis?"

"I suppose. But if he were close by, surely he would have come to see his children." She hesitated. "Wouldn't he?"

"You'll have to talk to Francine about that. She reads these guys better than I do."

"He's not one of 'these guys.' He's their father."

"Even if he hasn't put a penny in a slot since he left, he's still an addict, who might do anything for a fix." *Even kidnap his children or assault his wife.*

The minute Randy left Streak he'd head down to the squad room and see if he could locate the present whereabouts of one Michael Norcross, Ph.D. One look at her closed face told him he'd gone far enough along that line of questioning for the moment. She'd think about everything he'd said after he left. He'd check back later to see if she could tell him anything else about her ex-husband and his friends.

"Next question," he said. "Can you tell me where you went, what you did and who you might have seen before it happened?"

"How long before? A day? A week? A year?"

"A decade might be nice." He needed more caffeine, but his coffee was cold. He held out his cup. "Could I have a refill?" Going to the kitchen would give Streak a chance to regroup and check on Milo and Vi. They were ominously quiet.

And then they weren't.

First Randy heard high-pitched screams.

Then a soprano howl. "Mom! Mommy!"

The back door slammed, and one of the kids pelted down the hall. Milo skidded into the living room. "Mommy! Come quick!"

Randy drew his gun and ran for the back door. In the yard Vi continued to howl.

His foot slipped on the threshold, but he caught himself on the doorjamb with his gun hand as his feet slid on the stoop. He grabbed the iron banister and narrowly avoided crashing down the stairs to the backyard butt first, gun in hand. The stairs looked treacherous. The ice was much thicker here than at his place downtown, where the Mississippi kept the air currents flowing.

He heard Streak and Milo behind him. "Stay inside," he snapped.

Still screaming, Vi crouched on her hands and knees on the sidewalk at the foot of the steps. Blood dripped from her forehead.

He checked the fenced backyard for an intruder, saw no one and shoved his piece back into the holster he wore at the small of his back.

He avoided the icy stairs by vaulting the railing, to land on the crusty grass beside the sidewalk.

"Baby!" Streak cried.

"Mommy!" Vi screamed.

"Don't try to come down here. You'll break your neck," Randy said. "I've got her." He dropped to his knees beside the child. Blood welled from a cut at Vi's hairline and ran down her face onto the ground. He yanked his folded handkerchief out of his pocket and pressed it to the cut. Vi stopped screaming and stared up at him with her dark fawn's eyes.

"I fell down," she said, and sniffled.

"She hit her head on the railing," Milo reported from behind their mother.

"I scraped my knees, and my elbow, *too*." Vi twisted far enough to glare up at her brother.

"I've got to see," Streak said, and started out onto the stoop.

"You do and we'll have two of you bleeding. Hold the door open. I can make it if I take it slow." Randy looked at Vi. "Think you can put your arms around my neck so I can lift you and carry you inside?"

"Uh-huh."

When he took his handkerchief away from her forehead, the blood flow had slowed to a steady seep.

He slipped his hands under Vi and lifted her. From a kneeling position, he'd never have been able to heft an adult, but she seemed to weigh no more than the angel on top of the Christmas tree. He leaned against the banister and placed his feet on the stairs carefully. If he fell with the child in his arms, she could be badly hurt.

Streak reached out to steady him as he crossed the threshold into the back hall. When he'd carried Vi into the living room and laid her gently on the couch, her mother brushed him aside and knelt beside her. "Baby, are you all right?" She began to feel Vi all over.

The little girl sniffled.

Randy went into the kitchen, filled his bloody handkerchief with ice cubes, wrapped it in a dish towel from beside the stove, went back and held the makeshift ice pack out to Streak.

His eyes wide and frightened, Milo hovered in the hall. Neither child was wearing outdoor clothes or boots. Randy wrapped an arm around the boy and pulled him over to the fire. He came reluctantly, carefully avoiding the couch and staying out of his mother's reach.

"She's going to need stitches," Streak said.

"Come on, I'll drive you."

"Her car seat's in my vehicle."

"Milo, go move your sister's car seat to my SUV. I have four-wheel drive. You know how to strap it in?"

The boy nodded, obviously grateful to have a task that took him out of his mother's sight.

"Put on your coat and gloves before you go, and don't break your neck," Randy called after him. "Stay on the grass."

Before Milo reached the hall archway, Helena looked up and asked, "What on earth were you two *doing* outside with nothing on?"

Milo made a sound that didn't resemble words, and disappeared in the direction of the garage.

Helena turned her attention to Vi. "You were supposed to be in the kitchen doing your puzzle."

The child still sniffled and occasionally hiccuped, but she'd calmed down. "Milo was bored. He started hiding my pieces, and then he said he was going out to make an ice prince."

"An ice prince?" Helena asked.

Vi nodded, grimaced at the pain and whispered, "He said we could break the icicles off the garage in back where the roof's low and melt 'em together and make a crown."

Kid was creative; Randy would give him that.

"I doubt he asked you to go with him. Did he?"

Randy watched as the child considered lying, then thought better of it. "Nuh-uh. He hates it when I follow him."

"But you did it anyway."

"I wanted to help!" Vi wailed. "And then my feet went out from under me on the sidewalk and I fell and hit my head on the railing." She began to tune up again. "It hurt."

Helena raised her eyebrows at Randy.

"Mom," Milo called from the door. "I strapped the car seat in Randy's car. I did it right."

Randy noticed Helena had become "Mom" again. Under stress, Milo had reverted to "Mommy." Randy didn't think the kid wanted to be reminded of that.

"Bring my down jacket and Mr. Railsback's coat from the rack by the front door."

"Should I get Vi's coat? It's upstairs."

"We can wrap her in that afghan," Randy said, pointing to the one over the back of the couch.

"Can you walk, baby girl?" Helena asked.

The child's eyes narrowed as she glared at her brother. "I want Randy to carry me. My knees hurt."

Big sigh from Helena. "You are perfectly capable of walking to the car."

Vi gave Randy a dewy-eyed glance. "He makes me feel safe on the ice."

Helena rolled her own eyes. Randy grinned at Helena and offered a prayer for all the males Vi's big brown eyes would annihilate once she hit puberty.

He wrapped the afghan around her and swung her into his arms for the trip to the car and the emergency room.

WHILE HELENA STAYED in the examining room with Vi, Randy sat in the nearly empty waiting room with Milo. He'd expected the place to be packed with ice-related injuries, but apparently most people had stayed safely indoors. The E.R. nurse had taken Vi straight in.

Milo's head was sunk into his chest. His weight rested on his tailbone and the back of his neck. His feet in their giant white sneakers kicked just short of the floor. "I hate her," he snarled.

Randy didn't look at him. "You're talking about Vi?"

"It's all her fault. It's *always* her fault. She runs after me all the time. She's always getting in the way. She does something dumb and I wind up in trouble. I hate her."

"Makes sense," Randy said.

Surprised, Milo sat up. "I *told* her not to follow me outside. She's little and clumsy. Why couldn't she do the stupid puzzle and leave me alone?"

"Maybe because you were hiding her pieces."

"I was *bored!* And she whines at me and I want to stomp her into a puddle on the kitchen floor."

"Difficult to do effectively. She'd yell, for one thing."

Milo gave a tentative snicker. "Mom'll blame me. I'll be grounded until I go off to college."

"In that case, you might as well stomp Vi. Can't get any worse."

Milo tossed Randy a suspicious look to assess how serious he was, then said, "I don't really want to stomp her. I just hate her."

"Me, too."

He gaped. "You hate my little sister?"

"Why not? You're a pretty savvy kid. If she deserves to be hated, I get to hate her, too, right?"

"I don't really hate her, not *hate hate.*"

"Oh. So I can't hate her just because you don't hate her?"

"No, you can't."

They sat silently for a couple of minutes, then Randy

said, "She's probably going to have a black eye and stitches. She'll be the star of the third grade, or whatever grade she's in."

"Heck, she'll be the star of the whole school." Milo's chin sank onto his chest once more.

"You could have one, too."

"A black eye?"

"Sure. I could sock you one. We're in the emergency room already, so getting it treated would be simple."

Milo snickered. "You're crazy."

"No, I'm logical. You have a star sister with stitches and a black eye, and a mother who's going to blame you. Seems to me your black eye might help even the score."

Milo considered that seriously, then sighed deeply. "I shouldn't have gone outside, should I? Then she wouldn't have come after me."

"Bingo."

"She could have gotten really hurt."

"So could you. I don't think your mother would be happy about that."

"I better tell them I'm sorry."

"Yeah."

"What are you two talking about?" Helena asked as she came down the hall toward them.

"Whether Randy ought to give me a black eye," Milo said.

*"What?"*

"It's a guy thing," Randy stated.

"Is Vi okay?" Milo asked. "Can we go home now? I'm hungry."

Randy realized it was way past lunchtime.

"Small problem," Helena said. "Vi won't leave."

"Huh?"

"The hospital says she has to ride to the car in a wheelchair, but she wants you to carry her, Randy. They're afraid she'll pitch a fit if they force her, and upset the entire E.R."

"Milo, stay with your mother," he said. "Which room is she in?"

He needn't have asked. He could hear her the minute he opened the waiting room door.

"Knock it off, kid," said a man. "It's hospital policy. Get in the wheelchair."

"You can't make me," replied the child. "You're not the boss of me."

Randy parted the curtains. "Hey, Vi."

"Randy!" She held out her arms. The medics had split the legs of her jeans and the arms of her sweater, and bandaged both knees and her left elbow. The two-inch cut at her hairline was held together with butterfly bandages. She was already developing a magnificent shiner. Otherwise, she seemed fine. More than fine.

"You know what a compromise is?" Randy asked her.

She considered for a moment and shook her head. "I don't *think* so."

"When two people don't agree, both sides give a little and meet in the middle."

"I'm not giving."

"So, here's our compromise. You ride to the car in the wheelchair…" He held up a hand to forestall her. "And I push the wheelchair."

She considered, then nodded. "As long as you carry me inside when we get home."

"Deal." He'd handle that when they got that far.

He set her into the wheelchair, tucked the afghan around her, winked at the harried technician and drove Vi away in her chariot.

Before they reached the door to the waiting room, she looked back over her shoulder at Randy. "Maybe I don't not like you as much any longer."

"Thank you, I think."

# CHAPTER FOURTEEN

THE SUNSHINE HAD ALREADY melted most of the ice on the streets except for patches on the bridges. A few trees had lost limbs, but the power lines seemed intact. What water was on the roads would refreeze when the temperature dropped at nightfall, so driving might be even more hazardous for the morning commute.

"I'd guess no school tomorrow," Randy said as he negotiated the turn onto Helena's street. "What do you do with these two? Doesn't Marcie have to work, too?"

"I usually take them to school with me and park them in the library with Marcie, or in my office with plenty to read. I only have one class on Mondays, and I can finesse office hours in bad weather. We manage."

He pulled into their driveway as Marcie opened the front door.

"Stay there!" Helena called. She said to Randy, "I phoned her from the emergency room."

He carried Vi into the living room and sat her in the big chair by the fireplace. Marcie had built up the fire. She hugged Vi, then reached a hand back to Milo. "I was in the shower and didn't hear you scream," she said to Vi. "I'm so sorry."

"She really bawled," Milo stated.

"I'll bet she did. Now, I've got a big pot of bean soup I made last night on the stove. As soon as the bread comes out of the oven, we can have lunch."

Standing in the doorway to the front hall, Randy suddenly felt his position as outsider acutely.

"If you're okay," he said, "I guess—"

"Stay for lunch," Helena exclaimed. "Please, it's the least we can do."

"Randy has to carry me upstairs after lunch," Vi said with a blinding smile that was somewhat dimmed by her swollen eye and rainbow bruise.

"No, he doesn't," Helena replied. "You're *not* an invalid, kiddo. And you're not blameless in this mess. After lunch you can walk up the stairs to your room by yourself, get your pj's on, climb into bed and go to sleep."

"My head hurts."

"Serves you right," Milo said under his breath.

"I beg your pardon?" Helena frowned at him.

"I'm just sayin'…"

"Don't. This could have been way worse without Randy." She put a hand on Randy's arm. He felt the warmth of her fingers all the way down to his toes. "Please stay. You must be starved. You didn't even eat the doughnuts you brought and it's nearly two."

"I made enough soup for an army," Marcie said. "We'll have to eat in the dining room. The puzzle's still on the kitchen table. Come on, Milo, you can set the table." She gave Randy a nod of approval as she passed. His service today had apparently redeemed him in her eyes.

He didn't know whether he was redeemed in Streak's eyes. If he hadn't been questioning her, she'd have been paying attention to her children, and none of this would have happened.

"Come back to my office," she said. Once inside, she shut the door behind him and perched on her desk again. "When Vi screamed, you pulled your gun before you went outside. You thought it might be *him,* didn't you?"

"I wasn't taking any chances. If I hadn't been here, you'd have run out without thinking. A screaming child makes a dandy decoy."

She dropped her head in her hands. "I never considered that."

"I don't think he plans to ambush you. Shooting from a distance is not his style, but you never know." Randy rested his arms on her shoulders. "Give up this crazy idea of killing the guy. You're in way over your head."

She wrenched away from him. "As things stand, I have no other choice."

"Of course you do."

"What choice? You thought he could be stalking me right this minute."

"We'll protect you. *I'll* protect you."

"No, you won't. You can't. All you can do is catch him."

"Dammit, we're trying."

"By considering my ex-husband a suspect?"

"By considering everyone a suspect. That's why I asked if you had any way of knowing where you were and who you met before it happened. As I recall, we were interrupted."

She went around her desk and opened a drawer in the battered credenza behind it, rummaged in the drawer and handed him a thick manila folder. "This year I started keeping my appointment calendar, grades and notes on my computer, but two years ago I used a diary. I didn't write down the name of the guy who serviced my car, and I don't even *know* the name of my butcher, but I do keep track of scheduled meetings and the people who attended. Here's that entire year. Knock yourself out."

"Thanks." He took the folder, but didn't open it. He'd wait until he could spread the papers on his dining room table at the loft so that he could compare the names with the lists O'Hara had already compiled from her and the other victims. He doubted O'Hara's staff would have missed an obvious correlation, but Helena might have added a name she'd remembered. At this point he'd be grateful for a single match.

"Lunch!" Marcie called. "Come and get it."

Helena moved past him to open the door, but he put a hand on her arm. "I'm sorry I scared you last night," he murmured.

She leaned her forehead against the jamb and closed her eyes. "I'm the one who ought to apologize to you."

"Next time—"

Her eyes sprang open. "Next time?"

He repeated slowly, "Next time, you come to me."

"I'll never be able to do that."

He brought her hand to his lips. "You can if you want me—us—enough. I won't send you away."

## CHAPTER FIFTEEN

"As a general rule, I don't even like children," Randy said. He poured creamer into Jack Samuels's cup and handed it to him. At her desk, Liz Slaughter stirred bran into her yogurt. She was limiting her caffeine intake for the duration of her pregnancy. She had yet to switch to maternity tops, but the baby bulge grew more prominent every day.

"Most of the kids we see in here—" Jack took a sip of his coffee "—are one step short of feral. They'd have been better off if they *had* been raised by wolves. Wolves have a moral code."

"Half the kids expect to be dead before they hit twenty-five," Liz interjected.

"Too many of them actually are," Jack added. "My point is that they're anything but normal kids."

"The only kids I know are my cousins," Randy said. "They're loud, spoiled, selfish, have the table manners of warthogs and treat their parents with contempt."

"So do you," Jack commented.

"I think they're jerks, but I'm always polite when I get stuck at some family thing."

"Which you will kill to avoid," Liz said.

"My point is that I actually *like* Milo and Viola.

They're intelligent, well-spoken and fairly well behaved."

"Paragons," Jack said with a snicker.

"The heck with both of you. I'm headed out to an interview."

As he was leaving the room, he heard both Liz and Jack collapse into laughter.

Randy kept on walking.

"WHAT'S MICKEY DONE?" Dr. Lyman Pettigrew asked.

"What makes you think he's done anything?" Randy countered.

"The police would not be interviewing the chairman of his department—make that ex-chairman—about Michael Norcross for no reason." A tubby gray-haired man in a battleship-gray office the size of a broom closet, Dr. Lyman Pettigrew leaned forward and picked up a gold pen from the pristine blotter on his desk. He grimaced as his chair squealed.

Randy had not expected the office of the chairman of the department of economics in a community college to be palatial, but he'd been surprised to find Dr. Pettigrew's tiny office opened directly off the fourth-floor center hall of the ugly brick undergraduate classroom building. He didn't have so much as a clerk outside to announce visitors.

The books along one wall of the office were arranged as neatly as Streak's were messy, and not a scrap of paper, a family photograph or a potted plant cluttered the credenza behind the desk. Without his name on his door and his diplomas on the wall, Dr. Pettigrew's office could have belonged to anyone.

"The police routinely revisit old unsolved cases like

Helena Norcross's assault," Randy said. "Checking to see if there's anything we missed the first time." Without so much as taking a breath, he asked, "How come Michael Norcross didn't get tenure?"

Dr. Pettigrew dropped his gold pen. He managed to snare it before it rolled off his desk, and carefully put it into the center drawer. "Reports of the tenure committee are confidential. You'd need a warrant to see them. Why do you want to know?"

Randy shook his head. "You can give me broad generalizations, can't you? I don't need the official reports. I understand you don't have to document a denial of tenure action the way you do a dismissal for cause, do you?"

Dr. Pettigrew relaxed and smiled. Randy gathered that as long as he wasn't faced with revealing actual reports, he was happy enough to gossip about colleagues no longer employed at the school.

"After five years on a tenure track, you get it or you leave and the school brings in someone new. Up or out."

"Tough."

"Tenure isn't supposed to secure you a job for life, but that's generally how it works unless you get caught screwing coeds on the president's lawn."

"Did he?"

Dr. Pettigrew stared at Randy. "God, no. Michael never did anything *wrong,* precisely, but he didn't do anything outstanding, either. His students gave him adequate but not glowing reviews. He didn't publish articles in professional journals or present papers at conferences or volunteer to serve on faculty committees or work for the Community Chest. Helena did all those things and more over at Weyland. Frankly, he was something of a golden boy who thought he could win on his charm, as he always had. I wouldn't have hired him if I'd realized he was lazy."

"Why did you?"

Pettigrew took a deep breath and let it out slowly. "He was knowledgeable and intelligent. His dissertation was brilliant, although I suspect now that Helena wrote a good deal of it. I thought he would step up to the plate. So, I suspect, did Helena, whom I like very much, by the way, although I haven't seen much of her since her accident and the divorce. When Michael was here we saw a good deal of each other at faculty functions of both our respective schools.

"When Michael was denied tenure," Dr. Pettigrew continued, "I doubt anyone was surprised except Michael himself. He was furious, because Helena had been granted tenure several months earlier, and he expected to follow close behind. Instead, he knew he'd lose his job at the end of the semester, and economics jobs aren't easy to find."

"Did he blame Helena?" Randy asked.

"He blamed me, actually. Said I betrayed him. Threatened to appeal." Pettigrew wrinkled his nose. "Stupid. That just pisses the committee off." His watch chimed, and he clicked it off. "I have a class in ten minutes. Walk downstairs with me."

As Dr. Pettigrew closed his office door behind them, Randy asked, "Do you lock your door?"

"When I'm not inside."

"Start locking it. I could be a sniper who resents the F you gave me last semester."

The academic stopped in his tracks and turned to Randy, shocked. "I've never... You're right, of course. Security is always chiding me that I'm too lax."

"Do you know where Michael is now?" Randy asked as they started down the stairs. Several girls with heavy book bags over their shoulders ran up past them, chattering. A tall blonde in a skirt so short he caught a glimpse of her panties eyed him as she passed. Most of the time he forgot he was almost forty, but suddenly, he felt very old. At least she hadn't said, "Excuse me, sir."

"Possibly Pass Christian."

Randy registered what the chairman said as they reached the bottom landing and stopped in front of an open classroom door. The din from inside made Randy's ears hurt.

"That's where he was six months ago," Dr. Pettigrew said in a voice loud enough to be heard over the racket. "One of my colleagues saw him in the new casino they built after Katrina. He was losing at blackjack, and asked Alan—that's my colleague—to lend him two hundred dollars so he could continue playing." Dr. Pettigrew shook his head. "Alan refused."

"Was he always a gambler?"

Dr. Pettigrew nodded at a scrawny young man entering the classroom. "Only the occasional trip to the casinos in Tunica, so far as I know. After Helena's—uh, accident and the tenure thing, I suspect he wanted to show her he could make more money gambling than she did teaching. He couldn't, of course. His ego was terribly bruised, poor man. I heard rumors he had significant gambling debts, was seeing other women and drinking, too. No one was surprised by the eventual divorce."

"Was it ever a good marriage?" Randy hoped Dr. Pettigrew wouldn't realize he wanted the answer for himself.

"In the beginning I think it was. They met in grad

school, married after they graduated, and managed to find jobs in the same city. Good luck, really, although they weren't hired at the same schools or the same level. They seemed like the perfect faculty couple, same goals and ambitions, on their way up. Two beautiful children. Helena bolstered Michael's ego, but what woman wouldn't? She may not have acknowledged even to herself that he was a lightweight. The tenure thing coming so soon before her assault broke the marriage apart, but eventually the cracks would have come to light." The chairman glanced over his shoulder at his classroom, which was beginning to quiet down as the students waited for him. "I have to start my lecture."

"If you think of anything you consider relevant, would you call me?" Randy gave Dr. Pettigrew his card and shook his hand. "Thanks for your insights."

"Anytime." He called after Randy, "Oh, Detective, I promise I'll lock my door from now on."

TWENTY MINUTES LATER, Francine Bagby, Amanda Donovan's savior, met Randy at the front door of M'Dear's Day Care. The place was spotless, smelled of lemon rather than dirty children, and was freshly painted inside and out in yellows and peaches. Kids' art adorned the walls of the central hall. He could hear children laughing and singing in the rooms behind the closed doors. "We're not a large operation," Francine said. "We got a waiting list long as my arm. I'd like to take everybody, but I'd be short-changing the ones who are here if I did. Come on into my office. Want some coffee?"

"Thanks, but I'm already on a caffeine high." Francine's office was neat, with shelves of bright children's books low on the walls where little hands could reach them. No desk, just a hot-pink conference table surrounded by yellow vinyl chairs and a couple of shabby sofas loaded down with throw pillows in primary colors.

"I can give you twenty minutes, although I'm so busy I'd rather give you ten."

"Then tell me again what you remember about Amanda's assault. Fast."

She sighed, and the bosom of her green scrubs rose and fell like an ocean tide. "I have told the tale so many times it's like running a movie. What I know, you know."

"Relax, close your eyes and put yourself back to that night. Did you catch even a glimpse of someone in the parking lot as you and Amanda were getting into your cars?"

She shook her head. "Not many lights in that lot, with bushes and trees all around."

"But nobody came in from across the street."

She shook her head again, but kept her eyes closed. "He must have been waiting down behind Amanda's car."

As Randy walked Francine back through Amanda's attack, it seemed unlikely to have been random. The guy must have shadowed the women to the restaurant, waited for them and taken his chance when Francine drove out first.

"What if I hadn't seen what was happening?" she asked. "What if I'd driven away?"

Randy shrugged. "Don't beat yourself up. This guy plans. Stalking is part of the thrill."

"Just because of how they look?" Francine said. "Crazy."

"What they do, as well. Professional women. Managers. At some time he may have worked for a female boss who pissed him off or fired him. Could be remembering a schoolteacher, an abusive mother or aunt."

"Why does he go after strangers? Why doesn't he just go beat up the boss or the teacher?"

"He doesn't dare. Even if she's dead, she still has too powerful a hold on him. So he victimizes substitutes. That's what Bundy did, what a lot of serial killers do. What we haven't been able to figure out is how he identifies them in the first place."

WHY NOT DROP IN to Streak's office to ask his questions? He might be able to take her to lunch. Randy parked in the visitors' lot at Weyland and wandered around until he found a student who directed him to Professor Norcross's office.

It was on the third floor of a building that looked on the outside like a medieval castle, and on the inside like every educational building he'd ever been in. Smelled the same, too. Dust and mildew, sweaty young bodies and disinfectant.

Her office was at the end of a narrow hall that would have benefited from more light fixtures. She answered when he knocked, so he opened the door and went in. Just like Pettigrew, he thought. Anybody could walk in unannounced.

Unlike Francine's neat, bright and organized space, Streak's office here was as chaotic as her one at home. She had fitted bookshelves everywhere she could and crammed them full. The room was larger than Dr. Pettigrew's office, but seemed smaller. Unlike Pettigrew's big window, this room had only a tiny arrow slit and didn't look as though its vomit-green walls had been painted since the school opened in 1873. The threadbare industrial green carpet didn't look much younger than the First World War.

"Streak? Dr. Norcross?"

He heard a thud from behind the desk. "Ow!" She surfaced rubbing the back of her head. "Don't *do* that! I think I have a concussion." She set an untidy sheaf of papers onto the desk. "What are *you* doing here?"

"I called and left a message."

"I just got back after class. I haven't listened to my messages."

"Couple of questions. Strictly business." He sat in the straight chair the students must use for consultations. It was as uncomfortable as the "perp chair" in the Cold Cases interrogation room. "First off, why the hell is your office door unlocked? Anybody could walk in. I just did."

"These are my scheduled office hours, *Detective*." She slid open the center drawer of her desk. "I have a pistol here as well as a panic button to call Security. I'm not a total dimwit."

"Have you timed security to see how long it takes them after you hit that button? Or how long it takes you to get that gun out of your drawer and aimed?"

She raised an eyebrow. "Yes, and I normally do not leave my office door unlocked."

"Don't. Not ever."

She didn't take direction well, even when it was for her own good. "Now that I've had my chewing out for the day, what are your questions?"

"Can I take you to lunch?"

"You drove over here for that?"

"Not entirely."

"No time for lunch." She smiled. "But thank you for asking. Now, what else?"

"I had somebody check your appointments in the old diary against the lists of contacts O'Hara got from the other victims. No correlations jumped out at us. You have any new ideas on how he could be identifying his victims?"

She flopped back in her chair and let her arms fall by her sides. "*I* don't know. Maybe he advertises on VictimsRUs.com."

"It's been done. If he drives around the streets checking for a woman who fits his parameters, how does he know she's not a waitress or a secretary? He wants women with clout. For instance, joggers mostly dress and look alike."

"You mean, what identifies an executive?" Helena asked.

"Designer clothes?"

"Not in my case," she answered. "I could never afford expensive clothes. I don't wear diamonds, my watch comes from Wal-Mart and my shoes come from markdown stores. I don't own a fur coat or a Fendi handbag."

"Was your appointment book a fancy leather one? You only gave me the innards, not the book itself."

"Nope. Cheapo fabric from the office products store."

"What about your laptop?" He pointed to where it lay open on her credenza.

"When I take it home, I put it in here." She picked up a maroon leather briefcase from the floor beside her desk. "He wouldn't be able to see the computer inside."

They stared at each other in silence until she looked

away, then he leaned across her desk and slid his fingers down her cheek. She froze, but didn't flinch. "Come to lunch."

She took his hand and held it against her cheek. "I can't. I promise I'm not avoiding you."

"If you say so." He stood and had started to turn away when he stopped and swung back slowly. "That briefcase didn't come from Wal-Mart."

"I splurged when I got tenure. Figured I deserved it." Her eyes widened. "Oh my God. Briefcases."

He grinned and sat back down. "Lawyers have them grafted to their hips. Amanda even brings her to class."

"Realtors live in their cars with all their stuff. Stockbrokers want Internet access 24/7, wherever they are."

"Doctors carry charts. I'll bet that Germantown society lady who was running that antiques bazaar kept her notes in a briefcase."

"Yes!" Helena punched the air, then sank back, deflated. "So he looks for women like me who carry nice briefcases. Where does that get us?"

"Depends. When and where did you buy it?"

"There's only one place in town to buy expensive leather luggage. Leyland's in Germantown. This thing cost half a month's salary."

"You remember who waited on you?"

"Randy, it's nearly three years ago."

"Think. Male or female?"

"Male."

"Black or white?"

"White."

"Description?"

She shrugged. "I don't remember anything unusual,

so he can't have been too tall or too short or two fat or thin. He didn't have scars or an obvious deformity. He must have been literally nondescript. Sorry." She stood. "Look, you have to leave. I have a student due any minute. I'll think about it some more and call you if I remember anything else."

"Promise me you won't go running into that luggage shop brandishing a gun and demanding to talk to the man who waited on you three years ago. It may be nothing."

"No. It's right. I can feel it." She followed him around the desk. Her smile looked absolutely radiant and made his heart flop around in his chest like a freshly landed carp. As they stood in the doorway, he said, "The heck with it," pulled her into his arms and kissed her hard.

For a second she held herself stiffly away from him, then relaxed so that her body molded to his and her lips parted to his probing tongue. He wanted to lay her back on her battered desk and make love to her right here and right now.

"Professor Norcross," he heard a female voice call, "are you here? Oh!"

Streak jumped away from him so fast he nearly fell. He was delighted to see the glazed look in her eyes. It only lasted a second, but that's all he needed. He grinned. "Thank you for the interview, Professor," he said, and stepped away from her. "See you in class tomorrow."

She jabbed him hard with the elbow the student couldn't see. "You're quite welcome, Detective Railsback. Anything I can do to help." She turned to the girl who stood gawking at them awkwardly from the head of the stairs. "Miss Jackson, you're early. Come in."

As he walked down the stairs, he heard Streak say,

"Your *Twelfth Night* paper needs focus," before her door closed.

He was passing through the front hall when someone called, "Detective Railsback, how nice to see you!" Al Barkley, the American studies professor Helena nicknamed "Oblivious Al," came down the transverse hall.

"Checking up on our Helena?" Al asked.

"Needed to ask her a couple of questions."

"Hmm. I'm headed across to the library. May I walk with you?" As they exited the building, he stated, "You've made a marked change for the better in our Helena. I do hope you're not trifling with her."

"Are you asking me my intentions?"

"She has no family except her children. I consider myself a surrogate parent." He shrugged. "She might not agree."

"Did you know the ex?"

Al snorted. "Indeed I did. Handsome and not nearly as smart as he thought he was."

"Why did she marry him?"

"They're scoping you out." Al nodded to a pair of pretty blondes. These girls wore jeans, not overly short skirts. "She loved him." The professor spread his hands. "But finally, Helena, who is both practical and a loving mother, kicked his unfaithful little ass out. I applauded."

"Could he be back in town?"

Al stopped. "I doubt it. He's wanted for unpaid child support in Tennessee. In any case, she wouldn't let him back in their lives."

"They're his children."

"She has custody. She can be hard, can our Helena. Once she does a thing, she doesn't second-guess herself.

I doubt she has ever changed a grade, although sometimes the pressure to do so is intense."

"From students?"

"Students, parents, administrators, coaches. Ah, here's your car. I recognize the antenna farm and the black sidewalls."

"Enjoyed talking to you, Al," Randy said.

"Remember what I said about intentions."

What the hell *were* his intentions toward Helena? Randy thought as he drove off the campus. Talk about baggage! Two kids, an ex-husband and psychological hang-ups, not to mention criminal intent.

*Let's be practical,* he thought. *She and the kids can't live in my loft, and I couldn't live in that crowded, cluttered little duplex. I don't see myself coaching Little League. Okay, so she seemed to enjoy the barbecue at Jud's, and I definitely enjoyed her faculty friends at the president's house. I think they liked me, too.*

But forever?

Yet he hated thinking she and the kids might one day live somewhere in the world without him.

Sex was important to him. Could he spend the rest of his life celibate because the woman he was in love with turned into a crazy person when he tried to take her to bed?

*In love with?* Where'd that come from? He didn't believe in love. Lust, maybe. Pheromones, hormones, chemistry. So how come he could see himself tottering into Viagra country with Helena tottering right beside him while he read *Good Night, Moon* to their great-grandchildren?

Someone honked behind him, and he realized he'd

been driving on autopilot. He pulled over to let the angry driver whip past him at fifteen miles over the speed limit.

Before he headed out to the luggage store, he wanted to talk to the surviving victims and the husbands of the three women who'd been killed.

Both he and O'Hara had worried they'd overlooked some point where the victims might have intersected. Nobody had asked about briefcases. Until now.

"NANCY, YOU BOUGHT YOUR term paper online, didn't you?"

It had taken Helena fifteen minutes of denials on Nancy Jackson's part to get this far. The girl said, "It's the first time, swear to God. I have to bring my grade up to at least a B or my parents'll kill me. Please, please, Dr. Norcross, I'll never do it again. I swear." A moment later she looked up with an expression that was both innocent and threatening. "Haven't you ever done anything…indiscreet that you don't want everybody on campus talking about?"

Helena sat back in her chair. "I was planning to give you a chance to rewrite your paper, but I don't blackmail well."

"Blackmail? Dr. Norcross, I'd never…" Nancy opened her eyes wide. Her innocence needed work.

"Please feel free to tell everyone on campus I kissed a police detective at my office door." She put her hands flat on her desk and assumed a serious expression. "I can turn you over to the honor council for discipline and possible expulsion—"

"You wouldn't!"

"If it happens again, I will."

Nancy let out a long sigh.

"Considering this F, you'll have to work hard to bring your grade for the semester up. You have two more chances to write an A—by that I mean your own— paper. With this F your high C has become a low D."

"But—"

"See you in class, Miss Jackson."

The girl knocked over her chair as she stood, backing toward the door. "The guy who raped you must have thought he stuck his prick into an iceberg." She slammed the door.

Helena gasped. How did Nancy Jackson know she'd been assaulted? Her identity was supposed to be protected.... Did *everyone* know?

Was that the way her students looked at her? As a cold fish who couldn't even satisfy a rapist? Mickey would have agreed with that assessment. Randy might, too.

She dropped her head in her hands and closed her eyes. She burned when Randy touched her. She wanted to let herself go. Why couldn't she? Other women who had endured much worse had managed to find love. Or at least find a lover.

Would killing the rapist truly free her? What if it didn't? She didn't want to wait to find out.

She had to do what Randy asked. She had to call him, go to him.

Control the situation.

## CHAPTER SIXTEEN

"I DON'T DARE DRIVE TO Randy's loft and walk in on him. What if he's there with another woman? I'd die of embarrassment, if I could even make it to his front door."

From the backyard a baseball thudded repeatedly off the house as Milo practiced his pitching.

Vi was playing an educational video game in the living room. Every time she got an answer right the game whistled and clapped.

Helena dumped a packet of sweetener in her chamomile tea, took a sip and closed her eyes. "Ah, the joys of parenthood." She rubbed her temples.

"Why *not* just walk in on him?" Marcie asked. "I'll put the kids to bed."

"You've been doing that all the time lately."

"If I'm not here, I'm working at the library. The way Dr. Voss hates me, he'll never recommend me to take over as head librarian when he retires next year. I have to convince the board of governors I'm indispensable."

Helena set her cup down. "You ought to be going out to dinner and bars and sleeping over with some gorgeous guy."

"I wouldn't sleep with a man who picked up women in bars, even if I was the one he picked up."

"Why not try one of those matchmaking sites?"

"Later, when I have time. When this is over and you're safe."

"But—"

"One romance at a time, okay?"

"Randy doesn't want a long-term relationship."

"Do *you?*"

Helena got up to dump her tea in the sink. "Don't *you* push me, too, Marcie. I can't go to his loft and I can't bring him here."

"Why not? I can have the kids for a sleepover in my side of the duplex. They'd love that."

"What if they want me in the middle of the night? All they have to do is go out your back door and into ours."

"So lock it."

"And have them pitch a fit until you come? And what if I'm in the middle of something?"

"Call the man, Helena. Invite him to dinner. You're a pretty fair cook when you put your mind to it. I'll take Vi and Milo out for pizza, bring them back to my place and put them to bed."

"It's too late to ask him for tonight."

"Then ask him for tomorrow night."

"We have self-defense class tomorrow."

Marcie rolled her eyes. "Enough with the excuses. Get him over and take him to bed." She grabbed Helena's cup and shoved it in the dishwasher so hard it cracked.

"I'll ask him to dinner, that's all. I will *not* issue a booty call. That's demeaning to both of us," Helena said. "One meal, period." *When I get my nerve up.*

"I THOUGHT WE WERE ONTO something with the computer cases," Randy said. He handed Dick O'Hara a longneck Coors and slid into the booth opposite him. "Three of the seven bought their computer cases at Leyland's Luggage. The doctor's husband doesn't know where his wife bought hers, and no longer has it. The stockbroker's husband says his wife bought hers online. I haven't been able to reach the Realtor yet."

"What'd the store say about employees?" Dick downed his beer in one long pull and set the empty bottle on the table, then signaled to the waitress for another. He gave a significant burp and tapped his chest with his fist. "Sorry."

"They have a large turnover. They're pulling names and addresses for me. I'll cross-check with AFIS tomorrow to see if anybody has a record of violence against women. It's slim, but it's the best we've got at the moment."

"This guy is a damn ghost."

"Got word back from the lab this afternoon," Randy said. "They got a partial from the inside of the glove, but no DNA results yet. If we find the guy, we'll be able to compare prints, but there aren't enough matching points to run it through the FBI fingerprint database."

"A couple of months ago, Dr. Norcross accused me of wanting another assault to get more evidence," O'Hara told him. The waitress set a second bottle in front of him and he nodded his thanks, then stood, drained that one just as fast and tossed a bill on the table. "I'm heading home before I'm too drunk to drive," he said. "You got a hot date?"

"I wish." Randy left his beer, tossed down a bill to cover his own tab and followed O'Hara out. On the sidewalk, he said, "I listen for the phone to ring every night and pray it's not our guy."

"Good luck on the employee list. Let me know if you find anything," the detective added.

Randy watched him go. O'Hara's depressed slump was more marked now.

No sense in going home. He went back to the squad room to check employment records.

AMANDA DONOVAN CALLED Helena on Tuesday morning. "Can you meet me for lunch? I want to talk, and I don't want the others to know."

"I have a class until eleven," she said. "But I could meet you somewhere around eleven-thirty."

"Could you come downtown? I'm in court this afternoon. How about The Peabody? I'll make reservations in my name."

Helena agreed. After she hung up, she printed out a list of her contacts and the counseling services she'd used in case Amanda wanted it.

When she walked into The Peabody restaurant, she was surprised to see that Amanda was not alone. A small, beautiful black woman sat with her. She looked familiar, but Helena couldn't place her. Amanda waved her over.

"Dr. Helena Norcross, this is Katherine Davis. She does the six o'clock news on Channel 4."

They shook hands and Helena sat.

"I also do an interview show at ten weekday mornings."

"I've seen it," Helena said. "I don't watch daytime television as a rule, but the shows I've caught have been interesting."

"Thanks." Katherine glanced at Amanda. "We've

known each other since university. Amanda, you want to take over here?"

She leaned forward and lowered her voice. "Remember when we talked about the public's need to be informed, but we couldn't figure out how to go about telling them?"

Helena nodded. "Your assault didn't even make the newspapers."

"I wish I'd heard about it." Katherine's head came up. "It would have made *my* show, but last week's crime is old news."

"If it bleeds, it leads," Amanda answered. "I'm no longer bleeding."

"My interview show isn't hard news," Katherine continued. "We schedule writers on book tours, singing groups, craftspeople—anyone with an interesting story to tell."

"And this is an interesting story," Amanda added. "Cobb salad," she told the waitress. "And sweet tea."

"I can't remember when I've had a Peabody Cobb salad," Helena added. "I don't come downtown for lunch often. I'll have one, too. But I want my tea unsweet."

"I'll have the poached salmon and sweet tea," Katherine told the waitress.

After the waitress left, Helena asked, "Which aspect of the story do you find interesting?"

"That he's been doing this for over two years and the cops are no closer to catching him than they were the first day."

Helena bristled. "They're working very hard to catch this bastard."

"No doubt."

"But they are definitely keeping quiet about it," Amanda pointed out.

"It's time somebody told the public the police are withholding information about a dangerous predator poised to strike again at any moment, and who comes back to kill."

Helena could hear Katherine writing copy in her mind as she spoke.

"So, will you do it?" Amanda asked.

"Do what?"

"Come on the show and tell the public about this guy, put women on alert, give them information about how to stay safe, what to look out for." Katherine's wide brown eyes glowed. She seemed to grow larger as her enthusiasm built.

"Me? Why me? I'm the oldest news possible. Why not Amanda?"

"We'll do it together," Amanda said. "That way people can see how similar we look."

"The police won't like it," Helena said.

Katherine laughed. "Ya think? That's the point. Nobody calls in tips when they don't even know there's a case."

"And what about the nutcases who call in crazy tips that have to be checked anyway?" Helena asked.

She waved a hand dismissively. "Comes with the territory. If even one of the tips pans out, if even one woman doesn't have to go through what you went through, don't you think it's worth ruffling some police feathers?"

Actually, she did. But ruffling the feathers of people she knew and liked…loved even…

Make that lust, not love.

"We want to help the police, not hinder them," Katherine said. "Helena, the public has a right to know—"

"Much less than they're told. Forgive me, Katherine, but that's an easy catchphrase for blabbing about matters that don't concern the public at all."

The woman leaned forward and laid her hand on Helena's. Helena gently removed it as their lunches arrived. After they were eating, Katherine continued, "Let's say I agree with you that the public doesn't necessarily have a right to know who wears pajamas and who wears nothing. This is different. You admit there are women out there at risk?"

Helena nodded. "I'm not sure yours is the proper venue for alerting them."

"Name a better one," Amanda said.

"My show has excellent local ratings," Katherine explained. "People watch it and talk about it over the water cooler."

"When would this be?" Helena asked.

"Soon as possible," Amanda replied.

"Usually we book guests a month to six weeks in advance, but we have people we can put on hold if something more important comes up. Say before the end of this week. Maybe Thursday or Friday."

"That soon?" Helena's heart sank. She stood in front of classes every day and considered herself competent on her feet, but telling the entire mid-South about her experience, discussing the way it had changed her life, actually admitting to the world she had been raped...

"Let me think about it."

Katherine nodded. "Think fast."

"Tell me tonight at class," Amanda urged. "One more thing. Don't mention this to anybody."

"We should discuss it with Randy."

"He'll have to tell his boss, who'll call his boss, who'll call the police commissioner, who'll call the mayor, who'll flip," Katherine said. "Railsback's safer if he doesn't find out until afterward. He'll have deniability."

Helena decided before she got back to school for her two o'clock class that she would do the show. She wanted to tell Randy, but he'd lose it. He would be forced to tell his boss, just as Katherine said, and it would hit the fan. She hated being sneaky, but Katherine was correct that if the show saved a single woman, it was worth it.

There was another bonus. If the bastard saw the show or heard about it, he'd realize that she was no longer cowed, but had turned downright confrontational. If that didn't prick his ego, nothing would.

She'd definitely be a target.

She'd better be ready.

# CHAPTER SEVENTEEN

"I'VE GOT A LIST of employees from Leyland's Luggage from the time the assault began." Randy laid a copy on the edge of Dick O'Hara's desk. "It's a Joe job. I've run the names and put the seven with records who were there at the same time on top."

"Any of these guys still work there?" O'Hara said as he picked up the files.

Randy shook his head. "They don't pay commission, so there's no incentive to stay. Barely pays over minimum wage. They haven't had so much turnover the last year since the job market imploded."

"So he may have begun marking victims there, but gone to pick up others somewhere else?"

"Right. It's something, anyway."

"Anybody jump out at you?" O'Hara began to flip through the printouts.

"Three, actually." Randy leaned back and propped his heels on the wastebasket.

"What, you're not going to tell me?"

"See if you agree. I don't want to prejudice you."

Neither man spoke until O'Hara laid down the records. "Okay. Here you go."

Randy picked up the three O'Hara had selected.

"Yeah. These look like the best bets. All white males, all with a history of domestic violence. Nobody too tall or too short. All fair-haired, not hairy. All husky. Not much, but I'm running off pictures to show to the victims."

"This is thin, not enough to bring them in on."

"Hey, it's more than we had before. I've picked out seven others who look possible. Take a look."

O'Hara fanned the seven photos across his desk. "Where'd you get the pictures?"

"Driver's licenses," Randy stated. "Pulled them off and enlarged them."

"Computers are miraculous," O'Hara said with a grin. He studied the photos. "These represent the local chapter of Bald Men of America."

"Might account for the lack of hair at the crime scene," Randy suggested.

"None of the three with a history is bald."

"He wears a stocking cap or a hood, so he may have hair on his head and not on his arms."

"So, you gonna go talk to these people?" O'Hara asked. "I've got my hands full at the moment with three killings and one murder."

"I've got local addresses on two. Several have dropped off the map. Probably left town."

"Or gone to ground, changed identities."

"Not so easy to do nowadays as it used to be," Randy said. "I'd give anything for one fingerprint with enough points to compare."

He spent the rest of the day in his car, driving from one frustrating lead to another. By five in the afternoon he'd talked to three, discovered another had died of a heart attack six months earlier, one had moved out of town when he quit his job at the luggage company, and two had disappeared.

Of those three, one had moved out of his apartment owing four months back rent.

One had sold his house for cash to move to Los Angeles.

Another had walked out on his wife and baby six months ago. The man's mother swore she hadn't been in contact with him since he'd left. Randy didn't believe her.

He knocked off at five, grabbed a drive-through cheeseburger and a soda, and headed for the gym in hopes of finding Streak and possibly Milo. He needed to be early, anyway, to get into his attack suit.

He was disappointed when Streak showed up alone only five minutes before the self-defense class started, and seemed to be avoiding him. The women were already assembled and doing their warm-up exercises.

"Oh," Ellen said, when he walked into the room. "You look like a *Star Wars* storm trooper."

"More like the Pillsbury Dough Boy or the Michelin man," Bunny said with a laugh. "To what do we owe the costume?"

The heavy padding in the attack suit was uncomfortable and hot, but it was better than having his nuts shoved up through his lungs.

"Most victims react tentatively," Randy said. "They hesitate a second too long and don't fight back hard enough. Women especially are afraid they'll hurt somebody. Most normal people are. But if somebody attacks you, he or she is *not* normal. You've come a long way since Streak tossed me on my butt the first night. You're really becoming comfortable with the moves, but for obvious reasons we have to pull punches with each other. Not tonight. Tonight I am the bad guy and you're going to beat the crap out of me."

"Oooh," Lauren said. "Fun!"

"Since I don't plan to wind up in the emergency room, I borrowed the attack suit from the SWAT team."

"Do we need attack suits, too?" Ellen asked. "Won't you be trying to beat the crap out of us in return?"

"I promise I can scare you plenty without hurting you," Randy said. "You wonder why martial artists shout when they break boards? The yell heightens both their physical and emotional response. Tonight you are going to think fast, react faster and smarter, go toward your attacker, use your softness against his hardness and scream like a banshee while you're doing it. Got it? Okay, let's start with Amanda."

He'd picked her because he figured she had plenty of pent-up rage.

"What do we do?" she asked. "How are you going to come at us?"

He grinned. "Your attacker is not going to say, 'Now, Amanda, I'm going to try to choke you from the front.'"

Over the next two hours he and the rest of the class spent time on the mat. At first he tried to go easy on Sarah Beth, but she'd have none of it. They each called up strength he didn't know they had.

He swung right crosses. They countered and side-kicked his knees.

He clotheslined them from behind. They raked down his shins with their heels, stomped his insteps, dropped their shoulders and tossed him onto the mat.

He grabbed their wrists. They lifted their hands, moved his center of gravity and tossed him back.

When he called a break to strip off the heavily padded jacket and cool off, he realized everyone in the main part of the gym stood outside the window to the exercise room, gawking at them.

The second session was shorter, but more intense.

After he called a final halt, he yanked off the suit, dropped it on the floor and sank to the mat in his gym shorts and muscle shirt. Bunny brought him two bottles of water and his towel, then all the women collapsed around him to swig their water.

And laugh.

"That was so much fun!" Lauren said.

"Did we hurt you?" Sarah Beth asked, and patted Randy's arm.

"You sure tried," he said. "I'm proud of you, but don't think you'll react the same way in a real attack. For most women, fighting back isn't instinctive. You have to train the way they do in the army, so it's second nature. Muscle memory."

"You're saying we're not there yet?" Bunny asked.

"You're a long way from there."

"But a lot closer than we were when we started," Francine said. "Just let one of those gangbanging daddies try take one of my babies. I will take him *out!*" She pumped her fist in the air.

He noted that both Amanda and Streak were quieter than the others. They kept glancing at each other, then away. Something was going on there, but he had no idea what.

Bunny rose to her feet in one smooth motion and

reached down to help Sarah Beth. "Come on, ladies. I, for one, do not intend to sit my sweaty rear in my fancy car without taking a shower first. We reek of Eau d'Aggression."

Lauren giggled. "I may terrify poor Walter. That'll teach him to work late."

Randy stopped Amanda and noticed that Streak stayed behind, as well. "Want me to walk you to your car?"

"My firm's giving me a bodyguard after dark. He's in the car. I'm being careful."

She nodded at Streak solemnly as she walked into the women's locker room.

"What's all that about?" he asked Streak.

She glanced away. "Nothing."

"Do you have time for a cup of coffee?"

She looked directly into his eyes and the pulse in her throat began to speed. "The children are spending the night with Marcie. Why don't we have a drink at my place?"

"I planned to follow you home and see you safely inside, anyway, so I might as well." *Casual. Don't make too much of it. Don't scare her again.*

She nodded and fled.

## CHAPTER EIGHTEEN

"I TOLD THE OTHERS what we're planning to do on the talk show," Amanda whispered. She stood in the center of the locker room with a towel wrapped around her. The others sat or stood in various states of undress.

"Y'all are crazy." Francine grimaced. "Am I right?" Her gaze raked the group.

"You two are already targets," Sarah Beth argued. "This is waving a red flag at a bull."

"And you are not bullfighters," Bunny added. "Call it off."

"Or at least tell Randy," Ellen begged. "Listen to his advice."

"He'll have a fit." Lauren shook her head in dismay.

"It's bad enough for Amanda with her bodyguard," Ellen said. "She doesn't have children. You do." She pointed at Helena.

"That's why I have to do this," Helena told them. "I've put my life on hold for two years. I've crept around and frightened my kids with anxiety attacks and phoned it in at my job and run away from everybody, while I waited for the other shoe to drop." She sank onto the bench that ran down the center of the room. "Randy said many abused women orchestrate when their men beat them up. It's because they can't stand waiting any longer."

"It's the only choice they have," Amanda added quietly.

"Listen to yourself," Francine said. "Who gets the black eyes and the broken ribs? The husband? The boyfriend? She may pick the time, but she's still the one who winds up in the emergency room."

"Or the morgue," Sarah Beth said softly.

Ellen put her hand over Sarah Beth's and held it tightly.

"The doctor had children." Helena knew she was starting to sound belligerent, but she couldn't help herself. "He didn't hurt them or her husband."

"They were out of the house at the time," Bunny retorted. "What if one of them had walked in on him? Does he carry a gun? Does anyone know even that much about him?"

"So they were out of the house." Francine rolled her eyes and waved her hand dismissively. "They still lost their mother and the daddy lost his wife. You want your children to lose their mama? You are crazy, girl." She glared at Amanda. "You, too. Lawyer ought to have better sense."

"So we wait until he rapes and possibly murders somebody else?" Amanda demanded. "Until he comes back to kill that real estate agent or that woman in Germantown with the charities?"

"How about he sees that TV show and comes back and kills *you?*" Francine snapped. "You happy with that?"

"I'll be happy when he's put away," she answered.

"Or dead," Helena said. "Better dead."

"Let the police handle it," Ellen implored. "Let Randy."

"Like they're doing such a fabulous job." Amanda

pulled on a dry shirt and pushed her hair off her face. "The definition of insanity is doing the same thing over and over and expecting a different result. The police are going over the same ground repeatedly, and it's not working. We've got to force his hand and be ready for him. We're not stupid. We're not going to walk down dark alleys or stroll into empty parking garages at midnight."

"The cops can use us to set up a sting." Helena pulled on dry socks and stuck her feet in her Nikes. "That's what they do, isn't it?"

"Not with civilians." Bunny took out a compact, frowned at her reflection and began to powder her face.

"They won't have a choice," Amanda said. "My firm isn't going to pay for private security for long and I can't afford it on my own. I can't hide. My job is public. Sooner or later he's going to come back to finish what Francine interrupted. We have to catch him or none of us will ever have closure."

Sarah Beth let out a deep sigh. "There is no such thing. The men who killed my daughter will rot in prison without parole until they die, but that doesn't bring her back or make it any easier without her."

"They're not killing anybody else's daughter, though, are they?" Amanda picked up her briefcase and her jacket, then dropped to her knees before Sarah Beth. "I am so sorry. What an awful thing to say."

"But true." The older woman touched Amanda's cheek. "He could kill one or both of you and still get away."

"He'll have less chance if we orchestrate the confrontation." Helena pulled Amanda up to stand beside her. "That's all we're doing."

"Won't he realize it's a trap?" Ellen asked. "That's

assuming you get the police to take you seriously and set one up."

"Of course he will," Amanda said. "I don't think he'll be able to resist the challenge."

"He can't admit that any woman could put one over on him," Helena added. "*Of course* I'm worried about my children and Marcie, but I don't know what else to do to protect them. I don't have any family, so I can't send them to stay with grandparents or relatives, and Marcie lives right next door. I am not going to try to find my ex-husband to look after them. He'd lose them in a poker game."

"I'll do it." Francine nodded, decision made. When they all looked at her, she raised her hands. "What? Am I a qualified caregiver for children? Am I a widow-woman with a huge house with nobody in it but me? Am I not the absolute best cook in west Tennessee and possibly the world?" She shrugged. "One damn raping serial killer is small change compared to some of the low-life gangbanging drug addicts I've handled with one hand tied behind my back."

"I couldn't ask you—"

"You are not asking. I am offering."

"Who knows how long—"

"We'll worry about that later. Marcie and I between us can get them to school and back to my house."

"Marcie may not want to leave her house."

"You let me worry about that," Francine said, and smiled. "Be nice having a roommate who doesn't leave dirty jockey shorts on the floor and whiskers in the sink."

"I can't simply abandon Milo and Vi. Their father did that."

"You won't. You call every day and come by every chance you get, and I'll bring 'em with me to class. Won't be for long."

"Francine, you're the best."

"Don't I know. I think there's a policeman out there waiting for you."

"You better keep him close until this is over," Ellen said.

"And beyond," Bunny added.

"If we survive." Amanda shrugged.

"We'll survive," Helena added. *But that bastard won't.*


"COFFEE OR A DRINK?" Helena asked Randy, seated on her couch before the fire. Her very molecules seemed to be alive with fear and anticipation. No more what-if's. Crunch time.

She wanted Randy. He wanted her. The house was theirs for the night. The fire was crackling, the lights were low. Even as the rational part of her mind screamed *cliché,* the emotional part screamed *shut up.*

"Got any white wine?"

"Do you really like it?" she asked.

He grinned. "I'd rather have a beer."

"I have German beer," she said. "In bottles with long necks." She brought him one from the refrigerator, poured herself a glass of white wine and curled on the couch beside him.

"You did well this evening," he said as he settled beside her. "You've learned to control your anger, make it work for you instead of get you into trouble."

"Part of the time. Did we hurt you?"

He laughed. "You bet you did, but not as badly as you would have if I hadn't worn the attack suit."

"When can we go back to the firing range?"

"Maybe next week. You could go alone, you know. You don't need the class."

"I need an instructor."

"They always have an instructor on the firing line."

"Not the same as having you."

They sat quietly side by side, not touching. Helena was aware of Randy and assumed he was aware of her. He'd warned her she'd have to make the first move.

Why was that so hard?

"Tell me," he said softly, and took her hand.

She set down her wine and stood up, pulling him with her. "Will you please come upstairs and make love with me right this minute before I lose my nerve?"

He came to his feet so quickly he nearly knocked over her glass.

Upstairs, they stood face-to-face in her dark bedroom, but he made no move toward her.

"You're not going to make this easy, are you?" she whispered.

He shook his head.

She ran her fingers down his cheek, caressed the stubble that had grown since his morning shave.

He closed his eyes and kissed her palm. "Tell me what you want from me."

"I don't know. Men always demanded what they wanted from *me*. I tried to be what they wanted, feel what I was supposed to feel."

"Did you?"

"Sometimes."

"It's not a test, love. You don't get a grade on the length of your orgasm or even whether you *have* an orgasm. Feel what you feel. Trust me tonight. If you get scared, tell me. Hold on to me and try to ride it through. If you can't, then we'll try tomorrow or next week or next month."

"I can't ask you—"

"That's all right, too. I won't make you ask anymore. Lie naked with me, hold me and let me hold you."

"I want you."

He took her hand and ran her palm down to feel his erection through his jeans. "Pretty obvious I want you."

He kissed her gently, and she parted her lips to taste him. She felt as though her body was melting and reforming to fit the contours of his body. She moved her hips against him as she pulled her shirt over her head, unhooked her bra and slid the straps off her shoulders.

She didn't remember losing the rest of her clothes, or how he got out of his. After what seemed an eternity, he slid down beside her and joined his nakedness to hers. Her heart raced and she felt the start of the old panic. *Hold on, hold on.*

She caught her breath when he kissed her nipple and a shock not of fear but of pleasure shot through her. She ran her hands down his body, searching for him, but he stopped her. "Tonight is about you," he whispered. "Trust me." His lips slid over her stomach and below. She dug her fingernails into the tops of his shoulders.

A moment later, when his lips touched her, everything dropped away but sensation. Waves of pleasure, as though every nerve was centered where his lips touched, his fingers caressed.

And when the climax came, it rolled over and

through her with spasm after spasm while she could only grasp the bedposts and shudder.

Her first coherent thought was *not yet, not yet, there's more. I want the rest.* He slid up her body, careful not to lean over her, until he lay beside her. She found him and hugged him. He was still strongly erect, but it seemed he was willing to endure even that for her.

She lifted herself above him, straddled him. His eyes widened as his hands slid under her hips. "Wait," he said.

"You said I had to come to you," she whispered.

"Condom." He reached for his pants beside the bed and found the packet.

She couldn't remember ever watching Mickey. She'd always closed her eyes while they made love, but she watched Randy. When had her fear gone?

When he'd ceased to be all men and became only himself, the man she had learned to love.

She lowered herself onto him, chose to take *him,* not to be taken. He'd already given her an orgasm. She expected only enjoyable payback, but at some point her conscious mind flew away again as they drove harder and harder until they both came together. She held him inside her as long as she could before rolling over beside him.

She felt tears running down her cheeks.

He brushed one away. "Are you okay?"

Laughter bubbled up inside her, and a moment later she was laughing and crying at the same time.

He raised himself on one arm, careful not to loom over her. "Streak?"

She threw her arm across his chest and snuggled against his side with a sigh.

He wrapped his arms around her and kissed her hair. "Now, was that so hard?"

She giggled. "As a matter of fact…"

"Hey! You know what I meant."

She lifted her face and kissed his chin. "Thank you."

"The pleasure was all mine."

"No, it wasn't. I was so afraid I couldn't go through with it, that I'd make a fool of myself again. You gave me space to try, then held on to me until I forgot my fears. After what happened the last time, you had every right to reject me."

"A man would be nuts to reject such a beautiful, passionate woman." He slid his hand down her hip.

"Not beautiful, and I didn't have a clue I was capable of feeling this way. I never have before." She moved her leg across his thigh.

"I saw that first night that you were beautiful, and that the passion was waiting to burst out."

"Even in baggy sweats and droopy hair?"

"I sensed it the first night at the gym. You felt it, too. The electricity between us crackled like corn popping at a movie theater."

"So you knocked me down," she said with a chuckle.

"I always knock down people who are trying to kill me."

She rose up on one elbow and said seriously, "I was trying to kill what you represented."

"You're not still planning to kill *him,* are you?"

She avoided his eyes.

"Even if it really was self-defense, you wouldn't like what it does to you." He stroked her back.

"Have you ever killed anyone?"

He flinched and drew away from her. "Not the way you mean."

"What other way is there?"

He rolled off the bed, and she reached out to him. "Randy? Whatever I said, I'm sorry."

"It's okay."

"No, it's not." She climbed to her knees, wrapped her arms around him from behind and leaned her cheek against his back. "Please, don't pull away."

"I'm thirsty. How about I go get you another glass of wine and me another beer?"

"Please come back."

He reached behind him and stroked her hip. "Hey, lady, my clothes are up here. I *have* to come back."

She could tell his flippancy was an act. Something she'd said really got to him.

When he came upstairs again, she accepted her wineglass, never taking her eyes from his face. He sat on the side of the bed and stroked her hair. "You didn't say anything wrong. Just stumbled on my family skeleton."

"Come to bed. I don't care about your skeletons."

He stretched out beside her and pulled her against his chest. With his chin on her hair, he said, "Trust me, you don't get over being responsible for a death."

"If you shot someone, I'm sure you had no choice. You could never do anything wrong."

"I didn't shoot anybody, but I'm still responsible. I was eleven, old enough to tell my family to go screw themselves."

She sat up and stared down at him. "Eleven? That's only two years older than Milo."

"I told you policing is my family profession. Unfortunately, alcohol is the family curse. My dad is a member of AA, but Uncle Norman, also a cop, was a mean, stupid drunk. I didn't know until years later that the reason we couldn't eat toast for breakfast when he was around was that the crunch made his hangover worse."

"You're kidding," Helena said.

"Scout's honor." Randy leaned back against the pillows, and she snuggled against him once more, with her arm across his chest.

Now that he'd started, he seemed to want to continue, to let the whole story come out in that space of time after making love when men allowed their vulnerability to show. Whatever his burden of guilt, he couldn't have done anything too bad at eleven, could he?

"We lived next door to Uncle Norman and Aunt Jean," he continued. "Dad was on duty. Mom and Aunt Jean were at some meeting. Uncle Norman was supposed to be watching me and his six-month-old daughter, Irene, but he preferred beer and ESPN. I came in the house for a glass of water and heard her crying, really angry. I figured I'd change her and give her a bottle."

"You?" Helena asked.

"Hey, I can change a diaper." He sighed. "As I got to the nursery door, she went quiet. Uncle Norman was holding her over her crib, shaking her like a rag doll."

"Oh my God!" Helena tightened her hold on him.

"He didn't recognize me for a second, then yelled to call 911. She died in the E.R. When I told my dad what I saw, he said to keep my mouth shut, because they'd think I'd done it."

"You didn't talk to anyone else?"

"Dad said I must have been mistaken, that Uncle Norman would never hurt his own child, and I'd ruin his marriage, kill his career. When I tried to talk about it again, he slapped me. First and last time Dad ever laid a hand on me. He said Uncle Norman and Aunt Jean were suffering enough, and where was my family loyalty."

"So you shut up."

She heard the despair in his voice as he said, "They were all cops. I was a kid. The year I made detective I checked Irene's death certificate. It read 'sudden infant death syndrome.' No autopsy. Uncle Norman eventually blew his brains out."

"The guilt?"

Randy lifted his free hand and let it fall. "Who knows? That's why I angled for Cold Cases. I don't want any more Uncle Normans to get away with it."

"He didn't."

"He messed up a lot of lives. A year after Irene died they had a son, my cousin Norman Junior. Nobody including my mother or my aunt Jean ever left Uncle Norman alone with the kid."

"She *stayed* married to him?"

He nodded. "A couple of years ago I talked to an ADA buddy about what would have happened if I'd officially told the police what I saw. She said probably nothing. My evidence wouldn't have been enough. The rest of the family would have closed ranks. Other cops would have supported them."

"Couldn't it have been SIDS?"

He ran his hand over his hair. "I saw what I saw."

"You didn't shake the baby. It's not your fault. You didn't kill anyone."

"They might have done an autopsy. I should have told my dad to go to hell."

"You obeyed authority."

"That's what the Nazi storm troopers said."

"They weren't eleven years old."

"My father has never forgiven me."

"Forgiven *you?*"

"For knowing what he did, what we all did."

She took Randy's hand. "I am so sorry."

He slid down and clung to her. "I warned you. Everybody's damaged."

HE LEFT BEFORE DAYBREAK to avoid running into the children. Helena felt pleasantly achy and languid. She stood under her shower until the hot water ran out, before dressing and fixing breakfast for Milo, Vi and Marcie.

In her limited experience, the only time a man let his guard down and really opened up about his feelings was the ten minutes after orgasm. No doubt, this morning Randy regretted what he'd told her last evening. She wouldn't be surprised if he pulled away from her, at least for a while, uncomfortable that she knew.

While she waited for Marcie and the children to come from next door, she fixed breakfast, and thought about what Randy told her.

How could Randy's own father hit him for trying to do the right thing? Shaken baby syndrome was murder, certainly involuntary manslaughter. An autopsy might well have confirmed that the baby had been shaken, but the law took care of its own.

How could Uncle Norman's wife stay with him?

The same way abused women everywhere stayed

with their abusers. They were convinced they couldn't survive alone. Mostly, it was their abusive men who convinced them.

Now, before this evening, *she* had to convince Marcie, Milo and Vi that moving to Francine's for a few days would be like a vacation.

## CHAPTER NINETEEN

"I HATE TO SAY THIS, but the best way we're likely to catch this guy is to set up a decoy and hope he bites," Lieutenant Gavigan said at the morning Cold Cases meeting.

"Decoys work if you know the seed area the predator hunts over," Jack Samuels argued. "Even then it's iffy. This guy strikes at random intervals and locations. You may put a decoy on the street for months before he tries to take her."

"If ever. I'll put out the word we're looking for a tall, dark, handsome policewoman to go undercover," Liz said.

"He stalks them after he chooses them," Randy interjected. "Maybe for months. Upstairs is not going to authorize that use of manpower to catch a serial rapist who's only hurt seven women and killed three times in two years."

"That we're aware of," Liz said.

"They won't even let the media know he's out there," Randy retorted.

"How about we set up your girlfriend?" Gavigan suggested.

"No way! She's a civilian with children." He was afraid Streak would jump at the chance.

"How about that lawyer, Amanda Donovan?" Jack asked. "She's divorced, no kids. She's his type. Since he missed her once, he's likely to try again, no?"

"I'll bet she'd do it," Liz said.

"Too risky." Samuels frowned. "Any more info on the ex–luggage store clerks?"

"I'm working on it," Randy reported. "No luck in tracking down the guy who sold his house and moved to Los Angeles. Maybe he changed his mind about moving."

"Or his name," Liz added.

"If so, he's not listed in our area, either. No tax rolls, no voter registration, no driver's license. He could be anywhere. I did talk to a couple of elderly neighbors who remember the family. Mother was a nurse, father some kind of auto mechanic. He died first. Mother wound up in a nursing home for a couple of years before she passed away."

"The son?"

"The woman didn't see much of him, but didn't like him."

"Why?"

"Long-haired hippie type. Said he and his mother used to have some major rows. Had to call the cops a couple of times because of the noise."

"Elder abuse?" Gavigan leaned back in his chair.

"Nobody ever got arrested. The minute his mother died, he put the house on the market. Sold in two days, even though it needed a lot of work."

"Before the real estate market went bust," Liz said.

"Who was his Realtor?" Gavigan asked.

"Guess," Randy answered. "The woman who was assaulted. He told his neighbor he was moving to L.A. He was sick of living in the South."

"What about the other two?"

"Same thing. No trace of them in this area."

"Every time we think we've got something, it winds up a dead end." Gavigan ran a hand through his brush cut. "Give it a couple more days, then move on."

"Until he attacks again or kills another woman?" Randy said. He heard the anger in his voice. The lieut was right, but that didn't make it any easier to take.

"O'Hara's a bulldog." Jack went out of Gavigan's office and returned with a fresh cup of coffee. "He's going to keep revisiting his cases until he comes up with another lead."

But O'Hara wasn't Randy. *He* had to be the one to catch the guy. He'd finally gotten Streak to trust him enough to let him make love to her, but that didn't mean she'd given up on enticing the guy in order to kill him.

More likely be killed *by* him.

Streak's phone went straight to voice mail. Wednesday was her busy day, but she got through early enough to pick up the kids after school and spend time with them. Too cold to play catch with Milo, but maybe Randy could pick up takeout and join them for dinner. He could build his relationship with Vi, now that she'd decided she didn't dislike him. With both children home, he wouldn't be able to get Streak alone for more than a chaste kiss.

He checked his phone messages after the meeting with the others finished. "Oh, jeez," he said.

On her way back to her own desk, Liz asked, "What? Trouble?"

"Who knows?" He'd turned his cell phone off when he'd walked into Streak's place and forgotten to turn it on when he'd left at five this morning.

He leaned back in his chair, closed his eyes and

listened. "It's Paige. I'm sorry for all the nasty things I said. We can make it work." Next, "Call me." Third, "Please, Randy, talk to me." Her voice sounded teary. Finally, at eight-thirty this morning, she'd left a text message: "whr r u."

The phone vibrated in his hand. Paige again. Either she had a short memory or she hadn't found moving on to a marriage prospect as easy as she'd hoped. He let the phone ring until it went to voice mail, then he sighed and picked it up. Might as well get it over with.

"Randy! I've been calling and calling. I was starting to get worried."

"Morning, Paige. How've you been?"

"Lonely. I miss you." She sounded pouty, but then she frequently did. The little-girl thing that had amused him now seemed artificial and cloying. "Meet me for dinner, okay?"

"I'm really busy at the moment. In the middle of a big case."

"You have to eat sometime."

"I'm teaching self-defense in the evenings." He didn't say which evenings.

"We both said some things we didn't mean. I said I'm sorry. Can't we start over?"

"I'm, uh, seeing somebody."

Silence. Then in a mature, non-little-girl voice, she said, "Bastard," and hung up.

He sat and stared at his phone, then asked Liz, "Am I a bastard?"

"I used to think so," she admitted. "Lately, not so much."

"I never lied to anyone I dated," he said.

"Most women have a hard time keeping sex friendly, whatever they say. Even if they broke it off, they're still hurt when it's over."

"So I *am* a bastard."

Samuels came over to perch on the edge of Randy's desk. "Vickie and I have been married for forty years, and I'm still as crazy about her as I was the day we married."

"And I'm nuts about Jud." Liz patted her belly. "Obviously. You want to spend your life in that big, cold loft all by yourself? You'll never have a real home, loving arms waiting for you, your children clustered around you…"

"And I'll never destroy all of it on a one-night stand. I can live with that." He dropped his phone in his pocket, picked up the stack of folders from his desk and walked out.

Behind him, he heard her say, "Ya think?"

ALTHOUGH RANDY EXPECTED Streak to pull back after their night in bed, and wasn't surprised when she told him she was working on a paper all evening, he was disappointed. Tonight he'd have to be satisfied with pizza and beer alone in his loft. If he couldn't be with Streak, he'd rather be alone.

Nobody would do but Streak. That had never happened to him before. Was he finally falling in love? He could understand why smitten teenagers spent hours texting or talking, even though they saw one another all day at school. He longed to hear her voice.

Heck, he wanted to hear Vi and Milo, maybe help them with their puzzle or homework.

Before he left for the day, he finally located Streak's ex, Michael Norcross, who hung up on him twice until

Randy left a message that his call had nothing to do with the divorce or child support.

When they did speak, Norcross sounded drunk. He was living in Reno, teaching sixth grade in a small private high school, and had not been to Memphis since he'd left almost two years earlier. He knew nothing about his wife's assault he hadn't told the police at the time.

"You see rape cases all the time, Detective. Don't you agree most women ask for it?" he practically demanded. "The way they dress, the airs they put on. Make anybody want to take them down a peg, give 'em what they're asking for, am I right or am I right?"

"Absolutely, sir," Randy said. He loosened his grip on his phone before he broke it, and realized he was grinding his teeth. For a man who could sound as though he empathized with an ax murderer, he was having trouble not jumping down the phone line all the way to Reno and beating the crap out of Mickey Norcross. "Do you happen to remember where you were the night Str—uh…your wife was attacked?"

"Why?" Now he sounded suspicious. "After two years? Come on, you got to be kidding."

"Most people remember where they were during important events."

"Okay, okay. I was at a faculty meeting from late afternoon on, then some of us went to dinner at that steak house, you know the one downtown on the river. That's where the cops found me. I went straight to the trauma center, then I had to go take the babysitter back and apologize to her dad for keeping her out so late. Like it was my fault. Had to pay her for the extra hours, too, although with an act of God, you'd think she'd cut me some slack."

"Do you know anyone who might have committed the assault?"

"Against my wife, you mean? Hell, no."

"Did you carry life insurance?"

"Yeah, we both did. What's that got to do with the price of tea?"

"Just checking."

They spoke for another five minutes while Norcross grew drunker and angrier, until he hung up. After Randy calmed down enough to pry the phone from his hand, he crossed Norcross off his list of people to interview, but with a pencil rather than a pen. If the creep had hired someone to kill his wife, he'd picked a sadistic incompetent. No wonder Streak kept Norcross away from the kids. He hadn't even asked how they were.

Randy broke down and called Streak when he reached his loft, which felt lonelier every day, with his pizza. If he sold it for what he paid for it, she could rent out both sides of her duplex and they could buy a house big enough for all four of them.

He hung up his coat, then leaned against the cold steel of his front door. He was tired of having too much space. He was fed up with neatness. He wanted Streak's books and the kids' toys around.

He was out of his mind.

He called Streak so the sound of her voice could make him realize how ridiculous his idea was. Milo answered.

"Randy, guess what? Me and Vi and Marcie are going to go stay at Miss Francine's for a couple of days. Like a vacation only no traveling."

Randy came to full attention. "How long are you

planning on staying?" He kept his voice casual. Something was up. Maybe Streak had received a threat she didn't want him to know about. Or decided on a suspect, which would be equally bad.

"Mom said a few days. We'll go to Miss Francine's after school. They've got tons of kids Vi's age, and enough kids my age for a real baseball team."

"Marcie's coming, too?"

"She says it'll be fun."

Randy hoped Streak was simply clearing the way for the two of them to have more time alone. Maybe to spend the whole night together. Have breakfast at her kitchen table.

But it might be more than that. Did somebody threaten her? Had she remembered something? He wouldn't put it past her to figure out who had attacked her, and set herself up. Surely she wouldn't be that dumb.

Yeah, she would. He might have inadvertently been the catalyst. She felt she couldn't be free to love him— *love?*—while the rapist remained free.

"Can I speak to your mother, Milo?"

"She's not home yet. She's picking us up in a few minutes, though. I'll tell her to call you."

He hung up and called her cell phone, but got voice mail. She was ducking him. The way he'd ducked Paige. He called Francine. She didn't volunteer the information that she was taking in Marcie and Streak's kids.

Whatever game they were playing, he intended to make sure Streak wasn't hurt. She was obviously making certain her family didn't get caught in the cross fire.

That meant a long, cold night sitting in his car at the corner, where he could watch both the front and back of her house. If he banged on the door and asked to spend the night, she'd put off whatever she was planning.

He checked to make sure Amanda's female body-guard was on duty, picked up his stakeout gear and left his apartment.

## CHAPTER TWENTY

THE NEXT MORNING, he left before Streak could spot him. His old basketball knee injury ached, as did the bruises the women had inflicted on him, but he'd snatched sleep during the night. A couple of cops in a patrol car checked on him at midnight, then passed the word along to the next shift, so he wasn't rousted again.

She'd hate knowing he'd watched her house.

Showered, fed and clean, but far from rested, he dragged himself to his desk five minutes before Gavigan's morning meeting. Randy was organizing his notes when Gavigan's door opened hard enough to slam against the flimsy wall. "Railsback, all of you, get in here now!"

They shared looks as they raced to Gavigan's office.

He was standing behind his desk watching the small television in the corner. It was seldom used except to monitor news events and police press conferences.

This morning, however, he was tuned in to the Channel 4 morning talk show.

"Railsback, you know about this?" He turned up the volume.

"As announced earlier, our next guests are two prominent local women who have a story to tell—a story of violence and police cover-up, a story that every woman in our viewing area needs to take to heart. May I introduce Ms. Amanda Donovan, one of Memphis's leading divorce attorneys, and her friend and fellow victim, Professor Helena Norcross."

"Oh my God." Liz sank into a chair.

"Hell and damnation," Jack Samuels blurted.

"Yeah," Gavigan said. "Railsback, if you knew about this, you'll be parking cars at the Forum by noon."

Randy shook his head, but didn't take his eyes off the screen. "I can't believe… What the hell are they thinking?"

They told their stories over the next ten minutes. Randy saw that Amanda and Helena were gripping each other's hands as though to draw strength.

"He's a coward," Streak said. "He warns his victims not to speak to the police. If they do, that means they haven't learned to be submissive. He'll come back and teach them another lesson. The final lesson."

"You mean…?" the host prompted. Randy couldn't remember her name. Katherine something?

When neither guest replied, the host continued. "Yet you both reported your rape to the police. What have they been doing to catch this monster?"

"Everything they can," Streak said. "They've worked diligently, but in a series of random events, it takes a while to connect them, much less find evidence about the perpetrator."

"Have they warned the public there's a serial killer on the loose? He has killed twice, I think you said."

"They have not warned the public." Amanda jutted her chin and her eyes narrowed. "Which, in my view, is unconscionable."

"It can't have been easy for you two to blow the whistle." Katherine Davis, that was it.

"We're not blowing any whistle," Streak countered. "The police are working as hard as they have been able to without public input. That's why we came on your show." She turned to look directly into the camera. "If you are a victim who didn't report your assault, please call the police. They'll get you to the proper detectives. If you are aware of anything that might aid in catching this evil man, then please call the authorities to tell them what you know. In both cases, your information will be kept confidential."

"Take a look at us," Amanda said. "We could be sisters. This monster goes after women who look like us, women with careers and prestige. If you fit his profile, be particularly careful, but be aware that he could decide to go after blondes with blue eyes next."

"I'm afraid we're running out of time," Davis said. "Do you have anything to add to your terrible story?"

Both women stared into the camera. "The man who assaulted us," Streak stated, "is a coward and a loser incapable of tolerating successful women."

"Give yourself up," Amanda added. "Because the police *will* catch you."

The station went to commercial as Gavigan's phone rang. So did Randy's desk and cell phones.

Gavigan put his call on speakerphone.

"Those two idiots have painted big red targets on their backs," said the angry voice at the other end of the line. Nobody had to be told who he was. "What is this, Dodge City? Who let those two on television?"

Liz, Randy and Jack sneaked out while Gavigan sat

at his desk with his hand over his eyes and listened to his boss tear him a new one.

Randy figured he was the next step down on the food chain. The call on his desk phone was from Dick O'Hara. He'd call back after he talked to Gavigan.

The one on his cell came from Public Affairs, no doubt trying to put a spin on the show that wouldn't make them all look incompetent.

He remembered when Liz had said, "You'll get yours, Randy Randy."

He'd made a joke about it. This was no joke. He felt as though he should pick his guts off the floor and stuff them back into his abdomen.

His heart, however, was a lost cause. It was spewing blood through so many holes it felt like lace, and his brain wasn't much better.

How long had Streak known she'd be doing the show this morning? Days? Weeks? Certainly while they were making love.

She hadn't said a word.

This would destroy his career. He loved this woman, dammit! He loved her children. He'd been considering how they could mesh households.

Not telling him, not giving him the chance to talk her out of it—hell, not giving him the opportunity to lock her in a closet to keep her from doing it—was unforgivable. She didn't love him back or she'd never have done this thing.

She might as well have committed suicide.

His cell phone rang again. He wanted to throw it across the squad room. Instead, he picked it up.

"Randy?" Streak sounded tentative. "I need to tell

you something. You may not like it. This morning Amanda and I—"

"I saw it." He whispered the words, but he wanted to scream at her. "My boss saw it. His boss saw it. I suspect all of west Tennessee saw it. If your attacker didn't see it, I'm sure he'll catch it on YouTube and Facebook."

"You're upset."

"No. I'm stunned that I thought I had fallen in love with an intelligent woman. Instead I find I've fallen for a lying idiot with a death wish."

"Love?"

"Oh, hell, what does it matter? I have one request for you before you barricade yourself in your house for the rest of your life. Get Amanda to draw up a guardianship agreement so I can raise Milo and Viola after the bastard kills you." Despite his efforts at self-control, his voice rose dangerously. Liz and Jack, the only other detectives in the room, turned their backs and talked on their telephones to give him at least the illusion of privacy.

"But Marcie—"

"Can't protect them. I can. I probably make as much money as she does, your ex won't cross me. Marcie and I can come to an arrangement."

"You're talking as if I'm dead," Streak said. Now she was getting angry. About time.

"I am going to do everything in my power to prevent that, but in case I fail the way I have so far failed to find this guy, get it done today for the kids' sake."

"You're joking, aren't you? I mean, you can't possibly be serious."

"Dead serious, excuse the expression. It would make things less complicated if you'd meet me in Judge Axom's chambers this afternoon and marry me. We wouldn't need the guardianship papers if I was their stepfather."

"You have lost your mind. You just called me a lying idiot."

"That doesn't mean I don't love you. Annul me after we catch him if you want."

"How can I annul a man I've slept with?"

"We slept together before you set yourself up as a target."

"Well, if I marry you, which I seriously doubt I will do, I intend to consummate at the first opportunity and continue consummating for the rest of my life, which, to hear you tell it, is very short, anyway. That shouldn't inconvenience you too much."

# CHAPTER TWENTY-ONE

"PHONE'S RINGING OFF THE WALL," Dick O'Hara said when Randy finally called him.

Instead of being angry, Gavigan had given him the "more in sorrow than in anger" speech, which was worse.

"I guessed something was up, but I never guessed this," Randy said. "So you're having to check out the tips?"

"Yeah, everything from attack by aliens in aluminum foil hats to panhandlers on Beale Street. Amanda Donovan called me to ask me to set her up as a decoy."

"And?"

"I said I'd discuss it."

"What? You can't be serious."

"I'm serious, all right. Hell, Railsback, what other choice do we have? He'll try for one or both of them, anyway. I won't be able to set up anything until tomorrow at the earliest, and she's got her minder, so she should be all right. Can you handle Helena Norcross?"

"Not on my best day," he said drily.

"Okay. I'll try to arrange for a couple of detectives from the drug task force to pick her up at her office this afternoon. They look like college kids and speak the lingo. When does her last class finish?"

"Four. She generally goes home to see her kids afterward, but they're not there, and after this morning, I doubt she'll want to take the chance of leading someone to them. She'll probably head straight to the gym to work out before class."

"Tell me whether you can follow her home after your class and stay with her. If not, we'll pick her up again when she leaves the gym, and stick with her until morning."

"Thanks, Dick."

"They may be crazy, those women, but they've got guts. Amanda Donovan says they just want it to be over. Don't blame her. So do I."

HELENA SHOULD NEVER have listened to Katherine Davis. She should have told Randy she and Amanda were doing the TV show. Did he really mean what he said about the guardianship of Milo and Vi? About marrying her? Even though he was *so* angry at her?

Katherine didn't give a damn about her and Amanda. She was probably salivating in the hope that one of them would be killed. But wasn't the exposure on TV what they had wanted? She'd felt confident when she'd tossed her challenge out there, but she'd betrayed Randy, and now she was as scared of losing him as she was of losing Milo and Vi. And her own life.

She had to hone her skills and get ready for the confrontation she said she wanted. She wished she could walk away and never think about the bastard again, but that had never been possible.

For now Marcie and the children were safe with Francine, but that couldn't go on for long.

Now that she'd tethered herself out for the tiger,

Helena was feeling the terror the goat felt. What made her think she could take on a man who had nearly destroyed her life once? A faceless stranger?

She pulled her pistol out of the center drawer of her desk and checked to see that it was fully loaded. From now on she would carry it in the holster on her belt, under her blazer.

The students for her three o'clock modern lit class only wanted to talk about the TV show. She gave up after twenty minutes, cut the class short and got away from their avid faces as soon as she could.

Three-thirty. Plenty of time to drop by the gun shop. He never struck in daylight. She ran into Oblivious Al on her way out.

"Playing hooky?" he asked. "Are you alone?"

"I'm headed for the gun range to improve my aim and shoot away some tension in a public place."

"Let me come with you."

"I'll be safe enough in a gun store, Al." She leaned over and kissed his cheek. "Thank you for worrying about me. I won't go off the grid, I promise. I intend to surround myself with people."

The minute she slid behind the wheel of her car, locked the doors and started the engine, she called Randy's cell phone. Busy. She left him a message about where she'd be, and said, "Please call me. We have to work this out. I love you and I'm sorry I acted like an idiot."

The parking lot at the gun store was surprisingly empty, so she was able to park in front of the door. She waved to the store manager and asked if the shooting range was open.

"Sure. Ten to midnight seven days a week."

"Anyone else shooting?"

He shook his head. "Any minute. The range master's back there." He turned back to his cash register receipts, and she walked through the heavy door that divided the store from the range itself.

Although the targets twenty feet down the range from the shooting stations were well lit, the stations themselves and the corridor behind them were in relative darkness. Her eyes took a second to adjust. She didn't see the range master, but after a minute he opened the door to the ammunition locker at the far end of the corridor.

"Hey. Aren't you Dr. Norcross?" he said. "Harley Bitler. I met you when your class came over to shoot."

He offered his hand. She'd have expected him to have rough hands, but when she shook it, his felt as smooth as a woman's.

"I want to get in some practice with a silhouette target," she said. "I didn't bring any extra cartridges, so I'll need to buy a box. Thirty-eight longs."

"Sure, no problemo," he said. "One box enough?"

"I don't have time for more than that."

"Pick any station you want. There's room under the shelf for your purse. Lay your weapon on the shelf so I can check it and get you started. Grab a set of goggles and some ear protection. Back in a sec."

Randy had been her instructor when she came with the class, but the others said Harley was competent. Seemed like a nice guy.

Bald, with an extra thirty pounds around his gut, he reminded her of an oversize baby. A couple of the instructors she'd met here on earlier trips looked like fugitives from a mercenary brigade.

She chose the center station, stashed her purse, took her weapon out of her holster and laid it on the shelf, then chose ear protectors and goggles from the box beside Harley's chair. The thingies were uncomfortable and gave her hat hair, so she always delayed putting them on until she was ready to fire.

She'd never been the only shooter practicing before. Dankness and cold seemed to emanate from the concrete-block walls that rendered the room soundproof, and the relative darkness in the corridor and shooting stations added to her sense of isolation. She hadn't intended to shoot alone. Maybe she'd go drink the range's coffee until some other shooters arrived.

She shivered and walked over to gaze out the window of the door that led to the sales floor. The manager still worked at his cash register, and a couple of people had wandered into shop. Not, apparently, to shoot. At least not right away. She really wasn't alone. Harley was here.

"Here you go. One box of .38 longs."

She jumped. "Sorry! I didn't hear you come up." She took the box and walked toward her station.

"You're my first customer since lunch hour. I've been back in the storage room cleaning stock," he said. *He* obviously didn't feel the cold. He wore a short-sleeved polo shirt. She didn't see any goose pimples on the baby-soft skin of his arms. She caught her breath and missed a step. Not baby-soft. Hairless. Freshly shaved. Like his head. Not bald. Shaven. Like his face. Like his whole body?

She felt his breath on the back of her neck and willed herself to relax and remain casual. He mustn't realize she sensed anything wrong about him, until she got out of the range and into the store with people and lights.

Once she was there, she'd call Randy. She might be overreacting, but she didn't intend to take chances.

"I need to check your weapon," he said, and reached around her.

"That's okay." She scooped it up and took a step toward the door. "I'll have to come back tomorrow. I've just realized I don't have as much time as I thought I did." She slid her hand down toward her holster.

"You sure don't," he whispered. He grabbed her wrist and twisted. She tried to hold the gun, but it flew from her grip and over the shooting stand into the target area. He grinned. "Not much time at all."

"TAKE A LOOK AT THIS," Liz said. "You've been looking for the guy who moved to Los Angeles, right?"

Randy nodded. "I checked on Google. No hits." He strolled over to stand behind her.

"Maybe not on *him,* but I got a hit on his mother. She was a nurse practitioner. Got some fancy award a few years back. There was a group photo in the newspaper."

"Yeah? And?" He bent closer.

"Check her out."

"Damn," he murmured. Not a particularly attractive picture, but clear enough to see that she was a tall brunette in a freshly starched lab coat, with her dark hair drawn back from her face in a tight bun. The group was applauding her for nursing excellence and extraordinary devotion to duty. The head of the hospital board was handing her what looked to be a fine leather briefcase. Randy thought for a minute he was having a heart attack.

"Can you bring up the people in the background?" he asked.

"Which ones?"

"That guy." Randy pointed. "He's the only one who's not applauding."

"Give me a minute. It won't be perfect, but I can improve it some."

Randy waited impatiently while she fiddled with the image.

"There," she said. "Better."

His scalp tingled. The man's face filled the screen. "Is it possible to remove the beard and the long hair? Say, make him bald?"

"Piece o' cake." It wasn't, obviously, from the time it took, but at last she rolled back in her chair and pointed. "A real techie could do better."

Randy stared at the photo. "It's him."

"Him who?" Jack said. He swung his chair around.

"That's the guy from the gun range."

"Same guy as from the luggage shop?"

"Different name, different look, but yeah. Liz, you got a current address on him?"

She shook her head. "Not so far. But maybe we don't need one yet—he could be at work."

Randy dialed a number on his cell phone. When Buddy, his friend and the manager of the gun store, picked up, Randy took a deep breath so that he sounded calm and asked, "That guy on the gun range who helped my class. What's his name?"

"You mean Harley Bitler? What about him?"

"I want to schedule another session, and wondered when he might be working."

"He's here now. Want to talk to him?"

"That's okay. I may come by tonight, anyway." He hung up and ran for the door. "Call O'Hara, tell him to meet me at the range with backup. No sirens, no lights. Call Amanda Donovan and let her know we have a suspect—a man she's met."

Liz ran after him. "Should I call Dr. Norcross?"

He hesitated and glanced at the big clock over Gavigan's office door. Three-forty. She was teaching until four. He shook his head. "Tell O'Hara to get his two undercovers to pick up Dr. Norcross at the door of her class the minute it lets out. They are not to allow her out of their sight. They must *not* tell her about the suspect until he's safely in custody."

Liz looked confused. "If you say so."

"I do." He prayed he'd convinced Helena to give up her crazy plan, but he couldn't take the chance she'd duck the undercovers and go after the perp if she knew who and where he was.

Randy used his siren and lights until he came within blocks of the gun shop, blasting through every intersection and around what felt like a million semis. He screeched to a halt in the parking lot of the gun store and climbed out, loosening his Sig Sauer in its holster as he ran.

Then he realized that the car parked closest to the front door was Streak's old BMW. She couldn't be here! He glanced at his watch. Her class wasn't over for another ten minutes.

An elderly VW Beetle sat in the shaded far corner of the lot. Parked beside it was an even older VW van with out-of-date California plates.

He should wait for O'Hara and some kind of backup, but he didn't dare take the time.

He burst through the door into the nearly empty shop with his gun drawn.

"Randy? What the hell?" Buddy froze behind the cash register, where he'd been counting receipts.

"Where is she?" he demanded.

"Who?"

"Dr. Norcross. And where's Bitler?"

"They're both on the gun range. What's the matter?"

Randy ran to the door and turned the handle. "It's locked!" he yelled.

"Shouldn't be, with just the two of them in there."

"Get it open before I shoot the lock."

"It's steel, man. You shoot it, you'll turn this place into a pinball machine full of live ammo."

"Key!" He held out his hand.

"Okay, okay." Buddy rummaged in the cash drawer until he found a key and took it to him.

Randy flattened himself against the wall beside the door while he turned it in the lock. He didn't want either Streak or Bitler to catch sight of him and spook. He hadn't even taken the time to put on a vest. O'Hara would give him hell.

At that point Detective O'Hara, a man and a woman who looked like fugitive preppies and four uniforms raced in with guns drawn.

"Will somebody please tell me what's going on?" Buddy shouted.

"Get everybody else in the store out of here," O'Hara told him.

"O-kay…" Buddy waved his hands at two startled customers who were staring at the policemen. "Go! Now!"

"Streak's in there with Bitler," Randy said as the customers left. He pointed to the gun range.

"No reason to think anything will happen in a public place like this. She doesn't know he's our guy, does she?"

"Not possible." How could she? They'd just figured it out themselves.

"It sounds quiet in there," O'Hara said. "Probably nothing happening."

"Man, it's concrete block and soundproof," Buddy retorted. "You wouldn't hear a machine gun in there. But we've got an intercom. Want me to turn on the lights inside so you can check? You can see through the window in the door, but only if the lights are on inside."

"No!" Randy roared, then said to O'Hara, "I'm not waiting. I'm going in."

The detective flattened himself on the other side of the door. "Stay cool. Casual. Like everything's normal. Get Helena out, then we take him."

Randy nodded and lowered his gun to his side. "And if it's not okay?" He was having trouble focusing from the sweat pouring down his forehead.

O'Hara shrugged. "Then we kill him."

Randy gripped the door handle and prayed he'd find Streak alive.

"HARLEY, LET GO of my wrist," Helena said, and was amazed at how calm she sounded. She sure didn't feel calm. She wanted to throw up.

He shoved her away, so that he stood between her and the door to the store. She cracked her head on the concrete wall and raised her hand to touch it. "Ow! Harley, what on earth is the matter with you?"

"Don't you play dumb with me." He sighed. "When you called the police that night, I said, well, they had to take her to the hospital. Only told 'em 'cause they forced her to."

"I don't know what you mean."

"You do, too!" His voice had risen and he'd clenched his fists by his sides. "I even let you get away with kicking your husband out. A man doesn't support his family, he has to go. Last time I checked you out—"

"You checked me out?"

"Hell, I check all my women out every couple of months. That's how I pick the lost causes who aren't ever gonna get it." He glared at her. "Way you hid in the house or that school, dressed all dowdy, scared as a rabbit, I told myself, okay, she gets it. And she's got two little kids. Leave her be, leastways for now." He gave a disgusted snort. "Then you show up here to shoot. You and that other one, that lawyer." He barked out a laugh. "Self-defense for women. Like you bitches could take down a real man. I figured I'd been wrong, you *didn't* get it, after all. When you went out all duded up for that party and started messin' with that cop…" He shook his head wearily. "Then when you ran your mouth on that TV show, I knew for certain."

"What didn't I get, Harley? Tell me so I can get it now."

"Too late. You only get one chance. This time I'm gonna *show* you."

*Not if I can help it,* Helena thought. "Harley, any

minute now somebody's going to walk through that door." She pointed behind him.

He snickered. "Nope. Locked it after I gave you the shells. Only takes a second to throw the dead bolt."

"They'll know something's wrong."

"We keep it locked a lot. Don't want strangers walking in when everybody's shooting. When I *do* open that door, you're gonna be tied up and gagged in the storage room. I'll swear you left while Buddy was in the back room."

"My car's outside."

"Keys bound to be in your purse." He hooked a thumb at her purse, lying under the shooting shelf. "I'll move your car outta sight when I take my break, and I'll offer to lock up. Buddy likes to get out of here early when he can. After that, we're gonna walk out real quiet and get in my van. No sense in carrying you that distance, big woman like you. Had a hell of a time before."

*Never let them take you to a second location. Take your chances where you are. Bullets can miss. His adrenaline is bound to be pumping as fast as mine. He's got to be nervous in a public place. Oh, God, Milo! Vi! My babies! Randy, my love!*

He took a step toward her.

"Wait! Please don't do this. I have two small children with nobody else to take care of them. Tell me what I didn't get. I swear I'll listen."

He shook his head and leered. "You'll get it, all right."

She watched his eyes, not the way his shoulders hunched or his hands flexed. Any moment now he'd go for her.

*Attack is the only defense. My softness against his hardness. Don't let him punch my lights out. Move first.*

Helena charged inside his reach, grabbed his wrist, pulled down and toward her and shoved. He flew backward a half-dozen steps, flailing his arms to keep his balance.

"Hey!" He caught himself. "You are a dead woman!"

"Not yet."

He ran toward her with his right arm cocked. She stepped into him and felt the rushing air and searing heat as his fist grazed her ear. She reached up to knock his arm away, twisted, struck his shoulder with the back of her hand, stepped behind him to catch his ankle, thrust her hip against him and shoved his shoulder before he could regain his balance.

He grunted in surprise, flew face-first into the concrete wall, howling in pain and rage.

Sooner or later he'd land a blow she couldn't avoid. She needed a weapon, but her gun lay in the shooting lane a dozen feet away.

He saw the direction of her glance, leaped to his feet with more agility than she'd given him credit for and ran toward the stand. If he could vault over it and grab her gun, he could put five Smith & Wesson .38 slugs into her.

That must not happen. She grabbed a half-dozen pairs of goggles from the box on the table and threw them at his head. Hard.

He ducked and tried to ward them off, but a couple caught him across his eyes.

She vaulted over the stand herself and dived for her pistol.

"No!" he screamed.

She rolled onto her back, clasping the gun as he landed on hands and knees in the spot where she'd been only seconds before.

She kicked him hard in the side of his knee and heard something pop. He screamed and grabbed his leg as she scrambled away on her rear. "I will kill you," she gasped. "You move so much as a pinky finger, I will blow your head off."

He was bunching his muscles to hurl himself at her from his good leg. "Bitch, you don't have the balls to shoot a real man."

"Well, you hardly qualify. Facedown or die." She let off a round at the ceiling. "I have four more bullets with your name on them."

He yelped and dropped on his face.

"Stretch your arms flat out on the ground above your head," she snarled. "Legs apart. Wider."

"I think my knee's broken," he sobbed. "You broke my damn knee."

She reached up, grabbed the edge of the shooting stand, still keeping the pistol trained on him, and hauled herself to her feet with her other hand. She was afraid her legs were trembling too much to hold her. So was her gun hand, but facedown, Harley couldn't see that.

"Don't shoot me," he sobbed. "For God's sake, don't shoot me."

"I will if I have to," she said. Her voice sounded amazingly strong and steady considering that she couldn't seem to draw a decent breath.

That's when the door opened and Randy and O'Hara slipped in with their weapons drawn.

"Streak, don't do it!" Randy shouted. "Drop the gun!"

"What? Oh." She set it carefully down on the stand. She looked at Harley and said, "Randy, the little wimp's not worth the cost of a bullet. I've already won, don't you see?" She frowned at the sobbing man. "He's simply not relevant to my life any longer."

A moment later her legs gave way, but that didn't matter, because Randy had leaped over the shooting stand to take her in his arms.

O'Hara cuffed Bitler and dragged him to his feet as he read him the Miranda warning.

"My knee!" the man wailed, but managed to put weight on it. "These cuffs are too tight! I didn't do anything! This crazy bitch assaulted *me*. Arrest *her*."

"Nice try, creep," O'Hara said. "Guess what? Your last victim gave us some DNA and half a fingerprint on you." He winked at Randy.

"It's not supposed to happen this way," Bitler sobbed. "She didn't get it. I'm the man. I'm supposed to *win*."

IT WAS AFTER MIDNIGHT. The bull pen where O'Hara's desk was located was virtually empty except for a couple of cleaners chatting quietly as they dusted and dry mopped. Helena felt worn-out, not to mention hungry, lonely and let down.

Randy and the detective had to interrogate Harley Bitler while he still refused a lawyer, but she wished they'd take her statement soon. She wanted to hear what Bitler told them. That had to finish it.

Randy had let her call Marcie, Amanda and the other members of the class to tell them they'd caught the guy, but asked her not to divulge any more information until she'd been interviewed.

She drank semichilled diet colas and ate stale peanut butter crackers from the vending machine until she ran out of change. Then she fidgeted. She wouldn't have been able to concentrate on a book or magazine even if she'd seen one in the room.

She moved around the desk and stretched out in O'Hara's big chair. She might be able to doze until they came for her.

But her mind wouldn't stop churning. Would Randy have shot her if she hadn't put her weapon down when he asked? Even *he* might not know. Thank God she didn't have to find out.

In the final moments, she hadn't *needed* to kill Bitler. She'd beaten him, but with Randy's help, she'd already won back control of her life. Even if Randy didn't love *her,* she loved him, and opening herself up to love had begun the healing process. If she had to face the pain of losing him, she'd manage somehow.

She heard his and O'Hara's voices coming down the hall from the interview room, and sat up.

"Stay there," the detective said, and pulled up a chair from the desk next to his.

Randy came around to bend and kiss her. "Sorry, babe. We didn't think we'd need more than a few minutes with Bitler before we got to you. You should have caught a cab." Since she'd ridden to the precinct with Randy, her car still sat at the gun store.

"I wanted to find out what he said."

Randy pulled another chair close to her. "The state's attorney general just moved us to the top of the lab food chain. The partial print is Bitler's. We'll have the DNA match in a couple of days."

She looked over at O'Hara. "You told him you had it already," she said.

"Oh, yeah." The big man grinned. "Gee whiz, I guess I lied. Doesn't matter much. He's confessed."

"Confessed?" She sat up so fast the chair tipped forward. "I never dreamed he'd do that."

"Wanted to explain to us in detail what a real man he is."

"He kept saying I 'didn't get it,' but wouldn't teach me what I didn't get."

O'Hara stretched his legs out. "I love this part. Like after satisfying sex. Tired but elated." He glanced at Helena. "Oh, sorry."

"No need to be."

"Says he didn't plan to go for you until later this week, if he could get you alone. But he saw the way you looked at his arm, and decided not to take a chance you'd put two and two together. He'd just shaved his body in case he got lucky with either you or Amanda Donovan. He planned to take care of both of you within a couple of days."

"To reinforce his warning to the others not to say nasty things about him," Randy added. "He's definitely decompensating."

"And that means...?" Helena asked.

"Coming apart at the seams," O'Hara told her. "Not waiting as long between attacks, taking chances, making mistakes."

She shivered. It was harder than she'd thought, listening to them speak so calmly. Once they'd arrested Harley Bitler, they were ready to move on to another case, track another criminal. This might be her only brush with crime, but Randy and O'Hara lived with it every day. Randy cared deeply about her, but he cared for all the victims. He wasn't simply doing his job as a cop.

She looked from one man to the other. That caring defined them both. If she and Randy stayed together, could she understand and accept that part of him that belonged to the victims?

"I still can't believe you took him down," O'Hara said. "Way to go, Streak."

"So I'm Streak to you, too, now?"

The detective waved his hand at the vacant desks. "To everybody. You're stuck with it."

She smiled at Randy. "I *feel* like Streak now. You gave me the tools to save myself, you know. He never expected a woman to fight back, much less win. But he never gave me the answer to why he did it in the first place. Did he tell you?"

"It's always somebody. Sister, aunt, girlfriend... In his case he hated his mother, a nurse-practitioner." O'Hara rubbed his hand down his cheek. His beard made a scratching sound. "She ran off the father he idolized after he'd assaulted her one too many times. Called the police on him. A truck driver, he lost his job, and was killed in an accident not long after. He'd taught little Harley that uppity women deserved to be knocked around until they shaped up."

"And tattling to the cops was a betrayal," Randy added.

Helena caught her breath. That's what he'd said to her that awful night—that she had got above her station.

"Mama must have been one tough cookie," O'Hara said. "Harley didn't have the balls to face his mother even when she got old and frail. Must have been scared spitless of her. After she died, he sold everything and moved to California. Picked up forged ID, registered an old VW van and drove it back here. California plates."

"Which is why we couldn't trace it locally," Randy pointed out.

"He was free," Helena said. "He'd escaped. Why didn't he stay in California? Why come back to Tennessee?"

"Says he missed the South." O'Hara shrugged. "Go figure."

"Maybe if he'd never taken the job at the luggage store—who knows?" Randy mused. "Something else would have triggered him, I guess. He was already on the edge, studying up on forensics and trace evidence. Ready to explode. After she died, he burned his mother's briefcase. When that young ADA who reminded him of his mother bought an even more expensive one and treated him like dog doo—his words—he decided to teach her a lesson."

"We always wondered why his schedule seemed so erratic," O'Hara said. "He just confessed to a dozen sexual assaults that were never reported. He didn't need to come back to punish them." Randy's mouth twisted. "I hate this guy."

"The way he planned to punish me," Helena said.

HELENA AND RANDY FINALLY left the squad room a little after three in the morning. The moon was long down, but the false dawn had lightened the sky with the promise of a sunny day. Helena could feel spring. She'd seen her first jonquils growing beside the road on her way to work.

"I'm still mad at you," Randy said as he started his car, "but I'd be really mad if you were dead."

"Would you have shot me? Technically, I was no longer in danger when you came in."

"If you had shot Bitler before I could tackle you or knock the gun out of your hand?" He laid his hand on her knee. "Never. The man tried to kill you. I'd have arrested you, then pulled in every favor I could beg to keep you from being indicted."

"Do you still want to be Milo and Vi's guardian if something happens to me?"

"I meant what I said. Marry me."

"We barely know each other."

"Well enough for me to want to spend the rest of my life with you." He turned the corner into her street. "Are Marcie and the kids still at Francine's?"

She laughed. "Is that a question or a proposition? They're at Francine's."

"Then consider it a proposition." He cut the engine in her driveway and followed her all the way to her bedroom. Then he turned her to face him, and put his hands on her shoulders. "I'm asking you to let me be your husband, your children's stepfather, your lover, your…"

"Protector?"

"You've got this crazy idea that you have to face life alone."

"For how long?"

"How long what?"

"How long do you want to be my husband, my children's stepfather, my lover, my protector?"

"Well, for this life, anyway."

AFTER THEY MADE GENTLE love in her bed, she cuddled drowsily against his chest. "What if I bore you?"

He kissed the top of her head. "Never happen. You play bridge?"

She propped herself on one elbow and stared down at him. "Is that a deal breaker?"

He pulled her back beside him. "You learn to play old maid in elementary school, and poker and gin rummy in junior high. Then you learn to play bridge. Suddenly other games are boring. Bridge never gets boring. What I'm saying is that for me *you're* bridge. Other women are gin rummy."

"Do you love me?"

"Without you I'd turn brown and die like that poor starved philodendron on your kitchen windowsill. When I thought I might lose you tonight, I wanted to tear that damn shooting range stone from stone to get to you."

"What about the kids? Having them underfoot isn't a deal breaker for *you?*"

"Being without them would be."

"Truly? Sports and dance lessons and homework?"

"If you'll handle the dance lessons, I'll handle the sports."

"Deal." She crawled out of bed and returned with two glasses of ice water. After she'd settled down beside him again, she asked, "Can you trust me to come to terms with your job?"

"I'll have to, but an insurance salesman doesn't come home and tell his wife about every policy he sold."

"Most insurance salesmen aren't emotionally involved in their policies. You are, just as I am with my lazy students," she said.

"If I ever give you the impression that I think my job is more important than yours, call me on it."

"You're assuming I'll say yes."

He took the empty glass of water from her and set both on the bedside table. "I'm going to keep asking until you do."

"Isn't that called stalking?"

"I'm a cop. I can work the system."

"When you love someone…"

"Hah!" he said. "So you admit you love me!"

"This has to be love. I can't figure out what else it could be. Do you by any chance love *me?*"

"With all my heart forever, even though you tried to knock my head off and kick me in the balls."

"But with love."

He pulled her into his arms. "Is that a yes?"

"I've been stalked. Marriage is better."

"How do you feel about consummation before ceremony?"

"Consume away, handsome. And remember, the first time I catch you so much as smiling at another female, you're going to think you've run into Jet Li. I know self-defense. I had a good teacher."

\* \* \* \* \*

*Rancher Ramsey Westmoreland's temporary cook*
*is way too attractive for his liking.*
*Little does he know Chloe Burton came to his ranch*
*with another agenda entirely....*

That man across the street had to be, without a doubt, the most handsome man she'd ever seen.

Chloe Burton's pulse beat rhythmically as he stopped to talk to another man in front of a feed store. He was tall, dark and every inch of sexy—from his Stetson to the well-worn leather boots on his feet. And from the way his jeans and Western shirt fit his broad, muscular shoulders, it was quite obvious he had everything it took to separate the men from the boys. The combination was enough to corrupt any woman's mind and had her weakening even from a distance. Her body felt flushed. It was hot. Unsettled.

Over the past year the only male who had gotten her time and attention had been the e-mail. That was simply pathetic, especially since now she was practically drooling simply at the sight of a man. Even his stance—both hands in his jeans pockets, legs braced apart—was a pose she would carry to her dreams.

And he was smiling, evidently enjoying the conversation being exchanged. He had dimples, incredibly sexy dimples in not one but both cheeks.

"What are you staring at, Clo?"

Chloe nearly jumped. She'd forgotten she had a lunch date. She glanced over the table at her best friend from college, Lucia Conyers.

"Take a look at that man across the street in the blue shirt, Lucia. Will he not be perfect for Denver's first issue of *Simply Irresistible* or what?" Chloe asked with so much excitement she almost couldn't stand it.

She was the owner of *Simply Irresistible*, a magazine for today's up-and-coming woman. Their once-a-year Irresistible Man cover, which highlighted a man the magazine felt deserved the honor, had increased sales enough for Chloe to open a Denver office.

When Lucia didn't say anything but kept staring, Chloe's smile widened. "Well?"

Lucia glanced across the booth at her. "Since you asked, I'll tell you what I see. One of the Westmorelands—Ramsey Westmoreland. And yes, he'd be perfect for the cover, but he won't do it."

Chloe raised a brow. "He'd get paid for his services, of course."

Lucia laughed and shook her head. "Getting paid won't be the issue, Clo—Ramsey is one of the wealthiest sheep ranchers in this part of Colorado. But everyone knows what a private person he is. Trust me—he won't do it."

Chloe couldn't help but smile. The man was the epitome of what she was looking for in a magazine cover and she was determined that whatever it took, he would be it.

"Um, I don't like that look on your face, Chloe. I've seen it before and know exactly what it means."

She watched as Ramsey Westmoreland entered the store with a swagger that made her almost breathless. She *would* be seeing him again.

*Look for Silhouette Desire's*
*HOT WESTMORELAND NIGHTS*
*by Brenda Jackson,*
*available March 9 wherever books are sold.*

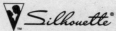

# ROMANTIC
## SUSPENSE

**Sparked by Danger, Fueled by Passion.**

Introducing a brand-new miniseries
# Lawmen of Black Rock

Peyton Wilkerson's life shatters when her
four-month-old daughter, Lilly, vanishes.
But handsome sheriff Tom Grayson is
determined to put the pieces together and
reunite her with her baby. Will Tom be able
to protect Peyton and Lilly while fighting
his own growing feelings?

Find out in
## *His Case, Her Baby*
by
# CARLA CASSIDY

*Available in March wherever books are sold*

**Visit Silhouette Books at www.eHarlequin.com**

SRS27670

# REQUEST YOUR FREE BOOKS!

## 2 FREE NOVELS PLUS 2 FREE GIFTS!

HARLEQUIN®

*Super Romance*®

## Exciting, emotional, unexpected!

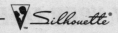

# SILHOUETTE

# SPECIAL EDITION

## FROM *USA TODAY* BESTSELLING AUTHOR
# CHRISTINE RIMMER

BRAVO FAMILY TIES

# A BRIDE FOR JERICHO BRAVO

Marnie Jones had long ago buried her wild-child impulses and opted to be "safe," romantically speaking. But one look at born rebel Jericho Bravo and she began to wonder if her thrill-seeking side was about to be revived. Because if ever there was a man worth taking a chance on, there he was, right within her grasp....

*Available in March*
*wherever books are sold.*

---

**Visit Silhouette Books at www.eHarlequin.com**

SSE65511

# VOCAL TECHNIQUE
# FOR CHILDREN
# AND YOUTH

Abingdon Press ♪ New York • Nashville

# VOCAL TECHNIQUE FOR CHILDREN AND YOUTH

MADELINE D. INGRAM
WILLIAM C. RICE

VOCAL TECHNIQUE FOR CHILDREN AND YOUTH

*Copyright © 1962 by Abingdon Press*

*Library of Congress Catalog Card Number: 62-9994*

SET UP, PRINTED, AND BOUND BY THE
PARTHENON PRESS, AT NASHVILLE,
TENNESSEE, UNITED STATES OF AMERICA

# PREFACE

*Singing is for everybody, and singing should be fun!* We have long been committed to this philosophy, and we are pleased that it is increasingly the belief of most persons who are charged with the responsibility of exposing children and young people to the delights of singing. We must admit, however, that some teaching, many books, and much choral material seem to be based upon an entirely different philosophy, namely that singing is for the select—those who possess unusual ability and who have had a great deal of training.

We have attempted in the following pages to discuss methods and materials in terms of children and youth rather than from the viewpoint of adults who see the situation as they wish it to be instead of the way it actually exists. Our experience has been that *every person* can benefit greatly from learning how best to use his voice, and this book is based entirely upon that premise.

We have tried to express our thoughts in such a way that parents, musically untrained church and public-school teachers, and church and school musicians will all be able to find usable ideas in what we have to say. We humbly dedicate our efforts to children and youth everywhere in the hope that they will increasingly benefit from the unique values of singing, and that as a result their lives will be much more satisfying than they might otherwise have been.

MADELINE D. INGRAM
WILLIAM C. RICE

# CONTENTS

7

# CONTENTS

chapter one

# The Preschooler

Many an adult has been heard to deplore the fact that he cannot "carry a tune," yet this same adult may be guilty of doing nothing to help his children escape the same fate. In this day of radio and television accessibility we find listeners rather than singers in most homes. Gone are the days when the family gathered around the piano and discovered deep contentment in singing together, yet most people think of those days with nostalgia. A parent who sings for the sheer joy of singing makes a marked impression upon a child, who will immediately want to join in with him and share the fun. Even a baby will try to sing like mother, and it is apparent that he finds pleasure in so doing.

Because children respond so readily to music, trying to sing and moving their bodies rhythmically when it is heard, we may assume that they have a genuine, even instinctive, liking for it. We know that if children are to receive the utmost pleasure and satisfaction from making music they must first learn to sing well; we know that proper singing habits must begin forming while the child is still very young.

It is doubtful if there has ever been a child who did not

make musical sounds from babyhood, even when there was a lack of encouragement in the home. These first sounds are made on various pitches and are vague and unconnected. But very early a variety of sounds (tones) uttered at random will produce a kind of song-chant that appears to come spontaneously from the child. As he feels the necessity he adds words to his tunes, and while we cannot call his creations songs, we recognize that they are actually the beginning of his song-singing experience. During an hour of watching small children at play one hears them sing about what they are doing, what they see or hear, what interests them, and so on. In doing this they are merely singing their thoughts instead of speaking them. The very young child will not be able to reproduce these fragments of song—it is likely that he does not even hear them— but as he continues this automatic singing he can be led into a gradual recognition of the correlation between singing and hearing. When his vocal and aural powers merge he can then reproduce his own songs and the songs of others. Spontaneous singing should be encouraged as a means toward helping children develop control over their singing voices. This, in turn, will help them to reproduce other songs accurately.

Although there are as many individual differences in little people as there are in adults, we may say that at five years of age—and in some cases even at four years—children are ready to begin to receive well-planned musical instruction. Home environment and physical, mental, and emotional growth all shape the child and in turn help to determine his music learning readiness. Just as children do not all develop the ability to walk and talk at the same age, they do not develop equal singing skill at the same time. The teacher who works with preschool children must study them individually and be prepared to deal patiently and lovingly with them. He must also remember the great body of adults who became so discouraged with their singing abilities as children that they gave up all efforts to sing. Most of this discouragement was brought about by teachers—and relatives—who unthinkingly had made them conscious of their deficiencies. A sensitive child, seeking and needing the approval of his elders, can be deeply and permanently affected when he feels that his singing is inadequate.

We have indicated that for some time the young singer cannot reproduce his own songs or the songs of others. For many children the process of learning to duplicate pitches is a slow one; during this period they are sometimes mistakenly called "monotones." A true monotone—exceedingly rare—can sing only one tone, never moving higher or lower. Many children who move about from tone to tone but do not match the pattern tones are assigned this unfortunate appellation and are the despair of the unskilled teacher. Given patient encouragement and training *every child*—unless he has a physical or mental defect—*can learn to sing*.

In a group of five-year-olds very few—if indeed any—can sing accurately. What are some of the reasons why a young child has singing problems?

1. He has not learned to distinguish between singing and speaking.

2. He has not learned to listen to and detect differences in pitches.

3. He is immature—physically, emotionally, mentally.

4. He is timid.

5. He does not speak well.

6. He is trying too hard.

7. He is trying to imitate an adult whom he admires.

8. He lacks family encouragement and understanding.

In order to learn to differentiate between pitches and then

to organize them a child must learn to hear individual sounds. His first experience with hearing music will have caused him to react to the pleasure he felt in the conglomerate or total sound. He will probably show his reactions by facial expression or bodily movement. It is the teacher's responsibility to help him listen not only to the general sound but to specific sounds as well. He must be trained not only to listen but to *hear*.

Quiet music frequently played during the several rest periods needed by young children provides a topic for discussion after the listening time. The lively imaginations of children are quickly set in motion and their hearing abilities sharpened when they are asked to tell what the music was saying. At other times subject matter may be suggested before the listening period with such statements as "Listen to the way the music sounds like wind in the trees"; or "Do you hear the waves on the shore?" This music may be played on a piano or other instrument or it may be a recording, but it must be remembered that the listening span is very short in this and other similar situations.

Record players and pianos used with children must be of the very highest order. When we remember that we are developing the musical ear of these people for all time to come we realize that only the best is acceptable. A portable record player capable of playing records of all three speeds, 33 1/3, 45, and 78, is necessary. An automatic record changer is not recommended for the use suggested here, but a flip-over needle is required so that the various speeds may be accommodated. Diamond-point needles are preferred, and though they are expensive, their life span is long enough to justify such expense. A so-called hi-fi set is not necessary for young children, because the added color produced by extremely low and high frequencies means nothing to them and may, in fact, be a liability.

The player must have a good, steady motor, however, in order that pitch and quality remain constant. The tone must be clear and completely undistorted.

Records must be given careful treatment. When not being played they should be kept covered as a protection from dust and should be stored in a dry, cool place. They must be handled at their edges only so that fingerprints are not made on the grooves.

Pianos should be kept in good tune; a visit from the tuner three times a year is desirable—twice a year is a necessity. Instruments kept in rooms that do not have a steady temperature will be out of tune most of the time. This is especially true in a church where certain rooms are not heated except on Sunday and rehearsal days. On the other hand, rooms can be kept so hot that great damage is done to the instrument. Children cannot learn to sing in tune with a poor piano that is out of tune.

It is unfortunate that few church-school pianos are purchased by the church—most of them are gifts that should have been junked! The average family that owns an old, never-used, never-tuned piano is inclined to look—with the best of motives—upon the church as a logical repository for what has once been a good instrument. Somehow this well-meaning generosity should be guided into other areas and the intended gift forgotten.

Films and filmstrips can be effective teaching aids, provided consideration be given to the preschooler's short span of attention and to his level of maturation. No film or filmstrip should ever be presented without a careful preview. Projectors and screens should be of high quality. Unfortunately, much eight- and sixteen-millimeter equipment does not reproduce sound adequately. Poor sound is quite likely to retard the child's musical development. The teacher must, therefore, be very certain that films and filmstrips are appropriate, of good quality, and of the proper length, and that the equipment is the best that is available.

Learning to match single pitches is accomplished by matching a voice rather than an instrument, and since children learn by imitation the teacher must use a child's (head) voice when singing to or with them. Many adults feel they cannot sing well unless they use what they term their "natural" voices. What they fail to recognize is that mature voices and those of children differ mainly in ability to produce fullness of volume and color. Any teacher who uses a full voice will cause the children to strain as they attempt to match her tones. This straining will, in turn, cause flatness of pitch and will actually injure the imitating voices.

In order to be a correct model an adult must sing *mezza voce* or half voice, the quality thus produced being more nearly that of a child's voice. Any adult with average singing ability will be able to use this quality, but those whose vocal training has been meager will need much practice in the use of a light voice. *Mezza voce* must be used by both men and women teachers. Although an adult male will be singing an octave lower than children, difficulties of pitch-matching rarely exist if he sings half voice. The male falsetto is effective with children if properly and easily produced. If, however, as is too often the case, it is breathy and completely lacking in vitality, the children may produce a dull, muffled tone as they try to imitate this completely unnatural quality. A good falsetto tone is difficult to distinguish from a *mezza voce*.

By example and precept children must be encouraged to sing lightly at all times. We do not mean, however, that they should sing so softly as to produce a weak, devitalized tone, but rather that they sing easily with no tenseness or strain in throat or neck. In this connection we must see to it that the piano accompaniment—if any—is played softly. It is one thing to insist upon light singing and another to play such a loud accompaniment that the singers automatically strain to be heard! In addition to being quiet, the accompaniment must be extremely simple; rich, colorful chords or "running" patterns serve only to confuse the children. For practical purposes, most of their singing should be without accompaniment.

The singing—and speaking—voices of preschoolers are usually high pitched, light in quality, flexible, and colorless. Properly produced, they will all be nearly identical, that of boys and girls being indistinguishable. The voices have a pleasing quality and surprising carrying power despite the preschoolers' inability to produce much volume of tone.

Just as children vary in singing skills so there are deviations in the ranges of their voices. In general, however, the range lies within the treble clef, though some can sing the G on the space above the staff and some can sing the C and D below. Notes at either extreme should be sung infrequently.

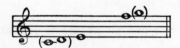

There must be constant practice in matching single pitches, then groups of pitches. As much variety as the teacher can invent will keep these drills from becoming monotonous. Individual participation in drills should be for all singers alike, not just for the inaccurate. Those who are more accurate serve as good models for the less competent.

A pitch-matching device commonly used is that of a singing

roll call in which the name of the child is sung and to which he responds by repeating the pattern.

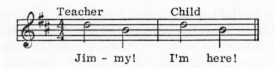

Jim - my!    I'm    here!

For the first few trials the pitch may be the same for each child; later it may be changed as the roll call progresses from child to child. Soon the pattern may also be varied.

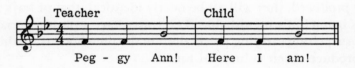

Peg - gy   Ann!    Here    I    am!

Questions and answers add the necessary variety.

Do  you  like  the  snow?    Yes, I  like  the  snow.

Songs in which a word or phrase is repeated are available, and the creative teacher can add to these songs of her own making that meet her special needs. A song such as the following in which the pitch of "hello" may be changed for each child at the will of the teacher illustrates this point.

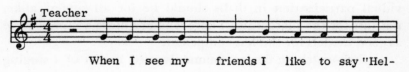

When  I  see  my    friends I  like  to  say "Hel-

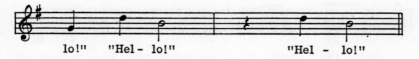

lo!"     "Hel - lo!"               "Hel - lo!"

This can be made an especially attractive game when individual children are asked to sing alone. Attentive listening results as each one is eager to hear what "hello" he is expected
to repeat and whether there will be one "hello" or a series
of them.

One of the characteristics of a young child is his disposition
to sing with the teacher as soon as she begins a song. It matters
not to him that he has never heard that song; he just joins in
anyway. To encourage him to listen, song material such as the
above mentioned can be helpful. He *must* listen in order to
echo exactly what he heard. Songs that incorporate train
whistles, bells, clocks, birds, and animal sounds are of interest.
If the children continue to bumble along during the teacher's
singing, she can say, "This time I am going to sing all by myself, and while I sing I want you to close both eyes and listen
with both ears. When I finish we will sing it together"; or,
"Then I will want to hear you sing it."

A simple song in which an echo may be employed is "Winter
Wind," from *God's Wonderful World*. The wind sound may
be repeated by children at the end of each line after being sung
first by the teacher.

### Winter Wind

A. L. M.                                                    P. B. O.

Win-ter wind blow through the trees,     Oo - oo, oo.

Howl as loud - ly as you please, Oo - oo, oo, etc.

From *God's Wonderful World,* by Agnes Leckie Mason and Phyllis Brown Ohanian, copyright 1954 by Agnes Leckie Mason and Phyllis Brown Ohanian. Reprinted by permission of Random House, Inc.

The following example has an echo in the second measure in each line.

### Pitter Patter

Lincoln School
Primary Group

Lincoln School Primary Group
Harmonized by W. Lawrence Curry

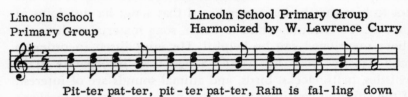

Pit-ter pat-ter, pit-ter pat-ter, Rain is fal-ling down

Mak-ing pud-dles, great big pud-dles on the ground, etc.

Reproduced from *Childcraft* with permission. Copyright © 1949 by Field Enterprises Educational Corporation. All right reserved. Harmonization copyright 1958 by W. L. Jenkins from *Songs for Early Childhood.* Used by permission.

A means of impelling children to listen and *hear* is provided by singing rather than speaking instructions to them. A church-school kindergarten teacher found that a perpetually happy atmosphere was created in her room when she sang more than she talked. Each child was greeted with a sung "Hello ———," to which he learned to reply, "Hello, Mrs. ———." Information such as "Come, let us go over here," "O sing a song with me," and "Let's have a story now" was sung as well as general comments such as "What a lovely day!" or "I am so glad to see you again." The children in this class enjoyed music and did not regard it as something set apart for use only at stated times.

A good teacher will be prepared to make sentence songs such as these and to stimulate the children to make their own. It is a perfectly natural skill for them and one which they enjoy. Together, teacher and children should make songs about daily happenings, the weather, birds and their songs, flowers, and the like. Guidance, not dictatorship, is the teacher's role. He must resist the temptation to "improve" upon a child's creation.

Physical response to music—moving a portion or all of the body in response to rhythmic pulsations—provides another step in music training. Children's need of motion can be a basis for musical growth when melodies and rhythms are used as motivating factors for action. Free, unregimented movement is all that should be expected or demanded of preschool children. They cannot quickly learn to walk "in step" or clap with rhythmic precision. Because their large muscles are developing faster than their small ones they make large sweeping motions that involve the whole body. Birds flying, leaves blowing in the wind, and trees swaying are types of motions children enjoy making. Normally there will be much variety in their interpretations. Before action takes place they should be stimulated to listen carefully to the mood of the music that they are to describe in motion. As they listen they become increasingly aware of differences in pitch, rhythm, melody, and mood; they are being given effective ear training.

Music for use in rhythmic activity must be well chosen. It should have the kind of marked rhythm that encourages action. It may or may not have accompanying words. Selections should be long enough to allow for a satisfying experience, since timid or unimaginative children are slow to make responses and need sufficient time to get under way. Conversely, children should not be kept in motion long enough to become overtired or over-stimulated. There should be a diversity of moods in the selections so that opportunity is afforded for a variety of expression.

Several things must be considered when choosing song material for preschoolers. These questions may be used as guides:

1. Is the range proper?

We have already discussed the range of singing voices of this age so that we need only to remember that notes to be sung should lie on the staff.

**Children Everywhere**

Lois H. Young        L. H. Y.

God   loves   chil - dren   ev - ery - where.

He has planned for  lov - ing care in  homes for all.

From *Kindergarten Bible Lessons*, words and music by Lois Horton Young, copyrighted 1951, permission of the Otterbein Press.

2. Does the melody contain simple progressions and easy skips?

Because young children are unable to distinguish between pitches that lie close togther, their early song material should avoid lengthy scale sequences. They learn to hear wide pitch differences such as octaves earlier than closer ones, yet they are not able to reproduce them accurately until they have had considerable singing experience. Skips such as do-me-sol and fa-la-do are easier for them to negotiate.

Tick, tick tock, Hear the clock tick - ing, tick - ing all the day.

3. Are the words within the vocabulary of this age?

Most preschoolers will have small vocabularies, and while it is the teacher's duty to help in their enlargement, more familiar than unfamiliar words should make up song content. One and two syllable words are best. Since good tone is greatly dependent upon good enunciation, teachers must select words that are not too difficult for preschoolers to pronounce. Correction should be made at once on such mispronunciations as "chil-d*run*" for "children" and "Christ*mus*" for "Christmas."

### Softly, Tread Softly

Margaret B. Williams; alt

Margaret B. Williams
Arr. by W. Lawrence Curry

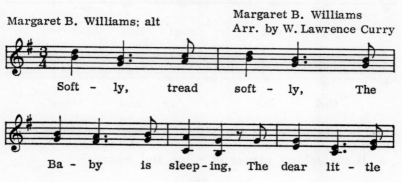

Soft - ly, tread soft - ly, The Ba - by is sleep-ing, The dear lit - tle

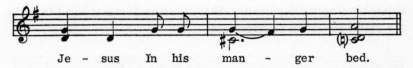

Je - sus In his man - ger bed.

Words and music copyright, 1951, by W. L. Jenkins; from *Growing*, October-December, 1959; used by permission.

**4. Do the words and music express the same feeling?**

Songs lack conviction unless the text and tune say the same thing. A text of joyousness sung to a quiet prayerlike tune would defeat its own ends. An example of restrained but glad thanksgiving in both words and music is found in the following example.

### Sing Thank You to God

Mary Edna Lloyd

Rosemary K. Roorbach
harmonized by J. Edward Moyer

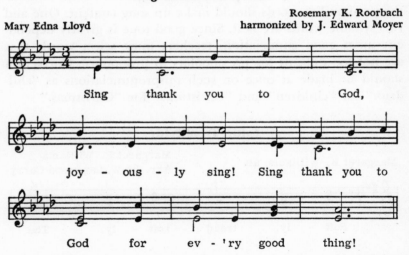

Sing thank you to God,

joy - ous - ly sing! Sing thank you to

God for ev - 'ry good thing!

Used by permission of *We Sing Together*. Copyright, The Graded Press.

**5. Is the subject matter of value and interest?**

Songs that tell of everyday experiences in language that is meaningful to preschoolers is preferred. Subject matter that will help to strengthen his ties with the church, establish his position with the family, increase his pleasure in beautiful and wonderful ways of nature, and provide opportunity for self-expression is desirable.

### It Is Very Good to Be Useful

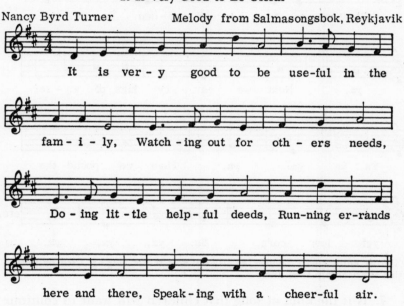

Nancy Byrd Turner                    Melody from Salmasongsbok, Reykjavik

It is ver-y good to be use-ful in the
fam-i-ly, Watch-ing out for oth-ers needs,
Do-ing lit-tle help-ful deeds, Run-ning er-rands
here and there, Speak-ing with a cheer-ful air.

6. Is the rhythm strong and vital?

Children are not accurate timekeepers, yet they respond well to music with marked rhythmic pulsations. Songs may sometimes be taught by having them speak the words in the rhythm in which they will eventually be sung. Accents on normally weak portions of a measure and any but the simplest syncopations should be avoided.

From Edith Lovell Thomas, ed., *The Whole World Singing.* Used by permission of Friendship Press. Inc.

7. Is it the kind of song that children will want to continue singing after it is once learned?

Tune and texts so expressive of the language and interests of children that they might have been made by them are the ones most often repeated. Moods of joy and happiness are predominant in children and song material that helps them toward the expression of these moods is effective.

### Singing

Miriam Dury            Miriam Dury

I sing at my work, I sing at my play, Tra-

la-la - la, La-la-la-la, La - la - la - la - la - la; I

sing ev - 'ry night, I sing through the day, Tra-

la - la - la, La - la - la-la, La- la - la - la - la - la!

Words and music copyright, 1935, by Presbyterian Board of Christian Education; from *When the Little Child Wants to Sing;* used by permission.

8. Will the music meet the qualifications for good music?

Children's tastes are being formed by the music they use, therefore inferior music must *never* be condoned. Oftentimes texts for children are very apt but they are coupled with poor music. Words and music must enhance each other and make of the whole song a delightful entity.

## Waiting and Waiting

Alice G. Thorn                                                     Satis N. Coleman

Wait - ing    and    wait - ing,    For

now    the    lights    are    red.    Start    the    car!

Here    we    go!    Green light    o - ver    head.

Songs will be taught by rote, using either the whole song or the phrase method. In the former the entire song is sung by the teacher and then imitated or joined in by the children. In the latter the teacher sings a phrase and the children repeat; then she sings another phrase and they repeat; then the two phrases are combined and repeated. This procedure continues for the length of the song. Both methods have merit and both should be used. The old style method of teaching words and tune separately and then combining them is obviously wrong. Not only is time wasted by this method, but a feeling of unity between text and tune is delayed and often never fully realized.

Teachers must remember not to sing constantly with children. It is, of course, sometimes advisable and necessary for her to do so, but it does not foster independence on the children's part nor does it permit the teacher to hear the pupil's voices as well.

Children are such mimics that they not only imitate the voice of the teacher, but also her posture, breathing, enunciation, and song interpretation. While little need be said to the children about any of these factors, they must forever be a part of every singing experience. Slumped bodies, labored breathing, faulty enunciation, and matter-of-fact singing have no place in the education of children.

We must make certain that no child is excluded from the joy of singing, no matter how "out-of-tune" he is. Singing must be made a happy experience in which everyone has a part and through which the whole world of music is opened to children. Methods may vary but the ultimate goals of all teachers should be:

1. To help children find use for music in everyday living experiences.

2. To help them learn to use their singing voices.

3. To establish the habit of finding emotional release in music.

4. To help them find many ways in which music may be made.

chapter two
# The Primary Child

Children in the first grade of school have many of the characteristics of the preschooler, but by the time they reach the second and third grades marked differences can be observed. Boys and girls are still eager to learn, and although they show much enthusiasm for learning, they sometimes become dreamy and seem to be detached from the group and its interests. These lapses are usually short, however, and can always be terminated quickly by a change of pace or subject matter. Both sexes love to clown and play pranks. They like to impress others with their knowledge, and in the process they do a great deal of "showing off." They need the approval of adults and are quite sensitive to praise and disapproval. They are warmly affectionate but less clinging than in earlier years; they show increased sensitivity to the feelings of others and are becoming more kindly in their dealings with them.

Improvement is shown in muscular co-ordination; hands, arms, fingers, and feet are able to function with increasing independence. Arms and legs are becoming longer. The eyes are able to do a reasonable amount of close work. Primaries seem to enjoy a certain measure of regimentation; having simple rules to follow gives them pleasure. They like to make plans and set goals to be reached. Vivid imaginations are characteristic of them, as is the desire to dramatize everything.

Action is a necessity for primary children; they are rarely still for any appreciable length of time. They wiggle, squirm, bounce about, and often run and hop instead of walking. Since motion is so important in their lives, it would seem wise to make use of it in the kind of rhythmic activity that will, in turn, contribute to their musical growth. Rhythmic response to music is developed in two ways: (1) Creatively, and (2) by following a prescribed form or pattern. In the first of these the child is encouraged to interpret freely in movement what he feels is called for by the music. He creates and executes his own interpretations.

Recorded music for interpretive movement may be presented in a variety of ways. A record may be played with no announcement of its title, and after a careful listening session, children may express their bodily interpretations as the record is played again. Sometimes a follow-up discussion of what each one said with his movements is helpful to those who find such expression difficult or who lack in imagination, but such an analysis—an accounting for—is not often desirable. Another approach is made by giving the title of a piece and then discussing it together after it has been played. Movement can then be made by the whole group, by small groups, or by individuals. Physical space is not always available for the entire group to move freely at the same time. Participation in smaller groups gives the timid and inhibited an opportunity to observe and imitate.

Recorded music is perhaps easiest for the teacher to manipulate but she can play the piano or other instrument to accompany the class. Children themselves may provide rhythms on drums, tambourines, wood blocks, triangles, and the like. They will profit by learning to select instruments which will best convey the mood to be expressed, the dynamic level needed, and the desired accent.

Creating response to song material affords yet another channel of interest. It is not necessary to create movement for an entire song. Words or phrases such as "Alleluia"; "Hosanna"; "Rejoice, give thanks, and sing"; "Joy to the world"; are examples of the kind of expression to which movement fits easily. Because it is more difficult to move freely when singing, it is advisable to divide the group into singers and rhythmic interpreters. Groups must be changed often enough for everyone to have opportunities to sing and to interpret. Simple movements—lifting the arms high as "Alleluia" is sung, swinging the arms wide from side to side for "Hosanna"—release children from the difficult task of sitting still and at the same time help them to feel the intent of the words. One may guide them at first by saying " 'Alleluia' is such a happy word it always makes me feel like opening my arms and reaching high." Or "When I think how the children waved palm branches in joy on the first Palm Sunday, I feel like waving my arms as they did when they sang 'Hosanna.' "

Children should be encouraged to seek their own interpretations of words and phrases as soon as they are able. Primaries can create effective interpretations of hymns, and the act of creation provides them with an understanding of and an affection for the text—and often the tune—that will remain with them all their lives.

Primaries resemble preschoolers in that they express themselves best with big sweeps of the arms and with other large body movements. The movements, however, are becoming more graceful and flowing. It is important to remember that small, jerky motions have no place in the activities of this age group. Most primaries can move in rhythm, but there are always a few who cannot, and those few must not be made to feel uncomfortable or conspicuous or be held up to the slightest kind of ridicule. A great deal of participation will usually solve their problem, since experience is more than the best teacher—it is the only one in this situation.

Music with planned action is valuable in that it emphasizes order and form. Songbooks for children usually contain songs that are to be accompanied by suggested movements. These are called "action songs" and are always enjoyed by young boys and girls. They are particularly valuable for these children who are less creative than others, because in these songs the children find an easy relationship between words, movements, and music. Children must constantly be encouraged to be rhythmically correct; this goal is best achieved when a minimum of action is required rather than action for every word or phrase. Because the words of action songs are often nonsensical, an atmosphere of relaxation is established that can bring disastrous results to musical pulsation. Properly guided, however, this free-and-easy attitude is a decided asset.

These benefits result from rhythmic experiences:

1. The child must first *listen* in order to make physical response.
2. He learns to distinguish moods.
3. He hears differences in dynamics.
4. He feels differences in tempi.
5. His imagination is stimulated.
6. He develops bodily poise and control.
7. He learns to express himself through a musical medium.
8. He learns that although there is form in music, there is also freedom.

The first benefit listed—learning to listen—is the one to which all the others contribute and upon which all of them depend. Since the development of the equipment of a good singer is strongly contingent upon his ability to hear pitches and then match them, it behooves teachers to spend much time in training for listening. This is a particular necessity today when radio and TV are sounding forth so continuously that one seldom *listens* to them. The length of the listening span will vary somewhat from one child to another but a five- or ten-minute period is about what can be expected from primaries.

It may be impossible to obtain absolute concentration from them for even this length of time; however, children can be encouraged to sit quietly and give reasonable attention for a short while. The volume at which a record is played is an important factor. Music played too loudly usually stimulates the children to action; when played too softly it causes them to lose interest at once.

Comfortable seats are a necessity—particularly when children are expected to sit quietly. Because their feet must rest on the floor and backs must be properly supported, primary children need chairs that are scaled to their size.

Music for children's listening should include selections by composers of all periods. It should never be restricted to music written only for children. They constantly surprise us with their response to music that we had thought too "adult" for them. Long compositions should be played a portion at a time, and we must be sure that the portion played comes to a satisfactory conclusion. Of course the teacher will set the example of attentive listening *at all times.*

The listening program can be made more varied and interesting by the occasional use of carefully selected films and filmstrips. The discussion on page 13 is applicable to all ages and should be read at this point.

What are some of the things for which primary children can learn to listen?

1. Dynamic changes
2. Melodies
3. Some of the more frequently heard instruments
4. Rhythms
5. Moods
6. Tempo differences
7. Children's voices
8. Adult voices
9. Melodies or phrases that recur frequently

As stated in the previous chapter, the record player—or instrument—used during listening sessions must be the very best possible, not something discarded from adult use.

While a certain amount of guiding is advisable the teacher should not spend too much time talking about the music before it is heard. Children will listen for and hear different things according to their previous musical training and experiences at home. Some will be interested in tunes, some in rhythms, some in dynamic changes, and so on. Questions which often come after a listening period give the teacher an opportunity to make instructive comments. An occasional "live" performance adds interest and pleasure.

As children develop their listening capacities they become more critical of their own singing—individually and as a group. They are more attentive to matters affecting the group—starting, ending, slowing down or speeding up, and the like.

The first paragraph in this chapter included the statement that there will undoubtedly be vast differences in the abilities of primary children. Many six-year-olds have not yet learned to sing on pitch. Normal eight-year-olds who have been well taught should be able to carry a tune accurately, and without help. In between are the seven-year-olds, some of whom belong in each of these categories.

The range of primary age voices will gradually extend from middle C to F or G in the octave above.

This range is an average one; children will undoubtedly be found in any group who can sing higher or lower. Strain at any place in the range, particularly at the highest and lowest points, must be avoided. Constant alertness in watching and listening for danger signs is necessary. Primaries are unable to make more than barely perceptible changes in dynamic level. They may be permanently harmed if more is expected of them than they are capable of producing easily.

We must encourage good breathing and good posture by example rather than by talking. Children who hunch over or slump in their seats or breathe noisily must, of course, be corrected. If, however, song material is chosen with short enough phrases to make an easy breath span, and if melodies are pleasing to children, proper breathing usually takes care of itself.

In addition to reasons given for poor singing in the previous chapter we can now add a few more:

1. Certain youngsters find learning to read a slow process.

2. The slow reader may develop a droning habit that will carry over into his singing.

3. Some, in their desire to be first in tone matching, will develop faulty listening habits.

4. The timid, shy child may be so overcome with self-consciousness that he cannot hear accurately.

5. Faulty listeners often sing too loudly in their efforts to match others.

6. Losing and regaining teeth make for problems in enunciation.

Many reasons why a child cannot sing well are psychological; we must, therefore, make every effort to understand him and his particular problems. First of all we must learn to know him as an individual instead of thinking of him as being "just another child." If at all possible we should become acquainted with his family and learn something of his home environment. When we recognize his special needs and difficulties we can then give him the special help he requires.

A sense of accomplishment is just as necessary to a child as to an adult. The very young child will blithely repeat a teacher's song and be quite happy about his achievement, good or faulty, but there will be a change of attitude when he becomes a little older. He may become uneasily aware of his deficiencies with the result that frustrations and inhibitions may appear and add to his discouragement. Children with pitch problems may be kept happily singing if the teacher exercises care in what she asks them to repeat. When she sings "hello" to a child who habitually sings low she can simplify his problem of imitation by dropping her voice to his level. Once his confidence in himself is established he will become more relaxed and at ease when he is asked to listen and then to sing.

Children always match the pitch of a voice more easily than a pitch given on a piano or other instrument, and, as has been said before, they can match the pitch given by another child more easily than one given by an adult. It is often a good practice to have one child sing a word or phrase and ask others to sing after him. (The same child should not be used too frequently as a leader.) Games using a good singer as leader may be devised. Echo games in which children are spaced at some distance from each other are very good for this purpose. Sometimes just the consciousness that what one sings has to travel distance will cause a child to "lift" his voice. We must help him to recognize that loudness is not needed nor is it desirable. It is important to remember that all of the devices used to help the poor singer will in no way harm the good singer!

Gone are the days of the "robins" and the "crows"—names which at one time distinguished the good singers from the faulty ones. No child should ever be isolated from the group when singing activities are in progress. It is not unusual for a child who has never sung well to find his singing voice quite suddenly. Such discoveries are most often made while a child is singing with his own age group.

Some children speak and sing vowel sounds well, others poorly. The same is true of consonants. Many children speak clearly; others may lisp or mumble and muffle their words. The speaking voices of children differ greatly in pitch range. Since correct diction is a requisite of good singing these problems must be solved by patient and kindly, but unrelenting attention to the niceties of proper vowels and clean consonants. Provincialisms or local idiosyncrasies should not be tolerated.

Proper pronunciation depends largely upon correct manipulation of the lips and tongue; it is, therefore, necessary to practice lip and tongue movements. Selected words or phrases may be practiced in song and speech. Drill is certainly more interesting when made a part of games or stories. Animal sounds such as "bow-wow," "meow-meow," "cluck-cluck," "tweet-tweet," "baa-baa," "hee-haw," are useful, as are "ding-dong," "tick-tock," "toot-toot," and the like. Songs that make use of these sounds are found in most music books for the young. The sounds may be spoken rather than sung when they are used in connection with storytelling. The child whose front teeth are missing has his own special problems that only time and nature can solve, but in his limited way he too can participate in this activity.

Dramatizing songs helps children to lose inhibitions as they become engrossed in reproducing sounds with or without accompanying action. Stories in which sounds of wind, a train whistle, or a siren are mentioned can be told with children supplying the sounds at each reference. Sounds that move in pitch are to be desired. Each teacher may make her own stories to suit the needs of her group.

A common adult mistake is that of not allowing a child enough time to hear the pitch properly before he tries to reproduce it. If the pitch is sounded by the voice—the preferred way—it should be on an easy syllable such as "loo." After it is sounded and sustained individuals or the entire group may be asked to reproduce it. It may be necessary to repeat the pitch several times in order to provide each child with plenty of time to establish it in his own mind. Frequently, however, it will be found that when a child substitutes a word for "loo" he also changes the pitch! In this case the first word of a song must also be established pitch-wise before the singing begins.

As we teach children to match pitches we must also help them to be alert to pitch changes. We should begin by referring to pitches as being "high and low" and "near and far." Since children rarely have innate conceptions of these terms we must use them repeatedly until they can be comprehended. A chord played on the upper register of a piano and named "high" may be played interchangeably with a "low" chord played in the low register. Playing one chord at a time and asking the group or various individuals to tell whether it is high or low makes a good game. Signals such as "stand up" and "sit down" in which two chords for each are played will induce alertness as they fit the action to the signal.

Standing high (tiptoe) when a high chord is played and bending low on a low chord may be extended to include medium range (sitting). There can be no singing of these extreme pitches because, in order that they can be quickly identified, they must be so far apart as to be out of singing range. For the "near-far" game, big chords played near each other or far apart may gradually be replaced by smaller chords and finally by single notes that are near or far apart. Song bells and xylophones may be used effectively. By gradually reducing extreme distances of pitches we can help children to learn to recognize thirds, fifths, and octaves. The eight-year-old can easily learn to recognize major and minor thirds and triads.

Parents and educators should recognize that, although children are lacking in experience, they do have ideas which they need to express in their own way. Art, drama, and music provide satisfactory media of expression; free use must be made of all three. Music is often employed as a background or as an aid to creative expression but the creation of music itself is sometimes omitted. While results of youthful composition may seem trivial to an adult they have inestimable value for the creator in the development of musical expression and understanding.

There are several ways in which interest in song-making may be fostered. The six- and seven-year-old may still be singing his thoughts and ideas as he plays. The alert teacher will be listening for these "songs" and when the situation warrants it will ask a child to sing his song again so that the other children may sing it with him. We need not be surprised if he cannot repeat the song, however, for he creates so spontaneously that he is often hardly aware of what he sings. Spontaneous song-making is to be as much encouraged at the primary level as it was in the preschool period.

What the children saw on the way to church or school provides material for song-making. If there is timidity about starting such activity the teacher can lead off with a song of his creation. Children may be inclined at first to use the teacher's tune for words of their own. Help may be given by the teacher's singing a first phrase for them, asking them the next one, and so on. At other times the entire group may make sentences that can be put together in a song. A wide range of subject matter is available.

Teacher: Aut-umn leaves are fall-ing down,

Children: fall-ing down, fall-ing down,

Teacher: And they blow all o-ver town,

Children: fall-ing, fall-ing down.

**A Choir Day Song**

Primary Choir of Memorial Methodist Church
Lynchburg, Va.

Wed-nesday is a good day, good day, good day,

Wed-nesday is a good day, We have fun.

**Valentine Party**

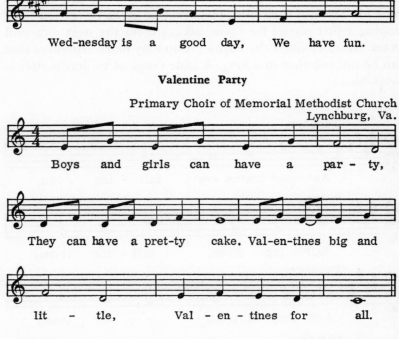

Primary Choir of Memorial Methodist Church
Lynchburg, Va.

Boys and girls can have a par - ty,

They can have a pret-ty cake. Val-en-tines big and

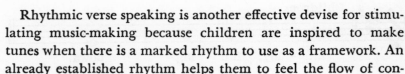

lit - tle, Val - en - tines for all.

Rhythmic verse speaking is another effective devise for stimulating music-making because children are inspired to make tunes when there is a marked rhythm to use as a framework. An already established rhythm helps them to feel the flow of con-

40

tinuous movement that is necessary to good music. The chosen verse should be spoken rhythmically a few times before the children are asked to make a tune for the first line. If several are forthcoming the group must decide upon the one they like best. Then the next line is considered, and so on. This method may make for lack of continuity because the parts are created independently, but despite technical deficiencies of the music, results will be quite beneficial to the children.

There are always some youngsters who lack the ability to create melodies; there are many more who need to be encouraged to try their skill. On the other hand, there is always the child who can make tunes as easily as he can speak and who is likely to dominate any period of composition. Here, as in all other dealings with children, the teacher must be tactful and patient.

Since singing is the medium which provides young children with most of their vocal training we must be certain to give them a variety of singing techniques in their songs. Slow, quiet songs will provide training in legato singing and in careful phrasing, while gay, fast songs will aid in the development of flexibility and lightness. Nonsense songs are good for the latter. A variety of song material is found in church-school songbooks, graded school songbooks, and in various publications for children and/or parents.

Primary children are not able to read music easily; they are taught most songs by rote, using the whole-song method or the phrase method. Both methods should be employed, and in such a way that the teacher radiates the joy of singing.

Until a song is well learned an accompaniment merely confuses young children. When the accompaniment is finally added it should be as a soft background—not in any way as a prop for weak spots or a prompting device. It need hardly be repeated that very simple harmonies are the only desirable ones for primaries. The autoharp—often played by the children themselves—can provide a good accompaniment for young voices. Independent singing should always be the goal of the teacher, however, the accompaniment being added only as a background to voices.

In selecting songs we need to keep these criteria in mind:

1. *The range should lie within the treble clef or not extend more than two notes below or one above it.* Sounds to be sung on notes E, F, G, in the upper range should be those that are produced by an open throat—ah, oo, oh—rather than sounds that pinch—ī, ē, ā. A sound that is difficult to produce will be unpleasing to the ear and will usually be flattered in pitch.

2. *The phrases should allow for an easy breath span.* If each phrase expresses a complete thought or idea it becomes natural to breathe at the right place. For example:

> Girls and boys, come out to play!
> We must have a holiday.
> Heigh-o! Heigh-o!
> Have a holiday.[1]

3. *A wide variety of texts should be used.* Songs about family, friends, school, church, and play all speak of things that interest children. The wonders of nature as displayed in the changing seasons provide excellent topics. Holidays provide song material as do also such aspects of religion as they are capable of understanding.

[1] Used by permission of Helen Hartness Flanders as published in *Vermont Folk-Songs & Ballads* (Stephen Daye Press, 1931), p. 187.

I like to think of Jesus
So loving, kind, and true
That when he walked among his friends
His friends were loving, too.[2]

O praise ye the Lord,
Praise him in his temple!
O praise ye the Lord,
Praise him for his mighty acts!

We thank you, God, for rain;
All growing plants need water too,
As much as growing children do.
We sing our song of praise to you,
And thank you, God, for rain.[3]

4. *The words used should be within the child's vocabulary.*
By this we do not mean that all texts should contain only words
that are in their present vocabulary, but words that are within
their comprehension and that are easily pronounced. On the
other hand, we need not lean over backward and give them
texts that are suitable for children younger than they. As in
the case of their understanding more complicated music than
we would expect, so they can grasp the meaning of many words
that we might consider to be too adult. We do not, for example,
consider "Rock of Ages" and "O Sacred Head now wounded"
to be appropriate, but "Joyful, joyful, we adore Thee," "For

the beauty of the earth," and "All creatures of our God and King" can certainly be included in the repertoire of primaries.

√ 5. *Words and tune must agree.* One of the reasons why spontaneous song-making is so successful is that one's verbal expression is immediately united with emotional expression. The child would never want to sing "Oh, I am so happy, happy, happy" to a dirge. If text is to be meaningful it must have an accompanying tune that says the same thing.

√ 6. *The song should be long enough to be a musical entity but not so long as to become tiresome.* Songs for primaries may have as many as four, five, and even six lines but they should not contain several stanzas. One set of words learned to a tune is easy enough but when a second stanza is added it becomes difficult to remember which words belong to each stanza. While they should certainly have some experience with this process, their repertoire should contain more single- than multiple-stanza songs.

It seems almost unnecessary to say that music and texts should be the very best available; that there should be no complicated rhythms in the melodies; that a variety of keys, both major and minor, should be employed. We know that *all* the music used is making a very definite impact upon highly impressionable young human beings. Their musical growth depends in a large part upon the musical food given them as children. Singing, listening, rhythmic activity, tone drills, and creativity must all be a part of the musical experiences of primary children.

How are all of these experiences related to a child's voice and his singing? When we teach him to listen, to feel, and then to interpret through one or more parts of his body we give him a good foundation for correct singing. No person, small or large, can really sing well until he has first heard, then felt, and then reacted.

chapter three
# The Junior Child

By the time children become juniors (grades four, five, and six) they are changing rapidly. They are in the beginning stages of growing out of childhood and into adulthood, and, as is to be expected, they show much variance in maturation. Girls usually develop more quickly than boys, most of whom seem awkward and clumsy. Both boys and girls may grow tall and lean or add weight instead of height and become chubby. Either extreme causes the child to feel self-conscious and gawky. Both sexes are restless and energetic and seem indefatigable so that a very occasional rest period is all that is needed before they are up and bursting with renewed energy. Active games of skill and endurance are popular and are made possible by the development of the large muscles and by better motor co-ordination.

Because juniors have an immense curiosity about everything, they are likely to be ardent learners. People—those of historic interest, those of other countries, and those close at hand—are of most concern and through this concern they develop a strong sense of responsibility to others. Hero worship is a dominant characteristic—the hero chosen being one whose skills or character traits are desired by the child in question.

A general spirit of friendliness prevails among juniors. While they often form close friendships with one other person of the same sex, they like to belong to a gang. For the first time all members of the gang want to do identical things and to dress and to talk alike. They are not content with expanding vocabularies, being prone to originate slang phrases and speech idiosyncrasies which they use endlessly—to the despair of their elders! Their healthy sense of humor is evidenced in teasing and in the making or repeating of silly jokes. They are less demonstrative in expressing their affections; they appear to be shy and to resent being given any verbal or physical caress before their contemporaries.

Juniors are perfectionists to a marked degree and are severely critical of themselves and others. This attitude helps them to produce beautiful, artistic singing. Many people believe that children's voices are at their best at ages nine, ten, and eleven. The quality of boys' and girls' voices is virtually the same—both speaking and singing—and it will remain so until the time of adolescent voice change. As children leave babyhood behind their voices attain a slightly fuller quality but one which cannot be compared in any way to an adult voice. Juniors can provide considerable dynamic contrast in their singing, but they must be restrained from any attempt to sing like adults. Days during which children feel particularly exhilarated—before a school holiday, for example—can be exhausting to teacher and students because their excitement may cause them to sing with all their might. The very exhuberance of their lives and their vigorous approach to all activities often leads into too-hearty singing—which is unpleasant to hear. Tones produced through strain are dangerous to a child's voice and must not be permitted—*ever*.

In our zeal to prevent children from harming themselves, we may swing the pendulum too far the other way and produce singing that is dull and lifeless. If we insist upon soft singing we may very well induce faulty enunciation and pitch inaccuracies, because, in an attempt to sing quietly, the children will fail to let their mouths open wide enough for the free and easy flow of tone. A tight jaw and a partially closed mouth will reduce the amount of tone until it sounds—and is—squeezed and pinched. When this condition exists high tones can only be approximated, and flat singing is an almost certain result. Such a tone is just as unpleasant and harmful as is an excessively loud tone.

When children sing within a range that is low for them— below middle C—they often change the quality and use what is termed a "chest voice." A break, or change of quality, distinguishes the "head voice" which we have used entirely to this point from the "chest voice" for which we must now be alert.

As the junior's vocal range widens his song material should begin to include occasional low notes. It is agreed by most music educators that all ages of children should use only the head voice. Careful selection of material and proper illustration of singing on the part of the teacher can keep this problem reasonably simple. A low note should not be repeated several times in succession for it is hard to continue using the "head voice" on more than one or two low notes at a time. Melodies that approach the low note from a fairly wide skip are easiest.

**Men and Children Everywhere**

Synagogue Melody

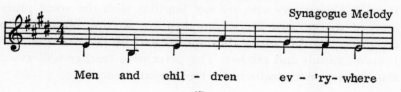

Men    and    chil - dren    ev - 'ry- where

When a low note is placed on the end syllable of a word it is very easy to touch it lightly, without strain or distortion.

**Be Thou My Vision, O Lord of My Heart**

Ancient Irish Tune

Be thou my vi - sion, O Lord of my heart;

Practice in singing descending scales with attention to maintaining the same quality throughout helps children to extend the head voice into a lower register. The singing range of juniors is:

Flatting—singing under the given pitch—is no more common to children than to adults. Sharping—singing above the pitch—is less likely to be heard in the songs of children. Flatting may result from any one of a number of causes. As has been previously stated, straining to reach high pitches is almost certain to produce a flatted pitch. Some sounds such as "ee" and "i" (ah-ee) tend to close the throat and should be avoided except in the middle voice range; "r" needs softening—more like an "ah"; a final "l" (as in "full") must not be permitted to become throaty. Composers who are not familiar with the vocal problems of the persons for whom they are writing often fail to recognize the difficulties that are created by certain combinations of sounds and pitches. The perceptive teacher will avoid music that is not conducive to free-throated singing.

Posture has a great deal to do with whether one sings on pitch. While it is true that singers must be free from tensions, we do not mean that they should be so limp and lifeless as to appear slouchy. Children should be comfortably erect when standing or sitting, with no sign of body stiffness. Heaving shoulders and chests result in pinched tones. Straight-backed chairs that prevent any leaning backward and that permit feet to rest squarely on the floor at all times are a valuable posture aid for all singers. Juniors are usually tall enough to use adult-sized chairs. When they stand to sing their arms should hang loosely at their sides, with hands relaxed.

Slouching posture may be due to lack of interest, a room that is too hot or full of stale air, or genuine fatigue. All of these will produce flatted singing.

Correct support is primarily the result of good posture. Most of the time and energy that might need to be devoted to the study of breathing can be diverted to other matters if proper posture is regularly maintained. Again, the teacher leads the way; he sets a good example; encourages without nagging; prevents boredom, irritation, and physical and mental weariness by providing frequent opportunities for changes of position— standing, sitting, moving. Occasional nonsense rounds that call for exaggerated action serve as relaxers.

Diction is a constant problem for singers and speakers of all ages. Most people have poor speech habits which most certainly will affect their singing because correct pronunciation is necessary for the production of good tone. Pure, "unchewed," undistorted vowels are the vehicles that shape and carry the tone. There must be no traces of sectional pronunciations (provincialisms). Special care must be given to word endings because of a general tendency to move the jaw, tongue, and/or lips long before the vowel sound is completed. A sustained "m" or "n" is musically incorrect; even worse is the nasal "ing" ("send*ing*," "walk*ing*") that is the result of placing the tongue against the palate. The singing mechanism should remain open and unmoving until the last possible instant. Even then the motion should be as small and as quick as possible.

Practice in reading aloud will make for diction consciousness. Some anthem books for juniors—notably those published by The Westminster Press—contain materials for speech choirs combined with singing choirs. Practice in reading psalms together, as well as the poetry and prose found in church-school literature, is both stimulating and interesting. The reading of one group for another commands critical attention. The children must learn to let their mouths open freely—but not in an exaggerated fashion; they must make the minimum lip and tongue motions that will produce correct consonants; and perhaps most important of all, they must develop the habit of speaking and singing pure, authentic vowel sounds. Fortunately, juniors, with their immense curiosity and their desire to attain perfection, respond quickly to the challenge of careful, clean diction.

Songs with long phrases may tax the breath span so that running out of breath will cause the pitch to drop. Failure to give adequate time for hearing a starting pitch may result in a slurred attack as the singer hunts for his tone. Slurring, scooping, or sliding, however, are generally the result of carelessness, inattention, or fatigue. An insidious challenge to good singing is the popular singer on radio and television who defies all the rules for correct use of the voice. The popularity of these singers is such that children will often seek to imitate them.

Finding suitable subject matter in songs for juniors is no problem because of their interest in so many things. More mature texts, songs with more than one stanza, freer rhythms, and wider range spans are needed now. The development of many vocal skills may be achieved through songs. Vocalization for its own sake is seldom used with juniors but they must not cease adding to their vocal attainments. Songs should incorporate the use of staccato, legato, scale-wise runs, diversified rhythms, and all manner of skips, hops, and leaps in the melody pattern. Many of the practices mentioned in the previous chapter may be continued and expanded. Juniors become intensely interested in musical form and analysis and because of this interest will begin to delve into many kinds of resource materials. For example, the junior will not only want to learn to sing hymns, but he will also want to know about the composer, the author, the tune name, and the meter markings.

Song material may be gleaned from many sources. We may certainly expect public-school graded music books to be kept as up to date and in line with modern educational methods as possible. In addition, the songs have been selected for their suitability to each age level. Unfortunately, church-school songbooks are often allowed to remain in use long after the contents have become outmoded. There are available, however, a number of fine church-school songbooks. Anthems, too—in octavo form or in collections—seem to be springing up like mushrooms all around. We must look at this abundance with a discerning eye and select those things that are best suited to our particular needs. Assuming that one's church hymnal is the best afforded that denomination, it is a never ending source of song material and one in which juniors delight. We are appalled at the thought of the wasted years when hymns were considered to be "over the heads" of children!

As always, texts that are within the comprehension of children who are to sing them must be of prime consideration. This is not to say that all words must already be in their everyday vocabularies, but rather that they may be readily understood and assimilated. Texts that make use of beautiful language make a lasting impression upon the singers.

Tunes for juniors should involve much rhythmic variety and more difficult melodic lines. In particular favor with them are folk songs, negro spirituals (which they sing with innate warmth of feeling), lively march tunes, and hymn tunes of almost all kinds.

Although they do not as a rule do much part singing, juniors must begin preparation for the time when they will. Descants sung by the entire group in conjunction with another group provide one manner of approach. Again, a simple two-part song in which all of the group sings together while the teacher sings the second part will give them added experiences. Simple rounds—first in two parts, later in three and possibly four— furnish an attractive introduction to part singing. No division of parts should ever be attempted until the group can sing well in unison.

Rote learning will still occupy only part of the juniors' singing activities, for they will also be reading songs. Reading readiness varies according to the general physical growth and early music training of each child. School music educators do not entirely agree as to when such activity should begin nor what process is best. It behooves each teacher who feels that her group is ready for song reading to study the suggestions offered by a variety of public-school music teachers so that she will be better equipped to follow the plan best suited to her group or to originate her own plan.

The listening span of juniors is considerably lengthened, and there are many new ways in which they can use the additional time. They may sing rounds and descants with recordings and they may listen to choral music in which parts are easily followed. They are interested in fugues—sung or played—in which melodies enter as they do in simple rounds. They enjoy identifying the qualities of various kinds of singing voices and instruments.

Larger choral and orchestral compositions must still be heard a portion at a time because of their length. An opportunity is here presented to acquaint children with oratorio, cantatas, and other religious works that they may not have a chance to hear in a "live" performance. If scores are available the group may have the added pleasure of following the music. This kind of study has another value in that it prepares the children for increased pleasure in singing and listening throughout their entire lives.

The discussion of films and filmstrips on page 13 is pertinent at this point since the selection and use of all aids must be in terms of the child's maturation level.

Creative rhythmic movement provides juniors with a satisfying means of expressing their feelings and emotions. Although they are able to express themselves verbally fairly well there are still many emotional needs that may not be met through language. Experience with life itself makes them more understanding of religious factors and more responsive to them. Interpreting the mood or central thought of a hymn through movement causes the words to take on added significance and helps the children to feel a personal response to the message. Study of the hymn in order to find its theme or mood encourages the interpreter to do more than merely pantomime the words. It is not necessary to interpret an entire hymn if one or more stanzas can convey the main thought.

Hymns such as "Joyful, joyful, we adore Thee," "Now thank we all our God," "All creatures of our God and King," and "Let all the world in every corner sing" offer opportunities for a wide variety of interpretive movement. There will be a diversity of ideas as to what movement best expresses the interpreter's reactions to the text, and this diversity is to be encouraged. When movement is used informally there need be no uniformity. If the group is working as a unit, however, there must be discussion, experimentation, and agreement as final movement patterns evolve. Anthems, songs, and instrumental music as well as hymns are all suitable for this kind of use.

All rhythmic experiences should add to the growing musical perception of children. Clapping can be a tool for teaching complicated rhythms, and varied clapping—loud, soft, finger tips only and so on—to indicate repetition of phrases and return to the original theme adds variety and interest.

Folk games are fun for juniors; they have an added value in that they provide a release for pent-up energies and at the same time focus attention on form and order. Children can be encouraged to provide original rhythmic accompaniments for their songs and movements. Drums, cymbals, tambourines, triangles, and bells are useful. Rhythm orchestras, as such, are definitely not to be recommended.

Juniors are able to work, play, think, and sing better than ever before, and this makes them ideal people to teach. The wise music teacher will use his precious time to its fullest degree, recognizing that they have attained a kind of perfection that will not be theirs again until they become young adults. Soon they will enter—and may already be entering—that disturbing, exciting period called adolescence. Wonderful opportunities are afforded the music teacher to prepare children for the vocal problems they will face in early adolescence. Changing voices can be thrilling and challenging. Every junior should understand the adjustments that occur in the singing mechanism and the way to handle these adjustments. In all probability a few sixth graders—both boys and girls—will be well into the period of change.

Emphasis must be placed upon certain items during the preparation period:

1. The changing voice is a natural development and a strong indication of approaching manhood and womanhood.

2. Free and easy singing should continue throughout the period of change.

3. The "new" voice will be better than the old one.

Enlarged pictures and good drawings of the singing mechanism can be used to explain the growth process. If all the mystery and uncertainty are removed there need be no worry, no fear, and no embarrassment.

The junior age is both the culmination of childhood and the beginning of adolescence. Methods and materials need, therefore, to be planned to serve two purposes of equal value if each child is to realize his full potential: (1) Provide a rich wholesome means of expression that is of real significance to the junior child, and (2) give him a foundation upon which he can build safely and securely as he moves rapidly from childhood toward adulthood.

chapter four
# Grades Seven and Eight

Early adolescence is a time of storm, stress, and excitement for all concerned—children, parents, teachers, and friends. It is also a time of worry and depression and of uncertainty and change. Someone has said that the only thing consistent about adolescents is their inconsistency. A typical group of twelve- and thirteen-year-olds will include some who show no evidence of puberty, a few who are far advanced into adolescence, and many who are just arriving. Because inconsistency is also an individual trait, an adolescent is about as easy to control as a drop of mercury. One minute he is gay, the next depressed; he will run for fifty feet and then collapse in a heap; he will seek affection and then turn upon the object of his love. This man- or woman-child is a braggart and a show-off, sometimes moody and often intense, at one moment an introvert and the next an extrovert, quarreling at the drop of a hat, crying (boys, too, much to their shame) without noticeable reason, giggling incessantly, and teasing unmercifully.

Mentally, the junior youth is entering a new and exciting period. While he or she will alternate between alertness and dullness, he is capable of reasoning on an adult level. Synthesis, aided by his extreme curiosity, becomes a delightful tool. He discovers the fun of thinking. Matters related to science and mechanics intrigue both boys and girls; their active imaginations are now aided by enough knowledge and ability to bring whole new concepts into their reach. Science fiction has an especial appeal for boys because it combines adventure with new areas of understanding. Cooking and sewing and their approaching womanhood and all its attendant implications and complications are increasingly attractive to junior girls.

Mental puzzles intrigue the junior youth; he will argue just to argue—a fact often ignored by irritated parents and teachers! He likes to be challenged and will tend to stagnate if no opportunities are given him to stretch his mental muscles. In the area of creativity he is capable of amazing accomplishments. Handwork, music, literature—he probably has abilities in most areas not involving careful, overall physical co-ordination. He can write passable—sometimes excellent—poetry and prose. Boys may resist developing this ability, however, because they shy away from anything that is not masculine, and poetry writing, they feel, is for girls. Girls, too, may be slow to write because they believe their efforts are not productive of usable materials. Exceptional teaching is required to lead these youngsters into this very challenging and rewarding area of creativity.

Very much the same can be said for the junior youth and music. Boys and girls can, and often do, produce some effective compositions. The ability that they possessed several years previously to create words and tunes is still present unless it has been completely subdued because of disinterest or lack of use. The six-year-old makes original music naturally and voluminously with only a little encouragement, but the twelve- or thirteen-year-old may have developed inhibitions which interfere with the natural outpouring of his emotions. As with writing poetry and prose, the composing of music by junior youth is the result of excellent teaching by someone who thoroughly understands the abilities as well as the limitations of his charges.

Many of the early adolescent's mental and emotional problems are due directly or indirectly to the changes that are occurring in his body structure. Social difficulties arise because girls usually enter puberty several months—sometimes a year or more—ahead of boys. Girls tend to be taller than boys during the seventh and eighth grades; arms and legs seem to shoot out overnight, resulting in faulty co-ordination and general awkwardness. Appetites are uncertain; great quantities of food will vanish one day while a candy bar and a soft drink serve the next. Both sexes suffer from acne. Junior youth may bubble with poorly controlled energy half the time and give evidence of great fatigue the other half. They need, but do not wish to take, lots of sleep. Not the least of their problems is the changing voice—of girls as well as of boys. This subject will be discussed later in detail.

Every day is filled with adventure. If none occurs they will invent something or find outlets in the adventure of others. They must have heroes—but not the same one for any great length of time. The boy in particular struggles manfully to show his regard for Jesus and God without doing anything that smacks of being "sissified." Songs about the virility of Christ appeal to him; he will often express his feelings in singing when he hesitates to let them be known in any other way.

Adolescents tend to go with a crowd because they must have social approval. The "gang" is all important, and within the gang each one strives for prestige and recognition. This tendency can be a liability, but the resourceful teacher can make it an asset by gaining the respect and unexpressed love of the gang's leaders. He will try to discover hidden abilities in these reluctant musicians that will offer them opportunities to obtain social approval. He is limited in his approach to the problem only by his resourcefulness, his imagination, and his enthusiasm.

Paradoxically, the youth both craves and dislikes control or guidance by his elders. Without it he is lost; with it he may become resentful. This characteristic is well illustrated by the fact that discipline is an accepted ingredient of junior-high choirs, bands, and orchestras—organizations which are very popular with youth. The discipline demanded by practice and by performance is at one and the same time despised and loved by members of the group. The writer heard two eighth graders from different schools discussing their musical groups. One said, "Mr. ——— is real tough. He means business. But we sure like it." The other said, somewhat ruefully, "Our director just doesn't care enough to make us want to work and to behave."

Youth's musical development echoes his mental, physical, emotional, and social patterns. For example, he may be able to hear, feel, and understand complicated rhythmic patterns, but be totally unable to reproduce them. He hears all kinds of harmonies and exciting melodies but his treacherous singing mechanism refuses to co-operate. The potential is great, but its realization demands skillful teaching, plus patience, understanding, and love.

Individual differences are nowhere greater nor of more significance than during early adolescence. The student with average ability usually gets along rather well because materials and methods are primarily "aimed" in his direction. Those with less than average ability or those whose musical development has been delayed for various reasons may find that music is boring and even repugnant. The effective teacher will call upon every available device and use every procedure that a lively

59

imagination can produce to bring these reluctant musicians into the group.

While the exceptionally talented child must be challenged to use and develop his musical abilities throughout all his school years, the most critical period for him occurs during early adolescence. If he goes into full adolescence without a growing appreciation of music and the ability to make it he will probably fade entirely out of the picture and become a musical "never-was."

It should be emphasized that the adolescent's love for, understanding of, and ability in music are strongly dependent upon his past experiences. If he has had a happy, unlimited musical life he will enter this new time with joy and anticipation. If, on the other hand, his music has either been dull and boring or very limited in extent, he will probably use adolescence as a good excuse to drop out—usually for life. A dedicated, efficient teacher—man or woman—can give this latter youth something he has never had before, but the task is indeed a difficult one. (A man is often considered more effective in a youth music program, but an understanding, competent woman can be just as successful.)

For the sake of convenience the early youth's musical characteristics are discussed under three principal headings: (1) Rhythmic, (2) Auditory, and (3) Vocal.

√ 1. Rhythm is as important to the twelve- and thirteen-year-old as it is to the primary child. Just as a stutterer can sometimes speak more easily when he establishes an artificial speech rhythm, so an awkward adolescent can find relief for his awkwardness in the smooth flowing movement of solid rhythmic patterns. Marching bands have their beginning in the seventh grade. Rhythmic games and activities of a more sophisticated nature than in previous years appeal strongly to both boys and girls, provided no embarrassing situations are permitted to develop. Boys, especially, must not be forced to do anything that they consider childish or beneath their dignity. Neither should they attempt activities beyond their emotional, physical, or mental abilities because failure is a terrible burden for an adolescent to bear. The resourceful music teacher will use the rhythmic demands of baseball, basketball, track, and other athletic ventures to illustrate the values of rhythmic activities of all kinds. The smooth, even movement of acrobats seen on TV is a good example of rhythmic movement in a very un-sissified profession!

Given a proper incentive and a solid challenge, the junior youth enjoys working out difficult rhythmic patterns in movement and singing. He can mentally master almost any pattern if his previous experience has been adequate. Physically his success may be somewhat more limited. The wise teacher will see that successes far outweigh failures because early adolescence is at best so full of frustrations that he may find music a convenient repository for all his discouragement.

Because he can hear and respond to rhythms which he is unable to reproduce, the junior youth enjoys recorded music as much as and possibly more than at any other age. The following list is representative of the hundreds of titles that are available. A more complete list will be found on pages 128 ff.

Brahms, Hungarian Dances, Cap. G-7209
    Kubelik and Royal Philharmonic. Over: Dvořák, Slavonic Rhapsody and Scherzo.
Chávez, Symphonie India, Dec. 9527
    Chávez and Mexico Symphony Orchestra.
Dvořák, Slavonic Dances
    Brendel and Klien, two pianos, Vox PI-11620

Reiner and Vienna Philharmonic, Lon. CM-9267
Over: Brahms, Hungarian Dances.
Greco, Flamenco Fury, MGM 3741
Milhaud, Scaramouche Suite, Dec. 9790
Vronsky and Babin, two pianos.

2. The musically experienced junior youth has auditory abilities equal to those of an adult. In fact, between twelve and thirty the ability to respond to pitch and color is at its highest. The primary child is confused by excessive tone color and pitch variations; the adolescent glories in them! He is pleased by lush harmonies and exciting dissonances. He particularly enjoys playing in brass and woodwind ensembles. The French horn and the double reeds are his delight. If he is a pianist, he will hunt for all kinds of new colors. Watch him the first time he is introduced to a pipe organ console!

Just as the twelve- or thirteen-year-old can understand many difficult rhythmic passages which he cannot reproduce, so color poses problems for him. And for the same reasons expressed previously, recorded music is extremely valuable at this age. The following brief list is but an indication of materials that are available. Additional titles are listed on pages 128 ff.

Khachaturian, Gayne Suites, Ang. 35277
Khachaturian and Philharmonic Orchestra. Includes Sabre Dance. Over: Masquerade Suites.
Mussorgsky, Pictures at an Exhibition, Col. ML-5401
Bernstein and New York Philharmonic. Over: Rimsky-Korsakov, Capriccio.
Rachmaninoff, Symphonic Dances, Col. ML-4621
Leinsdorff and Rochester Philharmonic. (Technically and musically a rare item. Also good for rhythm study.)
Stravinsky, Firebird Suite, Col. ML-5182

Bernstein and New York Philharmonic. Over: Tchaikovsky, Romeo and Juliet.

3. Vocally, the early adolescent is undergoing a period of insecurity and frustration. His entire singing mechanism, including the support muscles, is changing rapidly. It has often been said that more boys—and many girls—turn against music during the seventh and eighth grades than at any other time because most of the facility, the freedom, and the excitement of fifth and sixth grade singing diminishes during this critical time. Comedians have made capital of the boy—or girl—who is all hands, arms, legs, and feet, grown out of his clothes, and about as awkward as a Newfoundland puppy. Unfortunately this description also applies to the early adolescent voice because it is often as awkward as the picture just described. Where the range was once extended it is now limited—both the bottom and top may be gone. Where timbre was somewhat varied and under good control it is now much more varied and under little control. Is it any wonder, then, that even the very musical child may be disturbed by these changes although he has been properly prepared to expect them? Pity the poor youngster who comes into this period blind and deaf, as it were!

His extraordinary hearing ability is both an asset and a liability—the latter, because of the frustrations created by his inability to reproduce what he hears physically and mentally. In this respect, and contrary to popular opinion, girls and boys differ only in degree—not in kind. The tendency to give all our attention to the so-called boy problem has caused many a young girl to suffer untold miseries and often has resulted in the loss of part or all of her singing voice. Her feeling of inadequacy may have a further unfortunate result—she loses interest in singing and possibly in all phases of music.

Typical of statements to be found in most discussions of the changing voice is this one: "It is believed that girls' voices change also, but mostly in quality. There may be somewhat of a change in range, though not to the extent of lowering an octave as characteristic of boys' voices." [1] And thus the adolescent girl's voice is dismissed—there is no further comment.

What happens to the adolescent singing mechanism to create all these uncertainties? Quite briefly, the voice box enlarges, the vocal bands become longer and thicker, and all supporting muscles, such as abdominal and chest muscles, become stronger. It is as if a violinist were handed a violin whose size and shape had been suddenly changed and whose strings had been replaced with others of different texture, size, and tension. To make matters worse, he is given a larger, heavier bow with hair that is coarse and rough. Just how well can he be expected to perform without having an opportunity to become familiar with his new instrument?

Because so little attention is usually given to the girl's changing voice, her problems will be discussed first. The earliest indication she has of impending difficulties is a loss of ease in singing high tones. The F, G, and even A that had always floated out with little effort on her part suddenly demand a great deal of effort. The throat strains; the tones feel—and sound—heavy, breathy, and rough. If the girl has been previously warned to expect this new sensation and if she understands what is happening, she will immediately cease forcing her voice in order to let these new adjustments take place. She will not worry because her high tones feel strange; in fact, she may not try them except experimentally for several days or possibly weeks. She will discuss the situation with her teacher, who will, in turn, encourage her to sing easily within a comfortable range. She

[1] F. Andrews and J. Leeder, *Guiding Junior-High-School Pupils in Music Experiences* (Englewood Cliffs, N. J.: Prentice-Hall, Inc., 1953), p. 139.

may shift to a lower part until there is further indication of the kind of voice she will ultimately have.

Under no circumstances should she be permitted to sing loudly; however, she must be encouraged to sing with a vital tone, well supported by good posture and correct breathing. Properly supported and properly released, her tones will be firm, pleasant, warm, clear, and reasonably breathless.

Not every girl goes through a period of obvious voice change. Perhaps half are able to continue singing in the same range and with a similar basic quality as their voices become increasingly mature.

A word of warning is indicated at this point. We speak of "changed" voices. When is a voice "changed"? Not until it has attained complete maturity, and that condition is rarely reached before the early twenties and often not then. The young voice continues to change—though not so abruptly as in early adolescence—all through high school and college. The writer was told that Lawrence Tibbet sang professionally as a tenor until he was about twenty-seven years old, at which time he discovered himself to be a baritone, and as such he made his great reputation.

The twelve- or thirteen-year-old soprano has a comfortable range of

with a maximum range a step or so higher and possibly a step lower. An occasional high G or A, if sung lightly and easily, will not harm her. The unchanged boy-soprano has an identical range.

There is no such person—except in very rare instances—

as an adolescent contralto. The writer has known two twelve-year-old girls who were real contraltos. Both were physically mature and quite large, one being 5′ 11″ in height. Unfortunately, in an effort to produce beautiful (?) music, teachers are sometimes guilty of forcing young voices to sing much too low and much too heavily. Someone has said, "Cursed is the adolescent girl who can read music! She is forever condemned to sing alto." There is much truth in this statement. It should be obvious that forcing a voice down will ultimately limit and harm the singing mechanism as much as, or more than, forcing it up. The only way to solve the problems posed by a lack of altos is to select proper materials so that no young voice will be asked to do more than is good for it.

The low—not alto—voice—of both girls and boys—should sing only a note or two lower than the high voice:

This octave and one third will be comfortable for almost any young voice, whether high or low. An occasional low A or A flat will not be harmful but a series of such low tones could create real difficulties. In an effort to strengthen a weak section, teachers sometimes ask young altos to sing a tenor part, much of which will lie in the very low alto range. The writers consider this use of "girl tenors" to be an inexcusable offense at the junior-high level and a doubtful practice of any time.

The unchanged boy-voice has the same range as that of the girl, but there is a noticeable difference in quality as early as the tenth or eleventh year. By age twelve, boy sopranos and altos have a rich, warm quality which is extremely effective when used properly. It is this quality that has been responsible for the development of many famous boy choirs and all-male choirs. Because the unchanged voice becomes better with each year of use, certain directors have delayed the approaching change, and in the writers' opinion, have thereby harmed many young singers to the extent that singing became impossible after the delayed break occurred.

Without a doubt the twelve- or thirteen-year-old boy does pose vocal problems far beyond those of the girl. An average class of seventh- and eighth-grade boys will include some voices that have not begun to change—and may not for another four years or more—some that are beginning to change, and a few that are well on their way.

In order to simplify matters as much as possible it is often advisable to divide boys and girls at this age. The advantages far outweigh the disadvantages. First of all, social problems are almost eliminated because junior-high boys and girls work much better when there are no members of the opposite sex around. In a mixed group the element of social competition is a factor, and its elimination makes it possible to give attention to the matter at hand—singing. Self-consciousness in the presence of the other sex is a real factor, especially when voices misbehave. Girls are prone to giggle at the boy's breaking voice, with the result that the boy may cease trying to sing.

Second, materials suitable for girls are not always pleasing to boys; the converse is somewhat less true, but it is nevertheless an item. Third, while their vocal problems differ not in kind but in degree, the degree of difference is so great that much time taken up by these differences can be put to good use in separate choirs. Fourth, a boys' choir can include grades four through eight or nine without loss of effectiveness. Girls, on the other hand, do not work well together when the ages differ more than two or three years.

Some directors would add a fifth item—discipline. However the writers believe that problems of discipline will not arise if the groups, whether mixed or not, are kept interested, active, and challenged.

A problem of terminology must be considered. What shall we call the unchanged boy-voice? He is very resistant to anything feminine; therefore "soprano" and "alto" are not desirable. Certainly "tenor" and "bass" have incorrect connotations. Many directors use the simple and obvious "high," "medium," and "low" as identifying terms, limiting "baritone" to those who are well into the transition period. It is doubtful that "tenor" should be used at all, although "alto-tenor" has long been associated with the "in-between" voice. Another term, "cambiata," an Italian word meaning "changing," is receiving consideration but it has not been entirely accepted. The writers suggest that adolescent boys' voices be classified, after grade six, as *high, low, changing,* and *baritone.* Until publishers, composers, and teachers can agree upon terminology there will continue to be considerable difference, but it need not be of serious concern.

Until relatively recent times there was a generally accepted belief that boys should not sing while their voices are changing. This belief was perhaps fostered by the cathedral choirmasters who kept their boys on soprano and alto parts until the voices actually "broke," sometimes as late as age fifteen or sixteen. Most of today's trained choral directors—at least those trained in the handling of young voices—agree that, under proper guidance, a boy's voice is not harmed by his singing during the change. On the contrary, his voice is improved. Of equal importance is the fact that his interest is maintained and probably heightened because of the exciting challenge of his new voice and all the wonderful new music he can sing or soon will be able to sing.

The most important principle to remember in handling any young voice—whether boy's or girl's, changing or not—is that singing *must be easy* and it *must be fun!* If it is easy and if it is fun all the hard work that goes with good choral singing ceases to be work! In order to put this principle into practice, we should remember and use a very important word—perhaps the most important word for singers—*"let."* We must teach our people to sing with good, comfortable posture in order to *let* the *breath* flow into the lungs and then *let* the *tone* flow out. The young singer will save himself many hours of unlearning if he absorbs this basic concept. The actual sound producing mechanism has only one task: To vibrate freely at the frequencies demanded by pitch and color. All the real work should be done by the rest of the body and the tones permitted to find their proper resonance areas without hindrance from tight jaws and throats.

The principle "easy and fun" and the word "let" are pertinent at this point because the boy whose voice is changing must be able to evaluate his situation at all times, often without help from his teacher. He must be so well informed about the development of his voice that there is no mystery nor uncertainty. He knows what will happen and what to do about it. At the first sign of discomfort he must be prepared to "ease off" on the high notes and perhaps ask for a slightly lower part. His range may become quite limited—possibly as little as the five or six tones centered around middle C. However, he should sing down through "the break" for as long as he is able to do so without strain. As the additional lower tones become singable, his need for the "unchanged" higher tones will decrease. Finding good materials which are satisfactory in terms of range and

69

*tessitura* is especially important and somewhat difficult. The lists that start on page 141 have been carefully prepared with these problems in mind, but some editing of parts may be needed to solve particular problems.

The word "break" is an uncertain term; it is, however, generally understood to mean that area of the voice in which the quality abruptly moves from an unchanged quality—usually soprano—to a more mature tone in the new, changing color. The voices of most girls and some boys become gradually lower, heavier, and darker without producing an audible "break." Others undergo all kinds of squeeks and squawks that can, but need not be embarrassing.

A word of warning is needed at this point. Many boys and girls can continue to sing much higher than they think they can long after the first real or imagined signs of range difficulty appear. The tendency to give up and say "I can't reach it" must be resisted by the teacher, usually in private consultation. All evidence of strain should, of course, be eliminated.

The alert teacher will arrange private sessions at which time the emerging voice will be explored and discussed and questions answered. In a surprisingly brief time the quality of this new voice—speaking as well as singing—will give some clue as to its ultimate destination: bass, baritone, or tenor. Range provides no help at this point or for some time to come. In fact range is often a negative guide. Both student and teacher should "make haste slowly" in working with the emerging voice. No two will respond alike or move according to the timetable. The speaking voice is often the best guide in determining the rate of change and destination of the voice. No permanent classification should be considered until the voice is well into maturity, many years hence.

The implications of the word *tessitura* should be examined

because they become increasingly important as materials are discussed. The word literally means "texture." It refers to the way a selection "lies" in the voice—how the average position of its notes relates to the voice or instrument. Range has to do with the extremes of high and low and has little or no bearing upon *tessitura*. A song may have one or two extreme pitches, with most of the notes lying within a comfortable range. On the other hand, a song may have no extreme pitches but most of its notes lie fairly high or fairly low. For example, at first glance a song may seem perfect for a young soprano because its highest note is F and its lowest is C. Closer examination discloses its disturbing tendency to remain on or near the upper D and E. Obviously our young soprano will soon tire; she will strive without success to maintain the pitch level; and temporary or permanent harm may result. It is quite important then, that the average range (*tessitura*) fall well within the middle compass of each voice.

Occasionally a seventh- or eighth-grade class will include singers at both extremes—high soprano and low bass. The writer has had two thirteen-year-old students who were real basses; one sang a comfortable low F, and the other an E flat. Generally, however, the adolescent "bass" has a light baritone quality, with

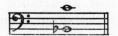

as his comfortable range. He will be able to touch a low A or A flat—and occasionally a D above middle C—but with little tone or volume.

The high soprano is found with reasonable frequency. In fact, an average class of twenty-five girls will usually include one and perhaps two who have an easy B flat and, rarely, a C. These girls should be given additional attention and encouraged to sing a few songs that offer them a special challenge.

The teacher whose class is blessed with exceptional voices can easily turn the blessing into a curse if she permits her singers to push their voices beyond the natural, easy limits that go with the maturation process. Parents and friends must often be held in check by someone who understands the young voice. The singers themselves are often impatient and do themselves irreparable harm by trying to "grow up" too fast. Imitation of popular singers, or any adult voice, is to be prevented at all cost—an item to be considered in the use of recorded music.

The singing of solos may provide an answer to the problem of the precocious adolescent. However, the writers believe that few twelve- and thirteen-year-olds will benefit from individual public performances. Occasionally a solo passage in a choral number may be sung to advantage by one voice. Individual study can often be a real value to selected students if emphasis is not placed upon solo singing. This matter is discussed more fully on page 114.

Vocalises are quite important for both boys and girls during the period of voice change. Descending scale passages and occasional arpeggios are most effective and offer few technical problems. During the time that both changed and unchanged qualities exist in the same voice, simple descending scales are especially useful in helping to "bridge the gap" between the two voices and in speeding up the maturing process. The emergent voice needs to be explored, expanded, and made flexible as fast as possible. No excessive effort should be made to hasten the change, but neither should there be a hanging on to the old voice. Let's say that its departure should be politely encouraged.

Vocalises

1.

All vowels; legato and staccato; also with *lah, mah, nah, loh, moh, noh,* and the like. Use within a comfortable range, and at tempos varying from moderately slow to fast, but always slow enough to be even and clean. May be repeated in one breath.

2.

Same instructions as for number 1.

3.

Same instructions as for number 1.

4.

Sustain one or more voices on the starting tone as the other voices sing the scale according to instructions given in number 1.

5.

Same instructions as for number 4, except sustain one or more voices on each note of the chord.

6.

ah    aye    ee    oh    oo

Use a light, but well-supported flowing tone without any "chewing" motion of the lower jaw. The vocalise may be extended thus: *mah, may, mee, moh, moo; lah, lay, lee, lo, loo.* The lips and tongue should form the consonants with little or no jaw movement so that the tone continues its even flow.

Voice lessons, as such, are not advisable at this age. What, then, can we teach them? Basically three things: Correct posture, correct support, and sensible diction. Perhaps most important of all is good posture, and it is a tricky item with which to contend. We cannot nag a slumping, circular youngster. He strongly resents any suggestion of pressure. Displaying pictures of an outstanding athlete who is a local hero and pictures of feminine movie and TV stars may have value—as will also a few "horrible examples." The adolescent is quick to grasp the humor of a situation if his attention is not forced upon it.

Correct posture carries with it a feeling and appearance of comfortable, springy erectness. It must be habitual. To assume a "singing posture" only as the occasion demands is to create tensions and a kind of rigidity that is the antithesis of good posture. *Balance, ease,* and *resilience* are the key words to remember in any discussion of good posture.

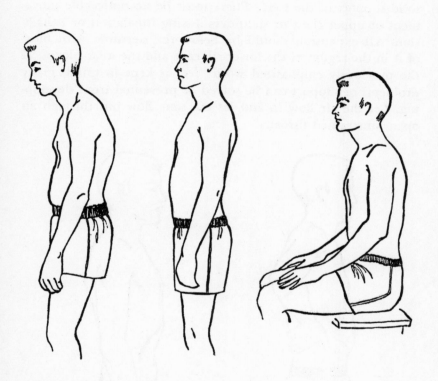

Proper breathing habits are about as difficult to promote as is good posture. Ask an adolescent to take a deep breath. How does he react? Almost certainly he will heave with his upper chest and his shoulders. Is it not paradoxical that we talk of teaching "natural breathing"?

Despite the danger of creating additional tensions, attention must be called to this matter of easy, noiseless breathing and solid support of the tone. There must be no noticeable movement of upper chest or shoulders during inhalation or exhalation. All expansion should be below the sternum, with most of it in the region of the lower rib cage and the solar plexus. If the previously emphasized word *"let"* is kept in mind, many problems of support can be solved or prevented from developing. *Let* the air flow in and *let* the tone flow out through an open, unstrained throat.

Diction appears to be the least difficult of the three to teach but it is probably the one least successfully taught. Private teachers try to combat, in a thirty-minute lesson, all the habits of the rest of the week and of the years gone by. Class teachers have the same problem. Constant, but non-nagging, attention to crisp consonants and pure vowels is a must.

A good tape recorder is an excellent teaching aid. It is not easy for the singer to hear minute gradations of vowel color such as one finds in the *Mary, merry,* and *marry; wonder, wander; color, collar.* Since English vowels tend to be diphthongs (my=mah-ay-ee) it is necessary that the young singer learn how to sustain the most singable portion of each vowel and then attach the necessary consonant (s) in one instantaneous movement. An agile tongue, a relaxed jaw, and quickly moving lips will make clean, sensible diction relatively simple to master.[2]

A tape recorder is an excellent teaching aid for all aspects of singing—color, pitch, rhythmic accuracy, blend, balance, and the like. Only equipment of good quality and reasonably high fidelity should be used since inferior machines cannot give a fair reproduction of tone and color.

As has been previously stated, early adolescents are excited by and respond to colorful, rhythmic music, but because they are not capable of reproducing more than a limited amount of what they can hear, carefully chosen recorded selections can and should play an important role in their over-all musical development. Their home, church, and school background will determine the kinds of music which best suit them. Under ideal circumstances and with proper guidance, they will respond positively to any good music that is artistically and correctly performed. They may even go so far as to enjoy songs and operatic arias sung in foreign languages. The writer observed a seventh-grade mixed group as they listened in open-mouthed

2 A more detailed discussion of posture, breathing, and diction will be found in William C. Rice, *Basic Principles of Singing* (Nashville; Abingdon Press, 1961).

awe to a recording by Korjus of the so-called "Bell Song." Her unbelievable accuracy enthralled them because they knew how, and for what, to listen. On the other hand, the writer has seen other junior youth break into guffaws of merriment while listening to similar recordings. The difference lay in their preparation for listening.

It should be obvious that excellent equipment is absolutely necessary. Many families possess and listen to the finest records and record players available. It would not be surprising to find that more than one boy in the class had built his own hi-fi set. Equipment that was more than adequate for primary and junior children will not satisfy these young people. An elaborate, fancy record player with all kinds of patented eyecatching devices is not recommended, however. Neither do the writers believe that stereophonic systems are necessary or even advisable in the school room for several reasons, three of which will suffice: (1) For proper effect stereo speakers must be placed in such a position that only a few people can hear properly. (2) The added cost of the equipment is not justified in terms of improved sound. (3) Maintenance is a major item when sound equipment becomes increasingly complicated.

The writers recommend the purchase of a simple, manually operated monaural record player that works effectively at these speeds: 33 1/3, 45, and 78 revolutions per minute. It should have a strong motor which runs evenly and smoothly so that distortion from speed variance will not be a problem. It should reproduce sounds at least as high as 12,000 and at least as low as 100 cycles per second. If the local electrical supply is not consistent and the motor runs unevenly as a result, a voltage regulator should be used.

Since the listening potentialities of early adolescents are almost unlimited, only general categories of recorded music will be described. Each teacher should choose according to the abilities and interests of his own group. He must be on the alert to prevent his students from attempting to imitate the mature voices and complicated structures produced by professional musicians.

1. *Folk music.* Many excellent recordings, artistically performed and technically near-perfect, are available. Such names as Harry Belafonte, John Jacob Niles, and Burl Ives are usually "safe," although each title should be checked and the record played before a purchase is made. Records made in the Thirties by Paul Robeson are perhaps musically superior to many others now being pressed. Technically, however, his records will be somewhat inferior to later recordings. Roland Hayes has released many fine spirituals through Vanguard. Occasionally, the recordings of popular singers can be used, but great care should be exercised in choosing their works because the texts and music they use are not always of very high quality.

A number of choral groups have prepared excellent folk records. The Robert Shaw Chorale and the Roger Wagner Chorale are two that come to mind. There are others and will be more. The alert teacher will constantly search for new and different recordings of groups and individuals. He will avoid highly commercialized recordings, especially of negro spirituals. There is nothing more sincere, moving, or beautiful than a good folk song that is presented in a natural, unincumbered setting. And there are few things more irritating—at least to these writers—than a "jazzed-up," "souped-up" spiritual or other folk song.

2. *Sacred music.* There are hundreds of sacred titles available for purchase. Unfortunately the number of acceptable recordings is relatively small. All too often the text is obnoxious, tune and harmonies are objectionable, or the performance

is in poor taste. So-called popular sacreds, such as "He," "I Believe," "The Man Upstairs," and the like have, in the writers' opinion, nothing to recommend them to anyone. For adolescents their value is completely negative.

A few reputable companies are making an effort to provide good, sensible recorded sacred music—both instrumental and vocal. For example, The Methodist Publishing House is bringing out new items as fast as is practical while giving careful attention to the quality of text, music, and performance.

Under proper guidance, junior youth will respond well to good recordings of oratorios. It is advisable to start with the best known of all—*The Messiah*—using the familiar choruses "Hallelujah," and "Lift up your heads." Such solos as "He was despised," "He shall feed his flock," and "Comfort ye" are serviceable but the other more florid arias are of doubtful value.

3. *"Classics."* This term is used with its accepted meaning—classic as opposed to popular. This whole area of vocal and instrumental music is rich and rewarding if carefully explored and exploited. For example, the story of Wagner's *Parsifal* makes a fine springboard for listening to much of that opera's great music. Certain selections from Mozart's *The Magic Flute*, though somewhat pagan in concept, are good for a church-school listening situation. Of particular interest is the beautiful and appealing prayer of the priest—"O Isis and Osiris."

Brahms wrote many fine sacred choruses and a few sacred solos. Hugo Wolf's "On looking at an old picture" and "Go forth, now sweet Mary" are hauntingly beautiful. A translation should be in the hands of the young people as they listen.

Junior youth will respond enthusiastically to good, carefully selected films and filmstrips. Materials must be selected with extreme care and equipment must be of very high caliber—

both sight and sound. The number of available films that can be used with this age is increasing rapidly. Early adolescents should never be shown a film that has not been previewed, however, despite the glowing descriptive material that may accompany it.

Being a romanticist, the youth is interested in creativity far beyond his generally accepted ability to write poetry and prose and to compose and arrange music. He enjoys working out "different" interpretations of hymns, using such devices as pantomime, tableaux, and rhythmic movement. The last named is not often popular with boys unless they had been introduced to it at an earlier age and had continued to use it. However, both sexes enjoy a related art—choral reading. (See page 118 for a discussion of choral reading).

It is extremely important that materials for singing be chosen with the interests and limitations of a particular group in mind. Music selected for a class of young girls may not interest the boys at all. If boys and girls are together the problem is compounded.

Ensembles of various sizes have many values for early adolescents. The girls' trio or sextet can be a fine musical group, giving pleasure to listeners, but giving much more to the participants. The niceties of good singing can be studied and various effects explored in a small ensemble. Because their voices are somewhat uncertain, junior-high boys are not so successful with quartets and trios; however, the boys' choir at this age can be exciting and rewarding.

Ideally a class of twelve- or thirteen-year-old boys should sing four-part music. In actual practice much of the singing will be unison and two parts because few such groups are able to sing even three parts consistently unless most of the boys have had better-than-average training in previous years. But whenever possible four classifications should be set up: *High, low* (these first two are unchanged), *changing,* and *baritone.* When there are only three use *high, changing,* and *low;* if two, merely call them *high* and *low.* In every case both range and *tessitura* must be carefully considered in the selection of music so that no voice will be strained.

The twelve- or thirteen-year-old girls' choir is capable of some very effective singing. Three-part music, properly arranged, is not beyond them. The voices are rather small, but the quality is clear and warm—in fact, very pleasing. Songs demanding extreme vocal agility must not be used; emphasis should be placed instead upon legato singing with occasional fast passages of short duration.

The mixed choir is perhaps the least effective at the junior high age, but a limited number of students, a shortage of teachers and/or teaching time, and other factors may make it necessary to depend upon such a group. The director of a mixed choir will need a great deal of patience, ability, and knowledge —especially of repertoire. Because all his energies and his full attention must be given to maintaining the choir's interest and to the development of an effective singing group, he should have the assistance of an excellent accompanist. He should himself play the piano only if competent help is not available.

The junior-high mixed choir can sometimes sing four part music in one of its varied forms (SATB, SSAB (T), and SAA (T) B), but SAB and two-part selections are much more practical because of the limitations of the voices.

Certain additional principles, if properly applied, can aid the teacher in the selection of songs for early adolescents.

1. Texts should be well written and meaningful, with a flowing rhythm far beyond the jingles of primary years. Junior youth are capable of responding to the very best poetry. Young

people will not give more than passing attention to texts that are shallow, meaningless, and/or jingly if they are properly introduced to more effective materials.

Texts should be concerned with adventure, people, life, mysticism, God, brotherhood—the world which beckons the adventurous spirit to go, to see, and to do. Love is interesting, but emotionalism tends to repel boys and sometimes girls. Standard show tunes, however, such as "Smoke gets in your eyes," from *Roberta* and most of the love songs from *Porgy and Bess* and *Show Boat,* are so well known that both boys and girls enjoy singing them, the love element seeming not to concern them greatly.

2. Rhythms must be varied. The steady beat of a marching song or of a folk dance should be contrasted with exciting Spanish-American syncopations. Even slow, calm music needs a flowing rhythm. Adolescents will not tolerate monotony unless it be deliberate monotony, such as in Ravel's "Bolero."

3. Melodies, too, must be varied. Under proper guidance the twelve- and thirteen-year-old will respond to almost any good melody provided it does not demand a great deal of vocal agility. The boy's voice is even less agile than the girl's. Scale- and chord-wise movement still has appeal, but boys and girls crave the thrill of chromaticism; augmented and diminished intervals please them, provided the patterns are sensible and musical. Great care must be exercised, however, to hold ranges and *tessitura* within the limitations of their voices. This one principle, when combined with the foregoing concepts, greatly restricts the amount of usable material. Not too many effective composers are concerned with—or have knowledge of—the early adolescent voice. The joy of singing an appealing melody can be permanently destroyed by a few seconds of strained voices and squeezed tones.

4. Harmonies may be rich and colorful or straightforward and plain. If his previous singing experience has been varied and reasonably complete he will respond to the lush color of Tchaikovsky, the brilliant harshness of Bartok, or the transparent beauty of Haydn. As with all matters—musical or otherwise—variety is his basic demand.

The comment made previously about folk song recordings that are in poor taste can be related to choral music. Arrangers and publishers are grinding out thousands of offensive arrangements of hymns, folk songs, and other kinds of music that, in the original form, have real beauty and are in good taste. Arrangements which depend upon excessive use of rhythmic and/ or harmonic devices will be rejected by the discriminating director.

The selections listed on pages 141 ff. have been used successfully with twelve- and thirteen-year-olds. A few are especially attractive to boys; girls will, as a rule, respond to any music that the boys like to sing. It is important to remember that the number of parts being sung has little or no bearing upon the effectiveness of the music or the enjoyment of the singers. A good, solid unison is exciting to sing and to hear, especially if the accompaniment is well composed and well played. An unaccompanied unison, such as the Niles setting of "I wonder as I wander," or MacGimsey's "Po' li'l Jesus Boy" can be equally thrilling.

It should be mentioned in passing that band and orchestra instruments can be used often to great advantage if performers are available within the group. Variety, added interest, and considerable incentive for increased practice by the young performers result from such use.

Because their bodies are in a state of uncertainty and change, junior youth tire easily. Their singing must be carefully paced with frequent interruptions and a wide variety of songs if vocal strain is to be avoided. The basis for successful adolescent singing is enjoyment. Good teaching will make the striving for goals just as exciting and pleasing as is their attainment. The wise teacher knows when to ignore poor tones, incorrect singing, and especially wrong notes. It must not be inferred that standards should be low—on the contrary they should be quite high—but they should be flexible. The adolescent is a daily illustration of the cliché that "success breeds success." These young people need encouragement; frequent failures cannot be allowed to dampen their enthusiasm. They cannot be pushed; they cannot even be crudely led. Teaching junior youth is indeed an adventure in learning.

chapter five
# The Ninth Grade

The fourteen-year-old has been called an "in-betweener." He is quite likely to be squarely in the middle of adolescence; in some public schools he is top man in the junior-high school (grades seven, eight, nine) ; in others he is the lowest of the lowly—a freshman (grades nine, ten, eleven, twelve) ; sometimes he is the underling of the hated sophomore (grades seven, eight; nine, ten; eleven, twelve) . In still another set-up he is also a poor freshman (grades nine, ten, eleven; twelve, thirteen, fourteen) .

Most textbooks include ninth graders in junior-high discussions. They are given passing attention in senior-high books, but no real effort is made to understand them. Since church schools—and choirs—are about equally divided between the junior-high (seven, eight, nine) and senior-high (nine, ten, eleven, twelve) plans, it seems advisable to look at the four-teen-year-old as an individual in his own right, who possesses many of the characteristics of the two preceding years and just as many of the following three. Much depends upon his place in the public schools. He will show more emotional, mental, and possibly physical maturity in the seven-eight-nine plan than in the nine-ten-eleven-twelve plan. The reason is fairly obvious; in the former he is the junior-high leader; faculty and students look to him for guidance. In the latter, however, as a freshman he is expected to be and therefore is, less than nothing! Many junior-high schools have a ninth-grade glee club which is the envy of seventh and eighth grades; just as many senior-high schools have a ninth-grade glee club which is of no great consequence because it is strictly preparatory. If no ninth-grade glee club is available, the fourteen-year-old will find it necessary to sing with the senior-high group, often with doubtful success.

Churches are as inconsistent in their treatment of the ninth grader as are the public schools. He may have to sing with a mixed-age junior-high choir; he may sing with the adult choir; the boys may be part of an extended-age boys' choir, sometimes including grades four through nine; the girls may be in a similar group, or in one less extended—seven, eight, and nine. Unfortunately we find that more often than not he is in *no* choir! He may have dropped out of music sometime during the preceding two years, or possibly earlier. There seems to be a relatively current opinion that boys must choose between athletics and music about this time and athletics naturally gain the most converts. It is too bad that both activities are not generally given a part in his very busy schedule, because a normal boy needs both. The virility of music must constantly be stressed if his interest is to be retained. Since he is inclined to associate music with women teachers, and therefore with femininity, it is important that more properly trained men assume responsibilities in this area.

The fourteen-year-old has advanced far beyond the twelve-year-old—physically, emotionally, mentally, socially, and musically—but the differences are of degree and not of kind. Keeping in mind that exceptions are to be expected, we can generalize with some degree of surity.

1. Boys are catching up with girls in height and social problems of the two preceding years are nearer to being solved. Romance is in the air!

2. Most girls' voices are sufficiently changed to give some indication of their ultimate development. Muscles are still young and growing, however, and lack endurance. The singing mechanism must be treated with care.

3. A very few boys' voices are reasonably well established. Most, however, are still insecure and therefore demand constant supervision.

4. Posture and support (breathing) are no more difficult to control than in previous years, but unceasing attention must be given to these problems. There is one difference—the fourteen-year-old is becoming interested in and proud of his body. He will accept posture and other health suggestions more easily than will his younger brothers and sisters. The ideas expressed in Chapter 4 can be expanded and given added emphasis.

5. Awkwardness remains a problem, but, perhaps it is not too serious. He is becoming acquainted with the potentialities as well as the limitations of his new body. Muscular and nerve tissues are a bit more secure; he is not quite so self-conscious. In all probability he is able to respond physically, with considerable success, to various rhythms which for the two previous years had caused him no end of difficulty. He can sing reasonably complicated passages involving syncopation and changing accents. A pattern such as the following has real meaning to him:

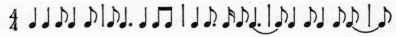

He can maintain a regular, unvarying beat—something quite impossible in the seventh grade and difficult in the eighth grade. Rhythmic movement is an attainable skill, to be enjoyed, not dreaded. Playing a drum is fascinating again, for the first time since his "childhood." If he plays piano or other instruments he discovers that his technique is improving noticeably, sometimes almost overnight. He makes a valuable contribution to school bands and orchestras and enjoys playing in numerous kinds of small ensembles. Girls' vocal trios and other vocal ensembles can be delightful to hear, and are obviously enjoyed by the participants. While the vocal potentialities of boys are still a bit limited, quartets and trios can be successful at this age, and they provide an important item of interest.

6. His hearing is probably more complete than it has ever been. He can distinguish between tones that are very similar in color, and his sense of pitch is probably quite acute. Fortunately he has the ability to reproduce—vocally—more of the sounds he hears and visualizes than in previous years. His singing mechanism is growing up. Tones are increasingly clean, mellow, and warm. Range is widening.

7. Because his interests and abilities are broadening, he wants to *do*. This ambition can be a problem; he may attempt tasks that are beyond his abilities. He will try to sing songs out of his range and/or demanding more maturity than he possesses. He likes to imitate others; he must not be permitted to attempt to duplicate the sounds of an adult singer—something he is sure to try, especially if he is a record fan.

Many churches consider it necessary to use ninth graders in the adult choir, and if given careful guidance these youngsters need not be harmed. Unfortunately, they are usually given little or no guidance. Thrown suddenly into the middle of a situation for which they are physically, emotionally, and musically unprepared, they try their best to sing as loudly as those around them, with unfortunate results to themselves as well as to the music. Since they crave attention they may obtain it by becoming generally obnoxious. The timid ones may retire completely within themselves. Girls will make a successful adjustment more often than boys. Most boys will quit in disgust within a short time. We must remember that the fourteen-year-old boy is not a tenor nor a bass—he may not even be a baritone—and the girl alto is really a soprano whose voice is lowering a bit. The true soprano is sometimes able to fit herself naturally into an adult choir, but only if she is encouraged to sing easily, freely, and correctly.

The falsetto voice is a saving grace for all boys who find themselves in an adult choir. The young tenor-to-be can handle the tenor line of most anthems if he makes it a habit to slip into and out of falsetto as a regular matter of procedure. The young baritone may need to do the same, but much less often. In all probability he will be more comfortable if he sings bass rather than tenor, provided he sings easily and does not at any time depress his voice box to reach the low tones. He may, however, be more comfortable with the tenors if he has an easy falsetto. The director must give his young men a great deal of personal attention and guidance as they seek to find themselves.

8. Because boys and girls work easily together at this age, mixed singing groups are usually advisable; but because of vocal limitations great care must still be exercised in the selection of materials. Ranges and *tessitura*—to be discussed later—are factors to be kept constantly in mind. Passages demanding great vocal agility may be impractical. Sopranos can sometimes handle technical patterns of considerable difficulty, girl altos rarely, and boys almost never. Melodies must be interesting. Perhaps more important, other parts should also be interesting. All too

often they are extremely monotonous. Harmonies may be simple or complex provided voice leading is such that all parts are easy to sing. Unaccompanied singing is not often practical because the voices lack the color, variety, and stability that *a cappella* music demands. While accompaniments should be more than simple duplication of parts, they should not be so florid as to be in bad taste. Woodwind, brass, and string groups are particularly effective with ninth-grade voices and are often easily available since many youth are effective participants in bands and orchestras.

9. Song texts may run almost the whole gamut of literary expression. "Love" is no longer taboo; adventure is still the center of attraction; rapidly expanding horizons of understanding just about eliminate all barriers, provided the texts are in good taste, aesthetically pleasing, and strengthened by appropriate music.

10. Everything said in Chapter 4 regarding recordings, films, and filmstrips remains true during the ninth grade, except that because of increased interest and understanding fewer restrictions need be observed.

Individual and group inconsistency remains a characteristic through the ninth grade but perhaps not to the extent that it was a problem during the seventh and eighth grades. For example, some voices will show no signs of changing. A few boys, and fewer girls, will not yet have entered puberty. Overall differences will vary from community to community and from year to year, depending to a certain extent upon environment and/or past experiences.

The mental acuity so noticeable in the seventh and eighth grades is even more obvious now and much more consistent. Those active imaginations are under better control and there is less wasted effort. The fourteen-year-old is almost reconciled to the added responsibilities of approaching adulthood, but he still looks back occasionally with a bit of longing upon the freedom and joys of childhood. He may even try to revert to his former status when severely provoked or frustrated.

His creative abilities are extremely high—perhaps higher in some ways than ever again. He performs well on instruments, writes plays and poetry, and arranges music rather effectively. It is interesting to notice that he is more likely to arrange than to compose because he enjoys exploring various combinations of sounds and his own compositions may not satisfy him.

Voices at fourteen differ somewhat from those at twelve and thirteen. The girl soprano will have a slightly higher range; G should be a comfortable tone, and an occasional A will do her no harm. The boy soprano will probably produce a tone that is increasing in size and warmth. His range may also be increasing. The girl's low voice, while still soprano in quality and lacking in the depth of a true contralto, has become a little bigger and possibly a little lower. Under no circumstances, however, should she abandon her high voice; even an adult contralto has a high C available, although not often attained. The budding young alto must continue to sing her D, E, and occasionally a light F in order to retain the top quality and range that should be hers for life. Tones are to be produced easily and freely, as in every other situation, with the word "let" firmly in mind. With proper posture and support and an easy jaw there need be no tension.

It is a generally accepted idea that adult and senior-high tenors are scarce. They need not be. As the changing boy voice moves downward from soprano to its matured level it should be given an opportunity to develop according to nature's plans. The falsetto must be used at every opportunity. Unfortunately we are inclined to push the voice down too fast and too far in order to obtain that "manly" bass quality. Most fourteen-year-old "changed" voices are light baritones. Every effort should be made to keep as much of the high voice as possible, subject only to the limitations of easy singing. The "tenor" part—really a high baritone—should rarely go above a D and never above an E flat, with the *tessitura* centering around G:

The lowest tone can be C, or possibly a very light, quick B flat.

Once in a very great while a real fourteen-year-old tenor appears. The writer was one, and he was indeed unfortunate because he was treated as a mature singer before he was sixteen. One never completely recovers from the effects of that treatment. He should have been encouraged to sing lightly and easily at all times and especially in his high voice, but instead he blasted away with his overgrown body until the rude awakening occurred a few years later.

The so-called bass voice at age fourteen is only a little heavier and a little lower—about a minor third—than is the "tenor." The young bass will lose his high voice, too, about this time unless he is encouraged to use it often—lightly and easily, however. His *tessitura* centers around an E flat:

He should sing almost as high—but not so frequently—as does the young tenor.

While quite rare, the ninth-grade bass does occur often enough to recognize that he exists and that provision must be made for him. Actually he is quite easy to care for and he is a decided asset to any youth choir. His range will be limited, and he will find it advisable to use his falsetto quite often. He is often able to sing a respectable low E flat, but without much power. His highest comfortable tone for several weeks or months may be only middle C, or even B flat. If he sings easily his higher tones will reappear and his lowest tones may deepen—if he is a real bass—or become even lighter if he is really a baritone.

Whatever the voice may be, it should not be forced, squeezed, driven, or confined. Good posture and support and free, easy singing will permit his vocal mechanism to grow naturally and his voice to move without interference along the way toward maturity.

The unchanged boy voice—high or low—poses the same problems as during the two preceding years and needs no further discussion at this point.

Vocalises are still quite valuable if used discreetly and purposefully. While descending scales and arpeggios will still help to develop vocal security throughout the entire range, other patterns can now be of value. But the young singers must understand the purposes for which vocalises are being used if the time and effort are not to be wasted. Certainly they are not intended to kill time nor to gather the choir together. They should serve to obtain relaxation of tensions; to develop good posture and support; to produce pure vowels and clean, accurate consonants; and generally to help the entire singing develop naturally.

Suggested vocalises in addition to those found in Chapter 4:

**1.**

Use with all pure vowels, legato and staccato. May also be used with *lah, loh, lee,* et cetera, and *mah, moh, mee,* et cetera. Sing no higher nor lower than is found to be easy and unstrained. Tempo should be fast, but not fast enough to sacrifice accuracy and quality.

**2.**

Same instructions as for number 1. May be repeated.

**3.**

Same instructions as for numbers 1 and 2.

To summarize: the fourteen-year-old deserves much special attention because of the "in-between" position he holds. He can be a real asset to the choir program provided he is, and has been, given proper guidance and encouragement. Whether he is in his own age choir, sings with the seventh and eighth grades, or participates in the adult choir, he is at a critical period in his musical and church life. More young people withdraw from church and choir during the ninth-grade than at any other age. We must accept him for what he is, let him develop what he has, and hope that his ultimate potential will be realized.

chapter six

# Grades Ten, Eleven, and Twelve

The senior-high student has been variously described as an adult with adolescent overtones and as an adolescent with adult overtones. Both statements are quite apt because he is a grown-up child looking forward with pleasurable anticipation to his new life while somewhat reluctantly looking backward at the "old life" he is leaving. He feels that the joys of adulthood are not unalloyed; responsibilities not always of his seeking will be his. The relative freedom he has known cannot continue; youthfulness will no longer be accepted as an excuse for his sometimes unconventional actions.

Mentally the fifteen-, sixteen-, and seventeen-year-old is potentially an adult. He can meet all the demands of mature reasoning. His only lack—an important one, however—is experience and knowledge. He is often a dynamic leader and will venture fast and far, sometimes beyond his ability to handle the situation. His limited experience creates problems of perspective; the "thing of the moment" is inclined to be the most important event in his life—an event for which he may wish to sacrifice other more real but somewhat distant values. He dislikes taking time to master the details demanded if perfection or near-perfection is to be attained—perfection in his studies, in singing, in playing an instrument, in athletics, and in almost any other area that may interest him. Expert teaching is needed if the dash man is to be kept at the monotonous task of springing from his starting blocks over and over and over, if the scientist-to-be is to complete all those tedious experiments, or if the young singer is to go through the rigamarole of technique exercises, diction study, and plain hard work that makes the difference between excellence and mediocrity. A high-school choir can be an exciting group to hear, but not without many previous hours of tedious attention to the details of good singing.

Planning for the future is both exciting and boring—exciting as he contemplates the opportunities that are his and boring as he struggles with the inconvenience and drudgery of realizing the opportunities. He is disturbed to discover that life has a way of interfering with living.

It is difficult to discuss separately the mind and emotions of the senior youth. He, himself, is unable to understand the motivating force behind most of his actions. Everything he says and does is affected almost equally by what he thinks and by what he feels. His emotions are basically adult in kind, but their intensity and duration are greatly different. Like the early teen he is still a bit mercurial, but this later teen is also volcanic—and one never knows just what may trigger an explosion. For example, if he is asked to sing selections that are not suited to his present equipment and needs he may react in various unpredictable ways, most of them unfortunate. It is virtually impossible for the teacher to superimpose his tastes and interests upon those of his young charges unless he has established a basis of similarity with theirs upon which he can work.

Love—in the guise of boy-girl romances—is important to

him. Love of a different kind is perhaps more important—the quiet, firm, unassuming love of parents and teachers. The former shows itself in the patterns of early courtship; the latter must depend upon mutual respect, confidence, and appreciation. His emotions are strongly affected by his adolescent-adult and adult-adolescent status. His hero worship tends to become more lasting, although "crushes" still occur, as certain TV and recording personalities so very well and profitably know.

He depends upon respected adults for firm guidance. But this guidance—and, to a certain extent, control—cannot be of the "apron-string" or dictator varieties. He needs to participate actively in the making of decisions regarding his welfare and conduct. He must know so well from past experiences that these decisions will be fair and unprejudiced that he will accept decisions he dislikes at the moment. If he has complete confidence in his teacher he will work hard on music that may possibly repel him at first, knowing that he will develop an appreciation for the music as he comes to know and understand it.

The "gang" tendency remains an item of concern because the need for social approval creates serious problems. Conformity in actions, attitudes, dress, morals, and speech is the rule of life. The alert teacher will take advantage of this characteristic rather than fight it. If the leaders become interested in his work the rest will follow along. Certainly he must not bemean himself in order to attract the leaders. He can, however, adjust his musical standards and his rehearsal techniques to fit the needs of the students until he has gained their respect and loyalty. Then he can gradually bring them along to the point where his standards and theirs are very close together.

The social values of a high-school choral group can be overemphasized. They are quite important, however, and should be given proper consideration. The benefits to each individual from producing thrilling, beautiful music as a group can be a big factor in the development of complete young men and women. Great care must be exercised lest, in a highly successful situation, the feeling spreads that "anyone who is anyone" simply must belong to such-and-such a choral organization. A false value of this sort can damage those who "make" the group as well as those who do not.

The physical characteristics of the senior youth are of continuing concern for teachers, parents, and youth. The problems are not nearly so serious as in the three preceding years, however. Most basic changes in body structure and functions have taken place; physical maturity has not yet been attained but it is well on its way. Boys are now—as a rule—taller than girls. They are not quite so awkward as they have been. The rate of growth of both sexes has slowed considerably. Girls and boys are able to get acquainted with themselves and with each other because height, weight, body and facial structure, and over-all appearance remain relatively unchanged for long periods of time. Voices are showing some stability; the uncertainties of early adolescence are decreasing in number and intensity. Psychological problems are fewer in number as personalities begin to emerge.

The senior youth is addicted to "causes," most of which are of brief duration. He has many heroes, both real and imaginary. His inquiring, inquisitive mind causes him many unpleasant moments, particularly when he questions the existence of God and wonders if Jesus ever lived. He *wants* to worship, but he feels his own inadequacies. He is inclined toward realism; because he despises hypocrisy, the hypocrisy that exists among his elders disturbs him greatly. While his church life may absorb him completely, he is often prone to hold himself somewhat aloof from religious activities. He may scorn church or church-school choir because they seem lacking in virility and significance. The boy—more so than the girl—may be accused by his associates of being a sissy if he attempts to practice his Christian beliefs. His tendency to go all the way in almost everything he does often leads him off on unusual tangents. Getting him back in line may not be easy.

The hysteria engendered by the "rock-and-roll" craze is a good illustration of his all-out tendency. Not long ago, the craze was called "jitterbugging"; the "Roaring Twenties" provided a setting for the "Charleston." Every generation has its own eccentricities, and music seems to provide a convenient outlet for them. The alert, successful teacher does not fight these abberations; he accepts them for what they are and concentrates upon providing something that is not only better, but that youth will accept.

Because music is an excellent vehicle for worship and because it provides a means of emotional release, the senior-high choir is an exceedingly important part of the church and church-school program. Unfortunately it is the one most often omitted. Youth needs the choir more than does the church. He, perhaps more than anyone else, should be encouraged to sing, and sing, and sing! Choirs, quartets, solos—in every possible combination and in many situations he will contribute to the happiness of others, but what is more important, he will make his own life richer than it can otherwise hope to be.

Musically speaking, fifteen-, sixteen-, and seventeen-year-olds are at an exciting period in their lives. They are able for the first time to respond physically to almost any kind of rhythmic structure. They can "keep time" accurately and reproduce difficult patterns. Many of them play instruments quite well; bands, orchestras, and choral groups are capable of excellent performances. The high-school choir has great potentialities. Color, pitch, and dynamics are no longer unattainable descriptive terms because these young singers actually understand, hear, and are able to react—on a reduced level—to all of the musical demands of good choral singing. By "reduced level" we mean that they should not be expected to sing so loudly, so high, so low, nor so long as adults. But just as a certain great woman pianist was able to produce exciting effects equal to those obtained by her larger, stronger masculine peers by reducing her entire range of dynamics a little—the softest a little softer, and the loudest not quite so loud—so the high-school choir director can re-create great musical moments as he judiciously directs his fine, pliable young singers.

It should be mentioned at this point that the senior youth who has had very limited musical experience will be at a considerable disadvantage in a group of well-trained singers. In all probability he has difficulty "carrying" or even hearing a part; his singing mechanism has not been developed and his voice is, therefore, unreliable and possibly unpleasant to hear. His appreciation of music is quite limited; it has never been just plain fun, but something mysterious and unattainable. Because he sees and hears others doing easily the things he finds difficult or impossible, he may adopt a "sour grapes" attitude and turn completely away.

We must emphasize, however, that his case is far from hopeless. His teacher will find it necessary to be patient and perseverant as, without seeming to do so, he gives the inexperienced student much personal attention and a great deal of encouragement. Criticism—even constructive criticism—will be used rarely and always with discretion. The important factor to remember is that the catching-up process can and should be made both enjoyable and challenging.

How does the teacher go about salvaging such a youngster? First of all, the student must *want* to sing. Perhaps the desire is well covered, in which case other students as well as the teacher can provide encouragement and incentive. The social aspects of a choral group can be used as a device to break down his resistance. As this hesitant prospect observes the obvious pleasure that others gain from participation, he may try a bit harder to overcome his hesitation.

Second, he should be seated with more experienced singers whose voice quality is similar to his. They should be encouraged to welcome this musically shy newcomer and to help him as inconspicuously as possible. Third, the teacher must use a few selections that are "aimed" at less experienced singers—music that is quite easy, tuneful, and that is built on a marked rhythmic structure. Fourth, the teacher must somehow find time to give special help wherever it is needed without neglecting his other singers.

The writers would prefer to believe that most senior youth will have had a great deal of musical experience prior to entering high school, but such is not the case. A group of twenty-five in the senior-high department of the average church will be divided about 15-10 among the girls and 8-17 among the boys, with the first figure representing those who have had a reasonable amount of singing experience.

In certain communities the balance will be much more favorable, and in others much less; the size of the community seems to have little to do with this musical state of affairs. It follows, then, that much of the teacher's (director's) time will be spent in "selling" these would-be musicians a new concept of music and singing. He will use every possible device, method, and kind of material that can help to attain what sometimes may appear to be an unattainable goal—young people who sing at least reasonably well, but what is more important, who enjoy their singing. There *must* be enjoyment, and a feeling of success is a basic ingredient of enjoyment.

Two facts should be kept constantly in mind in any discussion of high-school singers: Their voices are still changing, although usually at a slowed-down pace; and individual differences are the rule, not the exception. Girls' voices at this age may be divided with some degree of certainty into sopranos and light altos—not contraltos. Boys are, on the other hand, quite likely to be 70 per cent baritones, 10 per cent tenors, 10 per cent light basses, and 10 per cent completely unchanged or beginning to change. Girls will be able to sing passages demanding considerable vocal agility; boys' voices will be a little less agile, although much more flexible than during the past three years—provided the music remains within a comfortable range.

The unchanged boy voice poses serious psychological as well as musical problems. The slow-to-mature youth is inclined to be quite conscious of his physical deficiencies; if we call him a soprano we add insult to injury. While technically incorrect, the writer has found it beneficial to call him a high tenor. It is often a simple matter to write in a special part that is basically the tenor line, although lacking the lower notes—G or below. He must be encouraged to sing easily. Sometimes the tenor part will need little or no adjusting. He can sing soprano, but only if his disposition is such that he is not disturbed by doing so. The youth who wants to sing must be permitted—encouraged —to sing. The resourceful director will see that he has the opportunity. If he shows musical talent, he may be given an instrument to play in the band or orchestra. Such devices as making him librarian or choir secretary can be used—but with great diplomacy.

Here is another point for emphasis: Every singer has a potential range, when he reaches vocal maturity, far greater than is generally accepted. Because of the lack of understanding on the part of choir directors and voice teachers this potential is almost never realized. There are two opposite and equally harmful practices in existence today: Pushing the young voice as high and as low as possible, and as fast as possible; or taking the path of least resistence and making no effort at all to expand the ranges. Young adult sopranos who sing G above "high" C—or even higher—and down to the contralto G need not be a rarity; contraltos with a free, usable "high" C; tenors with a low A flat and a high D flat; baritones with an F to B flat range; and basses who can sing a low B flat and a tenor G *should* all be relatively common among well-trained amateurs as well as among professionals.

Much of the damage—in terms of limitations—is done in the years between fourteen and eighteen when attitudes and physical, mental, and emotional habits are so firmly ingrained that their later adjustment becomes difficult if not impossible. Let us examine the following chart of ranges for high-school students and for adults.

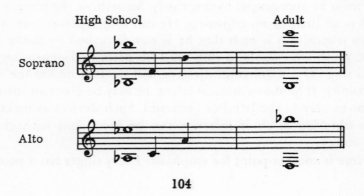

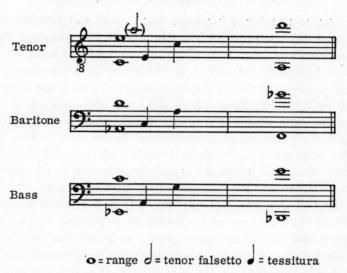

o = range  ♩ = tenor falsetto  ♪ = tessitura

We grant that the adult ranges are idealistic; however, the unrealized potential is present in many, many voices. We grant, also, that for practical purposes, most high-school sopranos should be expected to sing above A flat only on rare occasions. Many will feel uncomfortable above an F or G, or lower than a D. Most altos, baritones, and basses should be somewhat more limited than the chart indicates. Tenors, however, can use their falsetto quality easily and effectively and sing as high as A or B flat without strain. The tenor falsetto is a valuable aid in the development of the high voice; its proper use should be encouraged. Actually the falsetto can be gradually increased in size and warmth until it becomes a true head voice. It is unfortunate that some teachers are hesitant to encourage the use of this valuable part of the male voice. Not only does it provide the young singer with several easy tones that he could not otherwise sing, it also keeps his high voice open and flexible until such time as it becomes sufficiently mature to produce a *mezza voce* quality and later, a so-called full-voiced head tone.

Parenthetically, the writer is disturbed by a commonly accepted tendency to divide the voice into sections, some of which are to be ignored while others are used and developed. The singer has *one* voice. There are areas where certain minor changes are made in production and in resonance, but these changes will occur naturally and easily and the total voice will become effective if attention is constantly given to the premise based on the word "let," and explained in Chapter 4.

If the fact that every singer has only one voice is accepted, it follows that no part of it should be neglected. High-school sopranos and tenors are quite prone to avoid the chest voice entirely because it is coarse and breathy. Such avoidance was advisable in earlier years, but it is not a good practice at this age. All senior youth should be encouraged to investigate carefully their low voices and to use them occasionally. While sustained loud singing in a chest quality is not now advisable, the low voice will later become a real asset—something upon which the singer can build a fuller, richer quality throughout his entire range.

As has been previously mentioned, *tessitura* is perhaps more important than range. Young voices should not be expected to sing even medium-high tones for any extended period of time. Most of the singing should be done in the middle of the range.

The properly motivated high-school student is inclined to be a perfectionist. It is very important, then, that he be given as much instruction in proper techniques of singing as time and interest will permit. The director must know about and be able to explain and demonstrate correct posture, correct support, good tone production, and sensible diction. The concepts discussed in *Basic Principles of Singing* [1] can be applied to high-school singers, but always with due regard for their emotional, physical, and musical limitations. It is at this point that many teachers fail because they ignore the adolescent characteristics of this adolescent-adult. Endurance, range, and volume are *not* at an adult level, and while the color potential is becoming evident, it is not yet of adult proportions.

It is vitally important that high-school students develop proper posture and support in order to prevent the growth of throat, jaw, face, and body tensions. (See illustrations pp. 75, 76.) Voice teachers and choral directors use much energy and spend much time undoing bad habits that result from incorrect posture and support before they can do any positive teaching. Most of these bad habits are formed between ages fourteen and nineteen. It follows, then, that these years are critical years for the developing singer. A mirror and a tape recorder will provide help that is especially valuable just now. The student should be encouraged to watch critically and impersonally for signs of tension. It is not easy for adults to watch impersonally, and it is extremely difficult for youth to sing in front of a mirror without becoming embarrassed to the point of laughing or giggling. It can be done, however, if the teacher will perservere, in firm but kindly fashion. It is necessary only for the student's curiosity to be sufficiently aroused for him to become a mirror addict—at least in relation to his singing.

What can the singer look for? A tight, immobile jaw or a constantly moving jaw that "chews" every vowel; corded muscles in the neck and face; lips that are tense and too close together; a raised head or one that moves up and down with the pitch; rounded shoulders; a slumped body; a heaving upper chest. His goal should be to appear comfortable as he sings, with his whole

[1] Rice, *op. cit.*

107

person radiating a kind of springy resilience that has its origin in reliable posture and correct breathing.

A good tape recorder, especially if used in conjunction with a mirror, will tell the singer by aural means what the mirror tells him through his eyes. He will be able to hear the difference between a good tone and one that is not so good. He may be reluctant to accept the recorder's verdict at first; no one hears his own voice correctly—at least until he has been trained to do so—and it is unfortunate that what sounds best to the singer is often a very poor tone. The converse is equally true. Much careful study of his recorded voice will enable the student to hear himself with reasonable accuracy.

All young singers must be encouraged to sing by "feel" more than by ear. It is safe to assure the student that a tone which feels free, easy, vibrant, and strong is almost certain to be a good tone. One problem must be faced, however, if the singer has been moderately successful while singing incorrectly. As his bad habits are broken down, he may actually sound less pleasing during the time he is acquiring better methods of tone production. He is almost certain to feel insecure. Consider, for example, the difficulties of a baseball player whose batting average is good (260) despite very poor form. When his coach makes him change to a more effective form his average is almost sure to drop, but only for a time, after which he becomes the 300+ hitter that his ability predicted. Similar examples can be made of track, basketball, and other activities—whichever one is most familiar to the student. It is, of course, necessary that the young singer (or athlete) have enough confidence in his teacher to accept his teaching despite the temporary regression.

The successful director obtains beautiful, effective singing from his high-school students by scaling everything to meet their needs. As indicated previously, loud passages need not be so loud when soft passages are very, very soft. Music demanding adult tonal effects should not be used. Brilliant, high tenor or somber, low bass and contralto parts must be rewritten or the music discarded. Emphasis should be placed upon brightness, accuracy, blend, and technical facility. Selections that tend to be quite emotional need to be handled with considerable restraint because youth may sometimes understand and respond to the extent that their voices are harmed. For example, portions of "A German Requiem" by Brahms are perhaps technically within the grasp of high-school singers. The emotional demands are at times far beyond their capabilities, however. Another example is Bach's "Passion according to St. Matthew." A large, competent youth choir *can* sing those great choruses, but if the writers' reaction and the observed reaction of others is a reasonably safe guide, this great work is not to be recommended for use with younger than college-age singers.

It seems advisable to mention the tendency of directors to use simplified versions of great works, such as Handel's *Messiah,* because of community pressure or because of an honest desire to give their young people the experience of singing selections from "the masters." While it is perhaps advisable to protect young voices in such a fashion, the writers are inclined to believe that a few years of waiting will make the experience much more meaningful. So much good music within the technical and emotional grasp of youth is available that attempting the unattainable is really unnecessary. Occasionally, high-school students can combine with adults in an effective and beneficial performance of music that is otherwise out of their vocal reach. They must be cautioned, however, and cautioned frequently, to sing easily and not to try to keep up with the older singers.

Youth is impatient. The desire to move fast—to become adult—is often a musical liability unless properly channeled by a wise teacher. Youth listens to an adult choir and attempts to sing as adults do; youth observes a TV star whose style is the antithesis of correct singing and trys to imitate him. The teacher must always be ready with interesting, challenging materials and procedures to counteract these and other unfortunate influences, keeping his impatient and talented young people happily busy with productive work that is on their physical, emotional, and musical level.

Because of the popularity of TV and records, a good listening program for youth is perhaps even more important than in earlier years. The use of records was explored in each of the preceding chapters, but the emphasis in the present discussion is so different that it is almost a new subject. In the primary grades the word of the teacher is law and never to be contradicted, even by parents! His presentation of music, and particularly of recorded music, is simplified by this fact. Juniors are a little less prone to accept without question everything the teacher gives them, but they are still very receptive. The first actual resistance is usually encountered in the seventh grade. If handled properly even this resistance can be overcome completely so that it ceases to be a matter of concern.

The senior youth poses an entirely different problem, however. He is "from Missouri," and he will remain "from Missouri"! He accepts nothing except on the basis of his own wishes, likes, and dislikes. While the early adolescent resembles a piece of mercury and merely avoids that which he wishes not to accept, senior youth is inclined to "take a stand" and become the proverbial immovable object if he is pushed toward anything—even in matters of which he secretly approves!

The high-school director must recognize the need to proceed wisely and to "make haste slowly" in planning the listening program. Titles, artists, and reproducing equipment must be selected with great care and understanding. Any obvious attempt to substitute Bach for "boogie," Rachmaninoff for "rock-and-roll," or Palestrina for "progressive jazz" will fail even before it starts—in singing, too, for that matter. But he need not be obvious if he carefully selects and just as carefully presents excellent recordings of good music having characteristics which will appeal to youth. For example, the Pavanne (second movement) from Morton Gould's "American Symphonette Number Two" has an easily followed *ostinato* bass (boogie-woogie?) as has also Chopin's "Polonaise in A-flat Major." Gershwin used the same device in his second and third "Preludes." Ravel's "Bolero" is rhythmically exciting to the musically uninitiated. "Scaramouche," by Milhaud, is both rhythmically and melodically pleasing and easy to listen to. The jazz element is present in several of Aaron Copland's works, notably his "El Salon Mexico." "Symphonie India," by Carlos Chavez, is so full of syncopation that it will excite the most blasé listener.

Records made by the singing groups mentioned on page 79 will have particular appeal to high-school students because they can sing many of the songs they hear without attempting to sound like adults. Many fine so-called "classical" singers have made recordings of good popular music. Dorothy Kirsten is a fine example of one who is equally at home in either field. Ezio Pinza proved many times during his long career that great artists can sing many kinds of music effectively and musically. His "South Pacific" is, of course, a "classic" in another sense of the word; the youth who learns to enjoy this recording will be quite likely to accept Pinza's "Don Giovanni." Eileen Farrell sings, with good style, a haunting "blues" and an equally effective art song or aria. She has successfully worked with, and even substituted for, Louis "Satchmo" Armstrong.

Film and filmstrips are particularly valuable teaching aids

for senior youth. The amount and quality of effective materials is increasing rapidly. Used with discretion, the combination of sight and sound can enrich the whole program of music—provided the equipment is of very high quality.

Senior-high students can profit from voice lessons—class or private—but only if the teacher thoroughly understands what he is doing. It is not wise to ask someone whose whole experience has been with adults to teach adolescents how to sing better. He may be successful, even famous, but unless he knows and is able to use the limitations as well as the assets of the fifteen-, sixteen-, and seventeen-year-old he is quite likely to be, himself, a limiting factor in their growth.

He must always remember that, however mature they may sound, these young voices are still changing because the whole singing mechanism will continue the process of maturation for several years to come. Boys and girls are alike in this respect, yet differ in one important and little understood way. The boy's body, including his abdominal muscles, is probably far ahead of his voice box in the growth process. In fact his body may be strong enough to do lasting harm to the tone producing mechanism. The girl's situation is exactly the opposite—her voice box is probably far ahead of her supporting muscles, and she is therefore prone to use a squeezing action of the throat to supplement her inadequate support. This problem is quite obvious when she sings too high and/or for too long a period of time.

Both boys and girls must be shown by visual and aural means how to produce tones with a balanced effort—the correct amount of body pressure for the condition of the tone producing mechanism. This matter of balanced effort remains a problem throughout a performer's entire singing life and may determine more than any other factor the length of his career. It will, of course, affect his over-all success as well.

Another problem that the teacher of adults may not recognize is that of resonance. Few senior youth are able to produce tones that give more than a good hint of their potential resonance. Bones and cartilage are soft and growing; resonance areas in the head, throat, and chest are changing in composition, in size, and in shape. While a few of the young singer's "better" notes may resound with overtones, most of them will be relatively simple in structure. An even scale is the goal of all singers, but high-school students will become thoroughly frustrated and confused if an issue is made of this matter because their mechanism is just not ready to be consistent! The teacher must help his students to produce tones which are unincumbered by unbalanced effort, by tensions, or by any kind of interference such as may result if a wrong idea of "placing" a tone is permitted to develop. It is better to avoid using the term "placement" because the singer may unconsciously try to "put" his voice somewhere instead of understanding that he must "let" it find the proper resonance areas. The writers prefer to use the term "focus" for the reason that less action is thereby implied.

Youth respond positively to the challenge of developing their voices. They will even practice their vocalises occasionally! Simple scales—five, nine, and eleven notes in both ascending and descending patterns—help to develop accuracy and facility and to extend their ranges. Arpeggios are also effective for the same purposes. A sequence of vowel sounds, such as *ah, ay, ee, oh, oo,* or of words sung on one pitch, or possibly as an arpeggio, will aid in bringing good focus and an even quality to their singing. (See pages 73 ff.) Material contained in the sections on "Vocalises" found in *Basic Principles of Singing* can be applied with discretion to high school students.

113

Additional vocalises suitable for use by senior youth.

ah   ay   ee   oh   oo   oh   ay   ee   ah

Sing with a continuous, flowing tone, with each vowel appearing in full bloom out of the preceding vowel. Use this vocalise to explore both high and low areas, but avoid strain.

The   day   is   calm

Use this exercise to eliminate excessive jaw movement and to encourage clean, active lip and tongue movement. The tone should flow from vowel to vowel. Sing within a comfortable range. Use various combinations of words to solve particular problems. For example, "What did he do?" can be sung with *no* jaw movement.

ee   ah -----------------------------------

Start with a good, firm tone and slur it up with the breath providing the lift. Use within a comfortable range and with various combinations of vowels. If support is adequate and the singing mechanism free of tension, the upper voice may be explored with this vocalise.

The junior youth may occasionally benefit from solo singing

but only on rare occasions because he is neither vocally nor emotionally ready to sing alone. The senior youth, on the other hand, is ready to do a great deal of solo singing. The resourceful teacher will use interesting solos as teaching devices while at the same time stimulating his students to more effective vocal activity. It is unfortunate that unexciting songs, hackneyed beyond belief and entirely lacking in youth appeal are the customary and accepted vocal diet of most young singers. Teachers are either too lazy to find interesting materials, or they lack the ability to do so. Solos should be of good quality textually and musically and able to satisfy and to challenge the young singer. The writer has often served as a critic at high school festivals; his accumulation of "horrible examples" is extensive. Two such examples will suffice: (1) Schumann's "The Two Grenadiers" sung by a sweet-faced ninth-grade boy whose clear soprano voice carefully proclaimed "but I've a wife and child at home on me for bread relying"; (2) The familiar and too-well-known "Asleep in the deep" sung by a girl who struggled with her light soprano voice to complete both stanzas, two refrains and the coda which "ding-dongs" down the scale to a bass F.

The same principles that govern the selection of music for adults will apply to music for senior youths. The poetry—good and sensible, properly strengthened by logical melodic, harmonic, and rhythmic structure; range and *tessitura*—correct for each voice; voice leading—musically correct and easily singable. Perhaps more than at any other age variety is demanded by fifteen-, sixteen-, and seventeen-year-olds—variety in text, color, rhythm, harmony, melody, and style. Senior youth will enjoy and therefore sing easily and effectively a wider variety of materials than will any other age group, including adults. Folk songs of all lands, art songs, songs of Bach, pre-Bach, Handel, Mozart, Beethoven, Schubert, Brahms, Strauss (both Richard and Johann), Milhaud, Copland, Stravinsky, Pfautsch, Love-lace—any music that is well written, well composed, well arranged, and within his vocal grasp can answer his needs effectively if he is properly guided and motivated. Most of the selections listed on pages 154 ff. have been used successfully with high-school students. The resourceful teacher will search unceasingly for more.

In addition, the music listed on pages 144 ff. will provide a new kind of satisfaction as senior youth discover beautiful effects not attainable by junior youth. Good music is not necessarily difficult music, and difficult music is not always good music.

It is dangerous to expect too much of young people; it is equally dangerous to expect too little. Youth demands a challenge. He needs to strive for goals that are always being moved ahead. He epitomizes the statement that "A man's reach should ever exceed his grasp." It is necessary that he succeed, and often, but success that comes too easily is no success at all.

Another danger, often ignored, is that of trying to "keep up with the Jonses." No director should select his music in terms of an organization other than his own. While the titles listed by the authors have been used successfully, each director must, himself determine whether or not a particular selection is right for his students.

Ideally the attainments of high-school singers can be measured in terms of their near-adult status. They are capable of delightful sectional and full-choir unisons; they can sing effectively in four, six, and eight parts. Their interpretations are full of dynamic and color contrast; they can master extremely difficult rhythmic structures. Careful attention must be given, however, to their vocal limitations. Ranges are important; *tessitura* is more important. Because of these limitations it is necessary that all parts be interesting and challenging. A monotonous tenor, alto, or bass line will create all kinds of musical and personal problems for the director.

Three-part music for mixed voices (SAB) and sometimes four part in the guise of SSAB or SAAB are receiving increasing attention. A little of it is good, some passable, and much quite poor. In their efforts to simplify, arrangers and composers often produce music that sounds contrived, especially when the selection was originally designed for other combinations of voices. The baritone line of an SAB selection can be quite musical, interesting, and within the vocal and musical grasp of young tenors and baritones. Quite often it is not. The writer has found it necessary to discard hundreds of SAB titles for every one that he could use.

Girls, alone, sound best with three-part music, boys with three or four. Both enjoy and do well in various mixed or unmixed small ensembles, accompanied and unaccompanied. Unisons, unisons with descant, and two-part music sound well and are pleasing to sing provided the accompaniment is well written and well played. Unaccompanied folk songs can also be effective.

The prejudiced attitude long held by choral directors against the use of unusual accompanying instruments is fast being broken down. A well-played guitar, dulcimer, accordian, or even a mouth organ (French harp) can add variety, beauty, and interest to choral singing.

Senior youth enjoy preparing and presenting cantatas and operettas. The number of such publications is enormous, but the number of good ones is quite small. The director must, therefore, be very certain that the time given to such activity is not taken from something of greater value.

Many directors are discovering the benefits of the high-school speech choir. To those who say that they have no time for anything new others reply by emphasizing the time-saving values of a speech choir. Improved diction is an obvious result; the attainment of a better concept of dynamics and tone color is equally significant. Young people enjoy the challenge of obtaining choral effects without the use of music. A few minutes may profitably be taken from each rehearsal for the study of this interesting and different way of projecting ideas and emotions.

With high-school students, "practical attainments" and "ideal attainments" are a bit difficult to separate. Because every choir or glee club has its own personality, the potential of each one must be properly evaluated by the director as he establishes standards, selects materials, and determines procedures. With one group he will exceed even "ideal" attainments; with another he will struggle in vain to reach minimum standards. Much depends upon his adaptability, his knowledge of methods and materials, and his love for and understanding of these delightful, challenging, exciting, almost-adults that we call senior youth.

The writers have been a bit rough at times in their evaluation of current practices in the handling of the voices of children and youth. Actually the situation is a hopeful one. More children are being trained in music under the guidance of competent teachers than at any previous period. More adults are singing in church choirs than ever before, and this number will continue to grow as children move toward adulthood through an increasingly effective music program in churches and schools.

If nothing else is remembered from the preceding pages, the writers hope that two basic ideas will be accepted and applied: *Singing is for everybody, and singing should be fun!*

# RESOURCES
## BOOKS, ARTICLES, AND RECORDINGS

### Books

Andrews, Frances M., and Joseph A. Leeder. *Guiding Junior High School Pupils in Music Experiences.* Englewood Cliffs, N. J.: Prentice-Hall, Inc., 1953.

Andrews, Gladys. *Creative Rhythmic Movement for Children.* Englewood Cliffs, N. J.: Prentice-Hall, Inc., 1954.

Association for Childhood Education, 1200 Fifteenth Street, Washington, D. C.:
*Children and Music,* 1948.
*International Nursery School Portfolio,* 1953.
*Music for Children's Living,* 1955.

Baldwin, Lillian. *A Listener's Anthology of Music.* Vols. I and II. New York: Silver Burdett Company, 1948.

_____. *Music for Young Listeners. The Green Book, The Crimson Book, The Blue Book.* New York: Silver Burdett Company, 1951. (Companion records are available for each volume.)

Bartholomew, Wilmer T. *Acoustics of Music.* Englewood Cliffs, N. J.: Prentice-Hall, Inc., 1942.

Bernstein, Martin. *Introduction to Music.* Englewood Cliffs, N. J.: Prentice-Hall, Inc., 1950.

Brown, Helen A., and Harry J. Heltman, editors. *Choral Readings for Fun and Recreation.* Philadelphia: The Westminster Press, 1956.

————. *Choral Readings from the Bible.* Philadelphia: The Westminster Press, 1957.

Cain, Noble. *Choral Music and Its Practice.* New York: M. Witmark & Sons, 1932.

Christy, Van A. *Glee Club and Chorus.* New York: G. Schirmer, Inc., 1940.

Coleman, Satis. *Your Child's Music.* New York: John Day Company, 1939.

Davison, Archibald T. *Choral Conducting.* Cambridge, Mass.: Harvard University Press, 1940.

Driver, Ann. *Music and Movement.* London: Oxford University Press, 1936.

Dykema, Peter W. and Hannah Cundiff. *School Music Handbook.* Boston: Summy-Birchard Publishing Company, 1955.

Egbert, Marion S. *Keyboard Experience, A Handbook for Classroom Teachers.* New York: Bourne, Inc.

Eile, Marjorie, and Leila Davis. *Carols for Acting.* London: Novello, 1951.

Faulkner, Anne Shaw. *What We Hear in Music.* Camden, N. J.: RCA Victor Company, 1931.

Fields, Victor A. *The Singers Glossary.* Boston: Boston Music Company, 1947.

Fishburn, Hummel. *Fundamentals of Music Appreciation.* New York: Longmans, Green & Company, 1955.

Fox, Lillian, and Thomas Hopkins. *Creative School Music.* New York: Silver Burdett Company, 1936.

Fuhr, Hayes M. *Fundamentals of Choral Expression.* Lincoln, Neb.: University of Nebraska Press, 1944.

Gesell, Arnold, *et al. The First Five Years of Life.* New York: Harper & Brothers, 1940.

Henry, Nelson B., editor. *Basic Concepts in Music Education.* Fifty-seventh Yearbook of the National Society for the Study of Education. Chicago: University of Chicago Press, 1958.

Hoggard, Lara. *Improving Music Reading in the Choral Rehearsal.* Delaware Water Gap, Pa.: Shawnee Press, 1947.

Howerton, George. *Technique and Style in Choral Singing.* New York: Carl Fischer, Inc., 1957.

Huls, Helen Steen. *The Adolescent Voice; A Study*. New York: Vantage Press, 1957.

—————. *Song List for Adolescent Voices; Beginning Students*. Mimeographed by the author; St. Cloud State College, St. Cloud, Minn., 1959.

Ingram, Madeline D. *Organizing and Directing Children's Choirs*. Nashville: Abingdon Press, 1959.

Jacques, Reginald. *Voice-Training in Schools*. London: Oxford University Press, 1945.

Jones, Archie N., editor. *Music Education in Action*. Englewood Cliffs, N. J.: Allyn and Bacon, Inc., 1960.

Jones, Archie N., and Lois and Raymond Rhea. *First Steps to Choral Music*. New York: Bourne, Inc., 1957.

Krone, Beatrice Perham. *Music in the New School*. Chicago: Neil A. Kjos Music Company, 1950.

Krone, Max T., *The Chorus and Its Conductor*. Chicago: Neil A. Kjos Music Company, 1945.

Lamperti, Giovanni. *Vocal Wisdom*. Published by the editor, William E. Brown. Distributor: L. Strongin, 22 Stoddard Place, Brooklyn, N. Y., 1953 (1931).

Landeck, Beatrice. *Children and Music*. New York: William Sloane Associates, Inc., 1952.

Leeder, Joseph A., and William S. Haynie. *Music Education in the High School*. Englewood Cliffs, N. J.: Prentice-Hall, Inc., 1958.

Lovelace, Austin C., and William C. Rice. *Music and Worship in the Church*. Nashville: Abingdon Press, 1960.

McKenzie, Duncan. *Training the Boy's Changing Voice*. New Brunswick, N. J.: Rutgers University Press, 1956.

McMillan, L. Eileen. *Guiding Children's Growth Through Music*. Boston: Ginn and Company, 1959.

Marvel, Lorene. *Music Resources Guide*. Minneapolis: Schmitt, Hall, & McCreary Company, 1961.

Mathews, Paul W. *You Can Teach Music*. New York: E. P. Dutton & Company, 1953.

Michigan Education Association. *Essentials in Junior High School Music Education*. Lansing, Michigan (935 N. Washington Ave.).

Miller, P. J. *Youth Choirs*. New York: Harold Flammer, Inc., 1953.

Missouri State Department of Education. *Instruction in Applied Music*. Publication No. 80, 1951. Jefferson City, Missouri.

Morsch, Vivian Sharp. *The Use of Music in Christian Education*. Philadelphia: The Westminster Press, 1956.

Mursell, James L. *Music and the Classroom Teacher*. New York: Silver Burdett Company, 1951.

*Music for Living.* New York: Silver Burdett Co., 1956-59. (A series of song books and teacher's manuals for kindergarten through junior high.)

New York State Education Department. *Handbook for Applied Music.* Albany, 1956.

Nordholm, Harriet, and Carl O. Thompson, *Keys to Teaching Elementary School Music.* Minneapolis: Paul A. Schmitt Music Company, 1949.

Nye, Robert E., and Vernice T. Nye. *Music in the Elementary School.* Englewood Cliffs, N. J.: Prentice-Hall, Inc., 1957.

Rice, William C. *Basic Principles of Singing.* Nashville: Abingdon Press, 1961.

Roark, Genevieve. *Choral Teaching at the Junior High Level.* Chicago: Hall & McCreary, 1947.

Roggensack, D. *Pertinent Factors in Monotone Correction.* Washington, D. C.: Music Educators National Conference, 1939.

Scott, Ch. Kennedy. *Madrigal Singing.* London: Oxford University Press, 1931.

Shakespeare, William. *The Art of Singing.* Bryn Mawr, Penn.: The Oliver Ditson Company, 1898, rev. 1921.

Sheehy, Emma Dickson. *There's Music in Children.* New York: Henry Holt and Co., 1946.

Stanley, Douglas. *The Science of Voice.* New York: Carl Fischer, Inc., 1932.

Stanley, Douglas, and J. P. Maxfield. *The Voice and Its Production and Reproduction.* New York: Pitman Publishing Corporation, 1933.

Stringham, Edwin John. *Listening to Music Creatively.* Englewood Cliffs, N. J.: Prentice-Hall, Inc., 1946.

Thomas, Edith Lovell. *Music in Christian Education.* Nashville: Abingdon-Cokesbury, 1953.

Thorne, Margaret. *The Young Child and His Music.* New York: Arts Cooperative Service, 1950.

Turfery, Cossar, and King Palmer. *The Musical Production.* New York: Pitman Publishing Corporation, 1953.

Vennard, William. *Singing: The Mechanism and the Technic.* Los Angeles: Published by the author, 1950.

Westerman, Kenneth N. *Emergent Voice.* (2nd edition). Ann Arbor, Mich.: Privately published, 1955.

Whittlesey, Federal Lee. *A Comprehensive Program of Church Music.* Philadelphia: The Westminster Press, 1957.

Wolfe, I. W., *et al.*, editors. *Together We Sing.* Chicago: Follett Publishing Company, 1955-59. (A series of song books and teacher's manuals for kindergarten through junior high.)

Wright, Frances. *Elementary Music Education.* New York: Carl Fischer, Inc., 1941.

## Articles

*American Childhood,* published by Milton Bradly Company, Springfield, Mass.

Corrigan, G., "Monotone," January, 1944.

*American Music Teacher, The,* published by the Music Teachers National Association, 775 Brooklyn Avenue, Baldwin, New York.

Lemonds, William W., "Church Youth Choirs," November-December, 1958.

Smith, J. Dayton, "The Boy's Changing Voice in the Four Part High School Chorus," November-December, 1956.

/ *Bulletin, The,* published by the National Association of Teachers of Singing, Suite 905, 2930 Sheridan Road, Chicago 14, Illinois.

Johnen, Louis J., "Singable English," December, 1959.

Keller, Esther, "Vocal Problems in the High School Vocal Program," February, 1957.

Koppel, Elia, "Freedom of Voice Production," May, 1956.

Rice, William C., "The Abuse of Very Young Voices," May, 1957.

Ross, William E., "The High Voice Mechanism," May-June, 1953.

Thomson, Virgil, "Singing English," May-June, 1953.

*Church Musician, The,* published by the Sunday School Board of the Southern Baptist Convention, 127 Ninth Avenue, North, Nashville 3, Tennessee.

Unit for Beginner Music Activity, each issue.

Unit for Junior Choir, each issue.

Unit for Primary Choir, each issue.

*Music Educators Journal,* published by the Music Educators National Conference, 1201 Sixteenth Street, N. W., Washington 6, D. C.

/ Bray, Bruce, "Making Music Enjoyable for the Junior High Boy," February-March, 1956.

D'Andrea, Frank, "Music and the Adolescent," February-March, 1961.

Rayme, Kenneth, "The Tape Recorder: A Second Teacher," January, 1961.

Ross, William, "The Importance of Good Technique in Singing," September-October, 1961.

Sur, William R., "Music for Teenagers," November-December, 1960.

———, "The Proper Care and Feeding of Changing Voices," November-December, 1961.

Swanson, Frederick J., "When Voices Change," February-March, 1960.
Zimmerman, George H., "Listen!" Summer, 1961.
*Music Journal,* 157 West 57th Street, New York 19, New York.
Snyder, Alice M., "Creating Music With Children," January, 1958.
*Music Ministry,* published by The Graded Press, 201 Eighth Avenue, South, Nashville 3, Tennessee.
Alford, Muriel, "Music for Juniors," October, 1959-September, 1961.
Branton, T. Ray, "The Junior Hi Choir," April-August, 1960.
Burns, William, "Youth Choirs," October, 1959-March, 1960.
Carlisle, Helen, "Music for Kindergarten," March, 1960; November, 1961.
Cloud, Fred, "Children's Choirs," October, 1961.
Gessner, Muriel, "Music for Juniors," October, 1961-March, 1962.
Goddard, Carrie Lou and Edwin, "Music for Primaries," May-September, 1960.
Ingram, Madeline, "Music for Primaries," October, 1959-April, 1960.
Kalstrom, Christine, "Creative Arts with Teen-agers," October, 1961.
Lovelace, Austin C.
"Consonants," March, 1960.
"The Singing Voice," January, 1960.
"Vowels and Diphthongs," February, 1960.
Maramarco, Phyllis, "Music for Kindergarten," April, 1961-March, 1962.
Milne, Dixie, "Music for Primaries," October, 1961-June, 1962.
Montgomery, Mary Elizabeth, "Pointers on Posture," April, 1960.
Morsch, Vivian, "Music for Primaries," March-September, 1961.
Queen, Dorothea, "Music for Primaries," October, 1960-March, 1961.
Roark, Basil, "Principles in Training Youth Choirs," October-December, 1960.
Rodby, Walter, "Training the Youth Choir," October, 1961.
*Parent's Magazine,* published by the Parent's Institute, Bergenfield, New Jersey.
Jackson, Grace, "No Child Is Tone Deaf," August, 1940.
*Religious Education,* 545 West 111th Street, New York 25, New York.
"Creative Rhythmic Movements in Religious Education," January-February, 1958.

## Recordings for Preschool and Primary
### (CHAPTERS 1 AND 2)

ABC Listen and Do Series (all 78's)

| | |
|---|---|
| Album 1. Friendly Train; Ginger and Josh | Grades 1-2 |
| Album 2. Handsome Scarecrow; Little Clown | Grades 1-4 |

| | |
|---|---|
| Album 3. Panda Balloon; Dancing Monkey | Grades 1-2 |
| Album 23. Traditional Singing Games | Grades K-1 |
| Listening Series (all 78's) | |
| Album AS 24 Lullabies | Grades K-3 |
| Album AS 20 Soft and Loud (Dynamics) | Grades 1-3 |
| Album AS 21 High and Low (Near-far range) | Grades 1-3 |
| BR Records for Rhythm (all 78's) | |
| Rhythm Is Fun | Grades K-3 |
| Singing Games, Album 1 | Grades 1-3 |
| Singing Games, Album 2 | Grades 2-3 |
| Rhythm Time | Grades K-3 |
| Holiday Time | Grades 1-5 |
| Brahms, Waltzes, Epic LC-3331 | Grades K-6 |
| CRC Haydn, Symphony No. 94, "Surprise," Col. ML-4453 | Grades 1-6 |
| Jum-A-Jingle (Rope skipping and ball bouncing, 45-78) | Grades 1-3 |
| Tchaikovsky, Nutcracker Suite, Col. ML-4729 | Grades K-6 |
| CRG Nothing to Do (Fundamental movements, 78) | Grades K-2 |
| Little Indian Drum (45-78) | Grades K-2 |
| Slow Joe (Fast and slow, 78) | Grades K-2 |
| Album EAD 2027 (Rhythm, fun, and songs, 78) | Grades K-2 |
| Music Listening Game (Hearing pitches, 78) | Grades K-2 |
| Golden Goose (Combining melodies, 45-78) | Grades K-3 |
| Whoa, Little Horses (Creativity, 78) | Grades K-2 |
| Bring a Song, Johnny (Improvisation, 45-78) | Grades K-3 |
| Pretending (Creativity, 78) | Grades K-2 |
| Mother Goose (Two records, 45-78) | Grades N-2 |
| Sing Along (Echoing, 45-78) | Grades K-3 |
| Debussy, Children's Corner Suite | Grades K-6 |
| Casadesus, Col. ML-4978 | |
| Stokowski and Philadelphia Orchestra, Vic. LM-9023 | |
| FR Children's Songs and Games FC-7307 | Grades K-3 |
| Music Time, Folk. 7307 | Grades K-3 |
| Songs to Grow on, Vol. 1, Folk. 7005; Vol. 2, Folk. 7020 | Grades K-3 |
| FPC Album RA 23 Rhythmic Activities (78) | Grades K-1 |
| GAC Album, Let's Sing and Play (33) | Grade 1 |
| Album, Let's Sing of Fun and Frolic (33) | Grade 2 |
| Album, Let's Sing and Be Merry (33) | Grade 3 |
| GP Growing Days (An album of six 45's with teacher's manual) | Grades N-1 |
| Haydn, Symphony No. 101, "Clock," Van. 492 | Grades K-6 |
| PJR AED 1, Animals | Grades K-3 |

AED 2, Free Rhythms                                                                     Grades K-3
AED 9, Dramatic Play                                                                    Grades K-1
(There are 15 albums of 78's in the series, covering everyday
activities.)
RCA Albums for Rhythmic Activity (One for each grade,
45-78)                                                                                         Grades 1-3
Anderson, Tiptoe March, Running Horses, High Stepping
Horses, 45-5002                                                                          Grades K-1
Brahms, Lullaby; Schubert, Cradle Song, 45-5024                        Grades K-3
Kullak, Evening Bells, 45-5029                                                    Grades K-1
RER Albums of Childhood Rhythms (all 78's)
Vol.    I   (Fundamental, animal, toy, playland)               Grades 1-3
Vol.    II  (Combinations, interpretative, balls)              Grades 1-3
Vol.    V   (Animals)                                         Grades 1-3
Vol.    VII (Nursery rhymes and singing games)                Grades 1-3
SBC Tiny Masterpieces for Very Young Listeners (78)                    Grades N-3
W A Joyful Sound W-3137
Singing Children W-3130

## Recordings for Juniors
### (CHAPTER 3)

(Many records for junior youth are effective with juniors, especially
those that are classified as folk songs. Particular attention should be given
to the records of Marian Anderson, the Robert Shaw Chorale, and the
Roger Wagner Chorale. See also "Records for Pre-school and Primary.")

Britten, Young Person's Guide to the Orchestra, Ang. 35135
Chopin, Waltzes, Vic. LM-5035
CRC Great Composers Come to Life, Milton Cross, Narrator (33's)
The Story and Music of Haydn, Vox MM-3610
The Story and Music of Mozart, Vox MM-3510
The Story and Music of Chopin, Vox MM-3520
CRG The King's Trumpet (Evolution of the trumpet. 78)
Licorice Stick (Clarinet) (78)
Said the Piano to the Harpsichord (45-78)
The Wonderful Violin (78)
DR Christmas with the Trapp Family Singers, Vol. 1, Dec. 9553; Vol. 2,
Dec. 9689
Tubby the Tuba (78), CU-106
The Symphony Orchestra (Four albums. 78's)
90, Strings; 91, Woodwinds; 92, Brass; 93, Percussion

GP Great Hymns for Children
> Album 4, Thirteen hymns. Richard Lapo and junior choirs, Catalina Methodist Church, Tuscon, Arizona.
> Album 5, Twelve hymns. Donald F. Jensen and junior choirs, Westfield, New Jersey.
> Album 6, Thirteen hymns. Mrs. Bonita West and junior choirs, First Methodist Church, Glenview, Illinois.

Grieg, Peer Gynt Suites, Nos. 1 and 2, Col. ML-5035

Grofé, Grand Canyon Suite, Vic. LM-1928
> Fiedler and Boston Pops. Over: Copland, El Salon Mexico

A Joyful Sound, Word W-3137-LP
> Twenty-six children's songs sung by children, Mabel Stewart Boyter, director.

The King of the Instruments, Vol. I, Aeolian Skinner Co.

Laidow, Folk Songs for Orchestra, Young Peoples Records YPR 405

Niles, American Folk Songs, Vic. Cal 245

Obernkirchen Children's Choir, Christmas Songs, Ang. 65021

PJR   AED 8, Branding Cattle (78)

RCA   Albums for Rhythmic Activity (One for each grade, 45-78)

RER   Albums of Childhood Rhythms (78's) ; Vols. III, IV, VI, VII, VIII

Saint Saëns, Carnival of the Animals, Ang. 35135

Schumann, Carnaval
> Casadesus, Col. ML-5146. Over: Fantasia
> Novaes, Vox P1-11160. Over: Kinderscenen; Papillons

Singing Children, Word W-3130-LP
> Twenty-eight children's sacred songs sung by children, Mabel Steward Boyter, director.

Tchaikovsky, Nutcracker Suite, Vic. LM-9023

## Key to Distributors of Children's Recordings
### (CHAPTERS 1, 2, 3)

ABC American Book Company, 351 East Ohio Street, Chicago 11, Ill.

BR Bowmar Records, 4921 Santa Monica Blvd., Los Angeles 29, Calif.

CRG Children's Record Guild and Young People's Records, The Greystone Corporation, 100 Sixth Ave., New York 13, N. Y.

CRC Columbia Recording Company, 1473 Branum Ave., Bridgeport, Conn.

DR Decca Records, Inc., 50 West 57th Street, New York 19, N. Y.

FR Folkways Records, 117 West 46th Street, New York 36, N. Y.

FPC Follett Publishing Co., 1010 West Washington Blvd., Chicago 7, Ill.

GP Graded Press, 201 Eighth Ave. S., Nashville 3, Tenn.

GAC Ginn and Company, Black Bay Post Office, Box N., Boston, Mass.
PJR Phoebe James Records, Box 124, Pacific Palisades, Calif.
RCA RCA Victor Educational Series, Dept. 390, Camden, N. J.
RER Ruth Evans Records, 326 Forest Park Ave., Springfield, Mass.
SBC Silver Burdett Co., 45 East 17th Street, New York 3, N. Y.
W Word Records, Inc., Waco, Tex.

## Recordings of Sacred Music
### (CHAPTER 4)

Ambrosian Hymns, Vox DL-343
    Choir of Polifonica Ambrosiana. Hymns and other songs of Ambrose, Bishop of Milan. An excellent and authentic recording.
Marian Anderson Spirituals, Vic. LM-2032
    Described under folk songs.
Augustana Choir, The
  Vol. 1, Word 4001
    Britten, Hymn to St. Cecilia
    Brahms, Der bucklichte Fiedler
    Dawson, There Is a Balm in Gilead
    Traditional, Tryggare Kan Ingen Vara
    Williams, Lord, Thou Hast Been Our Refuge
  Vol. 2, Word 4005
    Bach, Blessing, Glory, and Wisdom
    Britten, A Ceremony of Carols
    German Folk Song, Gute Nacht
    Grieg, The Great Angelic Host
    Kodaly, Jesus and the Traders
    Kountz, Come to the Manger
    Luncholm, Tonerna by Sjoberg
    Rachmaninoff, Blessed Is the Man
  Vol. 3, Word 4012
    Brahms, Mary Magdalene
    Fryxell, Christmas Wish
    Hanson, How Excellent Thy Name
    Schubert, La Pastorella
    Schubert, Wilderspruch
    Stenhammer, Sverige
    Vaughan Williams, Mass in g minor
    Vaughan Williams, Souls of the Righteous
Bach, Three Choral Preludes, Summy Band Series No. 2

Neilson and Chicago Symphonic Band. Includes seven additional band selections.

The Passion According to St. Matthew, Westminster, WAL 407
Schercken, symphony, soloists, and chorus. (Sung in German.)

Brahms, A German Requiem, Vic. LM-6004
Shaw Chorale and RCA Symphony. Steber, Pease. (Sung in German.)

Chorales for Winds, Cantate Records
Eight 7-inch 45 rpm records. Chorale settings of composers of various periods. Order from Cantate Records, 250 West 57th Street, New York.

Christmas in England, Vic. LPM-1568
A service of fourteen carols in a country church setting.

Concordia Choir, Conc. 3, 4
Music of Bach, Britten, Willan.

Life of Christ in Afro-American Folk Songs, Van. 462
Roland Hayes. Described under folk songs.

Morman Tabernacle Choir
The Beloved Choruses, Col. ML-5364
Nine well-known and very reliable choral masterpieces. Representative titles: Bach, Sheep May Safely Graze; Haydn, The Heavens Are Telling; Handel, Hallelujah.

Songs of Faith and Devotion, Col. ML-5203
Twelve standard choral selections. Representative titles: Clayton, Come, Come, Ye Saints; Handel, Sound an Alarm, from Judas Maccabaeus; Bach, The Sorrows Thou Art Bearing and Here Will I Stay Beside Thee, from St. Matthew Passion.

My Songs, Van. 494
Roland Hayes. Described under folk songs.

Moravian Festival Chorus and Orchestra, Col. ML-5427
Anthems and chorales of American Moravians.

Music of The Methodist Church, Word W-4018-LP
Representative music of The Methodist Church sung by the Southern Methodist University Choir, Lloyd Pfautsch, director.

Music for Worship, Cokesbury UR-201-2
Southern Methodist University Chorus. Representative worship music divided into four sections: Praise (Adoration), Confession. The Word, and Dedication. Twenty-two selections including hymns, organ solos, anthems, responses, and one vocal solo.

Praise to the Lord, Col. ML-5334
Hymns selected from the Episcopal Hymnal (1940). Sung by the choir of the Church of the Ascension and the choir of General Theological Seminary.

To Thee We Sing, Custom Col. 379-60M
The Gustavius Choir and Brass Ensemble. Twenty-four hymns. Available from Faculty Woman's Club, Gustavius Adolphus College, St. Peter, Minnesota.

Robert Shaw Chorale
Christmas Hymns and Carols, Vol. I, Vic. LM-2139; Vol. II, Vic. LM-1722
Forty-eight Christmas selections.

A Mighty Fortress, Vic. LM-2199
Fifteen ageless hymns. Representative titles: Glorious Things of Thee Are Spoken; Rise Up, O Men of God; O Worship the King.

Seventeen Sacred Songs, Vic. LM-2403
Described under folk songs.

Sixteen Negro Spirituals, Vic. LM-2247
Described under folk songs.

A Treasury of Easter Songs, Vic. LM-1201
Twenty hymns and spiritual songs of various national origins, including Dutch, Russian, Welsh, French, Scottish folk songs, and compositions of Brahms, Poulenc, Schütz, and Billings. Also two Negro spirituals.

Sing We All Noel, Cokesbury
Southern Methodist University Choir. Eleven lesser known Advent and Christmas hymns.

The Story of Christmas, Boston B-600
The choir of Old St. Mary's Seminary, Baltimore, Maryland. Eight hymns and carols and one motet sung by male voices.

Roger Wagner Chorale
Echos from a 16th Century Cathedral, Cap. P-8460
The House of the Lord, Cap. P-8365
An unusual collection of Jewish, Greek, Russian, and Negro traditional music, plus Palestrina, Watts, and Schubert. It is unfortunate that Malotte's setting of The Lord's Prayer is included. The writers do not recommend the use of this song under any circumstances.

Voices of the South, Cap. P-8519
Described under folk songs.

West Point Cadet Chapel Choir, Vox VX-25590
Twelve standard anthems sung by male chorus. Representative titles: Glarum, Sing Praises; Shaw, With a Voice of Singing; Thompson, The Last Words of David; Holst, Turn Back, O Man. (While not technically nor musically outstanding, these selections can be used to "sell" the boys on the virility of music.)

## Recordings of Classics
### (CHAPTER 4)

Beethoven, Symphony No. 6, "Pastorale," Vic. LM-1755
Toscanini and NBC Symphony.

Bizet, Carmen Suite, Rich. 19013
Collins and the London Philharmonic. Over: Bizet, L'Arlésienne Suite.

Brahms, Variations on a Theme by Haydn, Col. ML-5076
Walter and New York Philharmonic. Over: Cello Concerto and Tragic Overture.

Chabrier, Espana, Vic. LM-2270
Included in a collection entitled Pops Stoppers. Fiedler and the Boston Pops Orchestra.

Chopin, Waltzes, Vic. LM-1892
Rubenstein.

Chicago Symphonic Band, Summy Band Series, Summy-Birchard
Vol. 1, Clebanoff, cond.
Ten program selections in various styles.
Vol. 2, Neilson, cond.
Eight additional band selections. Excellent recordings. In good taste.

Copland, El Salón México, Vic. LM-1928.
Fiedler and Boston Pops. Over: Grofé, Grand Canyon Suite.

Lincoln Portrait, Col. ML-5347
Sandburg, Kostelanetz, and New York Philharmonic. Over: Barber, Vanessa.

Rodeo, Col. ML-5575
Bernstein and New York Philharmonic. Over: Billy the Kid.

Dvořák, Symphony No. 5, "From the New World," Bluebird LBC-1005
Malko and Danish National Orchestra.

Slavonic Rhapsodies, Nos. 1, 2, 3, Cap. G-7209
Kubelik and Royal Philharmonic. Over: Brahms, Hungarian Dances.

Enesco, Roumanian Rhapsody No. 2, Camden-Cal. 115
The Globe Symphony Orchestra. Includes: Liszt, Hungarian Rhapsody No. 6 and Smetana, The Moldau.

Gershwin, An American in Paris, Camden-Cal. 439
Bernstein and RCA Symphony. Over: Copland, Billy the Kid.

Gould, Interplay for Piano and Orchestra, Col. ML-4218
Gould and the Robin Hood Dell Orchestra. Includes: Cowboy Rhapsody, American Salute, Go Down Moses, and others.

Herbert, Music of, Col. ML-4094

Nineteen well-known selections arranged for and played by Andre Kostelanetz and his orchestra.

Mendelssohn, Symphony No. 4, "Italian," Ang. 35524
Cantelli and Philadelphia Symphony. Over: Schubert, Unfinished Symphony.

Oklahoma City University Symphonic Band, Summy Band Series, Vol. 3.
Neilson, cond. Seven program selections. Excellent recording, in good taste.

Prokofiev, Classical Symphony, Cap. G-7118
Kurtz and Philadelphia Orchestra. Over: Shostakovich, Symphony No. 1.

Ravel, Bolero, Rich. 19001
Munch and Paris Conservatory Orchestra. Includes: Berlioz, Overture to Benvenuto Cellini and The Corsair Overture.

Spanish Rhapsodie, Camden-Cal. 118
Warwick Symphony Orchestra. Also includes: Dukas, Sorcerer's Apprentice and Mussorgsky, A Night on Bald Mountain.

Respighi, Fountains of Rome, Vic. LM-1768
Toscanini and NBC Symphony. Over: Pines of Rome.

Rimsky-Korsakov, Scheherazade, Vic. LM-1002
Monteaux and San Francisco Symphony.

Schubert, Rosamunde Incidental Music, Elect. 90153
Furtwangler and Vienna Philharmonic. Over: Unfinished Symphony.

Songs, Epic LC-3648
Vienna Choir Boys.

Symphony No. 8, "Unfinished," Ang. 35524
Cantelli and Philadelphia Orchestra. Over: Mendelssohn, Symphony No. 4, "Italian."

Strauss, J., Music of, Camden 127
Fiedler and Boston Pops Orchestra.

Strauss, Johann and Joseph, Music of, Bluebird LBC-1008
Bohm and Szell and Vienna Philharmonic Orchestra.

Strauss, R., Der Rosenkavalier Suite, Bluebird LBC-1017
Barbirolli and the Halle Orchestra. Over: Grieg, Peer Gynt Suite No. 1.

Music of, Epic LC-3769
Jochum and Concertgebouw Orchestra of Amsterdam. Contains Don Juan, Till Eulenspiegel, and waltzes from Der Rosenkavalier.

Til Eulenspiegel, Vic. LM-1891
Toscanini and NBC Symphony. Over: Death and Transfiguration.

Taylor, Through the Looking Glass, Mer. 50081
  Hanson and Eastman-Rochester Orchestra.
Tchaikovsky, Overture 1812, Col. ML-5392
  Ormandy and Philadelphia Orchestra. Over: Borodin, In the Steppes
  and Prince Igor, and Mussorgsky, Night on Bald Mountain.

## Recordings of Musical Shows
### (CHAPTER 4)

Ben Hur, Soundtrack, MGM 3900
Brigadoon, Original cast, Vic. LOC-1001
  Peerce, Merrill, Powell, Vic. LPM-2275
Carousel, Munsel and Merrill, Vic. LPM-1048
  Original cast, Dec. 9020
  Soundtrack, Cap. W-694
Exodus, Soundtrack, Vic. LOC-1058
Flower Drum Song, Design 1011
  Original cast, Col. OL-5350
Hansel and Gretel, Soundtrack, Vic. LBY-1024
King and I, Original cast, Dec. 9008
  Soundtrack, Cap. W-740
Music Man, Original cast, Cap. WAO-990
My Fair Lady, Merrill, Peerce, Powell, Vic. LPM-2274
Oklahoma, Soundtrack—MacRae, Grahame, Cap. WAO-595
Porgy and Bess, Engel, Winters, William, 3-Col. OSL-162
Porgy and Bess, Symphonic Picture, Vic. LM-2340
  Bennett and RCA Victor Symphony. Over: Bernstein, West Side Story.
Roberta, MacRae, Norman. Over: Desert Song, Cap. T-384
Show Boat, Keel, Jeffreys, Grant, Vic. LOP-1505
  Merrill, Munsel, Stevens, Vic. LM-2008
Song of Norway, Original cast, Dec. 9019
Sound of Music, Original cast, Col. KOL-5450
South Pacific, Original cast, Col. OL-4180
  Soundtrack, Vic. LOC-1032
West Side Story, Col. OL-5230

## Recordings of Folk Songs
### (CHAPTER 4)

American Ballads sung by Peter Seeger, Folk. 2319
  Sung with a five-stringed banjo accompaniment. Use with discretion

as a motivating factor. Folkway records have many recordings of songs from various lands and cultures.

**Marian Anderson Sings Spirituals, Vic. LM-2032**
Twenty-one negro spirituals. Representative titles: Deep River, Roll Jerd'n, Roll; Let us Break Bread Together.

**An Evening with John Jacob Niles, Trad. 1036**
Fourteen American songs with dulcimer accompaniment. Representative titles: Carol of the Birds, The Turtle Dove, The Seven Joys of Mary, You Got to Cross That Lonesome Valley.

**Harry Belafonte Returns to Carnegie Hall, 2-Vic. LOC-6007**
Songs of various peoples. Used with extreme discretion, these and similar songs can serve as motivating factors.

**Fisk Jubilee Singers, Folk. 2372**
Selected negro spirituals.

**Gould, Spirituals for Orchestra, Mer. 50016**
Dorati and Minneapolis Symphony. Includes Gershwin selections.

**Irish Sing-along, Dec. DL-4053**
The Bill Shepherd Singers. A collection of Irish songs.

**Life of Christ in Afro-American Folk Song, Van. 462**
Roland Hayes. Representative titles: Prepare We Our Body, Three Wise Men, Lit'l Boy, He Never Said a Mumberlin' Word.

**Norman Luboff Choir, Songs of the South, Col. CL-860**
A collection of white and negro spirituals, Creole and other folk songs.

**My Songs, Roland Hayes, Van. 494**
An extensive selection of American negro folk songs. Representative titles: I'll Make Me a Man, Let My People Go, Witness, Steal Away, You're Tired Child.

**Susan Reed, Sings Old Airs, Elek. 116**
A wide variety of American songs with accompaniment by zither or Irish Harp; in very good taste.

**Robert Shaw Chorale**
Seventeen sacred songs, Vic. LM-2403
Mostly white spirituals or traditionals. Representative titles: Bright Canaan, Death Shall Not Delay, Pensive Dove, Zion's Soldiers.

Sixteen Negro spirituals, Vic. LM-2247
Representative titles: Deep River, I Wanna Be Ready, Soon One Morning, There Is a Balm.

**Songs of My People, Camden Cal. 597**
Yosselle Rosenblatt sings Yiddish folk songs.

**The Sounds of India, Col. WL-119**
Ravi Shankar. Apparently authentic and very interesting.

Roger Wagner Chorale
  Folk Songs of the Frontier, Cap. P-8332
  Folk Songs of the New World, Cap. P-8324
  Folk Songs of the Old World
    Vol. 1, British Isles, Cap. P-8387
    Vol. 2, Western Europe, Cap. P-8388
  Voices of the South, Cap. P-8519
    Representative titles: Go Down Moses, Deep River, Little David, Steal Away, Joshua Fit the Battle.

## Recordings for Senior High
### (CHAPTER 6)

(Most of the records listed on pp. 128 ff. can be used effectively with senior youth.)

Albéniz, Spanish Dances, Tel. 8027
  Olmedo and Orq. Lírica Museum, Madrid. Over: excerpts from Spanish Suite.
Anderson, LeRoy, Music of, Dec. 8865; Dec. 8954
  Anderson, and orchestra
Bach, Chromatic Fantasy and Fugue in D for Harpsicord, Ang. COLH-71
  Landowska. Over: Toccata in D and Partita.
  Organ Festival, with Brasses, Col. ML-4635
  E. Power Biggs.
Barber, Adagio for Strings, Col. ML-5187
  Ormandy and Philadelphia Symphony. Includes Borodin, Nocturne; Tschaikovsky, Serenade; Vaughan Williams, Greensleeves.
  Essay No. 2 for Orchestra, Van. VRS-1065
  Golschmann and Symphony of the Air. Includes: Music for a Scene from Shelley and Serenade for String Quartet.
Beethoven, Overtures, Col. ML-5232
  Walter and New York Philharmonic. Includes: Egmont and Lenore (3) and Brahms, Academic and Tragic.
  Symphony No. 9, "Choral," 2 vols. Vic. LM-6009
  Toscanini and NBC Symphony. Over: Symphony No. 1.
Bennett, Suite of Old American Dances, FSR 1209
  College of Pacific Band.
Borodin, Polvetsian Dances, Col. CL-751
  Mitropoulos and New York Philharmonic. Over: Ippolitov-Ivanov, Caucasian Sketches and Borodin, In the Steppes.
Brahms, Alto Rhapsody, Vic. LM-1146
  Anderson, Reiner, Shaw Chorale, RCA Symphony. Over: Mahler, Kindertotenlieder.

Lieder, Vic. LM-1784
Robert Shaw Chorale. Includes: Bach and Schubert.

Love Song Waltzes, Cap. P-8176
Roger Wagner Chorale. Over: Ten German folk songs sung in English.

New Love Song Waltzes, Dec. DL-9650
Mixed quartet, two-piano accompaniment. Over: Six additional vocal quartets by Brahms.

Songs
Any Fischer-Dieskau released by Decca, Angel, Elect.

Symphony No. 4, Vic. LM-1713
Toscanini and NBC Symphony Orchestra.

Copland, Appalachian Spring, ARS-26
Hendl and American Recording Society Orchestra. Includes Barber, Overture to the School for Scandal and Music for a Scene from Shelley.

Debussy, Afternoon of a Faun, Lon. CM-9228
Ansermet and Orchestra Suisse Romande. Includes Ravel, Rhapsodie and Debussy, La Mer.

Enesco, Roumanian Rhapsody No. 1, Vic. LM-1878
Stokowski. Includes Debussy, La Mer.

Falla, Nights in the Gardens of Spain, Vic. LM-2181
Rubenstein. Over: Granados, The Maiden and the Nightingale and Spanish Dance No. 5; Falla, Miller's Dance; Albéniz, Sevillana; Mompou, Canco Dansa.

Gershwin, Concerto in F for Piano, Col. CL-700
Levant, Kostelanetz, New York Philharmonic. Over: American in Paris and Rhapsody in Blue.

Grofé, Grand Canyon Suite, Mer. 50049
Hanson and Eastman-Rochester Orchestra. Over: Mississippi Suite.

Haydn, The Seasons, 3-Cap. GCR-7184
Beecham, Royal Philharmonic, Choral Society.

Hindemith, Kleine Kammermusic, Col. ML-5093
Philadelphia Woodwind quintet.

Symphonic Dances, Dec. 9818
Hindemith and Berlin Philharmonic.

Kern, Mark Twain, Col. CL-864
Kostelanetz.

Liszt, Hungarian Rhapsodies, Vic. LM-1878
Stokowski and NBC Symphony. Includes: Nos. 1, 2, and 3, and Enesco selections.

Les Preludes, Col. ML-5198
Mitropoulos and New York Philharmonic. Includes: R. Strauss, Salome and others.
Lotti, Crucifixus, Mus.Lib. 7065
San Jose State College a Cappella Choir.
Mendelssohn, Elijah, 3-Wander. 1103
Winfield Civic Symphony and Chorus.
Overtures, Lon. CM-9109
Schuricht and Vienna Philharmonic.
Mennin, Canzona for Band, Mer. 50084
Fennell and Eastman Symphonic Wind Ensemble.
Milhaud, Sketches for Woodwind Quintet, Es. 505
New York Woodwind Quintet.
Monteverdi, Choral Music, Dec. 9627
Boulanger, Vocal and Instrumental Ensemble.
Madrigals, West. 18765
Field-Hyde and Golden Age Singers.
Morley, Elizabethian Madrigals, Bach 577
Deller Consort.
Moszkowski, Spanish Dances, Lon. CM-9192
Argenta and London Symphony. Includes: Chabrier, Espana and Rimsky-Korsakov, Capriccio.
Mozart, Arias, Vic. LM-1751
Pinza. Over: Verdi arias.
Concerto in A for Clarinet, Vic. LM-2073
Goodman, Munch, and Boston Symphony Orchestra. Over: Clarinet Quintet.
German Dances, Col. ML-5004
Walter and Columbia Symphony. Includes: Overtures and minuets.
Wind-Instrument Music, DGG ARC-3121
A varied selection of solos and ensembles for wind instruments.
Mussorgsky, Night on Bald Mountain, Dis. 4101C
Stokowski and Philadelphia Orchestra. Over: Beethoven, Symphony No. 6.
Palestrina, Choral Works, Ang. 35667
De Nobel, Netherlands Church Choir. Includes: Monteverdi selections.
Pezel, Sonatas for 5 Brass Instruments, Per. 526
Schuman Brass Choir. Includes: Gabrieli selections.
Prokofiev, Love for Three Oranges, West. 18701
Rodzinski and London Philharmonic. Over: Peter and the Wolf.
Puccini, Arias

Bjoerling, Cap. G-7239

Farrell, Col. ML-5483

Tenor Arias, Eterna 724

Purcell, Anthems and Secular Songs, DGG ARC-3038

Oppenheim and Saltire Singers.

Rachmaninoff, Isle of the Dead, Col. ML-5043

Ormandy and Philadelphia Orchestra. Over: The Bells.

Ravel, Daphnis and Chloe, Nos. 1 and 2, Col. ML-4316

Ormandy and Philadelphia Orchestra, with Temple University Chorus. Over: Schonberg, Transfigured Night.

Mother Goose, Richmond 19007

Ansermet and Orchestra. Suisse Romande. Includes: Debussy, La Mer.

Valse Noble et Sentimentales, Cap. Telefunken P8132

Andre and Grande Orchestra Symphonique. Over: Debussy, Iberia.

Sarasate, Zigeunerweisen, Vic. LM-2069

Heifitz, Steinberg, and RCA Victor Symphony.

Includes also compositions of Chausson and Saint Saëns.

Scarlatti, Saint John Passion, Over. 1

St. Thomas Choir, Yale Orchestra.

Schubert, Songs

Any of the Fischer-Dieskau collections released by Elect. and Angel.

Schumann, Songs

Any Fischer-Dieskau released by Decca or Elect., or Flagstad by London.

Schütz, Music of, Col. ML-5411

Craft.

Seven Words from the Cross, Lyr. 91

Grossmann and Vienna Symphony.

Segova, Concert for Guitar and Orchestra, Col. ML-4732

Six selections, including compositions by Villa-Lobos, Ponce, and Castelnuovo-Tedesco.

Six Centuries of Song, Van. 448; and Van. 449

Roland Hayes. Songs from the fourteenth through twentieth centuries, including both art and folk songs.

Strauss, R., Death and Transfiguration, Vic. LM-1891

Toscanini and NBC Symphony. Over: Till Eulenspiegel.

Stravinsky, Petrouchka, 3-Col. D3L-300

Stravinski and Columbia Symphony Orchestra.

The Rite of Spring, 3-Col. D3L-300

Stravinsky and Columbia Symphony Orchestra.

Tchaikovsky, Capriccio Italien, Col. CL-707

Ormandy and Philadelphia Orchestra. Over: Rimsky-Korsakov, Capriccio Espagnol.
Sleeping Beauty Ballet, excerpts, Cap. P-8471
Levine and Ballet Theatre Orchestra. Over: Swan Lake.
Symphony No. 6, "Pathétique," Mer. 50006
Kubelik and the Chicago Symphony.
Thompson, Alleluia, Mus.-Lib. 7085
Weaver, Catawba College Choir. Includes music of Josquin and Lotti.
Peaceable Kingdom, Mus.-Lib. 7065
San José State College a Cappella Choir. Includes music of Lotti and Ginastera.
Vaughan Williams, English Folk Songs, Van. 1055
Deller Consort.
Greensleeves, Col. ML-5187
Ormandy and Philadelphia Orchestra. Includes Barber, Adagio; Borodin, Nocturne; and Tchaikovsky, Serenade.
Verdi, Arias, 3-Ang. 3525
Callas, Gobbi, Tucker, Barbieri, Serafin.
Wagner, Concert, Col. ML-4962
Beecham and the Royal Philharmonic Orchestra.
Concert, Vic. LM-6020
Toscanini and the NBC Orchestra.
Excerpts from Parsifal, Col. ML-5080
Ormandy and Philadelphia Orchestra.
Excerpts from Lohengrin, Dec. 9987
Jochum and Bavarian Radio Orchestra.
Parsifal—Good Friday Music, Col. ML-5842
Walter and Columbia Symphony. Includes Overture and Prelude.
Wolff, Songs. Any collection of Fischer-Dieskau released by Elect., Angel, or Decca. Also Lehmann by Camden.

## SONGBOOKS, ANTHEMS, AND SOLO MATERIALS
### Songbooks for Primary and Kindergarten
*(CHAPTERS 1 and 2)*

*Another Singing Time* (Coleman and Thorne), Day (K)
*Canyon Hymnal for Boys and Girls, The,* Primary Edition, Canyon (P)
*Child Sings, A* (Pooler), Augsburg (K)
*God's Wonderful World* (Mason and Ohanian), Random (K & P)
*Hymns for Primary Worship,* Westminster (P)
*Kindergarten Songs and Rhythms,* Bethany (K)
*Let Children Sing* (Licht), Flammer (P)

*Martin and Judy Songs* (Thomas), Beacon (K & P)
*New Songs and Carols for Children* (Grime), C. Fischer (P)
*New Songs for the Junior Choir* (Bristol & Friedell), Concordia (P)
*Our Songs of Praise* (Klammer), Concordia (P)
*Sing, Children, Sing* (Thomas), Abingdon (P)
*Singing Time* (Coleman and Thorne), Day (K)
*Singing Worship* (Thomas), Abingdon (P)
*Songs for Early Childhood*, Westminster (K & P)
*Songs for the Little Child* (Baker and Kohlsaat), Abingdon (K & P)
*Songs to Grow On* (Landeck), Marks (K)
*We Go to Church* (Marshall and Montgomery), C. Fischer (P)
*We Sing Together*, Abingdon (K)
*Whole World Singing, The* (Thomas), Friendship (P)

## Anthem and Songbook Collections for Juniors
### (CHAPTER 3)

*Anthems for Junior Choristers* (Lovelace), Summy-Birchard
*Anthems for the Junior Choir,* Westminster
  Books I, II, III, IV
*Canyon Hymnal for Boys and Girls, The* (Junior Edition), Canyon
*Echoes from Bethlehem* (Rohlfing), Concordia
*Green Hill Junior Choir Book*, E. C. Schirmer
*Hymns for Junior Worship,* Westminster
*Junior Choir Anthem Book,* (Holler) Gray
  Book I, 2 pt.; Book II, unison; Book IV, 2 pt.; Book V, unison
*Junior Choir Anthems* (D. H. Williams), Summy-Birchard
*The Junior Choir Sings,* Broadman
*Morning Star Choir Book* (Thomas), Concordia
*New Songs for the Junior Choir* (Bristol and Friedell), Concordia
*Thirty-Five Sacred Rounds and Canons* (Bristol), Canyon
*Second Allelujah Choir Book, The* (Hokanson and Michelson), Kjos
*Songs for Children's Voices* (Lenel), Chantry
*Songs from Luke* (Bristol), Canyon
*Songs from Matthew* (Bristol), Canyon
*Songs of Praise for Boys and Girls* (Dearmer, et al.), Oxford
*Treble Choir, The,* Schmitt, Hall & McCreary
*Twelve Sayings of Jesus* (Willan), Concordia
*Voices of Worship* (Malin), Wood
*We Praise Thee* (Willan), Concordia
*We Sing to Learn* (Marshall), C. Fischer

140

## Anthems for Juniors and Junior-High Youth
### *(CHAPTER 3)*
#### (Unison; Unison with Descant)

| | |
|---|---|
| Bach | *Come, Let Us All This Day*<br>E. C. Schrimer 500 |
| ———— | *Come Now, Good Christians*<br>Row 423 |
| ———— | *Come, Together Let Us Sing*<br>E. C. Schirmer 1001 |
| ———— | *Now Sing We, Now Rejoice*<br>Concordia 98-1189 |
| ———— | *O Saviour Sweet*<br>Gray 198 |
| Bitgood | *Wise Men Seeking Jesus*<br>Sacred Design SD 6005 |
| Caldwell | *Gifts*<br>Summy-Birchard 5033 |
| ———— | *Spring Prayer*<br>Summy-Birchard B-2113 |
| ———— | *Sweet, Holy Child*<br>Gray 2612 |
| Clokey | *Let Us with a Gladsome Mind*<br>Flammer 86129 |
| ———— | *Litany of Jesus*<br>Flammer 86147 |
| Copes | *Three Carols for Juniors*<br>Canyon 6005 |
| Darst | *O God of Youth*<br>Gray 2147 |
| Davies | *Easter Bell Carol*<br>Flammer 86101 |
| Davis | *Let All Things Now Living*<br>E. C. Schirmer 1819 |
| Giles | *To Be a Pilgrim*<br>Abingdon APM-118 |
| Handel | *Forever Blessed Be Thy Name*<br>Summy-Birchard B-2128 |
| ———— | *Lord of Our Being*<br>Gray 1965 |

| Haydn | *The Spacious Firmament* |
| | E. C. Schirmer 1829 |
| Hokanson | *Chime, Happy Christmas Bells* |
| | Concordia 98-1513 |
| Hughes-Jones | *Laus Deo (Praise to God)* |
| | Mills 5019 |
| Jacob | *Brother James' Air* |
| | Oxford OSC 1139 |
| Johnson | *Carol of the Singing Reeds* |
| | J. Fischer 7710 |
| Kettring | *God Watches Over All the World* |
| | Gray 1935 |
| Kinderman | *Dear Christians, Praise God Evermore* |
| | Concordia 98-1503 |
| Lenel | *All Praise to Thee, Eternal God* |
| | Concordia 98-1402 |
| ———— | *Lord, This Day the Children Meet* |
| | Concordia 98-1403 |
| Lewis | *All Things* |
| | Summy-Birchard B-1629 |
| ———— | *Father, We Thank Thee* |
| | Concordia 98-1497 |
| Lindeman | *Long Hast Thou Stood, O Church of God* |
| | E. C. Schirmer 1765 |
| Lovelace | *God Make My Life a Shining Light* |
| | Flammer 86170 |
| ———— | *Kindly Spring Again Is Here* |
| | J. Fischer 9019 |
| ———— | *O I Would Sing of Mary's Child* |
| | Augsburg 1247 |
| Luther | *Holy Is God the Lord* |
| | Concordia 98-1379 |
| Marshall | *Jesus* |
| | C. Fischer CM 7126 |
| Pfautsch | *Easter Bell Carol* |
| | Abingdon APM-168 |
| Powell | *Three Treble Choir Anthems* |
| | APM—198 |
| Reed | *The Saints of God* |
| | C. Fischer CM 7019 |

142

| | |
|---|---|
| Shaw, G. | *Worship* |
| | Novello MT 967 |
| Thiman | *Grant Us Light* |
| | G. Schirmer 10280 |
| Thomas | *Let Us With a Gladsome Mind* |
| | Gray 2686 |
| Wienhorst | *Four Christmas Settings* |
| | Concordia 98-1498 |
| Willan | *From Heaven High I Come to Earth* (from *Carols for the Season*) |
| | Concordia |
| ———— | *Snowy Flakes Are Falling Softly* |
| | Concordia 98-1098 |
| Williams, F. | *The Stars Shone Bright* |
| | Flammer 86167 |

**Anthem and Songbook Collections for Junior-High Youth**

*(CHAPTER 4)*

(See also page 140.)

*Anthems for the Youth Choir,* Westminster
*Birchard Two-Part Choir,* Summy-Birchard
*Carols for the Season* (Willan), Concordia
*Choristers, The* (Woodside), Boston
*Familiar Hymns with Descants,* Westminster
*Five Settings to Texts by Tiplady* (Lovelace), Canyon
*Gateway Choir Book* (Lundquist), E. C. Schirmer
*Green Hill Three Part Book* (Davis), E. C. Schirmer
*Intermediate Choir, The* (Holler), Gray
*Joyous Carols* (Whitner), C. Fischer
*Junior Choir Anthem Book, The,* Book III, 3 Part, Gray
*Little Church Anthem Book, The,* E. C. Schirmer
*Rejoice in the Lord* (Leupold), Augsburg
*SAB Chorale Book, The,* Parts One and Two (Thomas), Concordia
*Sing Praises, Parts One and Two* (Lenel), Concordia
*Sing Praises,* (Ehret), Broadman
*Songs of Devotion,* Augsburg
*Teen Tunes* (Ehret), Boosey & Hawkes
*Twelve Anthems for Soprano, Alto, Baritone* (Williams), Summy-Birchard

## Hymns for Junior-High Youth

### (CHAPTER 4)

Texts and tunes that express a feeling of virility will have an especially strong appeal to boys. Most of the following hymns will make excellent anthems. (See *Music and Worship in the Church, op. cit.,* p. 131, for twenty-two suggested ways to "anthemize" a hymn.)

All creatures of our God and King
All glory, laud, and honor
All praise to Thee my God
As with gladness men of old
Ask ye what great thing I know
Be strong
Blessed Jesus, at Thy word
Book of books, our people's strength
Christian! dost thou see them
Come, Thou long-expected Jesus
Come, ye thankful people, come
Fairest Lord Jesus
For all the saints
For the beauty of the earth
Glorious things of thee are spoken
Good Christian men, rejoice
Hail to the Lord's Anointed
Harken, all! What holy singing
He who would valiant be
Immortal, invisible
In Christ there is no East or West
Joyful, joyful, we adore Thee
Let all the world in every corner sing
Look, ye saints!
Master, speak

Not alone for mighty empire
Now, on land and sea descending
Now thank we all our God
Now the day is over
O brother man, fold to thy heart
O come, O come, Immanuel
O God, our help in ages past
O Jesus, I have promised
Once to every man and nation
O sacred Head, now wounded
O Thou who camest from above
O young and fearless Prophet
Praise, my soul, the King of heaven
Praise to the Lord, the Almighty
Rejoice, the Lord is King
Rejoice, ye pure in heart
Shepherd of tender youth
Sing praise to God who reigns above
Sing with all the sons of glory
The voice of God is calling
This is my Father's world
We come unto our father's God
We gather together to ask the Lord's blessing
When morning gilds the skies

## Two-Part Anthems (Treble and/or mixed)

### (CHAPTER 4)

(See page 141 for unison and unison with descant.)

Ahle-Bach    *Jesu, Joyance of My Heart*
Novello C. S. 75

| | |
|---|---|
| Bach | *Beside Thy Cradle Here I Stand* <br> Wood 227 |
| ———— | *Lord and Savior, True and Kind* <br> Flammer 86162 |
| ———— | *Lord God, We Worship Thee* <br> Summy-Birchard B-1270 |
| Barnard | *Let Our Gladness Know No End* <br> Summy-Birchard B-108 |
| Bauman | *Behold the Lamb of God* <br> Concordia 98-1088 |
| Borowski | *Angels of Light* <br> FitzSimons 5007 |
| Bortnyanski | *A God of Night* <br> Gray 1563 |
| ———— | *Savior, Like a Shepherd Lead Us* <br> J. Fischer 8786 |
| Brackett | *Jesus, Our Good Shepherd* <br> Birchard 1497 |
| Brook | *The Shepherd* <br> Oxford 149 |
| Castleton | *Father, We Thank Thee* <br> Boosey & Hawkes 1762 |
| Couper | *The Flute Carol* <br> J. Fischer 8586 |
| ———— | *Here With the Ox and Donkey* <br> J. Fischer 8658 |
| Davies | *Christ Is Born in Bethlehem* <br> Flammer 86135 |
| Dickinson | *O Nightingale, Awake* <br> Gray 213 |
| ———— | *Sleep, My Jesus, Sleep* <br> Gray 267 |
| Dvořák | *I Will Sing Thee Songs of Gladness* <br> G. Schirmer 8646 |
| Franck | *At the Cradle* <br> E. C. Schirmer 1533 |
| Garden | *Easter Carol* <br> Gray 2364 |
| Gregor | *Hosanna* <br> Brodt 200 |
| Handel | *Thanks Be to Thee* <br> J. Fischer 8827 |

| | |
|---|---|
| ———— | *O Lovely Peace* |
| | Gray 1995 |
| Harvey | *Nativity* |
| | Flammer 86159 |
| Haydn | *The Heavens Are Telling* |
| | G. Schirmer 10072 |
| Head | *Star Candles* |
| | Boosey & Hawkes 1698 |
| Hokanson | *A Joyous Christmas Song* |
| | Summy-Birchard 4160 SA (A) |
| ———— | *Good Shepherd of the Children* |
| | Kjos 6056 |
| Jordan | *Why Do Bells for Christmas Ring?* |
| | Summy-Birchard 5346 |
| Kite | *Noel of the Shepherds* |
| | E. C. Schirmer 1849 |
| ———— | *God Who Watchest O'er Us* |
| | E. C. Schirmer 1850 |
| Kodaly | *Christmas Dance of the Shepherds* |
| | Boosey & Hawkes 5172 |
| Kountz | *Carol of the Sheep Bells* |
| | Galaxy 1078 |
| ———— | *Rise Up Early* |
| | Galaxy 1701 |
| Larson | *Come, Children, Join to Sing* |
| | Schmitt 216 |
| Lipscomb | *Song of Praise* |
| | G. Schirmer 10657 |
| Lutkin | *Above the Clear Blue Sky* |
| | FitzSimons 5008 |
| Lynn | *O Come Immanuel* |
| | Mercury 217 |
| Marcello | *Give Ear Unto Me* |
| | Gray 1522 |
| Marryott | *The Lord's Day* |
| | Ditson 332-40067 |
| Martin | *O Sons and Daughters, Let Us Sing* |
| | Mercury 223 |
| Praetorius | *Lo, How a Rose E're Blooming* |
| | Mercury ZC219 |
| Rawls | *Touch Hands Around the Rolling World* |
| | J. Fischer 9075 |

146

|  |  |
|---|---|
| | *Long, Long Ago* |
| | Gray 2198 |
| Reinecke | *A Christmas Carol* |
| | Gray 1558 |
| Rockefeller | *In Thy Cradle* |
| | Gray 2105 |
| Schütz | *Sacred Concert* |
| | Mercury MC13 MC17 MC18 |
| Sowerby | *My Master Hath a Garden* |
| | Gray 2581 |
| Thomson | *My Shepherd Will Supply My Need* |
| | Gray 2562 |
| Viegland | *My Faith, It Is an Oaken Staff* |
| | Gray 2698 |
| Vogler | *Holy Is Thy Name, O Lord* |
| | Flammer 86107 |
| Vulpius | *All Praise to God, Who Reigns Above* |
| | Concordia 98-1142 |
| Warner | *Mary's Lullaby to the Infant King* |
| | Summy-Birchard B-1611 |
| | *The Sun Shines in Splendor* |
| | Gray 2589 |
| Whittlesey | *Bells of Christmas* |
| | Flammer 86165 |
| | *We Tread Upon Thy Carpets* |
| | Flammer 86153 |
| Willan | *Come Jesus, Holy Child, to Me* |
| | Concordia 98-1091 |
| | *Glory to the Father Give* |
| | Concordia 98-1382 |
| | *Holy Spirit, Hear Us* |
| | Concordia 98-1120 |
| | *Hosanna to the Son of David* |
| | Concordia 98-1118 |
| | *The King Ascendeth into Heaven* |
| | Concordia 98-1381 |
| Williams, D. H. | *A Hymn for Thanksgiving* |
| | Summy-Birchard B-218 |
| Williams, F. | *In Bethlehem's Lowly Manger* |
| | Flammer 86067 |
| Wolff | *Come, Holy Spirit, Come* |
| | Concordia 98-1356 |

### Three-Part Anthems
### (CHAPTER 4)

| | |
|---|---|
| Bach | *Jesu, Joy of Man's Desiring*<br>G. Schirmer 8388 |
| Bortnyanski | *We Thank Thee, Lord*<br>Kjos 7751 |
| Cherubini | *Like as a Father*<br>Summy-Birchard 5297 |
| Cook | *Gentle Mary*<br>C. Fischer 7072 |
| Davies | *Hark, The Glad Sound*<br>Willis 3917 |
| Davis | *Mary's Lullaby*<br>Summy-Birchard B-142 |
| ———— | *To the Manger*<br>Summy-Birchard B-122 |
| Dickinson | *O Nightingale, Awake*<br>Gray 230 |
| ———— | *Shepherds, on This Hill*<br>Gray 225 |
| Emig | *A Round for Christmas*<br>Flammer 88616 |
| Fisher | *Ye Watchers and Ye Holy Ones*<br>Ditson 14946 |
| Forest | *Little Lamb, Who Made Thee*<br>Choral Press 2338 (4 pt.) |
| Jacobson | *A Carroll*<br>Summy-Birchard B-965 |
| Johnson | *Carol of the Singing Reeds*<br>J. Fisher 7711 |
| Kite | *Say, What Is This Our Hearts Compelling*<br>E. C. Schirmer 536 |
| ———— | *Noel! Sing Good News*<br>E. C. Schirmer 540 |
| Kountz | *Hasten Swiftly, Hasten Softly*<br>Galaxy 1752 |
| ———— | *Rise Up Early*<br>Galaxy 1664 |
| Mozart | *Christmas Lullaby*<br>Row 241 |

| | |
|---|---|
| Niles and Sheppard | *Wondrous Love*<br>G. Schirmer 10710 |
| Reger | *The Virgin's Slumber Song*<br>Associated Music Press A91 |
| Williams, F. | *In Bethlehem's Lowly Manger*<br>Flammer 86067 |

## Anthems (SAB)
### (CHAPTER 4)

| | |
|---|---|
| A. T. D. | *Thy Wisdom Lord*<br>E. C. Schirmer 1703 |
| Bach | *Awake, My Soul, and Sing Ye*<br>Wood 548 |
| Barnby | *When Morning Gilds the Sky*<br>Abingdon APM-117 |
| Billings | *Shepherds Carol*<br>Gray 2667 |
| Blake | *In the Lonely Midnight*<br>Presser 312-40039 |
| Davis | *To the Manger*<br>Summy-Birchard B-34 |
| Emig | *A Round for Christmas*<br>Flammer 88616 |
| Gastoldi | *In Thee Is Gladness*<br>Augsburg 1231 |
| Jones | *Little Lamb, Who Made Thee*<br>C. Fischer CM460 |
| Jordan | *Late Have I Loved Thee*<br>Flammer 88603 |
| Lenel | *Come, Ye Faithful, Raise the Strain*<br>Concordia 98-1384 |
| Lotti | *Mighty Lord, Thy Faithfulness Abideth Ever*<br>E. C. Schirmer 1716 |
| Malin | *Our Master Hath a Garden*<br>Wood 768 |
| Milner | *Praise God in His Holiness*<br>Novello M2B |
| Nelson | *Hosanna to the Son of David*<br>Augsburg 1258 |

Pierce    *Christmas Hymn*
            Canyon 5902

Pitcher    *Through All the Year*
            Summy-Birchard B-2097

Roberton    *All in the April Evening*
            G. Schirmer 9988

Runkel    *The God of Abraham Praise*
            Ditson 332-15063

Wolff    *The Easter Carol*
            Concordia 98-1147

## Anthems for Boys' Choir
### (CHAPTER 4)

Bach    *Lord and Saviour, True and Kind*
            Flammer 86162

Beethoven    *Joyful, Joyful We Adore Thee*
            FitzSimons 5011

Brook    *Silver Lamps*
            Oxford OCS1134

Caldwell    *I Know a Lovely Garden*
            Gray 2578

Cope    *Pleasure It Is*
            Oxford E33

Croft    *Ye Servants of God*
            Kjos Ed. 5277

Davis    *Let All Things Now Living*
            E. C. Schirmer 1819

Eichhorn    *Master of Eager Youth*
            Brodt 528

Fryxell    *To the Christ Child*
            Gray 2356

Gregor    *Hosanna*
            Brodt 200

Haydn    *Praise the Lord, Ye Heavens Adore Him*
            Oxford OCS1557

Holst    *Christmas Song*
            G. Schirmer 8119

| | |
|---|---|
| Humperdinck | *Prayer from Hansel and Gretel*<br>Ditson 332-14218 |
| Lindeman | *Long Hast Thou Stood*<br>E. C. Schirmer 1765 |
| Lovelace | *Blessed Man Whom God Doth Aid*<br>J. Fischer 9059 |
| ———— | *God, Who Created Me*<br>C. Fischer CM 7149 (with TB) |
| ———— | *O Thou Eternal Christ, Ride On*<br>Abingdon APM-105 (with SATB) |
| ———— | *The Lord My Shepherd Is*<br>Augsburg 1284 |
| ———— | *Saw You Never in the Twilight*<br>Gray 2553 |
| Lutkin | *Above the Clear Blue Sky*<br>FitzSimons 5008 |
| Pfautsch | *The Lord Is My Shepherd*<br>Summy-Birchard 5025 |
| Pitcher | *Through All the Years*<br>Birchard 30 |
| Purvis | *What Strangers Are These*<br>Summy-Birchard B-969 |
| Reed | *Rise Up, O Men Of God*<br>J. Fischer 8004 (with SATB) |
| Roberton | *All in the April Evening*<br>G. Schirmer 8837 |
| Scull | *Rise Up, O Men of God*<br>Novello MT 1140 |
| Shaw, G. | *The Lord My Pasture Shall Prepare*<br>Summy-Birchard B-1182 |
| Teschner | *All Glory, Laud, and Honor*<br>E. C. Schirmer 1547 |
| Thiman | *A Song of Praise to the Creator*<br>Gray 2286 |
| Warner | *Let Us, with Gladsome Mind*<br>Summy-Birchard B-2063 |
| White | *A Prayer of St. Richard of Chichester*<br>Oxford 44P033 |
| Willan | *Jesous Ahatonhia*<br>Harris 1641 |

_____     *What Is This Lovely Fragrance*
                Oxford (with SATB)

_____     *Whither Now the Shepherds (Ou S'en Vont)*
                Harris

(Selections suitable for the boys' choir will be found in many of the collections listed on pages 143 ff. Many of the unison, unison-with-descant, and two-part selections are also effective with the boys' choir.)

### Anthems for Youth and/or Children's Choirs with Adult Choirs

*(CHAPTER 4)*

| | |
|---|---|
| Ahle-Bach | *Jesu, Joyance of my Heart*<br>Gray 253 |
| Anderson | *The Sleep of the Holy Child*<br>Summy-Birchard B-2049 |
| Bach | *Now Sing We, Now Rejoice*<br>Concordia BA-32 |
| _____ | *O Saviour Sweet*<br>Gray 82 |
| Bairstow | *The King of Love*<br>Oxford A46 |
| Beckhelm | *What Sweeter Music Can We Bring*<br>J. Fischer 9233 |
| Bitgood | *Hosanna*<br>Gray 1345 |
| Black | *As Lately We Watched*<br>Gray 1358 |
| Buxtehude | *God Shall Do My Advising*<br>Concordia 98-1449 |
| Candlyn | *Palm Sunday Procession*<br>Concordia 98-1064 |
| Chase | *A Psalm of Praise*<br>Summy-Birchard 1420 |
| Christiansen | *Lullaby On Christmas Eve*<br>Augsburg 136 |
| Clokey | *Soul of Christ*<br>FitzSimons 2140 |
| Curry | *Psalm 150*<br>Gray 2129 |

| | |
|---|---|
| ———— | *In Christ There Is No East or West*<br>Abingdon APM-104 |
| Faure | *Sanctus* (From *Requiem*)<br>FitzSimons 2119 |
| Gesius | *In Triumph Shouts the Son of God*<br>Flammer 84374 |
| Gibb | *O God of Earth and Altar*<br>G. Schirmer 8825 |
| Halter | *Now Let the Heavens Be Joyful*<br>Schmitt, Hall, & McCreary 1663 |
| Holst | *A Festival Chime*<br>Galaxy 8 |
| ———— | *Christmas Day*<br>Novello 983 |
| Kountz | *Carol of the Sheep Bells*<br>Galaxy 1575 |
| ———— | *Prayer of the Norwegian Child*<br>G. Schirmer 9703 |
| ———— | *Rise up Early*<br>Galaxy 1702 |
| Lang | *Christ the Lord Hath Risen*<br>Novello MT-1044 |
| Lapo | *O Holy Father*<br>Abingdon APM-163 |
| Larson | *To God All Praise and Glory*<br>Summy-Birchard B-2095 |
| Lockwood | *All Thy Works Praise Thee*<br>Gray 1067 |
| ———— | *Lightly, Lightly, Bells Are Pealing*<br>Gray 45 |
| Lovelace | *From Eastern Lands*<br>Summy-Birchard B-2119 |
| ———— | *God Is My Strong Salvation*<br>Canyon 5403 |
| ———— | *So Lowly Doth the Saviour Ride*<br>C. Fischer CM7195 |
| Lynn | *Why Thus Cradled Here?*<br>Abingdon APM-138 |
| Malin | *Above the Clear Blue Sky*<br>Summy-Birchard B-2092 |

|  |  |
|---|---|
| _____ | *Praise to the Lord*<br>Summy-Birchard B-1571 |
| Marryott | *Infant So Gentle*<br>Gray 1686 |
| _____ | *One Early Easter Morning*<br>Ditson 332-14814 |
| Marshall | *Fanfare for Easter*<br>C. Fischer CM7090 |
| Niles | *When Jesus Lived in Galilee*<br>G. Schirmer 9388 (with SATB)  9268 (with SSA) |
| Pooler | *Be Thou My Vision*<br>Augsburg 1155 |
| Pritchard | *Praise the Lord, Ye Heavens Adore Him*<br>Summy-Birchard B-1476 |
| Purvis | *What Strangers Are These*<br>Birchard 969 |
| Reed | *Rise Up, O Men of God*<br>J. Fischer 8004 |
| Rowley | *Praise*<br>Oxford A24 |
| Sowerby | *Away in a Manger*<br>Gray 2537 |
| Watson | *Light of the World*<br>Brodt 529 |
| Willan | *Sing to the Lord of Harvest*<br>Concordia 98-1454 |
| Williams | *Let the People Praise Thee*<br>Schmitt, Hall & McCreary 865 |
| Wood | *Slumber, O Holy Jesu*<br>Abingdon APM-147 |
| York | *Prayer*<br>Presser 312-40212 |
| Young | *My Master Was So Very Poor*<br>Galaxy GMC 2200 |

## Vocal Solos

### (CHAPTER 6)

Bach, Rise Up, My Heart, with Gladness (in *Solos for the Church Year*, Pfautsch) , Lawson-Gould—H

Banks, A Prayer of St. Francis, Gray—H M

Beethoven, Prayer (in *Solos for the Church Year*, Pfautsch), Lawson-Gould—H

Benedictine Plainsong, Humbly I Adore Thee (in *Solos for the Church Year*, Pfautsch), Lawson-Gould—H

Bitgood, Be Still and Know That I Am God, Gray—H M

Blair, Thou Wilt Light My Candle, Gray—Med. H

_____, As the Hart Panteth, Gray—H

Burleigh, My Lord, What a Morning, Ricordi—L

Byrd, Come Thou and with Us Dwell (in *Solos for the Church Year*, Pfautsch), Lawson-Gould—H

Charles, Lord of the Years, G. Schirmer—M H

Christiansen, Lullaby on Christmas Eve, Augsburg—H

Davis, Trust in the Lord, Galaxy—H M

Del Riego, A Star Was His Candle, C. Fischer—H M

Diamond, Let Nothing Disturb Thee, AMP—M

Dvořák, The Twenty-third Psalm, Galaxy—H M

Handel, Come to the Waters (in *Sacred Song Masterpieces*, Fredrickson), Row—H L

_____, Lead Me, Lord (in *Sacred Song Masterpieces*, Fredrickson), Row—H L

_____, Sing with Grace in Your Heart (in *Sacred Song Masterpieces*, Fredrickson), Row—H L

Haydn, Trust in the Lord (in *Sacred Song Masterpieces*, Fredrickson), Row—H L

Head, The Road to Bethlehem, Boosey & Hawkes—H M

Humphreys, Let This Mind Be in You, Willis—H

_____, Seek Ye the Lord, Willis—H

_____, The Lord Is My Shepherd, Willis—H M

Kountz, Little Bells Through Dark of Night, Galaxy—H M

Loeffler, Prayer (in *Solos for the Church Year*, Pfautsch), Lawson-Gould—H

Lovelace, Star in the East, Galaxy—M

_____, We Lift Our Hearts to Thee, G. Schirmer—M

Lully, Great Peace Have They (in *Sacred Song Masterpieces*), Row—H L

McGimsey, Think on These Things, C. Fischer—H M

Malotte, The Twenty-third Psalm, G. Schirmer—H M

Mendelssohn, Thy Secret Place (in *Sacred Song Masterpieces*, Fredrickson), Row—H L

Mozart, O Lamb of God (in *Solos for the Church Year*, Pfautsch), Lawson-Gould—H

Niles, J., Jesus, Jesus, Rest Your Head, G. Schirmer—H L
———, The Carol of the Birds, G. Schirmer
———, Sweet Marie and Her Baby, G. Schirmer
O'Connor-Morris, Alleluia, Boosey & Hawkes—H M L
Purcell, Blow Ye the Trumpet (in *Sacred Song Masterpieces*, Fredrickson), Row—H L
Quilter, An Old Carol, Boosey & Hawkes—H L
Roberton, All in the April Evening, G. Schirmer—M
Rorem, A Christmas Carol, Elkan-Vogel—M
Sanderson, Green Pastures, Boosey & Hawkes—H M
Sateren, When God Made His Earth, Augsburg—M
Thiman, The God of Love, Gray—Med. H
———, Thou Wilt Keep Him in Perfect Peace, Gray—H
Vaughan Williams, The Woodcutter's Song, Oxford—M
———, The Bird's Song, Oxford—H
Warlock, Bethlehem Down, Boosey & Hawkes—M
Williams, In the Bleak Midwinter, Gray—H
———, Our Blest Redeemer, Gray—H

### Anthems (SSA)
### (CHAPTER 6)

| | |
|---|---|
| Bach | *O Rejoice, Ye Christians, Loudly* Summy-Birchard 5345 |
| Balakirev | *Send Out Thy Light* Boosey & Hawkes 1924 |
| Berger | *In Days to Come* Row 610 |
| Bortniansky | *Glory to God in Heaven* C. Fischer CM645 |
| Bright | *Four Sacred Songs for the Night* Shawnee B-190 |
| Crappius | *O Father Full of Mercy* Concordia 98-1407 |
| Cruger | *Now Thank We All Our God* Boosey & Hawkes 1789 |
| Davis | *All in the Morning* Flammer 89132 |
| ——— | *Our God Is a Rock* Summy-Birchard B-1580 |

| | |
|---|---|
| Dougherty | *The First Christmas* |
| | G. Schirmer 10095 |
| Ehret | *The Friendly Beasts* |
| | C. Fischer CM6839 |
| ———— | *Shepherds, Shake off Your Drowsy Sleep* |
| | Mercury MC268 |
| Farrant | *We Sing Our Praises Now to Thee* |
| | Flammer 89127 |
| Gesius | *Help Us, Eternal God and Lord* |
| | Schmitt, Hall & McCreary 2539 |
| Gillette | *Bring a Torch, Jeannette, Isabella* |
| | Choral Press 2346 |
| Hallstrom | *Shepherds Awake* |
| | Shawnee |
| Handel | *All His Mercies Shall Endure* |
| | Witmark 2-W 3390 |
| Haydn | *The Spacious Firmament* |
| | E. C. Schirmer 1877 |
| Humperdinck | *Prayer from Hansel and Gretel* |
| | Flammer 83087 |
| Kodaly | *Christmas Dance of the Shepherds* |
| | Boosey & Hawkes 5172 (SA) |
| di Lasso | *O Lord of Heaven* |
| | Wick 318 |
| Luvaas | *Alleluia, Christ Is Born* |
| | Summy-Birchard B-1543 |
| Mackinnon | *Give to My Restless Heart, O God* |
| | Gray 844 |
| Madsen | *If Ye Love Me, Keep My Commandments* |
| | Fischer CM6603 |
| Mozart | *Alleluia* |
| | Flammer 89024 |
| Nelson | *Jehovah, Hear Our Prayer* |
| | Summy-Birchard 5052 (SSAA) |
| Nicolai | *Wake, Awake* |
| | Concordia Tr101 |
| Niles | *The Blue Madonna* |
| | G. Schirmer 10014 |
| ———— | *The Carol of the Angels* |
| | G. Schirmer 9674 |
| Palestrina | *We Adore Thee* |
| | Schmitt, Hall & McCreary 2529 (SSAA) |

| Pergolesi | *Glory to God in the Highest* |
| | Flammer 89041 |
| Pfautsch | *Balulalow* |
| | Wynn WMP2202 (SA) |
| Pitoni | *Cantate Domino* |
| | Bourne ES47 |
| Praetorius | *Rejoice, Ye Christian Men, Rejoice* |
| | E. C. Schirmer 1505 |
| Shumaker | *Christ Child, Divine* |
| | Schmitt, Hall & McCreary 2552 |
| Tchaikovsky | *A Legend* |
| | Schmitt, Hall & McCreary 2525 (SSAA) |
| Vree | *Fum, Fum, Fum* |
| | Presser 312-40379 |
| Willan | *O Christ, Thou Lamb of God* |
| | Concordia 98-1122 (SA) |
| Williams, F. | *Let There Be Music* |
| | Flammer 83209 |
| Young, G. | *Now Let Us All Praise God* |
| | Galaxy 2207 |

## Anthems (TTBB)
### (CHAPTER 6)

| Arcadelt | *Lord of the Living Harvest* |
| | Birchard 920 |
| Bach | *God's Loving Kindness* |
| | Boston 2658 |
| ———— | *Let All Give Thanks to Thee* |
| | G. Schirmer 8342 |
| ———— | *May God Smile on You* |
| | Peters 6079 (TB) |
| Beethoven | *Prayer* |
| | Boston 2664 |
| Bortniansky | *Holy Is the Lord* |
| | Summy-Birchard B-1339 |
| Cain | *Jonah Swallowed the Whale* |
| | Flammer 82155 |
| Cassler | *Infant Jesus* |
| | Abingdon APM-162 |

158

| | |
|---|---|
| Clokey | *Six Sacred Pieces for Men's Voices* |
| | Summy-Birchard |
| Davis | *O God, Our Help in Ages Past* |
| | Boston 2268 |
| ———— | *Our God Is a Rock* |
| | Birchard 1592 |
| Dawson | *King Jesus Is a-Listening* |
| | FitzSimons 4025 |
| Dickinson | *O Nightingale, Awake* |
| | Gray 220 (TBB) |
| Forest | *Little Lamb, Who Made Thee* |
| | Choral Press 3111 |
| Franck | *O, Jesus, Grant Me Hope and Comfort* |
| | Schmitt, Hall & McCreary 3507 |
| Gibb | *Nobody Knows the Trouble I See* |
| | Boston 1663 |
| Greene | *Sing We Noel* |
| | Flammer 85027 |
| Haydn | *O Worship the King* |
| | Choral Press 3110 |
| ———— | *Praise We Sing to Thee* |
| | Kjos 2505 |
| ———— | *The Spacious Firmament* |
| | Flammer 85020 |
| Huntley | *It's Me* |
| | FitzSimons 4030 |
| James | *Almighty God of Our Fathers* |
| | Wood 704 |
| Large | *Eziekiel* |
| | Kjos 5528 |
| Larson | *All Night, All Day* |
| | Summy-Birchard B-1528 |
| Laverty | *Psalm 100* |
| | Schmitt, Hall & McCreary 3509 |
| ———— | *Psalm 117* |
| | Schmitt, Hall & McCreary 3508 |
| Luvaas | *All Blessing, Honor, Thanks, and Praise* |
| | Kjos 2504 |
| Lwoff | *God Ever Glorious* |
| | Boosey & Hawkes 5046 |

159

| | |
|---|---|
| Manney | *Hark! The Vesper Hymn Is Stealing*<br>Wood 307 |
| Marryott | *Evening*<br>Ditson 15310 |
| Morgan | *An Instrument of Thy Peace*<br>Wood 770 |
| ———— | *O Hear These, Our Words*<br>Pro Art 1135 |
| Palestrina | *We Pray to Thee*<br>Kjos 5540 |
| Parrish | *Be Thou Very Welcome*<br>Birchard 519 |
| Pitcher | *A Child Was Born in Bethlehem*<br>Birchard 1018 |
| ———— | *All People That on Earth Do Dwell*<br>Birchard 1018 |
| Protheroe | *O My Saviour*<br>Boston 1919 |
| Ringwald | *This Is My Father's World*<br>Shawnee |
| Roberton | *All in the April Evening*<br>G. Schirmer 8356 |
| Schop | *Dearest Jesus, Draw Thou Near Me*<br>Gamble Hinged 1030 |
| Schütz | *Sing Praise to Our Glorious God*<br>Concordia 98-1400 |
| Shaw-Parker | *The Boar's Head Carol*<br>G. Schirmer 10179 |
| ———— | *Mary Had a Baby*<br>G. Schirmer 10191 |
| Talley | *Behold That Star*<br>Shawnee |
| Tallis | *If Ye Love Me*<br>Concordia 98-1520 |
| ———— | *The Virgin's Child*<br>Concordia 98-1366 |
| Tchaikovsky | *Pilgrim's Song*<br>Flammer 82071 |
| ———— | *Praise Ye the Lord*<br>FitzSimons 4050 |

| | |
|---|---|
| Teschner | *All Glory, Laud and Honor*<br>E. C. Schirmer 2135 |
| Tkach | *Hear Our Prayer, O Lord*<br>Kjos 7501 |
| Tschesnokoff | *May Thy Blessed Spirit*<br>FitzSimons 4062 |
| Tye | *O Come, Ye Servants of God*<br>Gray 1776 |
| Williams, F. | *Give Thanks*<br>Flammer 85049 |
| _____ | *Holy Lord of All*<br>Flammer 85032 |
| _____ | *Let There Be Music*<br>Flammer 82145 |
| Work | *He Never Said a Mumbling Word*<br>Presser 20884 |
| _____ | *Sittin' Down Beside of the Lamb*<br>Presser 20886 |

## Anthems (Senior-High)[1]

### (CHAPTER 6)

SATB unless otherwise indicated.

| | |
|---|---|
| Aks | *Come to Zion, Sin-sick Souls*<br>Marks 4038 |
| Allen | *Amen*<br>Row 737 |
| Auber | *O Loving Savior Slain for Us*<br>Gray 61 |
| Bach | *Be Calm and Peaceful*<br>Gray 1934 |
| _____ | *Chorales from "St. Matthew Passion"*<br>(Several editions available) |
| _____ | *Come, Souls, Behold Today*<br>Augsburg 1171 (SAB) |
| _____ | *Come Thou, O Saviour*<br>Summy-Birchard 5203 |
| _____ | *God, My Shepherd, Walks Beside Me*<br>Gray 216 |

[1] See pp. 133-7, *Music and Worship in the Church*, Nashville: Abingdon, 1960, for additional titles.

|  |  |
|---|---|
| _____ | *Now Winter Fades from Sight*<br>J. Fischer 7816 |
| _____ | *O Father, God of Love*<br>Summy-Birchard 1575 |
| Bairstow | *The Day Draws On*<br>Oxford E1 SAB |
| Barnby | *When Morning Gilds the Sky*<br>Abingdon APM-117 (SAB) |
| Bartholomew | *Little Innocent Lamb*<br>G. Schirmer 10049 SAB |
| Bell | *Let Us Break Bread Together*<br>Mills 85 |
| Berchem | *O Jesu Christe*<br>Willis 7479 |
| Bevan | *Two Short Anthems*<br>*O Thou Who at the Eucharist Did'st Pray*<br>*O Love of Whom Is Truth and Light*<br>Oxford |
| Billings | *When Jesus Wept*<br>Mercury MC 102 (Round for four voices) |
| Bitgood | *Except the Lord Build the House*<br>Flammer 84499 |
| Black | *Let Carols Ring*<br>Gray 1524 (SSAATTBB) |
| Bortniansky | *Lord, Grant Thy Servants*<br>E. C. Schirmer 1250 |
| Brahms | *Blest Spirit, One with God Above*<br>Wood 518 |
| _____ | *The Hunter*<br>E. C. Schirmer 1680 |
| _____ | *Let Nothing Ever Grieve Thee*<br>Peters 6093 |
| _____ | *The White Dove*<br>Wood 370 |
| Burleigh | *Couldn't Hear Nobody Pray*<br>Ricordi NY278 |
| _____ | *Hold On*<br>Ricordi NY2047 (SSAATTBB) |
| _____ | *Stan' Still, Jordan*<br>Ricordi NY1155 |

162

# RESOURCES

| | |
|---|---|
| Buszin | *O Holy, Blissful Night* <br> Concordia 98-1167 |
| Buxtehude | *Lauda Sion Salvatorem* <br> Chantry (SAB) |
| Byrd | *O Jesu Blessed Lord, to Thee* <br> Schmitt, Hall, & McCreary 1685 |
| Candlyn | *The Road to the Lamb* <br> Witmark W3532 (SAB) |
| _____ | *Child of Bethlehem* <br> Abingdon APM-114 (SAB) |
| Christiansen | *Lamb of God* <br> Augsburg 133 |
| Clokey | *Carol of the Psalms* <br> Summy-Birchard B-1322 |
| Copes | *For the Bread* <br> Abingdon APM-115 |
| Curry | *In Christ There Is No East or West* <br> Abingdon APM-104 |
| Davis, K. | *All in the Morning* <br> Flammer 84485 |
| _____ | *Alleluia, Come, Good People* <br> Galaxy 1132 |
| _____ | *As It Fell Upon a Night* <br> Galaxy 1291 |
| _____ | *God Adoring* <br> Flammer 84639 |
| _____ | *Good Folk Who Dwell on Earth* <br> Wood 731 (SAB) |
| _____ | *Lord God of Sabaoth* <br> Summy-Birchard B-1563 (SAB) |
| Dawson | *Ain' A That Good News* <br> Music Press 103 |
| _____ | *There Is a Balm in Gilead* <br> Music Press 105 |
| DesPres | *The Name of Jesus* <br> Concordia 98-1095 |
| Dickinson | *Is This the Way to Bethlehem?* <br> Gray 178 |
| Diercks | *Clap Your Hands* <br> Abingdon APM-103 |

163

| | |
|---|---|
| Dietterich | *O Love that Triumphs Over Loss* |
| | Abingdon APM-126 |
| ———— | *Wilt Thou Not Turn Again* |
| | Abingdon APM-134 |
| Engelbrekt | *I Lay My Sins on Jesus* |
| | Schmitt, Hall & McCreary 861 |
| Farrant | *Hide Not Thou Thy Face* |
| | Pro Art 1155 |
| ———— | *Lord, for Thy Tender Mercies' Sake* |
| | Kjos 5204 |
| ———— | *We Sing Our Praises Now to Thee* |
| | Flammer 88609 (SAB) |
| Ford | *Almighty God Who Hast Me Brought* |
| | Bourne ES24 |
| Franck | *O Jesus, Grant Me Hope and Comfort* |
| | Schmitt, Hall & McCreary 1544 |
| Frothingham | *Descants on Ten Christmas Hymns and Carols* |
| | Summy-Birchard 1328 |
| Gardner | *Dese Bones Gwine Rise Again* |
| | Staff 358 |
| Gaul | *The March of the Wise Men* |
| | Gray 2384 |
| ———— | *Praise God, Extol Him* |
| | Flammer 84120 |
| Gibbs | *Thee Will I Love* |
| | G. Schirmer 10402 Unison |
| Gilbert | *Praise to the Lord* |
| | Oxford E75 (SAB) |
| Gore | *Four Rounds for Christmas* |
| | J. Fischer 9106 |
| Hairston | *Who'll Be a Witness for My Lord* |
| | Bourne S 1029 |
| Hassler | *Cantate Domino* |
| | Bourne ES 18 |
| Haydn, F. | *Evensong to God* |
| | Boosey & Hawkes 1824 |
| Haydn, J. M. | *Tenebrae in E-flat* |
| | Schmitt, Hall & McCreary 1536 |
| Herman | *We Thank Thee, Jesus, Dearest Friend* |
| | Concordia 98-1148 (SAB) |

| | |
|---|---|
| Hummel | *Alleluia!* |
| | Ricordi NY1679 |
| Ingegneri | *O Gracious Saviour* |
| | Schmitt, Hall & McCreary 1692 |
| Johnson, A. | *The Song of the Shepherd Boy* |
| | J. Fischer 7713 |
| Johnson, M. | *A Gallery Carol* |
| | Sacred Design SD 5901 |
| Jordan | *Late Have I Loved Thee* |
| | Flammer 88605 (SAB) |
| Kalinnikoff | *To Thee Do I Lift Up My Soul* |
| | J. Fischer 7156 (SAB) |
| Kopyloff | *God Is a Spirit* |
| | E. C. Schirmer 1132 |
| ———— | *Hear My Cry* |
| | Ditson 332-13804 (SSAATTBB) |
| Lapo | *Christmas Lullaby* |
| | Abingdon APM-123 |
| ———— | *Christmas Meditation* |
| | Row 495 |
| ———— | *Lord of All Being* |
| | Row 445 |
| di Lasso | *Lord, to Thee We Turn* |
| | E. C. Schirmer 1688 |
| ———— | *O Lord of Heaven* |
| | Wick 253 |
| Lotti | *Surely He Hath Borne Our Griefs* |
| | E. C. Schirmer 1124 (SAB) |
| ———— | *Mighty Lord, Thy Faithfulness Abideth Ever* |
| | E. C. Schirmer 1716 (SAB) |
| Lovelace | *As Grain Once Scattered* |
| | Summy-Birchard 5347 |
| ———— | *Beneath the Forms of Rite* |
| | Brodt 526 |
| ———— | *Bless Thou the Lord, O My Soul* |
| | Canyon 6011 |
| ———— | *Breathe Into Our Souls* |
| | FitzSimons 2164 |
| ———— | *Child of the Sovereign Heart* |
| | Abingdon AMP-101 |

165

| | |
|---|---|
| _____ | *In the Lonely Midnite* <br> Volkwein |
| _____ | *O Thou Eternal Christ, Ride On* <br> Abingdon AMP-105 |
| Luvaas | *Thy Light and Peace* <br> Kjos 2036 |
| Lynn | *Coventry Carol* <br> Abingdon AMP-100 |
| McCormick | *He Shall Come Down Like Rain* <br> Shawnee |
| Maker | *Dear Lord and Father of Mankind* <br> Pro Art 1139 |
| Malin | *There Is A Holy City* <br> Birchard 1549 |
| Manz | *E'en So, Lord Jesus, Quickly Come* <br> Concordia 98-1054 |
| Marshall | *Awake My Heart and Render* <br> Gray 2515 |
| _____ | *Blessed Is the Man* <br> Abingdon APM-106 |
| _____ | *He Comes to Us* <br> C. Fischer CM6996 |
| Maschoff | *Behold the Lamb of God* <br> Schmitt, Hall & McCreary 1715 |
| Matthews | *O Heavenly Father* <br> FitzSimons 2153 |
| Miller | *When I Survey the Wondrous Cross* <br> Kjos Ed. 5302 |
| Niles | *The Little Lyking* <br> G. Schirmer 10110 |
| _____ | *No Room in the Hotel* <br> G. Schirmer 9981 (SSATBB) |
| _____ | *Wayfaring Stranger* <br> G. Schirmer 10040 |
| Olds | *Let Us Praise God* <br> Schmitt, Hall & McCreary 5512 (SAB with speech choir) |
| _____ | *St. Francis' Prayer* <br> Abbey 101 (with speech choir) |
| Palestrina | *In Monte Oliveti* <br> Schmitt, Hall & McCreary 1660 |

166

| | |
|---|---|
| _____ | *The Strife Is O'er*<br>Mercury MC 218 (2 pt.) |
| Pfautsch | *God of Might, We Praise Thee*<br>Abingdon APM-109 |
| _____ | *Sing Praise to God*<br>Summy-Birchard 5315 |
| Pooler | *Prepare the Way, O Zion*<br>Canyon YS6051 (SAB) |
| Powell | *Let Saints on Earth*<br>Abingdon APM-112 |
| Pritchard | *Praise the Lord, Ye Heavens Adore Him*<br>Summy-Birchard 1475 (SSAB) |
| Read | *Broad Is the Road*<br>G. Schirmer 910 |
| Roberton | *All in the April Evening*<br>G. Schirmer 8100 |
| Roff | *Lord Jesus, Think on Me*<br>Schmitt, Hall & McCreary 1759 |
| _____ | *O God of All Beauty*<br>Abingdon APM-133 |
| _____ | *Watch and Pray*<br>Ricordi R.C. 3 |
| Rowley | *A Divine Intercession*<br>Pro Art 1755 |
| Saint-Saens | *Praise Ye the Lord* (Christmas Oratorio)<br>Boosey & Hawkes 5050 (SSAB) |
| Schroth | *O God of Youth*<br>Kjos Ed. 5179 |
| Schütz | *O Trinity of Blessed Light*<br>Marks 4110 |
| Shaw, G. | *Worship*<br>Novello 1147 |
| Shaw, M. | *Let All the People Praise Thee, O God*<br>Novello 1267 |
| _____ | *Lord, Make Us Instruments of Thy Peace*<br>Novello MT 1377 |
| Shaw-Parker | *O Sons and Daughters*<br>G. Schirmer 9950 |
| _____ | *O Thou in Whose Presence*<br>G. Schirmer 917 |

| | |
|---|---|
| ———— | *Pensive Dove* <br> G. Schirmer 916 |
| Snell | *Thanksgiving* <br> Gray 2150 (Union) |
| Thiman | *A Hymn of Praise to the Creator* <br> Gray 2290 |
| ———— | *Immortal, Invisible* <br> Novello 1140 |
| ———— | *Grant Us Light* <br> G. Schirmer 10228 |
| Titcomb | *Jesus! Name of Wondrous Love* <br> Wood 669 |
| Turner | *Stand Up and Bless the Lord* <br> Oxford U38 (Unison) |
| Tye | *Laudate Nomen Domini* <br> Gray 1526 |
| Van Iderstine | *God Rest Ye Merry, Gentlemen* <br> Abingdon APM-124 |
| de Victoria | *Jesus, the Very Thought Is Sweet* <br> Bourne ES48 |
| Voris | *Blessed Is He That Cometh* <br> Gray 914 |
| Walter | *Blessed Are the Pure in Heart* <br> Abingdon APM-190 |
| ———— | *Christ Is the World's True Light* <br> Abingdon APM-174 |
| ———— | *How Firm a Foundation* <br> Abingdon APM-125 (SAB) |
| ———— | *Humbly I Adore Thee* <br> Galaxy 2012 |
| ———— | *O Lamb of God* <br> Abingdon APM-173 |
| Willan | *Arise, Shine, for Thy Light* <br> Concordia 98-1508 |
| ———— | *Jesous Ahatonhia* <br> Harris 2925 |
| ———— | *Lift Up Your Heads* <br> Concordia 98-2003 |
| Williams, <br> D. H. | *Draw Nigh to Jerusalem* <br> Novello 2410 |
| ———— | *Lo! He Comes with Clouds Descending* <br> Novello 2350 |

| Williams, R. E. | *Father Eternal*<br>Schmitt 834 |
|---|---|
| Wilson | *To Bethlehem, Singing*<br>Boosey & Hawkes 5056 |
| Winstead | *The Humble Heart*<br>Witmark 5-W3270 |
| Woodgate | *Six Carols for SAB*<br>Oxford |
| Young, C. | *Bread of the World, In Mercy Broken*<br>Kjos Ed. 5291 |
| ———— | *Come Thou Fount*<br>Kjos Ed. 5315 (2 Pt.) |
| Young, G. | *Now Let Us All Praise God*<br>Galaxy 2108 |

## FILMS

An extensive and complete list of films and filmstrips has been published by the Music Education National Conference, 1201 Sixteenth Street, N.W., Washington 6, D. C., with the title *Film Guide for Music Educators*. The compiler is Donald Shetler.

The Barber of Seville, Brandon
Black and white; 60 min. Soloists, orchestra, and choir of l'Opera Comique, Paris. Sung in French; English subtitles. Senior high.

Children's Corner, Hoffberg, Ideal
Black and white; 17 min. Pictorial fantasy. Kindergarten, primary.

Christmas Carols, CanNFB (SF)
Color; black and white; 11 min. Animated drawings illustrating familiar Christmas carols and songs. Kindergarten, primary, junior high.

Christmas Rhapsody, EBF
Color; 10 min. Familiar carols help to tell the story of a little fir tree. Kindergarten, primary, junior high.

Falsetto, The, Henry J. Rubin, M.D., 436 North Rosbury Drive, Beverly Hills, Cal.
Black and white; 18 min.
A careful and scholarly study of the vocal cords in action. Sound films, taken at 6-8000 frames per second and projected at slow speeds. Junior high, senior high.

Fidelio, Brandon
Black and white; 90 min. Vienna Symphony, singers of Vienna State Opera. German; English subtitles. Senior high.

Folksong Fantasy, CanNFB (IFB)
Color; 8 min. Puppets enact three familiar folk songs. Singer: Emma Castor. Primary, juniors, junior high.

Hoppity-Hop, CanNFB (IFB)
Color; 3 min. Animated comedy dance to music of calliope. Kindergarten, primary.

Inside Opera, TFC
Black and white; 25 min. Episodes in the life of a rising young opera star, played by Grace Moore. Teacher's guide available. Senior high.

Melody in Music, Coronet
Color; 13 min. Young orchestra members discover characteristics of melody. Juniors, junior high.

On the Twelfth Day, Brandon
Color; 22 min. Old English Christmas ballad. Juniors, junior high, senior high.

On Wings of Song, Brandon
Black and white; 15 min. Vienna Choir Boys and Vienna Philharmonic. Excellent for instruction in choir technique. Juniors, junior high, senior high.

Opera School, CanNFB
Black and white; 36 min. A young girl is followed through three years of study. Includes a portion of Mozart's "The Marriage of Figaro." Senior high.

Reading Music, Coronet
Color; three films; 11 min. each. I. Learning about notes; II. Finding the rhythm; III. Finding the melody. Primary, juniors.

Rhythm in the Zoo, McGraw-Hill
Color; black and white; 14 min. Large body movements in imitation of animals in the zoo. Kindergarten, primary.

Rhythm Is Everywhere, Mahnke
Black and white; 10 min. Rhythm in natural things: Horse's hoofs, boy walking, cow chewing her cud, and the like. Kindergarten, primary.

'Round the Mulberry Bush, CanNFB (SF)
Color; black and white; 10 min. Puppets and figures. Other songs: "Rock-a-bye-baby," "Chopsticks," and "One More River to Cross." Kindergarten, primary.

Singing Angels, Brandon
Black and white; 98 min. Joseph Haydn, composer, with Johann Holzer, music teacher, founds the Vienna Boys' Choir. German; English subtitles. Juniors, junior high.

170

**Singing Champions, CanNFB**
Black and white; 10 min. A famous boys' choir in rehearsal and at play. Juniors, junior high, senior high.

**Sounds of Music, Coronet**
Color; black and white; 10 min. Acoustical properties of music simply and easily demonstrated. Junior high, senior high.

**Stephen Foster and His Songs, Coronet**
Color; black and white; 16 min. Life, music, and times of Foster. Junior high, senior high.

**Tall Tales (American Folk Music), Brandon**
Black and white; 10 min. Folk characters impersonated by well-known folk-singers, including Burl Ives and Josh White. Junior high, senior high.

**Three Songs by Susan Reed, Brandon**
Color; 9 min. Animation. "The Fox," "Mother, I Would Marry," and "There Was an Old Woman." Accompaniment: Irish harp. Junior high, senior high.

**Vocal Music, EBF**
Black and white; 10 min. Study of basic techniques of singing. Junior high, senior high.

**Your Voice, EBF**
Black and white; 11 min. Describes process of voice production. Vocal folds shown in operation. Junior high, senior high.

### Key to Film Distributors

| | |
|---|---|
| Brandon | Brandon Films, Inc., 200 West 57th St., New York 19, N. Y. |
| CanNFB | National Film Board of Canada, 680 Fifth Ave., New York 19, N. Y. (order from NFBC, SF, or IFB as indicated.) |
| Coronet | Coronet Instructional Films, 65 E. South Water St., Chicago 1, Ill. |
| EBF | Encyclopedia Britannica Films, Inc., 1150 Wilmette Ave., Wilmette, Ill. |
| Hoffberg | Hoffberg Productions, Inc., 362 West 44th St., New York 36, N. Y. |
| Ideal | Ideal Pictures Corporation, 58 East South Water Street, Chicago 1, Ill. |
| IFB | International Film Bureau, Inc., 57 East Jackson Boulevard, Chicago 4, Ill. |

McGraw-Hill     McGraw-Hill Text Films, 330 West 42nd. St., New York 36, N. Y.

Mahnke     Carl F. Mahnke Productions, 215 East 3rd. St., Des Moines, Ia.

SF     Sterling Educational Films, 6 East 39th St., New York 16, N. Y.

TFC     Teaching Films Custodians, Inc., 25 West 43 St., New York 36, N. Y.

# INDEX

**173**

# INDEX

Here is a comprehensive study of the developing voice with a discussion of the problems and their solutions when training young voices to sing, individually or in groups. The training technique begins with preschool children and continues through senior high school, each chapter dealing with a specific age group. For complete understanding, the physiological and psychological factors of maturing are shown in relationship to the continuous growth process of the voice.

This book is the first to trace, in one volume, the development of the human vocal mechanism from its earliest beginning in childhood through adolescence to near-maturity. Another distinction is the wide variety of resources which include book and music listings, musical examples, graded lists of recordings, films and filmstrips, and illustrations.

Written in semi-conversational, non-technical style, the book will be of invaluable aid to parents, to church and school music teachers and directors, and to everyone who works with young singers.